He was never late for a date.

It's not a date, Josh reminded himself. It was just dinner with Em and some friends. The reminder did nothing to calm his nerves. And that was something else he'd never been before a date—nervous.

He was afraid Em would eventually figure out why he'd been acting like an idiot. But really, how could she? It wasn't as if she could see what was going on in his head. She'd made his heart race and his gut tighten with desire simply by holding his hand and giving him an innocent kiss. Feelings he'd never felt with any of the women he'd dated this past year. There'd been no chemistry. He'd felt like he was on a date with a friend.

Now here he was having feelings for a woman who was an actual friend. A woman who was still in love with her dead fiancé.

Praise for Debbie Mason and the Highland Falls Series

"Debbie Mason writes romance like none other."

—FreshFiction.com

"I've never met a Debbie Mason story that I didn't enjoy."

—KeeperBookshelf.com

"I'm telling you right now, if you haven't yet read a book by Debbie Mason you don't know what you're missing."

—RomancingtheReaders.blogspot.com

"If you enjoy multi-layered characters, humor, emotional twists and turns, and heart-tugging romance that will leave you eager for more, I enthusiastically recommend a visit to Highland Falls, North Carolina."

—TheRomanceDish.com

"It's not just romance. It's grief and mourning, guilt and truth, second chances and revelations."

—WrittenLoveReviews.blogspot.com

"Mason always makes me smile and touches my heart in the most unexpected and wonderful ways."

—HerdingCats-BurningSoup.com

"No one writes heartful small town romance like Debbie Mason, and I always count the days until the next book!"

—TheManyFacesofRomance.blogspot.com

"Wow, do these books bring the feels. Deep emotion, heart-tugging romance, and a touch of suspense make them hard to put down..."

—TheRomanceDish.com

"Debbie Mason writes in a thrilling and entertaining way. Her stories are captivating and filled with controlled chaos, true love, mysteries, amazing characters, eccentricities, plotting, and friendship."

—WithLoveForBooks.com

"Debbie Mason never disappoints me."

—FictionFangirls.com

"Mason takes her romances to a whole new level..."

—CarriesBookReviews.com

"Heartfelt and delightful."

—RaeAnne Thayne, *New York Times* bestselling author, on the Harmony Harbor series

Reunited on Sugar Maple Road

Also by Debbie Mason

THE SUNSHINE BAY SERIES

Summer on Sunshine Bay

THE HIGHLAND FALLS SERIES

Summer on Honeysuckle Ridge

Christmas on Reindeer Road

Falling in Love on Willow Creek

A Wedding on Honeysuckle Ridge (short story)

The Inn on Mirror Lake

At Home on Marigold Lane

THE HARMONY HARBOR SERIES

Mistletoe Cottage

Christmas With an Angel (short story)

Starlight Bridge

Primrose Lane

Sugarplum Way

Driftwood Cove

Sandpiper Shore

The Corner of Holly and Ivy

Barefoot Beach

Christmas in Harmony Harbor

THE CHRISTMAS, COLORADO SERIES

The Trouble with Christmas

Christmas in July

It Happened at Christmas

Wedding Bells in Christmas

Snowbound at Christmas

Kiss Me in Christmas

Happy Ever After in Christmas

Marry Me at Christmas (short story)

Miracle at Christmas (novella)

One Night in Christmas (novella)

Reunited on Sugar Maple Road

DEBBIE MASON

A Highland Falls Novel

FOREVER
New York Boston

This book is a work of fiction. Names, characters, places, and incidents are the product of the author's imagination or are used fictitiously. Any resemblance to actual events, locales, or persons, living or dead, is coincidental.

Cover art and design by Elizabeth Turner Stokes
Cover images © Shutterstock
Author photo © Annemarie Gruden Photography

Forever
Hachette Book Group
1290 Avenue of the Americas, New York, NY 10104
read-forever.com
twitter.com/readforeverpub

First Edition: September 2023

Forever is an imprint of Grand Central Publishing. The Forever name and logo are trademarks of Hachette Book Group, Inc.

ISBNs: 978-1-5387-2536-8 (mass market); 978-1-5387-2537-5 (ebook)

Printed in the United States of America

OPM

10 9 8 7 6 5 4 3 2 1

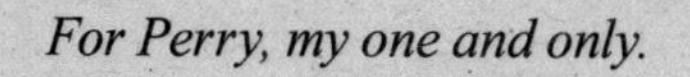

For Perry, my one and only.

Reunited on Sugar Maple Road

Chapter One

♥

"Do not make eye contact," Emma Scott muttered at herself as Gwen, her coworker at the Highland Falls Police Department, carried on an overly loud conversation with her daughter on the phone two desks away. Em wasn't the only one avoiding eye contact with Gwen. Half her coworkers were doing the same while the other half were discussing their Saturday night plans as they headed out the door.

"I'm sorry, honey. You know how much I want to be there but I have to work. Please don't cry. Yes, yes, I know. Okay. I'll see what I can do."

Em felt the weight of someone's stare and sent her nearest coworker and supposed friend a glare.

"Have a heart," Todd whispered as he got up from behind his desk. He looked like a clean-shaven Keanu Reeves. "The kid's crying."

"Me? What about you?"

"Can't." He took his jacket off the back of his chair and shrugged into it. "I've got a big date tonight."

"You're not the only one with plans, you know," Em said without sharing hers.

"Let me guess. You're taking Gus for a walk and then you're going to sit on your couch binge-watching *Stranger Things* while eating whatever's left of the fast food you ordered the night before. Am I right?"

"No, you're not." It was annoying how well Todd knew her. That was what she got for becoming friends with a coworker. When she'd taken the job with HFPD last fall, she'd vowed to keep everyone at arm's length. But Todd had blown past her defenses as if they were made of twigs and he was a gale-force wind.

He cocked his head. "Yeah? So where are you going?"

"The Fall Festival." She wouldn't be caught dead at the Fall Festival but it was the first thing that came to mind. Probably because Bri, her sister-in-law and best friend, had called an hour ago, trying to convince her to come.

Em didn't like crowds or making small talk. And while she might be a fan of the woo-woo on TV, she wasn't a fan of it in real life. Since the Sisterhood had organized the festival, a big helping of woo-woo was all but guaranteed. The group of women who made up the Sisterhood were some of the most influential women in town. Between them, they ran seventy percent of the businesses on Main Street and organized every single seasonal festival. They also considered themselves Highland Falls' resident matchmakers, and the last thing Em wanted or needed was someone else trying to set her up.

Todd smiled as if his boyfriend had just proposed.

"Finally. It's only taken you six months to take my advice. You'll see I was right, Em. Getting back out there is the only way for you to—"

That was what she got for moving back to her small hometown. Gossip spread faster than a five-alarm fire in Highland Falls, and everyone had an opinion on how to get over the loss of her fiancé, including her coworkers and the members of the Sisterhood.

Em raised her hand, cutting off Todd. "Don't you have a date to get to?"

"You're right, I do." He moved in for a hug.

She leaned back. She didn't do hugs.

He sighed and gave her a fist bump instead. "Have fun at the festival."

"Festival? Are you going to the festival, Em?" Gwen asked, coming to stand in front of her desk.

"Uh, yeah?" She couldn't say no with Todd still standing there. She frowned at him, wondering why he was making a face.

"You're a lifesaver. I didn't want to disappoint my daughter, but I didn't want to ask you to cover for me again."

Now she knew why Todd made a face. Gwen was working the festival. "Nope. No way. I'm not taking another shift for you."

"But why? You'll be at the festival anyway, and I promise, as soon as my daughter's swim meet is over, I'll relieve you." She pressed her palms together. "Please, Em. This meet is a big deal for her. It's the last one of the year."

Em felt bad for the kid but not that bad. Her own

mom had never made it to her swim meets, and she'd survived. Besides, it was past time Em put her foot down. She was everyone's go-to girl for shift changes and it wasn't fair. Just because she didn't have kids or a significant other didn't mean she didn't have a life. Okay, so maybe she didn't but that was her choice.

Em reached for her jacket hanging on the back of her chair and stood up. "Sorry, Gwen. I've put in my allowed overtime this month. Gabe won't be happy if I blow his budget," she said, throwing her boss, the chief of police, under the bus.

"Oh, okay." Gwen gave her a wobbly smile and brought her phone to her ear. Then she grimaced and held it out to Em. "Would you tell her? Maybe she'll take it better from you. At least she'll know I tried."

Em glanced at Todd, whose lips were pressed together as though he was trying not to laugh. "Fine. I'll do it. But if you're not at the festival in two hours to relieve me, I'm—"

"Thank you, thank you, thank you," Gwen squealed.

Em didn't step away fast enough and found herself enveloped in a patchouli-scented hug. She didn't know what was up with her touchy-feely coworkers. She'd never had this problem at her previous job in Nashville. Then again, other than Brad, she hadn't had a lot of time to get chummy with her colleagues. She'd been a detective on a big-city police force. So far, her most exciting cases in Highland Falls were a runaway bride, a dognapping, and equipment going missing at a summer camp.

Carefully extricating herself so as not to offend

Gwen, Em said, "Yeah, yeah, I know. I'm the best and you don't know what you'd do without me." She'd heard it before. At least twice a week.

Gwen already had her phone pressed to her ear and was heading for the exit doors.

"Two hours, Gwen. I mean it," Em called after her, texting Bri to let her know there'd been a change of plans. She'd pick up Gus at the festival. When Em was at work, the goldendoodle stayed with her sister-in-law, who was a family therapist and ran her business from home.

Bri responded immediately. Yay! We'll see you there. Bubbles came and went, and then a second later, I'm proud of you. So is Cal.

Cal was Bri's husband and Em's big brother. He hadn't come out and said it, but lately Em had seen signs that, like everyone else, he thought it was time she moved on from losing Brad.

It had been seventeen months since he'd died, and she still fought to save him in her dreams. And every morning when she woke up without him by her side, it was all she could do to get out of bed. She didn't know how to move on without him. If she was honest, she didn't want to.

But day after day, she went through the motions. She walked her dog, kept the house she rented on Sugar Maple Road relatively tidy, and got to work on time. She'd thought that would be enough to satisfy the people who loved her. But apparently as the months went by, their patience with her was wearing thin.

Maybe Gwen had done her a favor. If Em put on a

good show at the Fall Festival, everyone would leave her alone.

She frowned at Todd when he brushed her overlong bangs aside. She needed a haircut but couldn't be bothered. "What are you doing?"

"Rubbing 'sucker' off your forehead."

"Hey, you were the one who told me to have a heart." She batted his hand away and moved toward the exit.

"That was before I knew you were doing something fun for a change, and now you have to work." He held the door open. "Face it, Em. Under that hard-ass persona, you're a marshmallow."

Her, a marshmallow? She rolled her eyes and headed for her squad car. The black Camaro was a sweet ride and ranked as one of her favorite things about her job at HFPD. "Enjoy your night."

"Will do, and you know, just because you're on duty doesn't mean you can't have fun at the festival. I hear HFFD volunteers are in charge of the bonfires." He waggled his eyebrows. "Firefighters are hot."

One particular volunteer firefighter came to mind, Josh Callahan, her brother's best friend. He might be hot but he was also a regular pain in her butt. "Was that supposed to be a pun?"

"You're hopeless."

They got into their cars and drove off in opposite directions. Em wished her drive was longer. The Village Green was less than two blocks from the station. When she arrived at the gravel lot beside the green space, she decided she didn't want to get boxed in and parked alongside the curb.

In the distance, the sun looked like a ball of fire disappearing behind the mountains. She'd worn an HFPD T-shirt to work and zipped up her jacket as she got out of the car. It was late September, and while the days were still warm, there was a distinct chill in the air when the sun went down. She beeped the lock with the key fob and headed for the Village Green, taking a shortcut up a steep incline to avoid the people streaming onto the grounds from the parking lot.

Flickering flames from the bonfires lit up the grounds under the twilight sky. The fires' crackles and pops mingled with the sound of chatter and laughter and the distant whine of bagpipes coming from the stage at the far end of the green space.

Up ahead to her left, a line of colorful tents were lit up with fairy lights. The smells of cotton candy, candy apples, and corn dogs coming from a nearby food truck wafted past her nose, and her stomach grumbled. She was about to head that way when she got a look at the purple-and-white-striped tent beside the food truck.

Inside the tent, behind a wooden table, sat Bri's sister Ellie and their grandmother—a Betty White look-alike and a founding member of the Sisterhood. Ellie and Granny MacLeod were dressed like the fortune tellers they were pretending to be.

Supposedly, Ellie had inherited her psychic gifts from their grandmother. But Em didn't buy that they had psychic abilities, no matter how many stories she'd been told to the contrary. Going by the line outside their tent, she was in the minority.

"Let the woo-woo times begin," she muttered.

"Em!"

She turned to see Bri waving her over to where she sat around a bonfire with a group of teens, including Cal's stepdaughter, Izzy. Izzy was seventeen going on thirty with long, curly black hair. She was one of Em's favorite humans.

Bri smiled, patting the rock beside her. The firelight cast her best friend's hair and face in a golden glow. Em's sister-in-law and brother could pass for Barbie and Ken.

Em looked over the Village Green and demurred. "I'd better not. I'm on duty."

Bri's shoulders drooped, and Em was pretty sure she heard her sigh. Reminding herself of her goal for the night—to convince everyone she was moving on from her loss—Em said, "I guess I could sit for a minute." She took a seat, acknowledging Izzy's wave hello with one of her own. "Where's Gus?"

"He's with Cal and—" Bri broke off and waved. "Over here."

Em bowed her head when she saw who Bri was waving at. Her brother, Cal, and his best friend Josh. Heads turned as the two men weaved their way through the crowd, people calling their names in greeting. Cal and Josh were over six feet and stood out in the crowd. Cal with his head of golden hair was a perfect foil to his dark-haired best friend.

Em's brother was a renowned surgeon who headed up the trauma team at Highland Falls General. Josh, a former star athlete, taught gym at the local high school and coached the varsity football team. With Josh at the helm, the team was on a three-season winning streak, which probably accounted for his popularity in town. Apparently, from the people offering congratulations as they walked by, his team had won their game the night before.

Although she imagined the flirty smiles and finger-waves from three twentysomething women didn't have anything to do with his coaching abilities. Josh was obnoxiously good-looking with his jet-black hair, sky-blue eyes, muscled physique, and tattoo sleeves. But what annoyed Em even more than his head-turning gorgeous face and body was his perpetual good mood. She didn't trust anyone that happy or easygoing.

"Freckles," Josh said with a grin, tugging on her ponytail before sitting on the rock beside her.

She wanted to push him off the rock. Her brother and Josh had been best friends since grade school, and he treated Em like his baby sister. "I'm not twelve, you know," she said.

"Sorry. *Officer* Freckles."

Em was about to elbow him when Gus, her sixty-pound goldendoodle, shoved his curly, apricot-colored head between them, greeting her the way he always did, with a hug. "Yeah, yeah, I missed you too." She patted him and then gently pushed him off her.

Even Gus's doggy hugs made her uncomfortable. She was a reluctant doggy mom, or at least a reluctant Gus mom. She'd inherited the goldendoodle from her fiancé. They'd tolerated each other for Brad's sake when he was alive. Cal and Bri had offered to take Gus when Em moved out of their place last year, but he was all she had left of Brad. And while she might not be enamored of his doggy hugs or kisses, he was good company.

Cal ruffled Em's hair. "Glad you decided to come."

"I had no—" Em caught herself and forced a smile. "You know me, nothing could keep me away from the Fall Festival."

She waited for either her brother or Josh to call her out on the obvious lie, but Cal was helping Bri to her feet, and Josh was listening to whatever the kids were saying with a frown on his face.

"We're getting something to eat. You guys want anything?" her brother asked, including his stepdaughter in the question.

He knew better than to ask Josh, who considered his body a temple, Em thought with an eye roll. "Corn dog, thanks," she said, and Izzy asked for a candy apple.

"You've got to be kidding me," Josh said sotto voce as Bri and Cal walked away holding hands, Gus loping after them.

"I like corn dogs. What's the big deal?"

"I know you like corn dogs. You eat like half the guys on my team but that's not what I was talking about." Josh leaned into her, and she suppressed a shiver of awareness. She always got a tiny jolt when he got this close. He smelled like Brad. She'd thought about suggesting he change his cologne but then she'd have to tell him why.

"I was talking about the kids. Haven't you been listening to them?"

"No."

"I suggest you do. You're about to get a lot busier at HFPD thanks to this book they're talking about."

She tuned into the conversation going on around the bonfire. The kids were talking about Seaton House. An abandoned house up the road from Em.

"So you mean, if someone proves that the Seaton sisters were innocent, they can rest in peace?" asked a boy on the far side of the bonfire.

Another kid nodded. "That's what it said in the book."

"Seriously? There really is a book about the Seaton sisters?" Em whispered.

The Seaton sisters were Highland Falls' answer to the Sanderson sisters of *Hocus Pocus* fame. Except without the coming-back-to-life-on-Halloween-thanks-to-a-virgin part. Although the way rumors spread, that version of the story had probably made its rounds too.

"According to the kids, it's called *The Haunting of Seaton House*." He glanced over his shoulder, lifting his chin at a black-and-gold-striped tent. "Three Wise Women Bookstore is selling copies here tonight."

As several of the teenagers discussed whether there was any truth to the rumors that the Seaton sisters had been witches, someone on Em's right whispered, "If you ask me, the Sisterhood are witches."

Em couldn't tell who'd said it but she had to nip this in the bud. When she'd been in eighth grade, there'd been a brouhaha about the Sisterhood dancing in the woods to welcome spring. Everything had gotten blown out of proportion, and the town didn't need a repeat.

"Aunt Em, you live down the road from the Seaton House. Is it really haunted?" Izzy asked.

"No. It's a dilapidated, old house that needs to be torn down." Em might like to keep busy but the last thing she needed was the teenagers of Highland Falls going "haunting" as they used to call it.

"And it's off-limits to all of you." Josh glanced at an attractive redhead making a beeline for him, and he slid a muscled arm around Em's shoulders. "Just go along with it, okay?" he said out of the side of his mouth. Then he smiled at the woman. "Hey, how's it going?"

Em shook her head. The way Josh went through women, he probably didn't remember the redhead's name. He hadn't dated for a couple years after his divorce, but he'd been making up for lost time this past year.

Em spotted two men doing the chest-shove thing at another bonfire and jumped to her feet. "Duty calls."

Josh followed her gaze and stood up. "I'll give you a hand. You might need backup."

He was as overprotective as her brother. Something else that annoyed her. "I think I can handle it, thanks." Em eyed two other women headed their way. "You, on the other hand, might require backup."

It wouldn't be her. Unless a fight broke out amongst the three women, she supposed. Then again, Josh had charmed his way out of detentions in high school, and rumor had it, he'd even made their former principal laugh out loud. A big deal because no one could recall the woman ever smiling.

Em headed for the other bonfire, disappointed to see the two men hugging it out.

Izzy flagged her down with a couple of her friends in tow. "Aunt Em, are you sure you haven't seen lights at Seaton House? Or heard a woman screaming?"

"Positive. And, Iz, I don't want you near that place. It should be condemned." Now that she thought about it, that was something she should look into. "If you hear anyone planning to go, I want you to tell me."

Izzy glanced at her friends. "I'm not a narc, Aunt Em."

Em got it. Izzy had been living in Highland Falls for all of two years, and she wouldn't want to jeopardize her hard-won social standing at school.

"You're right. I shouldn't have asked. But do me a favor, the three of you—if you hear someone making plans to go to Seaton House, shut them down. Same goes for anyone talking smack about the Sisterhood."

The blonde beside Izzy ducked her head. At least Em knew who to look at if the rumor mill heated up. The teen's mother had been a mean girl in high school. "There are laws against defamation of character. It's a serious offense that comes with jail time." When the blonde raised her gaze, Em held it, letting her know she'd heard her.

Figuring she'd made her point, Em said, "Okay, I've got a job to do. I'll see you later, Iz."

Em walked the perimeter of the Village Green,

avoiding making small talk by staying in the shadows of the trees. Then her stomach grumbled, reminding her there was a corn dog with her name on it.

She spotted her brother and Bri. They were almost at the front of the food truck line, talking to a group of friends while Gus played with a golden retriever. Em spotted a line of teenagers outside the black-and-gold-striped tent and decided to grab a copy of *The Haunting of Seaton House* while she waited for her corn dog. At least she'd know what they were up against.

Retrieving her cell from her pocket, Em pretended she was engrossed in something on her phone. Someone walked into her, and she reached out to steady them. As a blue-veined hand closed around her fingers, Em raised her gaze, sucking in a breath when she met the vacant stare of Granny MacLeod.

It was said that all the woman had to do to see your future was hold your hand. It's why she routinely wore gloves. She wasn't wearing them now, and her viselike grip tightened around Em's fingers.

As Em struggled to free her hand, Granny MacLeod said in a disturbing monotone, "Beyond your sorrow, a man with hair the color of ravens' wings and a child with eyes the color of the morning sky wait for you. But your journey to the other side of sorrow shall not be an easy one. Only by dying will you free yourself from your past and find your future. This I see, so it shall be."

Em felt the blood draining from her face, and her knees went weak. Granny MacLeod hadn't seen her future. She'd seen her past. Brad and the baby weren't waiting for her. There was no such thing as life after death. It was a myth created to give people false hope. To give them something to hold on to when their world fell apart.

Brad and the baby were lost to her forever, and she was to blame.

Chapter Two

♥

Granny MacLeod's grip loosened, and Em jerked her hand free, stumbling backward. Gus grabbed a mouthful of her jacket, steadying her on her feet. When she regained her balance, he went up on his hind legs and gave her a hug. She bent over, wrapping her arms around him and burying her face in his fur.

"Em, what's wrong? What happened?" Bri asked, her voice laced with concern.

"Nothing. Nothing's wrong," she lied.

The sights and sounds of that bright blue April morning were like a runaway freight train, barreling toward her. Em knew, from those early months, when just a voice, a sound, or a smell brought everything back, what would happen next, and she needed to leave. She'd learned how to lock the memories of that day away. It was only at night, her barriers lowered in sleep, when they'd escape, coming back to haunt her. But Granny MacLeod's prophesy had unlocked the box.

"It was my gift, wasn't it? I said something that caused you pain, and for that I'm sorry. I can't help it, you know. I should've kept my gloves on but we've been doing readings for hours."

Em lifted her head. There was no longer a vacant expression on the older woman's face. She stood in her purple robe, wringing her hands.

"I'm fine, Granny MacLeod. I pulled my hand away before you said anything." Em stepped back. "I'm just worried about Gus. Something upset him."

"Was it the dog's future I read then?"

At any other time, Em might've laughed. She supposed if she did, it would explain the tears welling in her eyes at the memory of Brad's smile minutes before he'd rushed to the woman's rescue.

Em tipped back her head, blinking up at the fairy lights to keep the tears and memories at bay, focusing instead on the fact that Granny MacLeod didn't remember what she'd said to her. "No. It wasn't you. Something must've scared Gus. Probably all the noise." She looped her fingers through Gus's collar, looking around as if searching for the culprit. As she did she noted the way Bri's troubled gaze moved over her face. Her best friend knew her too well. Em had told her things she'd never told anyone. But she hadn't told her about the baby she'd lost. She hadn't told anyone.

Em curled her fingernails into her palm, struggling to contain the memory of that rainy night when she'd miscarried, a week after Brad's funeral.

"What's going on? Em, are you okay?" her brother asked, coming to join them with a box of drinks, corn dogs, and candy apples in his arms.

"I'm fine. Why wouldn't I be?" she asked, her tone

more defensive than she'd intended. "It's Gus. I've gotta go."

Her brother frowned. "What about him? He looks fine to me, and you're on duty, aren't you?"

Her heart started racing at the thought of staying. She couldn't do it. The memory of the day her life had changed forever had begun clawing its way to the surface.

Bri placed a firm hand on Em's shoulder, grounding her. "It's okay. Gabe just got here. I'll let him know you had to take Gus home." She held Em's gaze. "I can come with you so you can hold him."

She knew. Bri knew this had nothing to do with Gus. "Thanks, but it's fine. He'll be okay."

"I'm sure he will. But you'll call me anyway. After you get him settled," Bri said, the tone in her voice brooking no argument. Her best friend wasn't about to let this slide.

Em nodded, ignoring the way her brother's narrowed gaze moved from her to his wife. Walking away with Gus at her side, Em focused on her feet, silently counting her steps. When she reached the shadows of the trees, she sprinted for her car. The moment she slid behind the wheel and Gus settled in the passenger seat beside her, the memories slammed into her.

Em fingered the lace on the cocktail-length pale pink dress, feeling a little foolish and a lot uncomfortable. She rarely wore dresses, especially a dress as outrageously feminine and as outrageously expensive as this one.

Brad glanced at her from behind the wheel of the

SUV and reached for her hand. "You're not having second thoughts, are you?"

"About marrying you? Not a chance. About this dress? I'm beyond second thoughts." She smoothed the fabric over the slight pooch in her stomach. "I don't know what I was thinking. It cost more than our rent."

He smiled and brought her hand to his mouth, pressing his lips to her palm. "It was worth every penny. You look amazing."

"You look pretty amazing yourself, and you didn't have to spend a small fortune."

It was true. Brad, with his olive skin, dark hair, and hazel eyes, was stop-and-stare gorgeous. She'd certainly stopped and stared when they'd been assigned to the same case three years earlier. But it wasn't his good looks that she fell in love with. It was his dry sense of humor, his confidence and compassion, his drive and street smarts. The way he listened to her, looked at her, and loved her.

"And unlike me, you'll actually get to wear your wedding attire again. Today, in fact." They'd gotten a break on a big case late last night, and they'd decided to go into work after their wedding at the courthouse. She had her own black suit waiting for her in the backseat.

"You're sure you don't want to take the day off? The case will be waiting for us tomorrow morning."

"But we might get lucky today, and the judge will sign off on the search warrant."

Brad waggled his eyebrows behind his aviators. "As long as I get lucky tonight."

"No doubt about that, Slick." She smiled, and he smiled back.

"You still want to wait until next weekend to tell Cal?"

She laughed. Brad wanted to share the news over the phone in case her overprotective big brother took his unhappiness out on him. Cal had been thrilled when Em had agreed to get married in their hometown. Eventually. *She wasn't a fan of big weddings but her brother had been looking forward to it. "Please, Cal loves you as much as he loves me. He won't care as long as we're happy. And if he's ticked, we have our secret weapon. He'll be over the moon when we tell him he's going to be an uncle."*

"Yeah, he…." Brad trailed off as he leaned forward.

Em was about to ask him what was going on when she saw what he did. There was a carjacking underway at the gas station on their left. A man was attempting to pull a screaming woman from her car, waving a gun in her face.

As Brad turned the steering wheel sharply to the left, Em unlocked the glove box, removing his Glock and hers. By the time he brought the SUV to a screeching halt half-on, half-off the sidewalk, she'd inserted a full magazine and chambered a round.

"Call it in, and stay in the vehicle," Brad ordered, holding her gaze as she handed him his gun. He slid it into his jacket pocket and got out of the SUV.

He'd become annoyingly overprotective since learning they were expecting three weeks before. In any other situation, she would've shared how she felt about him ordering her to stay put. But they didn't have time to argue about it now. The last thing she wanted was him distracted.

Still, she had to be prepared in case he needed her and loaded her own gun while calling it in. She disconnected from dispatch and scanned the parking lot as Brad slowly approached the vehicle.

"Just relax, man," Brad said, his stance and voice nonthreatening as he tried to de-escalate the situation. "Let the woman and her little boy go. Then you can take the car and drive away. I won't try and stop you."

"You a cop? You look like a cop." The man waved his gun, his free hand fisting in the woman's hair as he dragged her away from the car. She was crying and so was her little boy.

"Just a concerned citizen. If you let her and the boy go now, you might get away before the cops arrive. You're drawing attention. Someone will have called it in."

The guy was jittery, looking from left to right. Brad eased closer, sliding his hand into his pocket. He was going for his gun. He needed backup. He needed her. Staying low, she eased her door open and kicked off her heels. She was about to run to the right side of the vehicle and come up behind the gunman when she noticed a white sedan inching froward from the far side of the building. The carjacker wasn't working alone.

Brad must've noticed the white sedan at the same time she did. "NPD. Drop your weapon," he ordered as sirens wailed in the distance.

The man yanked the woman in front of him. Brad

didn't have a clear shot, and neither did Em. But one of the men in the white sedan did.

A warm tongue licked Em's cheek, dragging her out of the memory, but not fast enough that her screams weren't still echoing in her head.

"Thanks, boy," she said, her voice a hoarse whisper. She wondered if she'd screamed out loud and glanced at the fogged window. If she had, no one appeared to have heard her. No one but Gus. Resting his head on her thigh, he looked up at her with sad eyes. "You miss him too, don't you?"

The courthouse hadn't allowed dogs or they would've brought Gus with them that morning. It was another scenario she'd played over in her mind. If Gus had been there, he would've rushed the carjacker, and Brad would've had a chance. Same as if she'd stepped out from behind the door and distracted the gunman.

A truck's high beams lit up the interior of the Camaro, and she ducked her head, her fingers white-knuckling the steering wheel. She had to get out of there before someone noticed her sitting in the car with bloodshot eyes and a tearstained face. She pushed the vestiges of her memories back in the box and pulled away from the curb.

She lived fifteen minutes out of town in a small Craftsman bungalow on an old country road. She liked the quiet and the reasonable rent. If there was one drawback, it was driving the winding road along the river when the weather was bad. She'd have to trade in the Camaro for an SUV a couple of months from now.

As the lights from town disappeared behind her, Em

reduced her speed. A gray mist snaked across the dark, twisty road that was bordered by woods on the right and the narrow, fast-flowing river on the left. Her headlights illuminated the yellow deer crossing sign and the taillights of a vehicle up ahead. She noticed the out-of-state plates and the stick figures of a man, woman, and child on a sticker in the back window. She checked her speedometer. They were driving over the speed limit. Not by much but enough that it warranted a warning. The driver might not be aware of how dangerous this stretch of road could be.

She pressed the gas, about to turn on the light bar to alert the driver to her presence, when out of the corner of her eye she caught movement. She had no time to react before a deer darted out of the woods and into the path of the SUV. She braked hard, her car fishtailing before she regained control.

Up ahead, the SUV swerved to the left, hitting the shoulder and then losing control. Em watched in horror as it barreled toward the guardrails. She was out of her car and running for the rocky shore as the SUV flew through the air and into the river, the beams from the Camaro's headlights illuminating the driver's panicked face.

Em called it in, yelling their location into her shoulder mic before screaming at the occupants in the SUV. "Get out! Get your seat belts off and lower your windows!"

They had minutes before their vehicle was submerged. The water was already lapping midway up the doors. There was a little girl in a car seat in the back.

Em kept yelling, repeating the same instructions as she pulled off her boots and tossed her jacket and radio on the shore.

Gus danced in and out of the water, barking. "Stay!" Em ordered as she jerked the glass breaker off her utility belt and ran into the cold water.

The man frantically pounded on the window while the woman beside him leaned over the front seat to get to her crying child in the back. The SUV bobbed in the middle of the river, the current carrying it downstream. As Em swam after it, there was a loud *thunk*, and the SUV shuddered to a stop. It must've hit a rock. By the time Em reached the vehicle, the water had risen to the base of the still-closed windows. "I need you to stay calm. Throw the blanket over your daughter."

"Okay, okay." The mother nodded, tears streaming down her cheeks as she did what Em asked.

The second the blanket landed on the little girl; Em punched out the window with the glass breaker. "You need to get out now. I'll take your daughter."

"I can't swim," the woman said at the same time the man said, "My seat belt's stuck."

"Okay. Don't panic," she said as much for herself as for them. They wouldn't get out of this alive if she let the fear making her heart race win out. "I need you to climb over the seat and come out this way," Em directed the woman as she cleared the glass with the blanket, ignoring the water seeping into the vehicle. She leaned through the window to hand the father the glass breaker. "Flip the switch. There's a utility knife."

As the woman climbed into the backseat, Em smiled and unbuckled the little girl. "I'm going to take you and Mommy for a piggyback ride, okay?" She eased the child through the window, fighting the current and the numbing cold as she put her on her back. "Wrap your arms around my neck and hold on tight."

Treading water, Em put an arm behind her to hold the little girl in place while grabbing the door handle with her other hand to keep from being swept away. "Okay, Mom. Your turn now."

The car creaked and groaned, shifting on the rock. Water gushed through the window. Em looked toward shore, using a dead pine tree to mark the SUV's location.

The woman cast a frantic glance over her shoulder. "Steve, hurry! You have to hurry."

"I'm trying. But I can't—"

"I can help." The woman ducked her head back into the SUV.

"Jenny, no. Go. You've gotta go now. I love you. I love you both."

Em gritted her teeth at his emotional plea, the look of terror on his wife's face, and the little girl crying for her mommy and daddy. She reached for Jenny. "I'll come back and help him. But we have to go now."

Silent tears rolled down the woman's cheeks as she got onto Em's back, their combined weight nearly taking Em under.

"Jenny, I'm going to need you to kick and loosen your grip on my neck," Em said, pushing off the car and swimming toward shore. She fought against the current and the cold, shouting encouragement to the terrified woman and little girl on her back. She had to keep them calm. There was another loud groan and then a sucking sound. She didn't look back to confirm the SUV was now submerged.

"Look, we're almost there," she said in hopes of distracting Jenny and her daughter. "There's my dog. His name is..." A wave smacked her in the face, and she choked on a mouthful of water. "Gus. Do you see him?"

Headlights appeared on the road, and Gus raced toward the vehicle, barking. The car stopped, and an older woman and man got out. Gus grabbed the man's hand, tugging him toward the water's edge. "Mabel, call 911!" the man yelled, running into the water.

"I've got her," he said, helping Jenny off Em's back. She hadn't realized how close they were to shore. The water was at his waist. Em struggled to stand as she peeled the little girl's arms from her neck, bringing her around to her front. She carried her to shore, about to collapse on the rocks when Jenny broke free from the man screaming, "Steve! Steve!" She whirled on Em. "Please. You promised. You promised you'd help him."

Em nodded, wearily pushing herself to her feet.

The man reached for her. "Miss, you can't. You can't go back in there. Listen. Help is on the way."

She heard the sirens in the distance. "They won't make it in time."

Glancing at the dead pine tree on shore, Em waded through the shallow water, her movements sluggish. She rubbed her arms and legs to get the feeling back into them. When she reached the pine tree, she turned and walked up to her waist before diving beneath the water. Under normal circumstances, she swam fastest under water. But this was anything but normal. It felt like she was swimming through mud.

She came up for air where the SUV should be and treaded water, searching for some sign Steve had gotten out. The sirens were coming closer. She dove under again, stretching out her arms. Her fingers brushed against something. Hair or weeds, she wasn't sure. Her fingers were numb. Time was running out for both her and Steve. She didn't want to give up on him but she couldn't see more than a few inches in front of her. She'd barely completed the thought when a bright light illuminated the inky depths, and she saw Steve. He was alive.

He'd punched out the driver's side glass and was halfway out of the window. He pointed behind him. His foot had gotten caught in the shoulder strap. A surge of adrenaline gave her a burst of energy, and she swam through the backseat window and into the front seat. She struggled to free him, her vision dimming. Thinking of Jenny and his daughter, she got another surge of strength and a flash of insight. She pulled off his shoe.

As his foot slipped out of the shoulder strap, her vision went black. She could no longer see him, though she sensed he'd turned back to her. She shook her head, motioning for him to go. He wouldn't have the strength to swim her to the surface too. She wasn't afraid to die. She'd been half dead since losing Brad anyway.

"Em, open your eyes."

She startled at the sound of that deep, familiar voice. "Brad?" She struggled to lift her eyelids. His face swam before her, and she choked on a cry. "Oh Brad, I've missed you so much."

"I know, baby." His worried gaze roamed her face. "You don't have much time, Em. You have to fight."

She shook her head. "I have nothing more to live for. Not without you and the baby. I lost the baby. It was my fault."

"You have to stop telling yourself that. It's not true, Em. You couldn't save me, and you couldn't save her. You didn't do anything wrong. She's with me."

"I don't understand. How...You mean, the stories are true? There really is a heaven?"

He smiled and nodded. "Now come on. I know you're exhausted and cold but you can't give up. Not now."

"No. I want to stay here with you. I can't go on without you. I can't, Brad. You don't know what it's like." As hard as she tried, she couldn't keep her eyes open.

"Em, don't let go. Open your eyes."

She managed to open them a crack, enough that she could see his lips moving. "Em," he shouted.

She heard the urgency in his voice and fought to open her eyes wider.

"That's it. Keep fighting, Em. I'll stay with you. I won't leave you until you're ready to let me go."

"Promise?"

"I promise, baby. Just hang on. Help is on the way."

Chapter Three

♥

Josh scanned the river and the rocky shore as he jumped from the fire truck. He spotted a black Camaro with its headlights on and the door hanging open. It wasn't just any black Camaro. It was Em's.

"It looks like HFPD beat us to the scene," said Cody, a new member on their crew. He was a career firefighter who'd recently moved to the area. Like Josh, he wore a dry suit. They'd been told to prepare for a water rescue. The dive team wouldn't get there in time.

Josh sprinted toward the group huddled at the water's edge without responding to Cody, desperate to see Em lift her head and shoot him the look she reserved just for him. Her cherry-red lips compressed in a flat line, irritation flashing in her bottle-green eyes.

The searchlight hummed to life, illuminating the fast-moving river and the people on shore. Something inside of him had known she wouldn't be there.

An older man got to his feet. "I told her not to go back in but she wouldn't listen to me."

Of course, she wouldn't. Em was annoyingly contrary, frustratingly confident, and probably one of the most courageous people he knew, and he was going to shake her until her teeth rattled. "Can you show me where she went in? What direction she swam?"

"There. She looked like she was using that dead pine tree as a marker." The man pointed it out to him. Then he lowered his voice. "It's been at least two minutes since she dove in. The woman begged her to save her husband."

Josh shouted the location to the firefighter handling the searchlight. She immediately changed the angle, focusing the powerful beam of light in the middle of the river.

The older man's voice followed Josh and Cody into the water. "I don't know where she found the strength. She swam both the mother and her daughter to safety, the two of them on her back. Her lips were blue. She didn't notice that her dog went in after her."

"You know her. She matters to you, doesn't she?" Cody said as they battled the current to reach the middle of the river. "Don't bother denying it. I can see it on your face."

"She's family," Josh said, treading water in the center of the beam of light, searching for some sign of the husband, of Em and Gus. Something caught his attention, and his heart began to race. "There. On that rock. Is that a hand?" He didn't wait for Cody's response and swam downriver. It was a hand, but it didn't belong to Em. Gus had the man by the back of his collar, holding his head above water.

"Cody!" Josh waved, scanning the nearby rocks for Em while grabbing both Gus and the man. "Good boy. I've got him."

The man's eyes fluttered open as Josh rotated him onto his back, his voice barely a whisper. "Did she make it?"

"She wasn't with you?" He searched the shoreline as he placed the flotation device under the man. His head lolled, and Josh gave him a gentle shake. "Sir, where did you last see her?"

"Car...inside."

She was still down there. She had to be. Gus would've found her if she'd made it out. He lifted the dog onto the rock. "Stay here, boy." Gus whined, looking at him with his sad eyes. "I'll get her."

Cody glanced at him as he reached for the man. "Josh, it's been at least five minutes."

"You don't know Emma Scott. This is a rescue mission until I say otherwise." He'd never give up on Em.

Josh swam hard toward the beam of light, the current fighting him for every inch of progress. He caught a glimpse of a large shadow a few yards to his left and cut through the choppy, white-capped water with powerful strokes before diving under. The air constricted in his lungs. Em was floating inside the car. He wasn't too late. He couldn't be. Reaching inside the driver-side window, he grabbed her hand.

Hang on, Em. Don't give up, he silently pleaded as he eased her through the window and then pushed off the car with his feet, swimming as if his own life depended on it. He didn't know what he'd do if he lost Em. Or what his best friend would do, or hers. He shut down thoughts of Cal and Bri as he broke the surface of the water and turned Em onto her back, fitting his forearm under her chin. As he swam toward shore, he shouted at Em to stay with him, to fight. Cody swam out to him. Placing a flotation device under Em's back, he towed while Josh swam. The moment they reached shallow water, Josh lifted her into his arms and ran.

One of the paramedics helped load the man onto a gurney before rushing over and checking Em's pulse. "Hurry. Put her down." She grabbed a blanket and pointed to a grassy area on his right.

As soon as Josh laid Em out on the blanket, the woman tilted Em's head back, administering five rescue breaths before beginning chest compressions.

Josh knelt at Em's side and took her hand. The beds of her fingernails were blue. She was too wet for them to use a defibrillator. They'd waste precious time removing her clothes and drying her off. After the thirtieth chest compression, the paramedic checked for Em's pulse and then started over again.

"Em, come on. You're a fighter. You don't give up."

The chief, Cody, and the rest of the crew joined them, the blue and red lights from the emergency vehicles crisscrossing their somber faces.

"Mom, dad, and daughter are going to be fine," the chief said, the *whirr* of the departing siren confirming they at least were on the way to the hospital. In the distance, he heard the sound of another ambulance coming their way.

The older man walked over with Gus in his arms, placing him on the other side of Em. "Thought it might help them both if he was with her. They checked him over, and he's going to be fine." Gus whined, licking Em's hand. The man patted him. "He's a brave dog."

Josh drew his gaze from Gus pushing at Em with his nose and cleared the emotion from his throat. "He is." He thanked the man for all that he'd done. Then Josh glanced at the paramedic, who once again checked for Em's pulse.

She looked at Josh and shook her head.

Josh froze and then an anger unlike he'd ever felt before roared to life inside him. He moved the paramedic out of the way. "I've got this." He wouldn't stop until he got Em back. He'd read the stories about cold-water drownings. Some people had been brought back two hours after they'd been pulled from the water.

"I wasn't giving up on her," the paramedic said, leaning over to give Em two more rescue breaths.

"Good, because she wouldn't give up on you," he said, and restarted compressions. As he pushed down on her chest for the twenty-ninth time, his panic came out in his voice, "Damn it, Em. Fight!"

A small sound escaped from between her parted lips, and the paramedic quickly rolled her onto her side. Em coughed and then vomited what looked like a gallon of water. Josh had never been so happy to see someone puke in his entire life.

The second ambulance arrived, and within minutes, Em was on a gurney. "I'm coming with you and so is her dog," he informed the paramedics as they headed for the ambulance with Em. Josh scooped Gus into his arms and glanced at his boss.

The chief nodded and gave his shoulder an understanding squeeze. "Good job, son."

"Team effort," Josh said, lifting his chin at the crew in thanks. He didn't think he could talk without getting emotional. Now that he knew Em had a fighting chance, the tight reins that held his fear in check were letting go.

"If it's all right with you, Chief, I can drive Officer Scott's Camaro to the hospital," Cody offered. "Keys were inside."

The chief agreed, and Josh called over his shoulder without breaking stride. "Have a care, Cody. That's her baby. I wouldn't want to be you if there's so much as a scratch on it."

"Okay, which one of you told him I took out my muffler on the speed bump?" Cody said.

"You'd better be jok..." Josh trailed off as he jumped into the back of the ambulance and immediately clapped a hand over his eyes.

"Oh, come on. Don't try and tell us you've never seen a woman in her bra and panties."

"Not that woman, and if she ever found out that I did, she'd stick burning pokers in my eyes." Feeling for the chair with his foot, he lowered himself onto it.

"Did you hear that, Lottie?" the paramedic called to her partner in the driver's seat.

"Oh yes, I did. Now, coach, about my son making your team next year," Lottie said, a gurgle of laughter in her voice.

The teasing felt good, normal, and helped slow the panicked gallop of his heart. He had a feeling Lottie and her partner knew exactly what they were doing. "As if you'd have to blackmail me. The kid has great hands. I can't wait to have him on my team."

"You can uncover your eyes, Coach. She's decent."

"You sure about that?"

Lottie hooted. "The man actually sounds scared of her."

"Have you met Emma Scott?" he asked, completely serious as he lowered his hand from his eyes. Em was covered in a trauma blanket, and he was relieved to see a hint of color returning to her face.

"I have, and she's never been anything but professional and kind."

"Lucky you," he said, then glanced at the screen monitoring Em's heartbeat. "That's good, right?"

"Weak but steady," the paramedic said, looking up from adjusting an IV drip. "She's not out of the woods yet, but she's young and obviously physically fit. There's no way she could've done what she did tonight if she wasn't."

He hadn't had time to process the lengths to which Em had gone to rescue the family. There was part of him that still wanted to shake her for risking her life while the other part of him was in awe of what she'd done. In awe, yet not surprised.

She'd been as courageous in grade school as she'd been tonight. He'd seen her climb to the top of a thirty-foot tree to rescue a kitten and take on bullies twice her size. In high school, she'd faced off with the mean girls and spoke out against a teacher for fat-shaming a student. She was fierce and never backed down, even when the teacher threatened to expel her. Josh was pretty sure she'd given him and his best friend gray hairs before they were eighteen.

Thinking about Cal, he asked the paramedic, "Can I borrow your cell? I need to give Em's brother a heads-up."

He lowered Gus onto the floor. "Lie down, boy." He didn't want him getting in the way. Gus ignored him. But instead of facing Em, he sat and stared at the side of the ambulance behind Josh.

The paramedic nodded, handing over her cell. Then she went back to monitoring Em.

"Thanks." Josh glanced at Gus, who was sniffing the side of the ambulance. He didn't have time to wonder what was up with the dog as the call connected.

"Hello."

"Cal, it's me."

"Little busy here, bro. Ambulance is pulling in now."

"Yeah, about that." He wished there was a way to soften the blow. "Cal, it's Em." He gave him a quick summary of Em's heroics. "I'm with her in the ambulance. She's going to be okay, Cal." He glanced at Em, praying it was true.

Josh loved his siblings. They were close but nothing like Cal and Em. Their father had abandoned his family when Cal was ten, and their mother had taken on two jobs to make ends meet. She hadn't been around much, and though he was only two years older than Em, Cal had taken on the role of father and mother.

"Cal?"

"Yeah," his voice was tight, like he was trying to hold it together. "Let me talk to the paramedic."

Josh handed her the phone. "He wants to talk to you."

As she relayed Em's vitals to Cal, Josh hoped they were good enough to set his best friend's mind at ease.

"You forgot to mention you were a hero too, Coach," the paramedic said after disconnecting from Cal. "If it wasn't for you, his sister most likely wouldn't have made it."

"I was just doing my job. If it wasn't me, my partner would've got her. And give yourself some credit. She wouldn't be here without you. None of us do this alone."

"Told you he was a good guy, Robyn," Lottie said.

"Hey, you make it sound like someone's saying I'm not," Josh said.

Lottie winced. "Hate to tell you, Coach, but you've got yourself a reputation as a ladies' man. They call you the Heartbreaker of Highland Falls."

They had it wrong. He was the one who'd had his heart broken when his wife left him three years ago. He'd thought they had a good marriage. Sure, they'd had their ups and downs, but who didn't. His parents and Cal and Bri were an anomaly.

He'd been shocked when he'd come home from work to find his wife gone, their joint bank accounts cleaned out. Two days later, she'd filed for divorce. A week later, he'd learned she'd left him for her ex-boyfriend. It'd taken Josh almost two years to feel like putting himself out there again. But as much as he enjoyed women and dating, he wasn't up for anything long term. Which was probably how he'd earned himself the heartbreaker designation.

"Do you not hear the sirens, people?" Lottie grumbled, blasting the horn.

Josh was about to suggest she take the side street when he felt the weight of someone's stare. He glanced at Em, relieved to see her eyes open. She smiled, a beautiful, luminous smile, and it was a shock to his system. It was a very un-Em-like smile, especially when it was directed at him. There was something different about the way she looked at him too. A softness, a vulnerability in her eyes that he'd never seen before.

"You stayed," she whispered.

"Of course I stayed." He took her hand in his. It was still cold, and he clasped it between both of his. "You almost died, Em."

Her gaze moved to his, and she frowned, her dusky-pink lips turning down. And that's when he knew she hadn't been looking at him after all. But who had she been talking to, if not him? He glanced at Gus, who'd moved to Em's side and licked her cheek. Okay, so maybe she'd been talking to the dog. But something didn't feel right.

"You up to answering a few questions, Officer Scott?" Robyn asked.

Em nodded, looking at Josh with another one of those luminous smiles, and it freaked him out. "Ah, Em, Robyn asked if you know today's date," he said, repeating the question the paramedic had just asked.

"Saturday, September twenty-fifth," Em said, her voice a hoarse whisper.

She didn't seem to be suffering any cognitive impairment, which was great, but it didn't explain why it felt like she was staring at him but not really seeing him. He glanced over his shoulder and noticed that Gus was looking behind him too.

Josh returned his attention to Em. "How old are you?"

"Thirty," she said with a touch of attitude. Okay, that was more like the Em he knew.

"Do you know where you live?"

"Yeah, thirty-nine Sugar Maple Road."

"Do you know who I am?"

"Yeah, a pain in my butt," she said, drawing a guffaw from Lottie and a smile from Robyn.

Oh yeah, she was back to her grumpy self, and for some reason, that ticked *him* off. "Yeah, well this pain in your butt saved your life. A little gratitude instead of attitude would be appreciated."

She glanced at Robyn.

The paramedic nodded with a smile. "He did. At one point, he thought I'd given up on you, and he took over the last round of chest compressions. So if you have bruised ribs, blame him."

"I'm sure she will," Josh said, worried now that he might've cracked one of her ribs.

"Thanks," Em murmured, glancing up at him.

"You don't have to thank me, Freckles." He added her childhood nickname in hopes of getting a rise out of her. He didn't want her getting lost in her head, thinking about how she'd felt the seconds before she'd lost consciousness. He couldn't imagine how terrified she must've been. He didn't want to think about how close they'd come to losing her.

A *beep, beep* signaled the ambulance was backing into the hospital bay, and Robyn prepared for Em to be off-loaded. "Can you carry the IV for me, Coach?" the paramedic asked as the ambulance came to a stop, and the doors opened.

"Sure." He stood up, reaching for the bag.

Em turned her head in his direction and nodded. "I love you too," she whispered.

Josh dropped the IV bag on her chest.

Chapter Four

♥

Em's brain felt sluggish, her mouth dry, and every muscle in her body ached. She heard the rattle of carts and orders being called out in the hall outside her room over the steady hum of the machines monitoring her vitals. She was lying on an uncomfortable hospital bed, covered by a warm blanket. She didn't need to open her eyes to know it was morning. The room was bright, and she smelled bacon and eggs.

She placed a hand on her grumbling stomach, tempted to reach for the Call button and ask for something to eat. But then she'd have to open her eyes. She didn't want to. She was afraid last night had been a dream, and Brad had never been there. Her oxygen-deprived brain playing tricks on her.

She cracked open her eyes and turned her head. Brad smiled and moved to the side of the bed.

"You really are here," she whispered, smiling as she reached for his hand. Her fingers went through his, landing on the cold, metal rail instead. He looked so vibrant and alive, but he wasn't, and a ball of emotion clogged her throat.

He met her gaze, and she saw her own sorrow reflected in his eyes. "I wish I could touch you, hold you, kiss you, but I can't, Em."

"I don't care. I'm just glad you're here. That you didn't leave me."

"I was always with you. Even if you couldn't feel me or see me."

"But you're here now, aren't you? I'm not imagining this."

"I'm here, Em."

"And you'll stay. You won't leave me."

He hesitated, and her heart began to race, causing the monitor to beep. "You promised."

"I know I did. It's just that—" He looked away.

"It's just what?" She was so focused on Brad she didn't realize her brother had entered the room until he said, "Em, who are you talking to?"

If she told him Brad, she'd never get out of the hospital. "Myself."

Cal frowned and walked to her side. He leaned in and hugged her. "You scared the hell out of us."

She nodded, tamping down a defensive response. It wasn't as if she'd nearly drowned on purpose. But she would've felt and said the same if their roles were reversed.

Cal straightened and looked her over. "No headaches? No dizziness?"

"I'm fine. I just want to go home."

"Maybe later today. I've ordered more bloodwork,

another chest X-ray, and an MRI." He glanced at his phone. "Dr. Rashida, the neurologist, will probably want to run more tests too."

"No way." She threw back the covers with the thought of getting out of bed but the pinch of the tubes attached to her hand had her flopping against the pillow. "I don't need more tests. I feel like a pincushion. I just need to sleep, and I can't do it here."

It was true, but she also wanted to be alone with Brad. At home where she wouldn't have to worry someone would walk in and catch her talking to him. She fussed with the blanket so her brother wouldn't notice her sneaking a peek in Brad's direction. Brad lifted his eyebrows, nudging his head at Cal, who of course hadn't taken his eyes off her.

"Where's Bri?" she asked, hoping to distract him. Em also hoped her best friend could work her magic on Cal and get her released.

Cal drew his gaze from where Brad was standing, nothing in his expression indicating he saw anything out of the ordinary. Em wasn't sure but she figured that's how it worked. No one would see Brad but her. Still, underneath the relief that he was there, she had a niggle of doubt.

She couldn't quite accept that this was real. Maybe if she was into the woo-woo like the Sisterhood, she wouldn't be questioning that the man she loved was standing there with a half smile on his handsome face. But that wasn't her. She questioned, analyzed, and evaluated the facts. She took nothing at face value. Those traits were what made her a good cop but right now they were stealing some of the joy of being reunited with Brad. She needed evidence she wasn't imagining him.

"She went to grab you some breakfast," Cal said, looking, she assumed, at her chart on his iPad.

"Great. I'm starved."

"Figured you would be." He rolled his shoulders.

"Were you here all night?"

"Yeah, so were Bri and Josh. We took turns sitting with you. Gus was banished to my office when he jumped on the bed and took out one of your lines. Gabe and a couple of your coworkers dropped by. Izzy too."

Em had woken up once or twice in the night but had been barely able to open her eyes. She prayed it was the same for her mouth. "Did I talk to anyone? I don't remember."

"No. You were exhausted. You'll need to take it easy, Em. No playing superhero for the next week at least," he said, lowering the bed rail. "Same goes for Gus." He told her how Gus had rescued Steve and how Josh had saved her. "Josh took Gus back to his place."

She had a faint memory of seeing Gus and Josh in the ambulance, but it was foggy, and she'd been focused on Brad. "Steve, Jenny, and their little girl are okay?"

He nodded. "We kept mom and daughter overnight for observation and, like you, we'll run a few more tests on Steve before he's released. I'm sure they'll want to stop by and thank you before they leave."

"I was just doing my job. Right place, right time."

"You would think that, Freckles. But everyone around here thinks you're a hero, including Steve and his family, so you're just going to have to put up with the gratitude and accolades." He grinned when she groaned. "And you might want to prepare yourself for a parade of visitors. The nurses have been fielding calls since news spread around town. Including from Phil and Patsy, who didn't understand why they couldn't see you since you're family."

Em and Cal shared a smile. Josh's parents, Phil and Patsy, had basically adopted Em and Cal as members of their family. They'd had a standing invitation to all of the Callahan's holiday celebrations, and not just the major ones. If Patsy had her way, they'd be celebrating something every week, and Phil would be right there with her.

Bri walked in carrying two large takeaway bags, her smile turning into a frown as she came around the bed. She shivered. "You must be freezing, Em."

"No. Why?"

She waved one of the takeaway bags in Brad's direction. "You don't feel the draft?"

"Where exactly do you feel a draft?" Em asked, thinking this might be the evidence she was looking for.

Bri went and stood *in* Brad. "Right here."

Em mentally pumped her fist. If Bri could feel something, it was evidence Em wasn't suffering a hypoxic brain injury.

But then Cal, who was adjusting the hospital bed table over Em, glanced up at the ceiling. "You're standing under the air vent, babe."

And poof, just like that, her evidence disappeared. Thankfully, Brad didn't.

"Maybe you can get them to close the vent. It can't be

good for Em." Bri placed the takeaway bags on the table and leaned in to hug her. "We were so worried about you. When Cal told me..." She straightened, swiping a finger under her eye. "I'm just so glad you're here, and you're okay. I don't know what we would've done if something had—"

Em had been ready to give up. If it wasn't for Brad, she would have. She hadn't thought about her brother and Bri and what losing her would've meant to them.

Afraid the guilt tightening her throat would be reflected on her face, Em cut off her best friend. "Please tell me you got me coffee and breakfast sandwiches from Highland Brew."

"I did," Bri said, opening the bags. "I also got you chocolate scones." She held Em's gaze as she laid everything out on napkins. "I know you don't like sharing your feelings or dealing with anyone else's, but we love you, and we nearly lost you. So you'll have to get used to us being mushy and emotional for a little while."

Em focused on a breakfast sandwich and picked it up. "For how long?"

She sensed her brother and Bri sharing a glance and heard the amusement in her best friend's voice when she said, "Six weeks."

"One, but I'll give you an extra week if you can convince my overprotective brother to release me." She went to take a bite of the sandwich, muttering around it, "I love you too. Both of you."

* * *

"This is not what I had in mind when I asked you to convince Cal to release me," Em said from the Camaro's passenger seat. She glanced over her shoulder at Brad, who was sitting in the backseat, taking in the scenery. It was midafternoon, and the sun was shining on Blue Mountain. Bri had taken the long way around to avoid the scene of last night's drama.

"Making frowny faces over your shoulder at your brother isn't going to change his mind," Bri said, easing up on the gas as she approached a hairpin curve.

"I don't make frowny faces." She made them all the time, as evidenced by the indent between her eyebrows, especially when she was on a case and trying to figure something out. Like how her dead fiancé was here and hanging out in the backseat of the Camaro.

"But if I was, it's because I'm trying to figure out who's in the vehicle behind Cal." She hoped there was a vehicle behind her brother's Jeep. It was the only excuse she could come up with for why she kept looking back and frowning.

"It's Josh. He got a new truck last week. Or I guess I should say an old truck. He says it's a classic. Didn't you see it?"

"No. Why would I? But more important, why is Josh following Cal?" Then she deduced the answer to her question on her own. "Right, he's dropping off Gus."

"Not exactly." Bri glanced at her. "Cal has to go back to the hospital, and I have a client I can't cancel. Josh offered to stay with you."

"No way. I don't need a babysitter."

"Humor us, Em. It hasn't been twenty-four hours since Josh pulled you from the river."

"I realize that, which is why I agreed to go back for X-rays and whatever else my brother wants to subject me to tomorrow. Even though I'm feeling fine."

"That's part of the problem. We're worried you'll overdo it. And as much as Josh tried to hide it, I think last night was difficult for him. It'll be good for you guys to talk about it. He'll be able to understand what you went through better than anyone."

"I doubt that," Em said, thinking of Brad. "Besides, I'm sure he has better things to do with his time than hang out with me."

"I remember a time when all you wanted to do was hang out with Josh."

She crossed her arms. "I did not."

"Em, you were in love with him. You wrote Em Callahan inside your notebooks."

She totally had. It was annoying to have a best friend who'd known her since she was a tween. She glanced back at Brad. He grinned, moving his eyebrows up and down.

"I was young and stupid. And I wasn't in love with him. I had a crush on him," she said for both Brad and Bri's benefit.

"No. I distinctly remember, when we were sharing who our first loves were, you said Josh Callahan," Brad insisted.

"It has to be reciprocated for it to be love, and it wasn't. If anything, Josh treated me like an annoying little sister." Thankfully, her response to Brad wasn't totally out of left field.

"Not always. Remember the summer we were seventeen?" Bri said as she turned onto Sugar Maple Road. "He seemed interested in you then. The only reason he kept you in the friend zone was because he's Cal's best friend."

"Why are we even talking about this?" Em asked, anxious to change the subject. It felt weird talking about a man she'd once had a crush on with her fiancé sitting in the backseat, even though Brad was right. They had talked about it before. He hadn't been bothered about it then, and he clearly wasn't bothered about it now. If anything, he seemed to be mulling their conversation over in thoughtful contemplation.

Bri didn't answer Em's mostly rhetorical question as she pulled onto the side of the gravel road just down from the mailbox. And the reason Bri pulled onto the side of the road was because Em's driveaway was packed with cars. She ducked down. "Back up before they see us. You can take me to your house."

"Too late," Bri said, waving at someone. "But just think, you won't have to order in for a month, maybe two. You should probably reconsider Josh staying and hanging out with you though."

"Why would I do that?"

"Because if people stay for a while, he'll entertain them. Unlike you, he's great at small talk, and he actually likes people," Bri said.

She could tell her best friend was trying not to laugh

but Em was focused on what else Bri seemed to be implying. "What people? They're already here."

"I have a feeling this is just the beginning." Bri shrugged at Em's horrified expression. "You live in a small town. This is what people do. You know that."

She did. When their father had abandoned them, people showed up with food, helped with the yard work, and volunteered to take Cal to his football practices and games and Em to her swim practices and meets.

"You nearly died saving that family, Em," Bri continued while undoing her seat belt. "You're a hero in everyone's eyes but your own. This is their way of honoring you and letting you know they're proud of you."

Someone knocked on Em's window, and she looked to see Phil and Patsy's smiling faces pressed against the glass. "Fine. Josh can stay," she said through a clenched-teeth smile.

As soon as she got out of the car, Patsy smothered her in a hug. "Sweetheart, we were so worried about you, and those darn nurses wouldn't let us come visit."

"Didn't stop Patsy from trying though. She was five feet from your room when they spotted her. I told her she should've taken off her Crocs. They squeak," Phil said, giving his wife a toothy grin before nudging her aside to hug Em. "We were worried about you, Emmy. You and Josh."

"The two of you scared—" Patsy broke off as Josh approached, beaming at him as if he were the second coming. Phil and Patsy were doting parents. They thought the sun rose and set in their children. It was a wonder Josh and his siblings turned out to be decent, productive members of society and not narcissistic sociopaths.

"Mom, Dad, I thought we agreed you'd wait until tomorrow to see Em." Josh sent her an apologetic glance.

"We did, but then we looked on the community Facebook page, and everyone was talking about stopping by and what they were bringing. We didn't want Em to think we didn't love her as much as everyone else." She tucked her arm through Em's. "I went to the grocery store and picked up all your favorite things, sweetheart."

"In other words, she got you a crapload of junk food," Josh said.

"Got a crapload for herself too, son."

"You're such a tattletale, Phil." Patsy patted Em's arm. "Let's go. I'll unpack everything for you and get you all set up. We don't want you doing a single thing."

Em cast a frantic look around and spotted her brother and her best friend talking to Bri's family, including Granny MacLeod, who was staring at Em. No, she wasn't staring at her. She was frowning at Brad, who stood beside the car, taking it all in. And Granny MacLeod wasn't the only one looking at him—so was Gus. Em might've appreciated the evidence that someone other than herself saw—or at least sensed—Brad was there if she wasn't freaking out that people were going to enter her house. And not just any people, her brother and Bri.

"Uh, okay. I just need a minute," she said, and took off, running for the front door.

"Em!" her brother yelled. "You're supposed to take it easy."

"Don't you have to go to work? You too," she said to Bri. Then she unlocked the front door, hurried inside, and shut it behind her. She locked it just in case someone had followed her. Except apparently a locked door couldn't stop a ghost, she thought, as Brad walked through it.

"Em, what's going..." He trailed off as he looked around.

"Don't judge. I've been busy," she said, jogging toward the kitchen, wishing the bungalow didn't have an open layout. The only thing better than having a kitchen door to shut was if Brad could give her a hand. As soon as the thought popped into her head, she felt guilty, as though she were judging him and found him lacking in his ghost-state.

But her guilt was replaced by panic when she heard the jiggle of a key in the front door. The door opened, and she let out a relieved breath, which wasn't her typical response to seeing Josh.

"Hurry. Shut the door and lock it," she said.

He didn't argue or goggle at the mess. He did as she asked, putting the bag he'd been carrying on the coffee table. "Where do you keep the garbage bags?"

She opened the pantry door, reached up for the box, took out one for her and one for him.

Josh took both bags. "I've got it. You go sit down."

"No time," she said, taking a bag from him. "If we're lucky, we have two minutes before someone starts pounding on the door."

"Yeah, you're probably right." He nodded, then grinned. "Okay, go. Whoever fills their bag fastest wins."

"You're on." She swept the containers off the counter and into her bag. "Wait a minute, what do I win?"

"Bragging rights," he said, heading for the living room and a pile of clothes on a chair.

Em glanced at Brad. His head was bowed, and his lips were turned down at the corners, the picture of sorrow. As if sensing her attention, he lifted his gaze to hers, and she saw the worry in his eyes. She knew what he was seeing, what he was thinking. Her brother had looked at her the same way last fall when he'd come to bring her home.

But no matter what it looked like, she was better than she'd been then. She gave Brad a bright smile, hoping to lift his spirits, but an hour later, she was having a hard time keeping up a cheerful front.

Bri had been right. The afternoon had brought a steady stream of visitors, and Em had enough baked goods and casseroles to last at least two months. The freezer on the back porch that she'd never had reason to use was almost full.

Patsy was in her glory and in hostess mode, plying their guests with tea, coffee, and cookies. Phil, who like his son had been a high school gym teacher and varsity football coach, was timing everyone's visits. Every fifteen minutes, he whistled, signaling it was time for one group of visitors to leave and to allow another group in.

And then there was Josh, holding court. He didn't do it intentionally; people were just naturally drawn to him. Grudgingly, she admitted, if only to herself, that she understood the attraction. It had nothing to do with his looks. Okay, so for some of her visitors, they were definitely a draw. But Josh had a gift for making people feel at ease and appreciated.

Bri was right. Having him stay had been a good idea. He'd never strayed more than a few feet from Em and had saved her butt on a few occasions when she didn't know someone's name or when talk veered to her hero status. She'd noticed he was as uncomfortable as she was with the accolades, sharing them with his crew and EMS.

As though he sensed the direction of her thoughts, Josh glanced at her, smiled, and mouthed *You okay?* She didn't want to admit she was tired and nodded instead. His gaze roamed her face, and then he excused himself from her neighbors down the road and walked to where Patsy was placing a fresh batch of oatmeal cookies on the kitchen table.

Brad stood by the patio doors, a few feet behind Josh's mom. Em had been avoiding looking at him in case someone noticed. It was bad enough that Gus sat behind him staring. Whenever someone commented on it, Em said the goldendoodle was mesmerized by the wildlife in the backyard. Em allowed herself a quick glance at Brad and then wished she hadn't. His expression hadn't changed. If anything, he looked more depressed, and she was afraid she knew why. Abby Mackenzie sat at the table with two of Em's coworkers, Gwen and Todd.

The three of them weren't shy about sharing their opinion that she needed to get a life and get back in the dating game. As they'd told her five minutes ago, a near-death experience was a life-changing moment. They were probably hatching a plan now. And they weren't the only ones, Em thought when Brad lifted his gaze to hers.

Her fiancé was a man of action. There wasn't a problem he couldn't solve. It's what had made him an exceptional detective. And apparently, from that look in his eyes, she was the problem he had to fix.

Chapter Five

♥

Josh stood in Em's bedroom. There was something going on with her. Not because she'd locked herself in her en suite bathroom twenty minutes earlier; that had been his mom's doing. She'd suggested Em take a bubble bath after he'd mentioned that Em was done in. He'd figured she'd have better luck convincing Em to rest than he would.

He was a little surprised when Em agreed to a bubble bath but imagined that escaping from the steady flow of well-wishers had won her over.

He threw parties at least once a month, the bigger the better, and even he'd been ready for everyone to leave. And while Em telling him she loved him in the ambulance had freaked him out, it wasn't the reason he thought something was going on with her. Her confession was easily explained away. It happened a lot to first responders. It had probably even happened to Em. People confused their gratitude for love.

No, the reason he believed something was going on

with Em was happening behind that closed bathroom door. He'd heard her talking when he'd come to check on her. It sounded like a two-way conversation but there was no one in the bathroom with her. Gus was asleep on Em's bed, and her cell phone was sitting on the coffee table. He'd just come back from checking.

He pressed his ear to the door.

"Josh?"

He winced and backed away, wondering how she knew he was there. He opened his mouth to explain himself, but she continued talking.

"I should date Josh? Why would I do that? Why would you even want me to?"

Josh didn't know whether to be offended or relieved. Relieved, definitely relieved, he decided. Except Em was having an actual conversation with herself, and part of her apparently wanted to date him while the other part of her was arguing vehemently against it.

He scrubbed his hands up and down his face, wondering if he should mention this to Cal. And while the last thing he wanted to bring up with Em was her dropping the *I love you* bomb on him the night before, he didn't see any way around it. They had to deal with this head-on. He had to let her down gently, at least the part of her that thought dating him was a good idea.

He was about to knock when he heard the front door opening. He was glad for the interruption but he was debating how to break the news to Em that they couldn't date and doubted he'd be very good company.

"It's just me," his mother called out.

"Mom?" He walked out of Em's bedroom. "What's up? I thought you and dad were going to bingo." Tonight was the last night for drive-in bingo at the fairgrounds.

"We are, but when I went to put out pajamas for Em to wear after her bubble bath, I noticed she only had those silky ones. You know the kind, I mean?"

"No, Mom, I don't." And he really didn't want to talk about Em's silky pjs. Not after what he'd just overheard. Plus he'd seen enough of her underwear and bras when he'd been stuffing her laundry into the garbage bag. Lacy and sexy, they were very un-Em-like, and very distracting. Which was probably why Em cleaned up her part of the house faster than he had and won bragging rights.

"Oh, you know, the ones with the little strappy tops and shorty shorts? Your dad bought me a pair for Valentine's last year. They had the cutest—"

"TMI, Mom. We've talked about this, remember?" His parents had a very happy marriage and a very active sex life, and his mother had a tendency to overshare.

She laughed and breezed past him into Em's bedroom. "Emmy, I brought you a pair of cozy jammies to keep you warm. I'll just leave them on your bed, sweetheart."

"Uh, thanks, Patsy. But you didn't have to do that."

Josh glanced at the fuzzy orange pajama top and fuzzy black bottoms decorated with pumpkins that his mom pulled out of the bag.

"I know, but I wanted to. I bought them for Amber, and she never wore them."

When they were kids, their mom bought them holiday-themed pjs every year and continued the tradition into adulthood. A tradition that his ex, Amber, had refused to take part in. She wasn't a fan of the holidays. His mom didn't give up though, and it hadn't exactly endeared her to Amber. He had a feeling his family weren't disappointed when she left him. Upset for him, of course, but deep down, he imagined they were relieved.

"Oh, okay. Thanks, Patsy."

"No problem, sweetheart. You and Josh have a good night."

"He's still here?"

He was about to roll his eyes when he realized it was actually a good sign she sounded ticked he was there. "I'm on *babysitting* duty until Cal and Bri relieve me, remember?" He figured the *babysitting* jab would remind her why she wasn't interested in dating him.

"Don't you listen to her if she tries to make you leave," his mom whispered, closing Em's bedroom door behind them. "That girl puts on a good show but she has a soft heart. She's been through a traumatic experience, and so have you. You need each other." She patted his cheek with a look in her eyes that made him nervous. "You know, your dad and I always thought you and Emmy would end up together. Maybe now that you're both single—"

"Mom, you promised. No more matchmaking." He pulled his phone from his pocket and tapped the screen. "It's six thirty. You don't want to be late." He kissed her cheek and walked to the door, holding it open for her.

"Have fun, and thanks again for helping out today. I know Em appreciated it."

"You tell her I'll stop by tomorrow around two. We should be finished painting the kindness rocks by then." Her eyes lit up. "I'll have the kids paint rocks for Em, and we can put them in her front garden. It could use a little sprucing up."

His mom had taught kindergarten for thirty-five years. She'd retired two years ago but couldn't seem to stay away and volunteered three times a week.

Josh glanced at the flower bed. It needed more than a little sprucing up. The plants were dead. "You might want to give Em a call before you drop by. She's got an appointment at the hospital tomorrow."

"I'll do..." She trailed off as a car pulled into the driveway. "I wonder who that is? I posted visiting hours on the community Facebook page."

Josh recognized the man and woman getting out of the rental car and lowered his voice. "It's the family Em rescued." He smiled, raising his hand in greeting.

"Hi, Josh. I hope you don't mind us dropping by," Steve said as his wife got their five-year-old out of the car seat.

Josh had checked in on them a couple times last night and again early this morning before he'd left the hospital. They were pale and looked a little shaky. He imagined it had been traumatizing making the drive along the river so soon after the accident.

"Not at all. I'm sure Em will be happy to see you," Josh said. Happy was probably a stretch but he knew she wouldn't turn them away.

Steve took the little girl from Jenny and placed her on his hip and then reached for his wife's hand.

"Oh my, you poor things," his mom said, meeting them halfway up the walkway. "I'm Josh's mom, Patsy."

The couple smiled and introduced themselves. "This is our daughter, Charlotte." The little girl, her dark hair in pigtails, buried her face in her father's shoulder, a stuffed unicorn clutched in her hand.

"That's a beautiful unicorn you have there. Does it have a name?" Patsy asked, meeting Josh's eyes and nudging her head at the door.

He was glad his mom thought of it. A heads-up was probably in order. "I'll let Em know you're here." He left the door half open and then headed for Em's bedroom. He knocked on the closed door, surprised when it opened right away.

Em, her auburn hair in a messy topknot and a scowl on her face, was wearing the pumpkin pajamas. "You're not taking my blood pressure or my temperature," she said, brushing past him. Gus jumped off the bed and followed her to the kitchen.

Cal had left a blood pressure monitor, digital forehead thermometer, and a stethoscope on the kitchen counter before heading to the hospital. He'd asked Josh to send him updates every three hours, which would be now. He thought about asking his mom to take care of it but instead said, "No problem. You can do the readings yourself."

"You're right, I can." She looked up something on her phone.

"Let me guess. You're looking up normal readings for all three and then you'll text them to Cal."

"Nope, you will."

He shook his head. "No way. This isn't something to fool around with, Em. Besides, your readings probably shouldn't be normal yet, and Cal will know."

Her eyes went wide, and she looked at him. "Did you forget to tell me something?" she whispered.

He glanced over his shoulder. "You distracted me," he whispered back. Then he smiled. "Come on in."

Jenny hesitated, looking from Josh to Em. "Are you sure you don't mind?"

"No, it's fine. How are you guys doing?" Em asked, nudging him with her elbow as she walked past him to greet the family standing in the entryway.

"You're a pumpkin," Charlotte said, giving Em a shy smile.

Em looked down at herself. "Huh. I guess I am. Do you like Halloween?"

"Uh-huh. We're witches. It's our holiday."

"Oh, okay. Cool. I've never met a witch before. Do you want to come in and sit down?" Em gestured to the living room, ushering the family inside while sending Josh *a what the heck?* glance.

"Sorry, I should probably explain," Jenny began as she took a seat on an armchair.

Her daughter cut her off, frowning at Em. "But you're a witch too."

Em scratched her temple as she lowered herself onto the coach. "I have been called a witch before, so I guess you're right."

Josh worked to contain his amusement. Em didn't appreciate his sense of humor. "You guys want something to drink or eat?" he asked. "We've got a ton of food. There's a lasagna in the oven and chicken soup on the stove."

"Here, pumpkin, come sit on my knee," Steve said as he took a seat in the armchair beside his wife.

Em got a horrified look on her face, and this time Josh couldn't hold back a laugh.

Steve chuckled, pointing at Charlotte, who'd joined Gus on the floor by the patio doors. "I meant my daughter." Then he and his wife shared a silent exchange, and he smiled at Josh. "If you're sure it's not an inconvenience, we'll take you up on your offer."

Em cast a nervous glance at Gus and the little girl. Josh didn't understand why. The goldendoodle was great with kids. "No trouble at all. Em's got enough food to last for a few months, and no doubt it's just the beginning of the casserole parade."

"Thank you. We really appreciate it," Jenny said. "We've rented a place up the road from you, and with everything that happened, I completely forgot to go to the grocery store before we left town."

"Josh is right. I'll never be able to eat half of the food in my freezer. You can help yourself to whatever you need," Em said, casting another look over her shoulder at Gus.

"Em's brother and sister-in-law are heading back here in an hour. They'd be happy to pick up whatever else you need," Josh said as he opened the oven, lifting the foil to check on the vegetable lasagna.

"We appreciate the offer, but if you can spare some milk and some coffee, we'll be fine until tomorrow morning," Steve said.

"Got you covered," Josh said, putting on oven mitts.

"How are you for clothes and toiletries?" Em asked. Then she lowered her voice. "Have they recovered your vehicle from the river? Sorry, I shouldn't have brought it up," she added when Steve reached for his wife's hand.

"No, it's fine. We think it's important to talk about the accident so Charlotte is comfortable sharing her feelings about it," Jenny said. "And it's not like we can avoid driving by where it happened."

"You actually can," Em said. "It adds about ten minutes to the drive, but if you want, I can give you directions."

"We might take you up on that. More for me than for Jenny and Charlotte."

"Steve, it wasn't your fault. If it was anyone's fault, it was mine." She cast a sheepish glance at Em. "I'm pregnant, and I had to go to the bathroom. That's why Steve was going over the speed limit. I noticed you just before the deer ran out in front of us. I was going to tell him to slow down and then..." She trailed off.

"It wasn't anyone's fault," Em reassured the couple. "You weren't going much over the limit. I saw your out-of-state plates, and I was going to warn you about the road."

"All I can say is thank God you were behind us. If you hadn't been, we wouldn't be sitting here now," Steve said. "We can't thank you enough for what you did."

Em shrugged. "I did what anyone would do."

"No. Not everyone would have risked their life like you did." Jenny bowed her head and then raised her gaze to Em. "It wasn't fair that I asked you to go back for Steve. You nearly died because of me, and I hope you can forgive me."

"There's nothing to forgive, Jenny. I would've done the same thing in your place."

Josh counted down in his head as he placed the lasagna on the counter, positive that Em would change the subject in three, two, one...He smiled when she said, "Lasagna smells amazing, doesn't it? You guys must be hungry."

"Famished," Jenny agreed with a smile. "Can I help with anything, Josh?"

"All good here, thanks." He glanced at the table and then at Em. She looked beat. "Actually, there's a couple of TV trays in that corner." He nodded to the stand beside the TV. "If you, Steve, and Charlotte don't mind eating in the living room, you could set them up."

"Works for us," Steve said, moving to get two TV trays out of the stand.

Once Josh had everyone set up with drinks and lasagna, he took a seat beside Em on the couch. Charlotte was more interested in Gus than eating, so Josh had wrapped up a plate for her to take with them.

"The two of you risked your lives for us, and now you're feeding us too. You'll have to let us return the favor." Steve grinned. "Not the rescuing part. Jenny and I aren't the superhero types, are we, honey?"

She laughed. "Far from it. But I can cook, and we'd

love to have you both for dinner once we get settled. It'll be nice having you for neighbors."

"Yeah, we had no idea you two were together," Steve said. "That must've made it—"

"We're not together," Em said at the same time as Josh said, "Together? No way. Not us."

That came out more forceful than he'd intended but the memory of what he'd overheard Em say in the bathroom was still too fresh. Except just now she'd sounded equally horrified by the idea they were together, which was a relief.

"Josh is my brother's best friend."

"Yeah." He nodded. "We've basically grown up together. She's like a little sister to me."

Em rolled her eyes and then said to the couple, "So, what brings you to Highland Falls? If you don't mind me asking."

"I've written a book about my family, and the owners of Three Wise Women Bookstore invited me to do a signing. It's not until the week of Halloween, but I inherited a house here from my grandmother. It needs some work whether we decide to sell it or to keep it, so we're here for a few months at least."

"The book you wrote, it wouldn't be *The Haunting of Seaton House*, would it?" Em asked.

"It is," Jenny said, looking pleased. "How did you know?"

"Lucky guess," Em said, glancing at Josh.

He reached for the bag he'd moved under the table earlier and held it up. "I bought a copy for Em today."

He pulled the book out of the bag and set it on the table. "So you're a Seaton then?"

"I am."

Em picked up the book. "That's why Charlotte said you're witches."

Jenny smiled. "Yes, and no. The stories about May and Clara were passed down in my family for generations, and Charlotte has heard them. But I'm a professor at Georgia Southern University, and for several years, I've taught a course on witchcraft from the perspective of women and gender history."

"Including that all women should embrace their inner witch," Steve said with a grin.

"Ah, okay. Good to know she doesn't think I'm really a witch," Em said, shooting Josh a raised-eyebrow glance when he snorted. "And obviously the house you inherited is the old Seaton House?"

Jenny nodded. "We had no idea my family still owned the property until my grandmother died last year and we came across boxes of correspondence and journals. Apparently, my grandmother hadn't known either. I've always been intrigued by our family's history, but it was the journals that inspired me to take a sabbatical and write May and Clara's story."

"You're not staying at Seaton House, are you?" Em asked. "Because from what I can see on the outside, it's in pretty bad shape."

"That would be a firm no," Steve said. "From what we've heard, the place is haunted." Steve smiled at his wife. "I know they're your relatives, honey, but a ghost is a ghost. And you know how I feel about the woo-woo."

"Oh yes, I know." Jenny rolled her eyes. "My husband can't watch scary movies but the violence in his video games doesn't bother him a bit."

"The games I develop aren't that violent. They're also not based in reality."

"You're a video game programmer?" Josh asked.

"I am."

"Cool. Did you develop any games I'd be familiar with?"

"*Overlords* and *Last Man Standing*."

"Seriously? Those are like the top games of all time."

"Why am I not surprised you still play video games," Em said.

"I don't but ninety percent of the guys on my team do. If you're up for it, Steve, we have career day at Highland Falls High next month, and I know the kids would be stoked if you'd come."

"Sure. I'd love to. I was going to see if there was any interest in me offering an intro to programming at the community center, but if you think your principal would like me to start a club or something like that with the students at your school, I'd be happy to."

"I know the kids would be all for it, but let me ask. I don't see why our principal wouldn't be on board though."

"There you go, honey. Something to keep you busy while I'm helping May and Clara go to the light." Jenny opened her arms for Charlotte, who walked over yawning.

Em rubbed her forefinger up and down her right temple. "So you really think Seaton House is haunted?"

"According to everything I've read and the interviews I conducted with previous tenants, it is." Jenny smiled at Em. "You don't believe in ghosts, do you?"

Em hesitated. She was a skeptic. She didn't believe in ghosts or anything that couldn't be proven with hard evidence but Josh also knew she wouldn't want to offend Jenny.

"You have a ghost in your house," Charlotte said, looking at Gus, who hadn't moved from his spot on the floor in front of the patio doors. "You need to help him go to the light. I think he's sad. Mommy can help you if you don't know how. Can't you, Mommy?"

Chapter Six

♥

It took a lot for Em not to react when Brad disappeared. One minute he was standing by the patio doors, and in the next minute, he was gone. She focused on Jenny instead. Her mouth was moving but Em couldn't hear anything over the pounding of her heart in her ears. Jenny was looking at her now, waiting for a response.

"It's okay. I'm happy sharing my house with a ghost." She wanted Brad to stay with her forever. But after their conversation in the bathroom earlier, she was almost positive he didn't feel the same. He wanted her to move on, to let him go.

"Uh, Em, Jenny was saying they're going to head out. Charlotte's tired, and so are you."

"Sorry, brain's still a little foggy, I guess." Em went to stand up when the couple did but Josh placed a firm hand on her shoulder.

"Sit. I'll see Jenny, Steve, and Charlotte out."

She nodded, watching as Gus left his place at the patio doors. He went directly to her bedroom without so much as a glance their way, which wasn't like him. He loved kids, but he loved Brad more. Brad had rescued Gus as a puppy, and to hear her fiancé tell it, it had been love at first sight for both of them. Gus's and Em's relationship had been dislike at first sight, but they'd put on a good front for Brad. They'd both adored him. Gus had been as depressed as Em when they'd lost him.

Em's racing heart began to slow. Brad must be in her bedroom.

"I'm sorry, Em. We should've realized how tired you were," Jenny said, handing Charlotte to her husband.

"I'm fine, honestly. I'm glad you stopped by," Em said. "Let us know if you need anything."

Josh returned from the kitchen with a bag and handed it to Jenny. "This should hold you over until tomorrow."

"Thank you. Both of you. For everything," Jenny said and gave Josh a hug. Then she walked over and gave one to Em.

Em awkwardly patted her back. "You're welcome." She ignored Josh, who was grinning at her. He knew how she felt about huggers.

After they'd said their goodbyes, Josh walked the family outside, leaving the door slightly ajar. Em shot off the couch and ran to her room. Brad and Gus were lying on the bed.

She pressed her palm on her chest. "I thought you left me," she whispered.

"I wouldn't leave without saying goodbye, Em," he said, his voice quiet.

But he didn't say he wouldn't leave. Charlotte was right. Em had a depressed ghost on her hands. She had to do something. Even if she didn't want to move on, it's what Brad wanted. He'd be happy if he thought she was. For him, she could pretend. She'd go on a couple of dates. Brad had suggested Josh but he was a hard pass. Except, if she wouldn't fake-date Josh, then who? She didn't really know anyone...but she knew someone who was friends with practically everyone in town.

She heard footsteps in the hall. "Don't go anywhere," she whispered and then closed the bedroom door behind her.

Josh met her outside her room. "Are you okay?"

She nodded. "I wanted to check on Gus."

"Yeah. He's not acting like himself. Might be a good idea to have the vet check him over. I can bring him after practice tomorrow, if you want."

"Cal said the vet checked him over, and he was okay."

"Yeah, but he seems...I don't know, depressed?"

She followed Josh into the living room, thinking he might have a point. Brad was back but it wasn't the same. He couldn't cuddle or play with Gus like he used to. It had to be difficult for Gus, and for Brad. Maybe he wasn't just depressed about Em's inability to move on with her life.

She picked up her plate from the coffee table. "I'll keep an eye on him."

Josh took the plate from her. "Relax. I've got it."

She opened her mouth to argue but instead sat on the couch. She'd been tired before but her panicked reaction to the thought that Brad had left and her run to the bedroom had pushed her into the exhausted zone.

She rested her head against the back of the couch,

watching as Josh cleared off the TV trays. As much as he could get on her last nerve, she was glad he'd stayed. He hadn't been nearly as annoying today. He was a good guy, caring and kind. "Thanks, and thanks for everything you did today."

"Now you've got me worried," he said, as he walked to the kitchen with a pile of dirty dishes and utensils.

"Why, because I thanked you?"

"No, because you didn't argue with me." He returned with the blood pressure machine, digital forehead thermometer, and stethoscope. "And don't bother arguing with me about this," he said, holding the digital thermometer an inch from her forehead. It beeped. He checked the reading and entered it into his phone.

"If I have a temperature, it's because I'm basically wearing a blanket, so make sure you tell Cal that."

"Your temperature is below normal," he said as he pushed up her sleeve, fitting the blood pressure cuff over her bicep.

"Oh, okay. Don't mention the blanket pjs then."

"No talking."

She sighed and closed her eyes, wincing as the cuff expanded. She heard the *tick, tick* of the numbers going up. When the tension loosened around her bicep, she opened her eyes. Josh was adding another notation on his phone.

"If it's high, it's because of Jenny and her book." After her near panic attack over Brad, her blood pressure was probably off the charts. "There's no way this thing is going to die down when people find out she's related to the Seaton sisters."

"It's low."

"That's great."

"No, it's not. It's too low. Then again, I'm not the expert. You were hypothermic so this might be in the normal range. Can you turn around and pull up your top?" he asked without meeting her gaze.

"Why would I do that?"

He held up the stethoscope. She waited for him to make a joke, saying something about them playing doctor when they were kids. It wouldn't matter that they hadn't. Josh liked nothing better than to get a rise out of her. When he didn't follow up with a joke, she lifted her top. Obviously, they were both uncomfortable, so she might as well get it over with.

He pressed the stethoscope's cold drum to her back.

"Geez, you could've warmed it up."

That earned her a *shush* and an order to cough. She sighed and then did as he said. Three times.

"No crackles or wheezing." He added the positive news to the other readings before texting it to her brother.

Cal responded almost immediately. That couldn't be a good sign.

"I'm not going back to the hospital. I overdid it today but tell him I promise to rest tomorrow. I won't visit with anyone." It sounded like a dream day. No making small talk, and she could stay in bed with Brad all day.

"A perfect day in the life of Em," Josh said with a laugh. "You could stay in your pjs, not talk to anyone, and watch *Stranger Things* all day and night."

She shrugged. "So what if it is." She tapped a finger on his phone. "Tell him."

"Cal didn't say anything about the hospital. He just wanted to let me know that they'll be here in twenty minutes."

"Oh, okay, that's good." She chewed on her bottom lip. She didn't want to mention the dating thing in front of her brother and Bri. "So, I've been thinking I should maybe start putting myself out there again."

He stared at her like she was speaking a foreign language.

"You know, like dating. And I was wondering if you—"

With a pained expression on his face, he slowly shook his head. "I can't, Em. You're an amazing woman. I admire and respect you. But you and me, we're like family."

Her mouth fell open, and he took her hand in his. "This isn't what you want. You just think you do because I saved you. What you feel for me is gratitude, not love."

She pulled her hand free. "What are you talking about? I didn't say I love you or that I—"

"Yeah, you did. You looked right at me in the ambulance and told me you loved me."

There was no way she told Josh she loved him. She searched through her memories of last night. They were foggy but she faintly remembered telling Brad she loved him just before they off-loaded her from the ambulance... and Brad had been standing behind Josh.

"Whatever. I can't be held accountable for what I said last night. You were there, you'd saved my life, and I was grateful." She shrugged. "It's not a big deal."

"You sure about that?"

"Of course, I'm sure."

"Okay, but, Em, you just said you wanted to date me."

"No. I said I was thinking I should start dating. And before you interrupted me, I was going to ask if you knew anyone."

"You want me to set you up?"

She hadn't but the idea held some appeal. Josh could handle everything. All she had to do was show up for the date. "Yeah. I do."

He surprised her with a gentle smile. She'd expected him to tease her. "Are you sure this is what you want? I heard Todd, Gwen, and Abby telling you it's time you put yourself back out there but the only one who knows that is you, Em. There's no time line on grief."

"You think it's too soon?"

"Only you can say. Everyone's different. My situation wasn't the same as yours. Amber didn't die, but I did love her." He raised a shoulder. "I guess that makes me an idiot after everything I found out but the heart wants what it wants. It took me two years before I was ready to start dating again."

This was a side of Josh she didn't often see. "Did it help? Dating, I mean?"

He thought about it for a minute and then nodded. "Yeah, it did. Don't get me wrong, it wasn't easy at first. I'd been out of the dating game for almost five years."

He'd been out of the dating game a lot longer than she

had. Although he'd probably had a lot more experience than her to begin with. She'd only dated two other men before she met Brad.

Josh had started dating again around the time she'd moved back home, a little more than a year ago. "Is it easier now? Do you still miss Amber?"

"I thought it was going pretty well until last night." He angled his head to the side. "Have you ever heard anyone say I was a heartbreaker?"

"Man ho, a couple times. But heartbreaker, no, I don't think so."

"Seriously?"

He seemed genuinely baffled, and she held back a laugh. "It's a small town, and you do date a lot, Josh."

"I like women, and I'm a social guy. I like going out and having a good time. But I don't want anything serious, and around here, if you date someone more than a couple times, people start asking when you're getting married." He put his cell phone on the coffee table. "I don't know. Maybe it's a small-town thing. At our ages, people expect you to settle down and start a family. But it didn't work out very well for me the first time."

Em had moved to Tennessee for college, and after her mom died, she rarely visited her hometown so she hadn't met Josh's ex-wife. She hadn't been able to take time off work to come home for their wedding either. She'd heard stories about Amber, of course, but she wasn't big on gossip and routinely shut it down. Her brother was the same but she knew Cal hadn't been Amber's number-one fan. Although, like Em, Cal hadn't been living in Highland Falls when Josh was with Amber. Cal had moved back to Highland Falls only a couple years ago.

Em was so used to Josh and his easygoing charm and teasing smile that it threw her to see this serious, vulnerable side of him. "Do you still love her?"

"Good question." He rubbed his hand along the back of the couch. "In a way, I guess I'll always love her. At least the woman I thought I'd married."

"You don't sound like you've moved on."

"It's always harder to move on when you're the one who was dumped." He gave her a half smile. "But in the beginning there was a part of me that didn't want to. We had a lot of dreams for our future, for kids, and I found that hard to let go of."

Reflexively, she put a hand on her stomach. She knew how it felt to give up on dreams of a family.

"It was a loss, nothing like yours, but you have to take the time to sit in your grief for a while. I probably took longer than I should. I spent the first year trying to figure out what went wrong in our marriage and fighting the divorce. The second year, I was mostly angry about the whole thing."

"You did a good job hiding it. I never would've guessed you were angry," Em said, thinking back to when she and Brad visited. They'd come to help Cal and Raine move into their new place on Marigold Lane. The same street where Josh lived.

"It's not like you were around much," Josh said. "But yeah, I did my best to hide how I was feeling. No one wants to be around that guy, do they?"

"Or that girl," Em murmured, thinking of how she'd

pushed people away those first few months after Brad had died. It hadn't been an option when she'd moved back home last year. Her brother and Bri, even Josh, had seen to that. It wasn't enough though. She was still stuck. She knew it, her family and friends knew it, and more importantly, Brad knew it too.

"Don't sell yourself short. Everyone wants to be around you, Em. You just don't want to be around them," Josh said with a teasing grin, but she saw the sympathy in his eyes, the compassion too.

She hated people feeling sorry for her and wished she could be more like Josh. He'd gotten past his sorrow and anger. He'd done the work, taken the steps, and put himself out there again. "If everyone wants to be around me, it shouldn't be hard for you to find me a date then," she said, unable to hide the skepticism in her voice.

"If you're serious, I can think of at least three guys off the top of my head who'd jump at the chance to take you out."

Puzzled, she said, "Why?"

"Don't punch me, but you're hot, Em." Laughing, no doubt in response to the shocked expression on her face, he put up his hands. "Not that I ever looked at you that way. You also have no idea that you are, which is appealing. Plus you're smart, and I've heard you're also nice."

"I don't know if this is a good idea anymore."

"Don't overthink it or put pressure on yourself. It's just a night out with someone who you might like to hang out with again. Everyone could use a few more friends, right?"

"I have enough, thanks."

He rubbed his hand over his mouth.

"Are you laughing at me?"

"Nope," he said, but she could hear the amusement in his voice.

"Some people are happy with their own company, you know. There's nothing wrong with that."

"No, there's not." His voice took on a serious note. "But working all the time isn't good for anyone, Em. Or being on your own."

"Despite what everyone seems to think, I do have a life." Her brother and, obviously, Josh, didn't think so, and neither did Brad. And that's what had started this conversation. As much as she wanted to back out, she didn't have a choice. Not if she wanted to make Brad happy. "Just do me a favor and don't set me up with someone like you."

"I think I'm offended."

"I didn't mean it like that. I just meant set me up with someone more like me."

"So someone who eats like a sixteen-year-old, watches *Stranger Things*, true crime, and horror, prefers ordering in than going out to eat, and would rather stick a fork in her eye than go to any of the town's social events."

She nodded. "Yeah, that about covers it."

"Okay. It might take me a couple days, but I will find you the perfect match, Em."

"I don't need a perfect match. A live male body will do."

"Em, what exactly are you going to do with this guy?"

She felt the weight of someone's stare and turned her head. Brad stood there watching her, a tender smile on his face. This is what he wanted, for her to move on with someone else. Tears burned in the backs of her eyes. Not just tears of sorrow but of anger too. It wasn't fair. None of this was fair.

She got up from the couch. "I'm going to bed." Josh stared at her, and she remembered his question. "Jeez, Josh. I'm going to bed *now*, not with the guy you set me up with."

"Good to know because that would've added at least ten guys to my search," he said and got up from the couch.

"What are you doing?" she asked, when he followed her to her bedroom.

"Don't you hear Gus scratching at the door?" Josh reached around her to open the bedroom door, letting Gus out. The goldendoodle moved to Brad's side.

"Come on, boy. I'll take you for a walk. You've been cooped up all day," Josh said as he walked toward the living room, no doubt expecting Gus to follow him.

But Gus was looking at Brad, who gave him an encouraging smile. When Gus didn't move, Brad crouched by his side and went to pet him. Em saw the anguish on both their faces when Brad's hand passed through his dog's curly coat. Gus nudged Brad's hand, whining when his nose went through his beloved human's fingers.

"I know, buddy. It sucks. But I love you. It'll be okay. You go with Josh."

Gus tried to lick Brad's face and then his hand. Em pressed her fingers to her lips when Gus gave up, trudging after Josh with his head down.

Josh opened the front door and looked back at her. "That was nice, Em. We haven't talked like that for a while. It was like old times."

Chapter Seven

♥

Em nodded in response to Josh, unable to speak around the hard lump in her throat. She knew what she had to do but her heart and mind fought against it, trying to justify keeping Brad here no matter the pain it caused him and his dog.

Gus would get used to this new Brad and his physical limitations. Brad would too. At least he'd be with them.

"You're tired, Em. You need your rest," Brad said when the front door closed, his voice a dull monotone. His deep voice had always been vibrant, full of energy and positivity. He'd loved life and her and Gus so much.

"I don't know how to let you go. I know you're not happy and having you here like this makes Gus unhappy too." She looked at Brad through tear-filled eyes. "Tell me what I'm supposed to do."

"I think you know." He lifted his hand to stroke her face, bowing his head when his fingers drifted through her cheek. Then he raised his gaze and held hers, the look in his eyes as gentle as his voice. "Deep down inside that compassionate, loving heart of yours, you know it's time to let me go."

"What if I can't? Will you stay?" she asked as she walked into her room and lay down on the bed, unable to look at him. It was a selfish request of a man who didn't have a selfish bone in his body.

He lay beside her. "Yes. I'd stay."

She turned her head, studying his strong profile. "But you don't want to, and I don't understand why. If our positions were reversed, I wouldn't want to leave you."

"The only way you could truly know that is if you'd died instead of me." He turned his head and held her gaze. "I'm not supposed to be here. I don't belong here anymore. I belong with our little girl."

She squeezed her eyes closed, tears rolling down her cheeks at the thought of their daughter, alone and wondering what happened to her daddy.

"She looks just like you, you know."

"She has green eyes, not blue?" she asked, thinking of Granny MacLeod's prophecy.

He smiled. "Big green eyes and auburn hair."

"Is she by herself now?"

"I'm not sure, but time is different there. For her, it will feel like I've been gone seconds, not days."

"What's it like? Heaven?"

"I don't know how to explain it really. It's more of a feeling. It's peaceful, a never-ending space filled with a warm, loving light. But I'm not sure it's heaven. I feel like there's something beyond us, other people too. Every now and then I'll get a glimpse of—"

"Why? Why aren't you in heaven yet?" she asked,

angry at the thought Brad and their daughter were stuck in limbo. An innocent child and a good, heroic man deserved to be in heaven.

"It's not a punishment. It's just...I think it's because I can't let you go, and until I do, we're stuck between heaven and earth."

She searched his face. "It's me, isn't it? It's because I'm stuck that you can't move on."

"It's not just you. I didn't want to leave you, Em. I fought as hard to live as you did last night. Don't ever doubt that I loved you. I love you still, and because I do, I don't want you to waste another minute mourning me. I want you to grab on to life and wring out every ounce of happiness from it that you deserve. For me, for our daughter, but most of all for you."

She wasn't sure how to move on without him, but for Brad and their daughter, she'd try. "I will. I promise." She prayed it was a promise she could keep. "Will you stay with me until I fall asleep?"

He smiled as if he knew she planned to stay awake all night, drawing out every minute of the time they had left. On the other side of the door, she heard her brother, Bri, and Josh's voices. She reached for her phone, turning on a podcast, to cover her whispered conversation with Brad.

They talked about the morning she'd lost him, the night she'd lost the baby, grieving the loss of their dreams and what might have been together. As difficult as it was to talk about, it was cathartic, an absolution of the guilt she'd been carrying for the past seventeen months. As they continued talking deep into the night about the happy times they'd shared and about her life in Highland Falls, Em fought to keep her eyes open. But no matter how hard she tried, they began drifting closed.

"I love you. Tell our daughter I love her too," she whispered, a hot tear sliding down her cheek and into her hair.

The last thing she heard as sleep took her under was Brad whispering, "We'll meet again, my love. We're always with you. You carry a piece of us in your heart."

* * *

Em awoke to sunlight streaming through the blinds, the sounds of voices, and the smell of bacon frying. She opened her eyes, searching for Brad before remembering he was gone. She buried her face in her pillow, muffling her sobs, wishing she hadn't let him go, wondering how she'd ever keep her promise to him. But then she thought about what he'd said about him and the baby being stuck and rolled onto her back.

She had to figure out a way to move on, and she wasn't sure how. The words *fake it until you make it* came to mind. But wasn't that what she'd been doing for the past year? Pretending she was okay and moving on with her life when she really wasn't. She hadn't tried. She hadn't wanted to. But Brad had given her a reason to.

She got up and looked at the rumpled sheets on her side of the bed, expecting, or at least hoping, to see the imprint of Brad's head on the pillow. Some sign that he'd been here before all trace of him disappeared, but there was nothing. She ignored the niggle of doubt that none of it had been real and looked around for Gus. He usually slept in her bed until it was time to head to Cal and Bri's. They must've let him out. She glanced at her phone on the nightstand, pressing her lips together at thought of Gus searching for Brad. Brad would've said goodbye to him too but how was a dog supposed to understand if she couldn't?

She considered crawling back into bed and burying her head under the covers but her stomach grumbled. She'd have a shower and something to eat and then go back to bed and figure out a way forward. But she'd kind of done that last night when she'd asked Josh to set her up. Only she'd been planning to fake-date to keep Brad happy, to keep him here, and he was gone.

She reached for her phone to text Josh that she'd changed her mind. But then an image of Brad from last night reminded her of the promise she'd made. Except she'd promised to move on and be happy, which, as far as she was concerned, meant the last thing she should do was start dating. She didn't need a man to be happy. What she needed was to get a life.

She groaned at the thought she'd have to give up eighty-hour workweeks and quiet nights watching TV with only Gus for company. She'd have to put herself out there, become more involved in the community. Ugh, she'd have to make small talk. Maybe she could just get a hobby. She decided dating might be easier, especially with Josh doing all the work. She put down her phone and went to take a shower.

The bed was made when she came out of the bathroom fifteen minutes later. She knew who was responsible when she spotted the vase of sunflowers on the nightstand. Bri had also opened the window, a warm, fall-scented breeze clacking the slats of the wooden blind.

Em opened her closet, pulling a pair of jeans and a sweatshirt off the hangers while staring longingly at her uniform. She had a feeling the chief would take her off this week's rotation after her near-death experience.

She got dressed and wound her wet hair in a bun, holding it in place with a clip. Then she remembered what she'd looked like in the bathroom mirror and pinched some color into her cheeks before opening the door and heading for the kitchen.

Bri looked up from where she sat at the table, making notes and talking on the phone. She smiled and mouthed *client*. Em grinned at the two Pop-Tarts and bowl of Froot Loops laid out in front of the chair at the head of the table and gave Bri a thumbs-up. The bacon she'd smelled must've been for Cal.

She looked around for her brother as she pulled out the chair and took a seat. He must've left for work already. Pouring milk over her cereal, she glanced at the clock on the stove and nearly dropped the container. It was four in the afternoon!

"You're making great progress. You should be proud of yourself. Thank you, but you're the one who's doing the work." Bri nodded. "Yes, I'll see you then. Thanks again for agreeing to a phone appointment. I will. I'll tell her."

"How is it four o'clock? Did the power go out?" Em asked Bri as soon as she'd disconnected from her client.

"No. You were exhausted. I checked on you a couple of times, and you didn't move." Bri searched her face. "How are you feeling? And I want the truth. You look like you've been crying."

"Ragweed season. I'm allergic." She scooped up a spoonful of Froot Loops and shoved it into her mouth.

"You do remember who you're talking to, right? I've known you since you were twelve. You don't have allergies."

She shrugged. "Yesterday was a lot. It was overwhelming."

"Are you sure that's all it is? Josh mentioned he was setting you up with one of his friends." Bri laid a hand on Em's arm. "That's a huge step. It wouldn't be surprising if you're emotional. I'd be more surprised if you weren't."

"You don't think I'm rushing it?"

"Only you know that."

"Take off your therapist hat and put on your best friend hat. Tell me what you honestly think."

"That I'm proud of you, and happy for you. So is your brother. He's also relieved."

"Of course he is," she muttered around a mouthful of cereal.

"It's okay if you change your mind, you know. Just being open to the idea of dating is a good first step." Bri took a sip of coffee. "Do you mind me asking what brought it on?"

"I don't mind you asking but I don't have an answer." At least one she felt comfortable sharing. "Maybe because I nearly died?"

Bri nodded and took another sip of her coffee, meeting Em's eyes. She smiled.

Em was familiar with that particular look...and smile. Bri was in therapist mode, waiting for Em to spill her guts. Em wondered if she'd heard her talking to Brad. But she'd put on her podcast, the volume high enough that they wouldn't hear her whispering. Except now that she thought about it, when she'd picked up her phone to text Josh, it had been turned off.

"Did you turn off my phone last night?" she asked conversationally, picking up a pink iced Pop-Tart.

"Cal did when he checked on you."

She worked to keep the panic from her voice. "I didn't say anything to him, did I? I don't remember him coming into my room."

"You were out cold. He didn't want to disturb you. Right now, the best thing for you is sleep. He moved your appointment at the hospital to tomorrow." She nodded at the digital thermometer, blood pressure machine, and stethoscope on the kitchen counter. "We'll send him your vitals after you eat."

"He's at the hospital now?"

She nodded. "He had back-to-back surgeries. He left at eight."

"Huh. I could've sworn I smelled bacon cooking when I woke up."

Bri smiled. "You did. Patsy dropped off a Caesar salad. I think it's her way of making up for all the junk food she bought for you."

Em snorted. "Josh probably guilted her into it."

"I'm not sure her version of a Caesar would get his

stamp of approval. The ratio of bacon, croutons, and cheese to romaine lettuce is ten-to-one. She bought the salad at the grocery store and wasn't happy they used imitation bacon so she cooked up a pound of the real stuff here and added it."

"Sounds like my kind of salad," Em said, turning in her chair to survey the living room. "Where's Gus?"

"Josh picked him up an hour ago and took him to his football practice. He thought the kids and exercise would be good for him."

"Yeah, he's not been himself. Gus I mean, not Josh," Em said. "How did you find him today?"

"He seemed depressed. Cal tried to take him when he went for his run, but Gus wouldn't leave the house. He kept sniffing around like he'd lost something."

The lump in Em's throat made it difficult to swallow, and she put down the half-eaten Pop-Tart. Focusing on the empty bowl in front of her so Bri wouldn't see the tears swimming in her eyes, Em nodded. She should've woken up earlier. She was the only one who understood what Gus was going through.

"Charlotte thinks it's because he misses the ghost," Bri said in the same conversational tone Em had used only moments before.

"Steve and Jenny's Charlotte? She was here?" She sensed Bri watching her, waiting for a reaction for her to analyze. She wouldn't get one. Em was good at hiding her feelings under an impenetrable mask.

"Jenny and Charlotte stopped by this morning to borrow some sugar. You're eating her breakfast." Bri smiled. "She wanted to play with Gus instead of eating but asked me to save it for her. Jenny's bringing her by for a session in twenty minutes. They're worried about Charlotte. She won't talk about the accident. When Jenny found out I was a family therapist, she asked if I'd talk to her."

"I'd be worried too if the kid's seeing ghosts," Em said instead of coming to Charlotte's defense. Not everyone wanted or needed to talk about their traumatic experiences ad nauseam. But this was an opening to get her best friend's opinion on whether Em had been imagining Brad without outing herself. "You don't actually believe she's seeing ghosts, do you?"

"I believe Charlotte does, and that's all that matters. But I got the impression she wasn't seeing a ghost so much as sensing a presence."

"Tomato, tomahto. Do you think the kid saw a ghost or not?"

"Do you believe she saw a ghost?"

"It's annoying when you answer a question with a question. But you don't fool me. I know exactly what you're thinking."

"What am I thinking?"

"That it was Brad, and that's why Gus is depressed. And if you ask if I think it was Brad, I'm going to smack you with my Pop-Tart."

"You wouldn't want to waste a perfectly good Pop-Tart by smacking me," Bri said with a hint of a smile before it disappeared and she got a serious look on her face. "Are you upset because Charlotte and Gus might've seen Brad but you didn't?"

If she only knew. "No, not at all. I'm just trying to figure out what's real and what isn't."

"Okay. Let's go back to your original question. Is it possible Charlotte and Gus saw a ghost in your house? Yes, I think it is possible they sense something we can't. Children and animals are sensitive and more open and aware than adults. They don't have built-in biases."

"Yeah, but it's not only kids and animals. Plenty of adults see ghosts. I had a call not that long ago from an older woman who'd lost her dog. She talked like there was someone else in the room with us. When I asked who she was talking to, she told me it was her dead husband." It wasn't true but Em needed Bri to confirm she wasn't losing her mind.

"It's not uncommon for people who've lost a loved one to talk to them. It's a way of keeping them with them, of keeping their memory alive. I've worked with clients who believe their departed loved ones visit them in their dreams or swear they've received signs they're still with them. For the majority of them, they were comforting and healing experiences."

"But you don't think they're real? You think they were all in their head."

"It doesn't matter what I think. I believe we should judge by what happened as a result of their paranormal experiences. For my clients who maintained they were visited by their departed loved ones, it was an absolute gift, and they found peace." She covered Em's hand with hers. "It's quite common for people who've had a near-death experience to witness all manner of supernatural phenomenon. Some report seeing bright lights or angels or being reunited with departed loved ones. There's no definitive answer to why—"

"Oxygen deprivation causing hallucinations would be my guess," Em said, her throat tightening at the thought that what she'd shared with Brad wasn't real.

"You might not want to say that to Jenny and Charlotte," Bri said. "Or to my sister and grandmother for that matter."

"Share what? I never said I saw Brad or talked to him. Charlotte and Gus did." She wanted to throw her Pop-Tart across the room. In her panic, she'd said too much. "Before you say anything, I know Gus can't talk. Charlotte said Gus saw Brad, and he was sad."

She needed to stop talking. Charlotte hadn't referred to the ghost as Brad. The front door opened, and Em was glad for the distraction. Gus trotted in wearing a Highland Falls football jersey with Josh following behind in a black Highland Falls golf shirt that showed off his tattoo sleeves.

"Froot Loops and Pop-Tarts, the breakfast of champions." Josh reached for her half-eaten Pop-Tart. "Do you know how many additives are in this thing? It's not food."

"Hands off my Pop-Tart."

Josh raised his hands. "You'll have to elevate your palate, Freckles. Neil is a foodie."

"And why do I care that this Neil person is a foodie?"

"Because Neil is your date. If Cal gives you the all clear, he'll pick you up Friday at eight."

Chapter Eight

♥

Instead of giving him the third degree about her date like Josh expected her to, Em pulled Gus in for a hug. The way she was holding on to the dog, you'd think she hadn't seen him in a month and that he was her best friend in the world. Neither of which was true. It was weird, but a good weird. It looked like Em was finally bonding with the dog she'd inherited from her fiancé.

"Why is Gus wearing a Highland Falls football jersey?" Em asked, releasing the goldendoodle after one last squeeze.

"He's our new mascot, aren't you, boy?" Josh rubbed Gus's head, snagging the piece of Pop-Tart Em offered the dog. They both looked at him.

"No junk food." Josh tossed the pastry onto the plate. "It's as bad for him as it is for you. But you're an adult and not on my team. Gus is on my team and has to run drills. Before you say anything, he loves it, and the guys love him. He was a hit."

"He looks happier than when he left," Bri said, leaning in to give Gus a hug. The dog put his paws on her shoulders, hugging her back. As Josh knew, Gus gave great hugs.

Bri straightened. “So tell us more about Em’s date. Do we know him?”

“Em might.”

Em frowned. “How would I know him? Did I arrest him?”

Josh laughed, shaking his head. “Only you would ask that. He’s Gwen’s brother-in-law. Your coworker,” he said when she stared at him.

“I know who Gwen is, which is why I’m looking at you like you’ve lost your mind. What were you thinking, Josh? I can’t date a coworker’s family member. I won’t get a moment’s peace. That’s all Gwen will want to talk about, and not only her, Todd too.”

“Gwen and Todd are too busy with their own love lives to worry about yours.”

“You have met Gwen and Todd, right?”

Thinking she might have a point, he pulled out his phone. “I’ll text Neil and ask him to keep it on the downlow.”

Em’s phone pinged, and she looked at the screen and then up at him with her lips pressed in a flat line. “It’s too late.” She turned the screen, showing him a text from Gwen. It read BEST NEWS EVER!! CALL ME NOW! followed by a screenful of smiley-faced emojis with heart eyes.

“Maybe she has other news she wants to share with you,” Josh said lamely.

Em’s phone pinged again, and she held it up without looking at the screen. “I’ll bet you a hundred bucks it’s from Todd, and it's a meme of some guy dancing and screaming '*Best news ever!*'"

"I'll take your bet and raise you twenty."

"Really? It's not from—" She looked at the screen and scowled at him.

"What? You said a meme of some guy dancing and screaming '*Best news ever!*'"

"He made a video of himself dancing, and he's holding up a sign that reads *About damn time!!*"

"Technically, I'm right so I win the bet, but whatever. Gwen probably told Todd. They're like two desks away from each other, aren't they? No one else will care." And then his phone pinged and so did Bri's, making a liar out of him. Cal wanted the 411 on Neil, reminding Josh he'd promised to run Em's prospective dates by him first.

And at the rate Bri's phone kept pinging, the Sisterhood had heard the news.

Which Em had obviously figured out because she said, "That's it, the date's off. I'll get a hobby instead."

Josh winced. "I'm sorry. I didn't think you going on a date would rate this kind of attention. But, Em, Neil's a great guy. I'm sure you'll have a better time with him than you would if you took up baking or cooking."

"Baking or cooking? That's work, not a hobby."

"Fine. Neil will be more fun than knitting or painting or sitting at home binge-watching *Stranger Things*."

"Binge-watching *Stranger Things* is fun."

"You need to get a life, Em," he teased, expecting her to cut him down with a one-liner.

Instead, she got a serious look on her face and reached for Gus. "I know I do."

Now he felt bad for teasing her. He was always on the wrong foot with Em.

"I hate to say this but it might be easier for you to go on the date than it would be to cancel it at this point," Bri said.

"How do you figure that?"

"Well, for one, Gwen will be disappointed and try and change your mind. Todd too. Then there's Neil, who might think he's the reason you canceled. Not to mention everyone else will want to know why you did, and now that it's out there that you're open to dating, they'll probably try setting you up too."

Em glared at him. "Are you happy? You've ruined my life. I'll never get a moment's peace."

"Hey, it wasn't my idea. You're the one who asked me to set you up."

There was a knock on the front door. "If that's someone wanting to talk about me dating Neil, tell them I moved," Em muttered, pushing back her chair.

Bri glanced at her phone. "I'm pretty sure it's Jenny and Charlotte." She got up from the table. "Josh, would you mind taking Em for a walk?"

"I'm not a dog or a toddler. I can take a walk on my own, thank you very much."

"I'd feel better if someone went with you in case you had a dizzy spell or felt faint," Bri said. "Your blood pressure was a little low yesterday."

"I can guarantee that's no longer the case," Em grumbled.

"I wouldn't mind checking out the Seaton place if you're up for it, Em. I overheard a few members of my team talking about it in the locker room. It sounded like they were making plans to go to Seaton House this weekend."

"I wouldn't mind checking it out myself," Em said. "Come on, Gus." She patted her thigh.

"Would you mind if he stays, Em?" Bri asked as she went to answer the door. "Charlotte might be more comfortable opening up if he's here."

"Sure," Em said, and Bri let Jenny and Charlotte in.

They said hello as Josh, with Em following behind him, joined them at the door. "Em and I thought we might take a walk to Seaton House and check things out. You don't mind, do you?" he asked Jenny, smiling when Charlotte made a beeline for Gus.

"Not at all. I'd planned to ask Em how we can keep the kids away or at least keep them safe. I have a feeling my book has renewed interest in the house."

"Your book and Abby Mackenzie. She's going all out to promote it," Josh said, repeating what his mother had told him. She was a podcast junkie and never missed Abby's show.

"Abby's been wonderful, and she's so creative," Jenny said, taking a key out of her pocket and handing it to Josh. "Although I am a little concerned about a few of her ideas, especially considering the state of the house."

Josh was surprised Em didn't react and glanced over his shoulder. She was focused on Charlotte and Gus. The little girl was explaining to Gus that the ghost had gone home and why that was a good thing, not something to be sad about.

Bri glanced at Em and nudged Josh.

He nodded. “Em, you ready to go?”

“Yeah, sure.” She didn’t look at him so it was hard to tell, but he thought she had tears in her eyes.

“Are you okay?” he asked when he closed the door behind them.

“I’m fine, why?”

“You didn’t react when Jenny mentioned she was concerned about some of Abby’s promotional ideas for her book,” he said instead of bringing up Em’s watery eyes.

She’d be embarrassed that he’d noticed. Even as a kid, she hadn’t liked people seeing her cry. He wondered what had upset her but he’d let it go for now. He’d ask Bri about it later.

Em scrolled through her phone, and her eyes widened. “Have you seen this?”

He leaned in. “What is it?”

“Abby’s upcoming podcasts. She’s planning on doing them from Seaton House. And it says here the bookstore is running a contest for people to stay the night at the house. What a nightmare,” Em said, rubbing her hand up and down her face. She frowned and slowly lowered her hand, pointing at her garden. “What are those?”

The dead plants had been replaced with brightly colored rocks decorated with stick figures, smiley faces, and the word *hero*. “Gratitude rocks. Mom painted them with her class today. I got a few too.”

“Oh.” She looked at him. “Am I supposed to send them a thank-you card or something?”

“You could,” he said, keeping his amusement in check at the ill-at-ease expression on her face. “Or you could drop by their class and thank them. That's what I'm going to do."

"I won't have time, not with what Abby's got planned. Gabe will probably want me to work double shifts for the next few weeks." She looked pleased at the idea she'd be working nonstop. Obviously, Bri hadn't shared Gabe's news with her. Josh didn't blame her for putting it off.

"I'll ask your mom to thank them for me." Em frowned. "What?"

He thought he'd done a good job covering his reaction but he should've known Em would notice. Nothing got by her. "You might want to give your boss a call later. Now let's go check…," he began as he headed down the driveway.

She stopped him with a hand on his arm. "Why should I call Gabe?"

He sighed. As much as he didn't want to be the bearer of bad news, he might as well tell her. The woman was like a dog with a bone. She never gave up. "He took you off the schedule for this week, and he's—"

"Oh, okay." She nodded. "I figured he might. But if I get a doctor's note stating I'm fine, I'm sure he'll put me back on the schedule. He's going to need all hands on deck."

"You didn't let me finish. Gabe took you off the schedule for a week because of the accident, but he's insisting you take an additional two weeks."

"Why? I didn't do anything wrong. I just did my job."

"Em, it's not a punishment. You haven't taken your holidays, and Gabe wants you to. He says you've accumulated more overtime in the past year than the entire station has in the past two."

"Because they keep asking me to take their shifts."

"And you never say no."

She looked away. "I like my job. I like to stay busy."

And he had a fairly good idea why. He'd done the same when Amber first left. He draped a companionable arm over Em's shoulders. "You said you needed to get a life, so look at this as an opportunity. You'll have time to take up a hobby and go on a couple of dates."

"You always do that."

"Do what?"

"Look for the positive. It's annoying." She moved out from under his arm as they walked along the side of the gravel road lined with sugar maple trees. "So this Neil guy, what's his story?"

"He was married to Gwen's sister-in-law. He wanted to be around family after he lost his wife. They moved here three years ago. His son plays for me."

"Ah, how old is this guy?"

"I'm not sure. Around forty, I guess. Why? Is that a problem?"

"Josh, he's ten years older than me. We won't have anything in common." Her eyes narrowed. "You picked him because we both lost someone, didn't you?"

He had. He'd gotten the impression Neil was having a hard time moving on after losing his wife, and since Em was having a hard time moving on after losing Brad, he thought they'd be good for each other. He wasn't about to share that with Em though. "No, he's a nice guy and a good dad. He always shows up for our games and helps me out at practices sometimes. I think you'll like him."

"What's he do?"

"Contractor," he said as they reached a rusted gate, barely visible under the fiery orange leaves of choke-cherry bushes and sumac trees. A battered yellow *Keep Out* sign hung on the post.

"You should give Jenny and Steve his name. They're going to need a contractor," Em said, the gate squealing as she shoved it open and the house came into view.

It sat nestled among a stand of evergreens. It was a mishmash of architectural styles, but the stone stairs, stained glass windows, and turret made it look like it belonged in a fairy tale. As they walked up the dirt path toward the house, and he got a better look, Josh amended his first impression. The house looked like it belonged in a horror story.

Rubbing her hands on her thighs, Em glanced at the roof. "Are those crows or ravens?"

"I don't know, but whatever they are, there are a lot of them."

Em nodded while she looked around. "This place is creepy enough in the day. I wouldn't want to hang out here at night. Maybe that'll be enough to deter the kids."

"Some but there'll be enough of them who want to prove they're not scared to take up a dare, which is basically what Abby's doing." He headed for the front door. "You don't have to come in."

"I said it was creepy, not that I'm scared," she muttered, following him up the stairs.

He wondered if she realized her hand had slid to

where her gun would usually be. "Of course you're not," he said, pushing aside the bloodred vines to reach the door knob. The side of the house was covered in the vines.

Em let out a squeak, and her hands went to her head, frantically combing through her hair.

"What's wrong?"

"Something fell off the vine and onto my head."

"Beetle," he said, plucking it from her hair and tossing it on the ground.

"Thanks," she said, head bent as she scrolled through her phone. "Are the vines Virginia creeper?"

"I think so, why?"

"Because not only are these infested with creepy-crawly things, those"—she pointed at a clump of berries over his head—"are poisonous to humans and dogs, but not to birds. They like them, which is probably why there's a zillion of them hanging out on the roof."

"Okay, so the vines have to go. And," he said as the doorknob turned under his hand, "they need a new lock."

"Steve or Jenny must've forgotten to lock it."

"Or someone picked the lock," Josh said, looking around as he walked inside. The living room was on the right, the furniture draped in sheets that at one time must've been white but were now a dingy gray. The house smelled damp and dusty. He could practically taste it on his tongue.

"How long has this place been abandoned?" Em asked, closing the door behind her.

"About fifteen years, according to Jenny's book.

I read some of it last night," he said as he walked into the living room. "After May was charged with their neighbor Edward Henderson's murder, based primarily on evidence provided by his younger brother, Clara worked tirelessly to prove her sister's innocence. But the town had turned on both sisters over rumors they were witches, and no one would help her. A day after her sister died in jail, Clara's body was found at the bottom of the basement stairs. It was ruled accidental but the rumor at the time was that her sister's ghost, angry that Clara hadn't saved her, pushed her down the stairs."

"It doesn't make sense," Em murmured. "A ghost couldn't push her. Its hands would go through her body."

"You've had experience investigating murders by a ghost, have you?" he teased.

She glanced at him like she'd forgotten he was there. "No. It just doesn't sound plausible." She walked farther into the house. "And if her sister's ghost appeared to her, I doubt it would've scared her or that her sister would've wanted to scare her. They were close, weren't they?"

"According to Jenny's book, they were. Clara hadn't given up on May. She'd been trying to get the case reopened days before her sister died. She'd found evidence that she believed would prove May's innocence."

"It could've been suicide then," Em mused.

"I don't think so. May had a son, Willy. He was thirteen months old at the time of the sisters' deaths."

"What happened to him?"

"Their great-aunt moved here to raise him. She sold the house a year later."

"Because she thought it was haunted?"

"Yeah, and she wasn't the only one. The house changed hands at least thirteen times. The last owners were going to turn it into a tourist attraction but apparently the ghosts weren't happy about it. The owners couldn't afford to walk away from the house, and they couldn't sell it. They tracked down Jenny's family, and her grandfather bought it but he had a stroke just after the sale went through and hadn't told anyone, including his wife. No one knew about the house until Jenny discovered the deed with the letters and journals."

"I'd like to read..." Em began as she walked into the living room. She froze, and her eyes went wide.

"What?" Josh asked.

She raised her hand, pointing to something behind him.

He turned to see a sheet covering a couch rise in the middle, looking distinctly ghostlike.

Chapter Nine

♥

Em watched as Josh whipped the sheet off the couch, revealing one very large and ticked-off raccoon standing on its hind legs. It growled at Josh, and it wasn't alone. There was another equally large raccoon tucked in the corner, making a high-pitched screaming sound.

"Throw the sheet back on the couch!" Em yelled, but it was too late. The raccoons jumped off and headed straight for her.

"Open the door," Josh shouted, flapping the sheet at them like he was a bullfighter.

She lunged for the door and flung it open, taking a giant step backward in hopes of getting out of their way. It was hard to tell where they were with the clouds of dust generated by Josh frantically waving the sheet. She wasn't about to complain though. It appeared he'd successfully herded them out the door.

He slammed it shut, leaning his back against it. He was covered from head to toe in dust.

Em laughed. "You look like one of the ghosts in *The Walking Dead* or like you've seen one."

"Har har," he said, rubbing the dust from his eyes. "I would've preferred seeing a ghost. Those things were huge." He looked around. "Do you think they left any of their friends behind?"

"I'd think they would've shown up when their friend started screaming. I didn't know raccoons made sounds like that. It was freaky." She'd barely gotten the words out when a door slammed on the second floor. "Okay, so maybe they left one of their friends behind." She looked up the stairs. "I guess we'd better check it out."

Josh didn't look any more thrilled with the idea than she was. "There was a breeze coming through the front door when you opened it. When I shut it the—" Another door slammed on the second floor. Josh sighed. "Remind me again why we volunteered to check this place out?"

"To ensure the safety of Highland Falls' teenage population."

"Right. Well, I'd feel better if I had more than a sheet for protection this time." He walked into the living room and tossed the sheet onto the couch while looking around.

"There's a poker to the right of the fireplace," she said, turning to walk away. "I'll check out the other rooms on this floor."

"Hang on. We should stick together." He crouched to pick up the poker and then scrambled backward.

"More raccoons?" she asked, sidling toward the front door.

"No. Bats. A lot of bats."

"You know, that might be the answer. We'll spread the word the house is infested with rabid raccoons and bats."

"And rats," he said, joining her at the door.

"I guess it couldn't hurt to pretend we saw rats too. The more wildlife the better."

"I'm not pretending. I saw its tail before it disappeared into a hole in the wall."

"Steve and Jenny need to hire a pest control company," she said as they walked toward the kitchen.

"I don't know. Jenny and Steve don't seem like the animal-exterminating types."

"Not the ones who kill the animals, the ones who trap and relocate them. As long as they relocate them far from Sugar Maple Road."

"Em, duck."

"What? Is it a bat?" She covered her head and kept walking...into a gigantic spider's web. She yelped, attacking her hair with her fingers. "Are they gone?"

"If you'd stop raking your hands through it, I could get a look."

She dropped her hands to her sides, and he combed his fingers through her hair. "What's with you and bugs? You're more upset you might have one in your hair than you were about the bats, rats, and raccoons."

"You would be too if you'd had head lice. Twice." She'd been in fifth grade and had forgotten her winter hat at home. Her teacher had given her one from the lost-and-found box. Em's head lice had been particularly stubborn, and her mother had gotten fed up with nit picking and paying for the expensive shampoo.

Josh's dust-coated lips twitched. "You rocked your buzz cut."

She'd looked like Eleven from *Stranger Things*. "So did you and Cal." She smiled at the memory. Her brother and Josh had shaved their heads in solidarity.

He winked. "All for one, and one for all."

They'd been close back then. Josh had been her best friend as much as he'd been her brother's. Until he'd become the object of Em's teenage romantic fantasies, and she hadn't known how to act around him anymore. She'd used teenage attitude to cover her teenage adoration.

"You're as cheesy as you always were." Obviously, she'd grown out of her crush but not the snarky attitude. Except it wasn't just reserved for Josh anymore. Even she could admit she'd become something of a hard-ass since losing Brad.

"What can I say? I like the cheese." Josh looked around the kitchen. "It's kind of surreal, isn't it? It's as if whoever lived here got up one morning, walked out the door, and never came back."

"Or ran," she said, picking up an overturned chair. "I'm surprised no one squatted here."

"Someone might have tried but the ghosts or the wildlife probably scared them away." He nodded at what appeared to be a broom closet. "Open the door for me, will you?" He stood at the ready with the poker.

She opened the door, and he lowered the poker. "No bats, rats, or raccoons?"

"Not at the moment, but something has been hanging out in there." He rubbed his forearm under his nose.

Em got a whiff and muttered, “That’s putrid,” behind her hand.

Josh nodded, transferring the poker to his left hand and reaching inside. He handed her a broom before shutting the door, pointing his poker at a door across from them. “Now that we’re armed, what do you say we check out the basement?”

She moved to look around the half-open door. The basement was dark and smelled like mildew. The rough walls looked damp, and the wooden stairs that led to what appeared to be a dirt-covered floor seemed rickety. “I don’t even know if I’d call it a basement. I can understand how Clara fell down the stairs and died now. Maybe her death was accidental.”

Josh leaned around her to get a look. “Yeah, let’s leave it for pest control.”

He shut the door, and they took a quick look around the rest of the main floor. Other than spiderwebs and animal droppings, it was relatively clean and had the same surreal feel as the kitchen.

“It’s held up reasonably well, considering. I thought the wood floors and walls would be rotted,” Em said as she started up the stairs.

“Careful,” Josh advised from behind her. “The stairs look in okay shape but they might not be.” The steps creaked and groaned under his weight.

“Back at you,” she said, walking gingerly up the stairs.

“Did you see that?”

“See what?”

“A dark shadow flew across the landing.”

She looked up. There was a large window framed by floor-length blue drapes. "Maybe there's a window open up here and it blew the drapes? It would explain the slamming doors."

"No, it... Look, there."

By the time she looked where he was pointing, whatever he'd seen was gone. "Sorry, I didn't see it. But I hear that," she said, at the sound of someone screaming outside.

The front door burst open, and they both turned. Steve ran inside, slamming the door shut, barring it with his body, his arms spread wide, his glasses askew. "Raccoons. Really, really big raccoons," he said breathlessly.

"Yeah, we met them. They were hanging out on your couch. I don't think they were happy when we kicked them out," Josh said.

"They were here? In the house?" Steve asked, looking around.

"Yeah, but they're gone now. You're good." Josh gave Em a *zip it* look.

She supposed he was right. Steve probably wouldn't take the news that there might be more raccoons in his house well. "Yeah, pest control can take care of your bat and rat problem."

"We have bats and rats?" Steve said, his voice rising into teenage girl vicinity as he frantically looked around. He pressed his palms to the sides of his face, shaking his head. "I don't know if I can do this. I'm a city guy. I like condos and pavement. If I see a spider at our place, Jenny or Charlotte have to kill it for me. Except they don't kill it, they set it free."

Josh glanced at Em, clearly struggling not to laugh. But he still managed to send her a look that conveyed she wasn't to mention the gigantic spiderwebs.

Steve straightened his glasses, and his eyes went wide. "What was that?"

"What was what?"

"A shadow, a really big shadow. It floated across the landing," he said as he hurried to join them on the stairs.

"Em thinks one of the windows are open upstairs. We were just going to check it out."

"Oh, okay."

The man had gone as white as Josh's dust-covered face. "You don't have to come with us," Em said.

"Are you kidding me? I'm not staying down here by myself."

They continued up the stairs with Steve practically plastering himself against Josh's back. Another door slammed shut, and Steve screamed. Em turned. He had his arms wrapped around Josh's waist.

Josh rubbed his ear. "You're okay, buddy. It's just a drafty, old house. Nothing to worry about."

Splotches of red appeared on Steve's pale cheeks. "Try telling that to the contractors I called today. No one wants the job. I even offered above the going rate, plus a signing bonus." He glanced at the landing and shuddered. "It's because of what happened the last time someone tried to renovate this place. More than one person got hurt on the job, one even died." He returned his gaze to them. "What am I supposed to tell Jenny? She's got her heart set on this, and I can't hammer a nail without breaking a thumb." He held up his left hand, tapping a mishappen thumb with his forefinger. "This is from trying to hang a picture."

Em pressed her lips together to keep from laughing. She felt bad for the guy and didn't want to embarrass him any more than he already was. He clearly loved his wife and would do anything to make her happy.

"You didn't call Neil Sutherland, did you?" Josh asked.

"I had Sutherland Construction on my list, but after the first five shot me down, I was too depressed to keep going."

"I know Neil. He's a great guy and does great work." Josh glanced at Em, and she rolled her eyes. He grinned and then said to Steve, "I'll give him a call for you."

The other man's face lit up with a smile. "That'd be great, Josh. I really appreciate it."

"Not a problem." He lifted his chin at Em. "Let's get this done before we lose the light."

Josh was right. The sun was no longer shining through the trees outside the windows, and it was getting darker inside the house. When they reached the landing, Em handed Steve her broom.

"You're sure it's okay?" The way he was holding the broom to his chest, Em had a feeling he wouldn't give it back even if she changed her mind.

"Yeah, I'm good," she said, and headed for the first bedroom with Josh and Steve following behind her. She noted the painted furniture and the vintage bedside lamps as she walked into the room. "It's so weird that they didn't take anything with them when they left."

"It was part of the sale. Everything was ordered specifically for the house," Steve said, standing in the doorway. "They researched what it looked like when May and Clara lived here, from furniture to paint colors."

"Josh mentioned they were going to open it to the public," Em said, bending to look under the bed. There were animal tracks in the thick layer of dust that coated the floor. A lot of them.

"They were but not as a museum. Dark tourism had become popular around that time," Steve said, watching as Josh checked the window. "It still is."

"Dark tourism?" Em asked, having never heard the phrase before.

"Yeah. There's good money to be made opening murder houses and haunted estates to the public. They charge for daytime tours and for overnight stays, and sell merchandise too."

"Is that what you and Jenny plan to do?" Josh asked as they left the room.

"If Abby Mackenzie had her way, that's exactly what we'd do. But Jenny's hoping by the time she's finished"—Steve looked around and lowered his voice—"that Clara and May will finally be able to rest in peace, so I'm not sure the house will be a draw if they're no longer haunting—"

A red ball rolled out of a bedroom on their right, coming to rest at Em's feet. "Okay, so it looks like we have a playful raccoon."

Steve stared at the ball Em had picked up. "You said they were gone."

Josh, who'd gone into the room, came out shaking his

head. "It wasn't a raccoon or a bat or a rat. It's a little boy's room, and the window's sealed shut."

"Okay, so we have a playful ghost," Em said.

Steve looked like he wasn't sure whether to be relieved or terrified.

"I'm teasing." She crouched, rolling the ball back into the room. "There's a reasonable explanation for this." There was a *clunk*, and then the ball rolled back to her.

Josh snorted. "Yeah, you're playing ball with a ghost."

"No. Look. The floor's slanted. When the doors slammed, they must've dislodged the ball." Or a raccoon had but she wouldn't mention that in front of Steve.

His shoulders dropping from around his ears, Steve nodded. "That makes sense."

They searched the last two bedrooms and checked out the bathroom and a linen closet. They found nothing but more evidence that Steve and Jenny needed to call an exterminator ASAP. There were also some cracks in the ceilings and water damage on the walls and floors. But the one thing they hadn't found was an open window.

"We missed one." Josh pointed the poker at what must be the turret room. The door was closed. Steve raised the broom as they walked toward it. Josh went to open the door but it opened on its own with a drawn-out squeal.

Steve yelped, swinging the broom. Em and Josh ducked. Luckily, they both had fast reflexes.

"Good thing I didn't give him the poker or we would've ended up on the house's list of victims," Josh said for Em's ears alone, adding for Steve's benefit as he walked into the room, "You can relax. There's nothing in here."

"But we do have an explanation for the slamming doors," Em said, nodding at the open window. "And an explanation for how the raccoons got in."

"Now we just have to figure out who left it open," Josh said.

"Maybe some of the kids already came to check it out," Em suggested as she looked around. "It's a nice room." The floor and walls were a warm, honey-colored wood with built-in shelves. "It must have been a library. And that must be the Seaton family." Em angled her chin at the portrait on the wall. A handsome white man sat on a settee with a pretty Black woman sitting beside him. Behind the couple stood two beautiful women.

"Mr. Seaton and his wife, Beth," Steve said. "Beth was his second wife. She'd been the family's housekeeper. A year after his wife died, he sold his businesses, married Beth, and moved here to start a new life. The two women are their daughters, May and Clara."

"Did Jenny think the rumors they were witches had anything to do with May and Clara being biracial?" Em asked.

Steve nodded. "Partially, yes, but they were healers, and back then that was tantamount to being a witch, especially if you happened to be young, beautiful, and single, which May and Clara were. And then May got pregnant and wouldn't name the child's father."

Josh studied the family portrait. "They look like a happy family."

"By all accounts they were," Steve said.

"It must've been quite the showplace back in the day. This room's got a great view," Josh said as he closed the window. It looked onto the sugar maples lining either side of the road, rooftops peeking through the vibrant fall-colored leaves, and smoke from the chimneys rising to the violet-blue sky.

They left the door open and headed for the stairs. Steve looked at ease for the first time since he'd run into the house. Or at least he had until a black cat darted across the hall, chasing a rat.

Steve ran past them, yelling, "I hate this house!"

Josh and Em shouted, "Careful!" at the same time, but Steve ignored them, practically flying down the stairs.

"What do you think the chances are they'll keep the cat?" Em asked Josh as they walked toward the landing.

"If Steve gets a say, zero."

"Yeah, you're probably right. Black cats get a bad rap."

Josh grinned. "Especially when they live in a house supposedly haunted by witches." A door slammed, and then another. Josh raised an eyebrow. "Okay, how do you explain that?"

She leaned over the railing. "A draft. Steve just ran out the door and slammed it."

"So you don't think the house is haunted?"

"No. Do you?"

He looked around as they walked down the stairs. "I'm not sure but I believe not everything in life can be explained."

She was tempted to tell him about her experience

with Brad but immediately shut down the thought. Josh was the last person she'd tell. She decided to change the subject. "I'm curious if there were other reasons people in Highland Falls thought the Seaton sisters were witches, aside from the ones Steve mentioned."

"I know that look. You're not just curious, you're going to investigate the mystery of the Seaton sisters and their murders, aren't you?"

She shrugged. "I'm off for almost three weeks. What else am I supposed to do with my time? Wait a minute. You said the Seaton sisters' *murders*. Does Jenny believe both May and Clara were murdered?"

"That was my take on it." Josh stopped her with a hand on her arm before she opened the front door. "But, Em, if you get wrapped up investigating the Seaton sisters, when are you going to have time to date and have some fun?"

"Investigating the lives and deaths of May and Clara will be fun." She thought about her promise to Brad. Even if there was part of her that wondered if it had been real, she couldn't take the risk that Brad and their daughter remained stuck in limbo because of her. "But it's not like I'll be working on their case twenty-four seven. I'll have time to do other things." She couldn't bring herself to say *date*.

They found Steve waiting for them by the gate. He grimaced. "Sorry about that. You won't tell Jenny, will you?"

"Tell her what?" Josh said.

Steve smiled his thanks and then shot an *oh crap* look at the house. "I forgot to lock up."

"Give me the keys," Em said. "I'll do it for you."

"Thanks, Em." He dug the keys from his pocket and handed them to her.

"I can put the broom back in the house if you want," she offered.

He hugged it to his chest. "I think I'll just hang on to it, thanks."

"No problem." Em figured, now that he'd gotten a look at some of Highland Falls' wildlife, he wouldn't leave home without his broom for protection. She wondered if he'd heard they had black bears and bobcats. She smiled, imagining his reaction when he found out.

As she walked away, she heard Steve and Josh discussing Neil Sutherland. By the time she returned from locking up the house, Josh had organized a meeting between Steve, Jenny, and Neil for the next morning.

They leaned against the gate, watching Steve walk down the road. "Looks like you've got a new bestie. I thought he was going to kiss you when you told him Neil would take the job," Em said, then frowned. "You don't look happy though. What's wrong?"

"Neil backed out of your date." He raised an eyebrow. "You don't have to look so happy about it. He really is a great guy, Em. I was hoping you two would hit it off, as much for him as for you. He's having a hard time moving on after losing his wife, and I think it's having a negative impact on his son. On both of them, really."

"It's not easy moving on but he'll know when he's ready." Would she ever have been ready to move on without a push from her fiancé's ghost? She doubted it. She didn't even know if she'd be able to move on now.

She just knew she'd try for Brad and their daughter's sake.

"I'm sure you're right, but it's—" Josh began as he closed the gate behind them. "Ah, Em, look at the window in the turret room."

She looked up. There was a woman standing in the window. It was hard to tell from this distance, but it looked like one of the women in the painting. "Okay, so maybe Seaton House is haunted after all."

Chapter Ten

♥

Bri, there's no way Em will go tonight. She'd rather stick a fork in her eye," Josh said, tucking his phone between his shoulder and ear so he could finish loading the dishwasher. With everything that had happened since last weekend's Fall Festival, he'd let things at his place slide, and he was scheduled to work at HFFD tomorrow.

"She promised she would, and you know Em, she doesn't break her promises."

It was true, but still..."What did you blackmail her with?"

Bri and her friends had gotten together after learning Neil had canceled his date with Em. Apparently, they couldn't reach a consensus on a substitute candidate, so Abby Mackenzie had suggested a Saturday Singles Night at Highland Brew, with speed dating as the main event.

Josh had a feeling it wasn't a purely altruistic act on Abby's part. Did she want to help Em find a date? Of course she did. Abby was a bighearted woman who went out of her way to help anyone in need, whatever that need may be. She was the driving force behind the majority of charities in town.

But since their visit to Seaton House, Em had been focused on stopping the events Abby had planned for there. And when Em put her mind to something, she was a force to be reckoned with and almost always got her way. From what he'd heard, she already had Jenny, Steve, and her boss in her corner, and she was working her way through the members of the town council. So Josh imagined Abby's Singles Night had as much to do with distracting Em as it had to do with finding her a date.

Bri laughed. "There was no blackmail involved. I just suggested that if she took part in the speed dating, maybe everyone would back off."

"And she believed you?"

"After I made Abby and the Sisterhood promise that they would."

"Did they sign their promises in blood?" Matchmaking was the Sisterhood's favorite pastime. He couldn't see them giving up on finding Em a match, especially when she was standing in the way of Abby's plans to capitalize on *The Haunting of Seaton House*.

Bri snorted. "Em asked the same thing, only she was serious. But she's still going tonight."

"And you want me to go and keep an eye on her," Josh said, thinking about the overflowing laundry hamper in his bedroom and the footage from last week's game he wanted to review.

"You know Em. This isn't exactly in her wheelhouse. I'd feel better if you were there to support her, so would

Cal. And you know how she'd react if we showed up. But you have a legitimate reason to be there. You're single too. You never know, you might meet someone you'd like to date for more than a couple of weeks."

"Since when has my dating life become the topic of conversation in Highland Falls? Stupid question. Everyone's dating life is a topic of conversation in Highland Falls. But seriously, Bri, does everyone think I'm a serial dater?"

"Well, you have dated quite a few women in the past year."

"Okay, but it's not as if I'm not clear about my intentions. I don't ghost anyone."

"I know you don't intentionally mean to break anyone's heart, Josh, but—"

"So it's true, people really are calling me a heartbreaker." It bothered him that he had a reputation, and not one he was proud of. He didn't like the idea of his players hearing about it. A few of the kids on his team didn't have a male role model in their lives, and he felt strongly that, as their coach, it was his job to be one for them.

"You didn't know?"

"No, I didn't know. Not until last Saturday." He shut the dishwasher door. "As much as I want to support Em, given my reputation, a speed-dating event is probably the last place I should be."

He knew how bad it was when Bri agreed with him.

"Maybe you're right. But you could just hang out at the bar and keep an eye on Em."

* * *

Josh pocketed his keys as he walked toward Highland Brew. The brewery was housed in the old mill at the base of the falls and was one of the locals' favorite weekend hangouts, his included. At least, before his eye-opening conversation with Bri, it had been.

A hazy mist floated over the falls, putting a damp chill in the air, and he shrugged into his leather jacket. From the laughter and voices coming from the other side of the stone building, it sounded like Abby's first Saturday Singles Night had drawn a crowd. He supposed he shouldn't be surprised—any event Abby promoted on her social media channels drew one. But he'd thought dating apps had replaced speed dating.

Someone behind him let out a low whistle, and he turned. Todd, Em's coworker, grinned. "I was whistling at the size of the crowd, not you, but you are looking as fine as always, Coach."

"You're not looking so shabby yourself." It was true. Todd was always dressed to the nines, and tonight was no exception.

"I should hope not. This baby set me back a small fortune." Todd smoothed a hand down the brown leather blazer he wore over a cinnamon-colored turtleneck he'd paired with dark jeans and loafers. "You know everyone in town. What do you think my chances are of finding my soulmate tonight?"

Josh didn't know everyone in line, again not surprising when Abby was involved. She had a large following and drew people from as far away as Georgia and Tennessee.

"What happened with you and Matteo? You guys have been dating for months, haven't you?"

"And that's all he wanted to do. Date." Todd returned his attention to Josh. "You can't tell by looking at me—God bless my mother for introducing me to skincare at thirteen—but I'm thirty-six. I'm ready to settle down and have a family. Matteo made it clear he wasn't." He quirked his eyebrow and his lips, which Josh thought was quite the accomplishment. "Sound like someone you know?"

"Been there, done that, got the T-shirt, and I don't want another one, thanks," he said, taking his place in the back of the line.

"Says the guy who has a new lady on his arm every few weeks."

"I have a lot of friends who just happen to be female, and I enjoy spending time with them."

He should've stayed home. But Bri was right, Em might need his support. Putting herself out there like this was a huge deal. He still had no idea how Bri and Abby had convinced her to come. He looked over the people in line and didn't see her.

"Then I will also share with you that several of your *female friends* are at the front of the line." Todd made a face. "Awkward."

It might be for a couple of the women he'd dated over the past year but he decided against sharing that with Todd. "I'm here to support Em. I'll just hang out at the bar, grab a beer and something to eat."

"Color me shocked when she told me she was coming tonight. What happened with Neil anyway?"

Josh shrugged. "Not ready to put himself back out there again, I guess."

"Yeah, Gwen and her husband are worried about him. They were thrilled when they heard he'd agreed to go out with Em. And we were all thrilled you convinced her to put herself out there again. What's your secret? I've been trying to set her up for the past six months."

"It was Em's idea, not mine."

Todd nodded. "I guess almost dying has a way of putting things in perspective."

"Seems so," he said, as two women in the middle of the line drew his attention. They were having a heated conversation. He recognized the tall, dark-haired woman on the right. It was Cal's ex-wife, Raine Johnson. Raine was a talented and respected surgeon, who was heading up the trauma center expansion. She was also not one of Josh's biggest fans.

It looked like Raine's friend wasn't her biggest fan at the moment. She batted Raine's hand away from her shoulder-length, auburn hair. When the woman sidestepped Raine, Josh got a better look at her, at least from behind. She wore a black-knit turtleneck dress and a pair of knee-high black boots. The fairy lights strung through the trees glinted off the fiery red streaks in the woman's beachy waves, and Josh felt the pull of attraction. He'd always had a thing for assertive, confident women, and he liked the way she didn't let Raine steamroll her. He also liked the way she filled out her dress.

Raine pulled the woman back into line, and she

dropped her purse at the same time the crowd started moving forward. He couldn't hear what the woman said, but she looked like she was giving Raine crap while stepping out of line and bending down to pick up her purse.

Oh yeah, Josh thought, he really liked how she filled out her dress.

As though the woman sensed his attention, she glanced back, and a pair of familiar bottle-green eyes narrowed and her full cherry-red lips flattened.

And the buzz of attraction Josh was feeling seconds ago fizzled out and died an embarrassed death. He'd been seriously thinking about hitting on his best friend's sister.

Em straightened. "Callahan, were you checking out my butt?"

People turned, some of them going up on their tiptoes to see what, or in this case, who, was causing the commotion. He heard a couple familiar female voices at the front of the line mutter his name.

"No, I, um." He rubbed the back of his head. "Maybe?"

"He totally was," Todd said. "But can you blame him? You are looking gor-ge-ous."

Em waved the people behind her on and joined them. "What are you two doing here? You have a boyfriend," she said to Todd and then looked at Josh. "And far as I can tell, you don't need help finding a date."

I might after this, he thought, but instead said, "Todd's right. You look great, Em." She didn't look great; she looked amazing. He was used to seeing her in uniform or in sweats, hair up and makeup free. This new version of Em was unsettling to say the least.

"Matteo and I broke up, and Josh isn't here for the speed dating. He's here to support you. Isn't that sweet?"

The look she gave Josh made it clear she found the idea of him being here to support her the furthest thing from sweet but Todd and his breakup news took precedence. Josh was sure he'd hear about it later.

"What's wrong with you?" She lightly swatted Todd's chest with her purse, glancing at it as if she didn't know what it was, and then continued. "How could you break up with Matteo? He's a great guy."

"Ouch," Todd complained, rubbing his chest. "Why do you think it was me and not him?" When Em crossed her arms, Todd sighed. "Fine. It was me. But I wanted a commitment, and he wouldn't give me one."

"Of course he wouldn't. You've been dating all of six months," Em said, glancing at Raine who joined them. "Do not touch my hair or try to put lipstick on me."

"Dr. Johnson, you are looking fine tonight." Todd circled Em's face with his finger. "I'm sensing you had a hand in turning our diamond in the rough into this vision of feminine perfection we see before us. Am I right?"

Em groaned.

"You are." Raine pursed her lips at Em. "At least someone appreciates the effort I put into your makeover."

"Easy for him. He didn't have to sit—"

Raine talked over her ex-sister-in-law. "You should've seen what she planned to wear tonight, Todd."

Before Em smacked Raine with her purse, Josh intervened. "You're just about up, ladies." He nodded at Abby handing out cards at the door and, before he second-guessed himself, pulled out his phone and texted Em. Her phone pinged inside her purse. She took it out and read his text. "Conversation starters, really? How socially inept do you think I am?"

"Don't answer that," Todd murmured before saying to Em, "Your turn, sunshine."

Josh laughed, and Todd said with a grin, "No one does resting witch face better than Em, do they?"

"Not that I've seen," Josh agreed and then tuned into Abby and Em's conversation, which included Abby trying to convince Em to let her do at least one podcast from Seaton House. When Em started listing the reasons why she wouldn't back down, Abby sighed and handed Em her cards, plus a paper.

"What's with everyone giving me conversation starters?" Em muttered as she walked into the pub.

Josh rubbed his hand over his mouth so Em wouldn't see him laughing if she happened to glance back. He lowered it when she disappeared from view, smiling at Abby, who handed him a set of cards to rate his dates *yes*, *no*, or *maybe*. He figured he might as well take part. That way Em couldn't accuse him of being an overprotective jerk or a spy for her brother. Besides that, it would be easier to gauge how she was doing if he was one of the daters. It also sounded like there were some women he needed to apologize to. "Thanks, Abby. Great turnout."

"I know. I'm so excited. It was a spur-of-the-moment

idea but it really came together. I can't believe how many people signed up." She glanced over her shoulder and then returned her attention to him, lowering her voice. "I felt so bad that Neil canceled on Em. I wanted to do something to help. I think this will be easier for her, don't you? She only has to talk to someone for five minutes, and she'll meet twelve prospective dates before the night is over."

"Yeah, she should be able to handle that," Josh said, working to keep the skepticism from his voice.

But Abby must've picked up on it because she said, "You know, maybe you should be her first date. Kind of break the ice for her?"

"Might be a good idea," Josh said as his phone pinged with incoming texts. One from his mother, one from Cal, and one from Bri, the three of them wanting to know if Em had shown up, and if she had, how she was doing. He responded to all three of them as he walked into Highland Brew.

Em had already taken a seat at a row of tables. Within seconds of sitting down on either side of her, Raine and Todd crossed their arms and scowled. They put Em's resting witch face to shame. As Josh joined the men and a couple of women lining up on the opposite side of the bar, he discovered why.

Todd's ex, Matteo, a physical therapist who Josh saw regularly for his shoulder, and Raine's ex, Quinn, who looked like a thirtysomething Idris Elba, were leaning against the bar. From Matteo and Quinn's expressions, they weren't any happier to see Todd and Raine.

Josh walked over to say hello to the two men and

grab a beer at the bar, which is how he missed being Em's first date. His first date was a woman he'd gone out with last fall. "Hey, Lisa. How are you doing?"

She lifted her hands. "I'm here. How do you think I'm doing?"

"Ah...well. You look great," he said, going through conversation starters in his head. The problem was, he already knew everything about Lisa. Including that she was upset with him for not asking her for a third date. Two was his magic number, his line in the sand. "I'm sorry if I messed things up. I never meant to hurt you. I thought I was pretty clear when I told you I didn't want to get serious."

She played with the rating cards. "You did, but I was hoping you'd want more. I thought we had fun."

"We did, and I enjoyed getting to know you. But you told me you wanted to get married and have kids, and I didn't want you to waste your time with me."

They continued talking until Abby rang the bell, and Josh was feeling good with how it went. Until he saw Lisa's card. She'd put *yes* in capital letters with an exclamation mark. Now he felt bad for putting *no* on his.

His next four dates went about the same as with Lisa but he enjoyed his five minutes with Robyn, the paramedic who'd been on duty the night of Em's accident, and marked *maybe* on his card. He probably would've gone with an enthusiastic *yes* if not for coming face-to-face with his ex-dates.

During the refreshment break, Josh walked over to Todd to see how Em was doing.

Todd grinned and patted his chest. "Don't tease me, Coach. I don't think my heart can take it."

Josh laughed, which earn him a raised eyebrow from Em, who'd returned to her table with a chocolate cupcake and a bottle of water and was talking to Lottie the ambulance driver. On the other side of the bar, through a stone archway, Highland Brew sold specialty coffees, gift baskets, and baked goods from Bites of Bliss.

As Em and Lottie bonded over their love of everything chocolate, Josh leaned toward Todd and whispered, "How's she doing?"

Taking part in the event hadn't been as conducive to spying on Em as Josh had initially assumed. Since he'd apparently offended half the women here, not being fully present during their one-on-one times would've further cemented his reputation as a jerk. But from what little he'd observed of Em's interactions with her dates so far, it wasn't going well at all.

Todd raised a hand to the side of his face. "The first guy got up within two minutes of sitting down. I think she'd ticketed him for something because she had her cop-face on, and if you haven't seen it before, I can tell you from experience it's intimidating. I kind of missed what happened with her second and third dates because mine had potential. But from the look of relief on both their faces when the bell rang, it didn't go well. And then there was the pest control guy, who seemed into her. Em was really animated, so I thought he had potential until I heard what she was talking about. She spent the entire five minutes quizzing him about bats, rats, and raccoons."

A water bottle cap hit the side of Todd's head. "Stop talking about me," Em muttered, "and focus on your own date."

Todd rubbed his head. "I'd love to, but for some reason, he's more interested in you than me."

Geez, he couldn't go five minutes without hurting someone's feelings. "Todd, you know I'm not gay."

"I know, and I'm as invested in Em's dating success as you are." He sighed. "It's just that Matteo's here, and look." He waved a hand at a table five down from him. "The bell rang, and he's still sitting at that guy's table."

"Probably because, other than you, there's only two other guys here he could date. Did he come to your table?" Josh knew he had, just like he also knew Todd had turned his head.

"Maybe. I didn't want to look in case he thought I was still interested in him."

"Are you?"

"Of course I am. But I refuse to put my dreams on hold because he isn't ready for a commitment. It's not my fault his last partner broke his heart."

"No, but it took me a while before I was ready to date after my wife left me. If you ask me, Matteo dating you exclusively for six months says a lot."

"Of course you'd say that. The longest you've dated someone since your divorce is six hours." Todd filled out a ranking card and held it up. "But I'd still date you."

Josh laughed. "Thanks, but I'm done with dating."

"Yeah, me too. Wanna grab a beer sometime?"

"Sure," he said, standing up when Abby rang the bell.

The guy Matteo had been talking to got up from behind his table and walked over to Todd's. Todd grinned. "Maybe I was a little hasty."

Josh took a seat in the chair in front of Em. She held up her ranking card. She'd written his name, and underneath, *no* in capital letters with three exclamation marks.

He wrote her name, and underneath, *no* in capital letters with four exclamation marks. He held it up. "Now that we've cleared that up, can we just sit and talk?"

"About what?"

"About why you don't look like you're having fun," Josh said.

"It's stupid."

"Then why did you come?"

"I was trying to keep a promise to someone." She shrugged and looked away. "I need to go to the ladies' room."

Josh pulled out his phone and played Wordle while he waited for her to come back, looking up when the bell rang. Todd glanced at him. "Wanna bet she's not in the ladies' room?"

Todd was right. Nor was Em on the other side buying a cupcake or at the bar buying a beer. After confirming with Raine that Em had driven herself to Highland Brew, Josh searched the parking lot for her car. It was gone. And the more he thought about it, he realized there was something off about her voice when she said she was trying to keep a promise. He had a feeling it wasn't the promise she'd made to Bri. He didn't like the thought of her driving home on her own when she was upset and got into his truck.

Ten minutes later, he spotted her car, headlights on, car door open, in exactly the same place he'd seen it a week ago today. His heart raced the same way it had that night. Only this time, Em was standing by the water, her arms wrapped around her waist as she stared out at the fast-flowing river shimmering silver in the moonlight.

Chapter Eleven

♥

"You don't have to check on me. I'm fine," Em said without turning around. She knew Josh wouldn't be satisfied. He'd want to see for himself that she was all right. She brought her hands to her face, rubbing away the evidence of her tears. By the time she remembered she was wearing makeup, it was already too late. She probably had mascara all over her face. She supposed she could blame it on the mist hovering over the river but she wasn't up to explaining anything.

It was just a stupid dating game. Her inability to take part like a normal thirty-year-old out for some Saturday night fun shouldn't have hit her as hard as it did. It wouldn't have if she hadn't promised Brad. If he hadn't looked so happy at the thought of her moving on with someone else. If her inability to move on and enjoy life didn't affect his and their baby's ability to move on.

"I'm not checking on you," Josh said, coming to stand beside her. He tucked his hands in the pockets of his brown leather bomber jacket and looked at the river. "I needed quiet time communing with nature after communing with women who think I'm Highland Falls' equivalent to the guy Matthew McConaughey played in *How to Lose a Guy in 10 Days*."

She snorted. She'd been mad when she'd discovered him in line at Highland Brew, madder still that he thought she needed conversation starters, even though Abby had thought the same thing. It didn't matter that they'd been right. She'd spent her first three *dates* glaring at Josh. He hadn't noticed. He'd been too busy trying to make amends to the women who'd hoped for more from him than a couple dates.

She didn't blame them. The dating pool in Highland Falls wasn't that big, and Josh with his wavy black hair, sky-blue eyes, and chiseled jaw was the town's most sought-after bachelor. She imagined his inability to commit was part of the attraction. Everyone loved a challenge. But tonight would've been hard on Josh. He'd never intentionally hurt anyone. It wasn't in his DNA.

He was surprisingly oblivious to the impact he had on people, women in particular. He'd been the same way in high school. She'd always been fascinated by how easily he drew people to him, how easily he'd made friends. It was kind of comforting knowing Mr. Personality had had a lousy time tonight too.

"Is that a smile, Freckles?"

She shrugged. "I didn't know you were into rom-coms. All you and Cal ever watched was ESPN."

"Amber liked them. My sister and mom too." His smile faded, and he looked at the river. "A week ago, you almost died here, Em. Isn't it hard for you to be here?"

The air was damp and chilly, and she shivered,

hugging herself tighter as her gaze went to the middle of the river. They'd pulled Steve and Jenny's SUV from the water two days earlier. She considered his question before answering. "No. We all made it out alive."

Josh shrugged out of his jacket, laying it over her shoulders. "You're cold. I'm not," he said when she opened her mouth.

"I wasn't going to argue. I was going to say thanks." She put it on, the warmth from Josh's body and the smell of his cologne enveloping her like a hug.

"Huh, twice in a week," he said, then smiled. "You're welcome." His gaze went back to the river. "So it really doesn't bother you?"

She snuggled deeper into the jacket, and maybe because it smelled like Brad, she told Josh what she hadn't told anyone else. "I knew I was going to die, and I was okay with that, but then I saw Brad." She glanced at Josh, waiting for him to react, but he simply nodded.

"Why doesn't that surprise you?"

"I'm a first responder, Em. You're not the only person I know who's had a near-death experience. And we were with my grandma when she died. A few hours before she passed, she started talking to my grandfather like he was there. He'd died the year before." Josh shrugged. "It was nice, comforting even."

"But you don't believe she really saw your grandfather. You think it has something to do with oxygen deprivation, don't you?"

His gaze roamed her face. "You didn't just see Brad when you were dying, did you?"

"Why do you say that?"

"Because I was in the ambulance with you, and you told me you loved me. But it wasn't me you were talking to, it was Brad." He shook his head. "I knew something was off. It was the same with Gus."

Em could almost hear the pieces clicking into place and wasn't surprised when Josh asked seconds later, "The ghost Charlotte was talking about, it was Brad, wasn't it? That's why Gus was acting weird and why he's depressed."

She nodded. "It was." As the words left her mouth, a weight lifted off her shoulders. It was surprisingly freeing to tell someone the truth. She hadn't realized what a heavy burden it had been to bear by herself. Or how good it would feel to have someone validate her experience and not simply brush it off as a figment of her imagination.

If Josh had reacted any other way, she wouldn't have opened up to him. But now that she had, she couldn't seem to stop herself, and blurted out the rest. She told him about the morning Brad had died and about the night she'd lost the baby. She told him what Brad had said, and the promise she'd made.

She wrapped her arms around herself, waiting for him to respond. He'd stayed quiet the entire time she'd talked, sometimes bowing his head, sometimes silently nodding. Or like he was now, looking at the river. It made it easier to open up when he wasn't looking at her, and she had a feeling he knew that. But she wanted him to look at her now. She was afraid she'd told him too much, and he thought she'd lost her mind. She'd know as soon as he looked at her. She'd know exactly what he thought.

"Josh?"

He turned, lifting his gaze to hers, the moonlight illuminating his handsome face and the tears that had dried on his cheeks. He opened his arms, and she walked into them, surprising herself with how much she wanted to be held. Needed to be, if she were honest.

Closing his arms around her, he rested his chin on the top of her head. They stayed that way for several minutes, the only sound the quiet *sush* of the water against the rocks and the wind rustling the leaves on the trees.

"I'm so, so sorry, Em. I wish you would've told Cal or Bri or me—someone—about the baby. It guts me that you went through that on your own so soon after losing Brad."

"Talking about it would've meant reliving it, and I just couldn't do it then. And Cal would've blamed himself for not being there." She didn't blame him. He'd taken off two weeks to be with her, and he'd needed to get back to his family and work. He'd left that morning.

"Like you blamed yourself?"

She nodded.

He stepped back, moving his hands to her shoulders. "You don't anymore, do you?"

"No. Not like I did in the beginning. Not after talking to Brad." She glanced at him. "You believe me that he was here? That I saw him? That I talked to him? You don't think I was suffering from oxygen deprivation or something?"

"You didn't show any symptoms of oxygen deprivation. You're also one of the most skeptical people I know. So if you say you saw and talked to Brad; I believe you. Also, we saw a ghost at Seaton House, remember?"

She released the breath she hadn't known she'd been holding. "Thank you."

"Em, come on. You don't have to thank me." He draped an arm over her shoulders. "Are you ready to head home now?"

She nodded and went to take off his jacket.

"Wear it until you get home."

"You're following me, aren't you?"

"Yeah, but it's more for my benefit than yours. And I wouldn't mind checking out Seaton House. The kids have gone radio silent about their interest in the place, at least when I'm around. They know how I feel about it, so I figure they're keeping their plans on the downlow."

"I mentioned it to Izzy tonight when she was helping Raine with my makeover. She says she hasn't heard anything either. But it's Saturday night and not much else is going on in town, so who knows? It wouldn't hurt for us to check it out."

"Em, about tonight," Josh said as they reached their vehicles. "Don't put so much pressure on yourself. You didn't break your promise to Brad. You went tonight, and that's a big deal."

"Josh, I saw the guys' cards. They all put *no*, not a *maybe*, big fat *no*s."

"Did you put a *yes* for any of them?" She must've given herself away because he nodded. "Yeah, that's what I thought. Em, after years of not dating, you jumped into the deep end of the dating pool. You have to start in the shallow end, get comfortable..." He trailed off and angled his head. "You trust me, right? We're friends?"

She nodded. As much as he sometimes annoyed her, he'd been a big part of her life for as long as she remembered. And as she'd just proved by opening up to him, she trusted him. Maybe more than she'd even realized.

Grinning, he rubbed his hands together, which made her a little nervous. "Okay, hear me out before you shut me down. I'll be your practice date. We'll go out together, have some fun, and then in a few weeks, you'll be ready for a real date."

"I don't need a pity date. I mean, a pity fake-date."

"The last thing I feel for you is pity. I know what it's like to put yourself out there again." He scratched the back of his head. "If tonight was any indication, I didn't do a great job of it. But despite opinions to the contrary, I'm a fun date."

"I don't think that's your problem, Josh. The issue the women tonight had with you is that you cut them off at two dates for no apparent reason. I bet every one of them said they'd date you again." She crossed her arms. "I'm right, aren't I?"

"Yeah." He sighed, his shoulders drooping, and then he got a look in his eyes that made her as nervous as his gleeful hand rubbing. "This is the perfect solution for both of us. By fake-dating you, I can rehabilitate my reputation as a serial two-date dater. Okay, that doesn't sound right, but you know what I mean. And if everyone thinks we're dating, they won't try setting you up with half the single guys in town."

"Okay," she said slowly, thinking it over. "There are benefits for both of us, I guess. But Cal and Bri won't buy that we're dating."

"Yeah, no way I'm letting Cal think that we're actually dating. He'd disown me as his best friend, and I hate to tell you this, Freckles, but even for you, I wouldn't risk my friendship with your brother."

"You're right. I feel the same way about Bri."

"Wait a minute, are you telling me that Bri would defriend you if you were dating me? Because I get why Cal wouldn't want me dating you, especially given my reputation these days, but Bri loves me. Doesn't she?"

He looked so upset at the thought Bri didn't love him, that Em didn't have the heart to tease him. "Of course she loves you. She's the first one to come to your defense when someone accuses you of being a man ho." Okay, so she couldn't resist teasing him a little. It was about time he got a taste of his own medicine.

He groaned. "I can't believe people are calling me that. What are the kids on my team going to think?"

"Go, Coach?"

"Em, that's not funny."

"Relax, I'm teasing you. I'm also cold, so you must be freezing," she said, sliding behind the wheel of the Camaro. "We can continue our fake-dating conversation while we're checking out Seaton House."

"So we're really doing this," he said with a grin, rubbing his hands together again.

"If you keep rubbing your hands together like that, we're not."

"You're such a hard-ass, Freckles."

"Too much of a hard-ass for you to fake-date?" she said, then realized she'd asked it as a question and hadn't stated it as a fact, as she'd intended. And was that a hint of disappointment in her voice? She was beginning to think agreeing to Josh's fake-dating plan was a bad idea.

"Are you kidding me? It's one of my favorite things about you."

Em sighed. Obviously, Josh wasn't going to let anything stand in the way of his plan, including her snarky 'tude. As she backed onto the road and headed for home, she considered the benefits of going through with his idea. At least with Josh, she wouldn't have to fake it.

Except that wasn't entirely true. If they had an audience, she'd have to fake she was into him, and he'd have to fake he was into her. She had a feeling he'd be better at faking it than she would. As she'd discovered tonight, she sucked at faking it and dating.

She'd been right. This wasn't a good idea. She was about to call Josh and tell him she couldn't do it when her cell phone rang. She glanced at the screen. It was Bri, and she knew exactly why she was calling. Highland Falls' phone lines were no doubt burning up as word spread through town that Em had fled the speed-dating event.

Em didn't answer, and her phone fell silent, only to start ringing again a minute later. It was Abby. Em didn't answer and her phone once again fell silent, for all of fifteen seconds. The calls didn't let up. Text messages were also blowing up her phone by the time she pulled into her driveway.

She picked up her phone, scrolling through the increasingly worried texts from family and friends and went to the WhatsApp group chat she rarely used.

Just FYI, she typed. I didn't leave early because I was upset. Josh and I went... She deleted went and replaced it with are on a date so I don't have time to talk or respond to all your annoying calls or texts. She started to delete annoying but decided, just because all six women in their group chat cared about her, it didn't negate the fact that they were annoying, and she sent the text.

She got out of her car, looking up as Josh pulled into the driveway behind her. She supposed she'd better tell him they were having their first fake-date tonight. Their rendezvous at the river met the requirements of a date. It was a pretty location with the moon and mist adding a romantic atmosphere. Although some people might disagree with her. After all, she'd nearly died there. But she and Josh had talked, her more than him really, and she'd been completely open and vulnerable with him. Something she hadn't been with Brad for the first few months they'd dated.

Of course, Josh had an advantage in that he knew her so well. There'd also been physical contact—Josh had hugged her, and more important, she had hugged him back. She and Brad had dated six weeks before they'd shared a hug. Again, Josh had the advantage of sharing a highly charged emotional moment with her. And if a chivalrous act was included on a successful date questionnaire, Josh had checked the box when he gave her his jacket. All in all, Em decided, they were doing really well for their first fake-date.

Or maybe they weren't, she thought when Josh, who was on his phone, got out of his truck and shot her a look. Between the river and her place, she'd somehow managed to tick him off. She had no idea what…

She winced. He was talking to her brother. *Sorry*, she mouthed and texted Bri, filling her in on the fake-dating arrangement. She promised to call her in the morning.

"Yeah. Okay. We'll see you then," Josh said, disconnecting from Cal and walking toward her. "We've got a problem."

"It's okay. I told Bri about our arrangement."

"Would that be before or after you told your group chat that we were on our first date?"

"After." She glanced at him as she opened her front door. "They were annoying me, and I texted them all without thinking. Sorry. Again."

She caught the amused quirk of his lips. He'd never been able to hold a grudge for long.

"I'm not sure Cal believed me," he said as he walked into the house. "He and Bri are on their way over. But they're not our problem, at least I hope they're not." He closed the door behind him. "Izzy tried to text you, and when you didn't respond, she texted Bri."

"Right. She's on our group text too. But why would Izzy be upset we're dating? She's been trying to set us up since I moved back to town," Em said, accepting Gus's welcome home hug.

"That hasn't changed. I got a thumbs-up and a smiley face with heart eyes. I didn't know why until I heard you'd outed us in your group text. But that's not what she texted Bri about."

Em scrolled through her texts and found Izzy's. *911 Midnight.*

"The haunting of Seaton House is on." He grinned, crouching beside her to receive his own hug from Gus. "I told you dating me would be fun."

Chapter Twelve

♥

How does half the teenagers in town showing up at Seaton House at midnight have anything to do with our date and fun?" Em asked him.

Josh went to rub his hands together and remembered it annoyed her. Although, as he'd learned over the past year, there wasn't much he did or said that didn't annoy Em. Unlike when they were young. "Because we're going to scare the crap out of them so they don't come back, and since we'll be doing it together, it's a date."

"If that's your idea of a fun date, it's a wonder your ex-dates want to go out with you again."

He'd never have to worry about getting an inflated ego around Em. "You're the one who decided this is our first date, so I'm improvising. But trust me, you'll understand why they do when I take you on an actual date."

"We're fake-dating. You don't need to wine and dine me."

"I wasn't planning to." The last thing Em would enjoy was going out for a fancy dinner, and after witnessing the depth of her heartache at losing Brad and the baby, all he'd wanted to do was take away her pain. He'd been shaken seeing her like that. He couldn't remember the last time he'd seen Em cry. Even at Brad's funeral, she'd been stoic and remote.

But what had rattled him the most was the simple, quiet statement she'd made when she began opening up to him. It wasn't until he was following her home, replaying the conversation in his head, that he'd recalled what she'd said. She'd known she was dying, and she hadn't cared. He wanted her to care. He wanted her to feel like she could move on and be happy again, and not because she'd made a promise to her dead fiancé.

She turned on the lights, and he got a good look at her face. "You might want to wash your face before Cal and Bri get here."

"Why would I wash my face?"

"Because your mascara ran, and the last thing I need is for Cal to think I made you cry."

"Oh, right." She began walking toward her bedroom and then stopped and turned. "You won't tell anyone what I told you about seeing Brad or about the baby, will you?"

"Not if you don't want me to, I won't. But, Em, it might help to talk about it with Bri and Cal."

She shook her head. "It won't."

"Would you just think about it?" Not only was he uncomfortable keeping this from Bri and Cal, he thought it was important for Em's healing to open up about losing the baby.

"Nope."

Josh sighed. There was no sense in arguing with her.

He knew from experience that, once Em's mind was made up, there was no changing it. "I'll take Gus out."

"Thanks. Just watch him around the bushes. I spotted a mother raccoon and her babies in the backyard yesterday."

"Good to know," he said, attaching the leash to Gus's collar. But as soon as he opened the door, it was clear the goldendoodle had other plans, half dragging Josh to the side of the house. "Not tonight, boy."

He gave a light tug on the leash. Gus tugged back, and they played tug-of-war for a couple minutes before the dog sat on the lawn and whined, a pathetic look in his eyes.

Josh crouched beside him. "What's wrong, buddy?" The dog hadn't been himself since the accident, and after Em's confession at the river, Josh now knew why. "He's gone, boy. Brad's not coming back. But I'm here, and so is Em." Josh patted his chest. "Come on, give me a hug." Gus did as he asked, licking Josh's cheek as if he understood.

While he waited for Gus to do his business, Josh called his parents. The last thing he needed was for them, specifically his mom, to hear from someone else that he and Em were dating.

The call connected on the fourth ring. "Sweetheart, are you okay?" his mom asked, sounding breathless.

"Yeah, are you? I didn't wake you, did I?" He glanced at his phone. It was ten o'clock.

"It's date night. Your dad and I were—"

"Stop right there, Mom. I don't need or want to know what you two were up to. I'm just calling to let you know that you might hear a rumor about Em and me, and it's—"

"Phil, pick up the phone! Joshie has news about him and Em!"

"Mom, no, it's not what you—"

His mother talked right over him. "You don't know how long I've waited for you two to come to your—" His mom broke off, paused, then shouted, "I might've kicked it off the nightstand when—"

He groaned, raising his voice to cut her off. "Mom, Dad doesn't need to get on the other line. Em and I aren't dating. We're just pretending that we are so that everyone will stop trying to set her up, and..." He trailed off, thinking it best not to mention his dating reputation needing a reboot. "I'll take her on a few practice dates so she feels comfortable. But no one can know that we're fake-dating, other than you guys and Cal and Bri, okay?" He prepared for his mother's disappointment.

"Hmm, it probably has been a long time since Em went on a date. I imagine it will take a lot of practice dates for her to feel comfortable again, don't you?"

"I guess," he said slowly. "Mom, are you laughing?"

"It was your father. He tickled me. Stop it, Phil."

Josh didn't hear his father in the background, but just in case the tickling progressed to something more, he said, "I've gotta go. But you'll keep it quiet, right, Mom?"

"My lips are zipped. We'll do our part too."

"Umm, you don't need to do anything."

"Of course I do. We have to show everyone that we're fully supportive of your blossoming relationship with

Em. Everyone in town knows what I'm like. They won't believe you two are an item otherwise. They'll expect me to have you both for a family dinner. Maybe go on a couple of family outings. Yes, that should do the trick. I'll send you and Em some dates."

"No one will expect you to have us for dinner." He purposely didn't mention the family outings. He hoped she was joking. "You never invited any of the women I've dated this past year for dinner."

"Why would I? I knew they wouldn't last. But you know, son, you've acquired a bit of a reputation. This arrangement you have with Em will benefit you as much as her. You need time to figure out what you really want, and I'm sure spending time with Em will help you see the light."

At the sound of an approaching vehicle, he turned. The lights from Cal's Jeep nearly blinded him as he pulled in behind Josh's truck. When the spots finally cleared from his vision, he couldn't help but notice that his best friend looked a lot less enthusiastic about Em and Josh's plan than his mother sounded.

"I'll talk to you tomorrow, Mom." As he went to disconnect, he heard her say, "They're fake-dating like in the movie we watched last weekend. And we know how that turned out." He heard their gales of laughter just before the call ended. It was not a good sign. Then again, maybe they were tickling each other.

Bri and Cal got out of the truck and walked up the driveway. "Josh, what are you doing out here holding a leash?" Bri asked.

"I'm waiting for Gus to..." He glanced behind him.

There was nothing attached to the leash. The dog was gone. "Crap. How did he do that? I clipped his leash to his collar."

Bri gave his arm a commiserating pat as Josh turned on his phone's flashlight. "I've done it before," she said as she walked toward the front door. "You probably clipped the leash to his fur instead of his collar."

"Don't tell Em I lost him, okay?" He was almost positive Bri nodded as she walked into Em's and returned to searching the bushes with his flashlight.

Cal crouched beside him, shining his cell phone's flashlight under a bush. "So, you and my sister?"

"Are fake-dating, and I told you why. It'll be good for her, Cal." He straightened and headed for the road, calling for Gus. Quietly.

Cal followed him. "Unless she falls in love with you."

Josh turned, shining his flashlight in Cal's face. "Em? Fall for me? We're talking about your sister, right? The woman who looks like she wants to throw something at me every time I open my mouth." She hadn't acted that way tonight though.

"You're right. It's just that Bri looked a little too happy at the thought you two were dating."

"Probably because she knows it'll be good for Em to get out of the house and have some fun with someone you *trust*," he said pointedly.

"Yeah, but..." Cal grimaced. "You're right. I know you'd never do anything to purposely hurt Em. It's just that I'm worried about her. I can't shake the feeling that she's keeping something from me."

If Cal knew what Em was keeping from him, he'd

be beyond worried. "She nearly died last weekend. It's a lot for anyone to process, including you. Just give her some time. I'm sure she'll be fine." Josh intended to make sure that she was, and when he set his mind to something, he didn't give up.

"Now let's find Gus before Em finds out I lost him," Josh said, shining his flashlight into the bushes on the left side of the road.

Cal snorted. "Remind me never to let you watch my kids."

"Hey, I took Izzy to Asheville this summer and didn't lose her."

"She's seventeen. I'm talking about when Bri and I have kids."

"As long as you don't put them on a leash, I should be good."

Cal laughed and then turned at the approach of two vehicles, their headlights illuminating the gravel road.

Josh recognized the cars. "What are Raine and Quinn doing here?"

"I tried to call Izzy after she texted Bri. She's at a sleepover tonight. When I didn't hear back from her, I called Raine. And if Iz is ghosting her like she is me, Raine probably figures she's with the kids going to Seaton House."

"Ah, okay." It made sense why Quinn would be here with Raine. He'd raised Izzy for the first five years of her life. They had a great relationship. Actually, Izzy had a great relationship with all her parents, bonus and otherwise. Including with her aunt Em and with him. He was her honorary uncle.

As Raine and Quinn parked their vehicles behind Cal's, the front door opened. "Josh, what are you still doing out here?" Em asked, leaning halfway out the door.

Josh glanced at the empty leash, wondering if she could see it from there. "Just letting Gus sniff around." Under his breath, he said to Cal, "Don't shine your flashlight over here."

"We shouldn't be much longer," Cal said to his sister, covering for Josh like he always did. "Hey, Raine, Quinn. Any word from Izzy?"

"No," Raine said, looking at Josh with a frown.

He moved to his right, afraid from her vantage point she could see the empty leash. Unlike his best friend, Raine would totally out him. Raine said something to Em as she ushered the couple inside. Em nodded and then leaned against the doorjamb with her arms crossed. "It would serve you both right if I let you keep looking for Gus."

"What are you talking about? We're not—" Josh began.

Em patted her thigh, and Gus appeared beside her. She raised an eyebrow. "He was scratching at the back door, trying to get inside."

"Thanks a lot, buddy," Josh said as he walked to the door, standing back to let Cal go in before him. "So what's the real reason you didn't let us keep looking? I know it wasn't out of the goodness of your heart."

She jerked her thumb at the living room. "They're going to be here for a while. I don't know what to do with them."

Josh didn't tease Em about her social awkwardness. It didn't matter that they were all friends and had hung out together plenty of times in the past. Em had never invited them here. She wasn't big on entertaining. And not that anyone else would know it, but she'd had an emotionally draining night.

"What can I get you guys to drink?" he asked as he hung Gus's leash by the door.

They called out their orders, and he walked to the fridge, grabbing a few beers and a bottle of red wine.

"I've got it," Em said. "You go talk to everyone."

"I will," he said as he put the bottles on the counter and opened a cupboard.

At the moment, the *everyone* she referred to was texting on their phones and not paying attention to them. He figured they were trying to reach Izzy.

"Hands off my snacks." Em raised her hand to close the cupboard door.

"We have guests, Freckles. You have to share." He snagged a couple bags of cookies.

She looked at the cookies. "As long as you don't touch my Sour Patch Kids."

"I wouldn't think of it," he said, waiting for her reaction when he opened the freezer and pulled out a carton of Moose Tracks ice cream.

"No, no way." She tried to take it from him.

"Don't worry, I'll share with you." Ice cream was his one vice, and he knew how much Em loved it, which was the real reason he'd gotten it out of the freezer. It was Em's go-to emotional soother.

"And me," Bri said, raising her hand.

"You'd better buy me another carton," Em grumbled when everyone else placed an order for ice cream.

Ten minutes later, they were settled on the couch with their bowls.

Raine waved her spoon at them. "So, you two are dating now?"

Josh glanced at Em. She looked like she had brain freeze. "Ah, yeah, this is our first date."

"Their first *fake*-date," Cal said, shrugging when Josh and Em swiveled their heads to stare at him. "What? It's not as if Raine and Quinn will say anything."

He was probably right. Last year, they'd all kept Cal and Raine's secret in order to ensure that the hospital expansion went through. Until it had blown up in their faces. But what Josh and Em were doing wasn't at all the same.

It had been fun when Em and Bri moved into the house on Marigold Lane, all of them hanging out together. It was one of the reasons he'd decided to start dating again. But now that he thought about it, he'd never invited any of the women he'd dated to join him at Cal and Bri's or at his house when he'd had them over.

"Okay, I get why Em wants to fake-date you, but why do you want to fake-date her?" Raine asked.

"Gee, thanks, Raine," Em said.

"You know what I mean. You don't want to date, but Josh loves dating."

At least Raine hadn't called him a serial dater or a man ho. "I need to take a break. Revaluate my dating strategy."

Cal, Bri, and Quinn ducked their heads but not fast enough that they could hide the fact they were laughing at him.

"What's so funny?"

"The fact that you think you have a dating strategy," Em said. "Okay, enough dating talk." Then she looked at Quinn and Raine. "Unless you two have something you want to share."

"Why would we have anything to share?" Raine asked.

"Oh, I don't know. Maybe because you're both here. Together," Em said.

"Raine told me about Izzy's text and that she wasn't responding to her. So I decided to tag along." Quinn held up his phone. "She isn't responding to my texts either."

"Did you try contacting the parents of the kid's house she's staying at?" Em asked.

"I talked to them," Cal said. "The girls supposedly went to Kelly's to watch a movie. She's not answering her phone either."

"It's not like Izzy not to answer her cell or at the very least respond with a quick text," Bri said.

"They're probably out of cell range but we know they're eventually going to show up here, so for now, I wouldn't worry about it." Em leaned over and scooped a spoonful of ice cream from Josh's bowl. "Izzy said they're going to be at Seaton House at midnight so we have about an hour and a half until showtime. You might as well share with us how you intend to scare the crap out of the kids, Josh."

Chapter Thirteen

♥

Josh's ability to read a room hadn't improved with age, Em thought, noting the expressions on Bri and Raine's faces. Since he was using both his hands to describe what he'd do to terrify the unsuspecting teenagers, Em picked up his bowl of ice cream.

Bri and Raine gasped, and Em smiled around a spoonful of Moose Tracks. Josh was right. He was a fun date.

"See, I told you. Scary, right?" he said, clearly misinterpreting Bri and Raine's horrified gasps.

Bri shook her head. "No, Josh, just no."

"Really?" He shrugged. "Okay. If you give me a second, I'll come up with something that will really freak them out."

"Please, don't," Raine said.

"There you go. Raine thinks my plan will work. What about you guys? Quinn? Cal?"

Cal grinned. "Maybe a little too well, buddy. I think that's what Bri's worried about."

"Of course that's what I'm worried about. Josh, you can't go around terrifying the kids," Bri said.

"But that's the point. We don't want them hanging around Seaton House. If we scare the crap out of them, they won't."

This had been Em's main concern when Josh first mentioned his plan to her, but she hadn't had a chance to talk to him about it. "Or, it'll have the opposite effect, and have more kids wanting to check out the house."

"Hey, I saw you. When I was laying out the plan to these guys, you were smiling and nodding." He took his ice cream bowl back.

"You're entertaining. But think about it. The only reason the kids are going to check out a haunted house is because they want to be scared."

"Em's right," Bri said. "But the kids I'm worried about are the ones who are tagging along because they want to be part of the in-crowd. Think what it'll be like for them if they run away, crying."

"You sure know how to ruin a guy's fun," Josh said, dipping his spoon into the bowl. He looked down and then back at Em. "You ate my ice cream."

"Technically, it was my ice cream. So." She looked around the room. "What are we going to do?"

"The whole point is keeping the kids from getting hurt, right?" Bri asked.

"That and keeping them from coming back," Em said. "I looked into motion-sensor cameras with lights and noise for Jenny and Steve, but with the amount of wildlife in the area, we'd be fielding more complaints at HFPD than it'd be worth. Jenny and Steve ordered a new gate and a couple of *No Trespassing* signs, but the property's too big to completely fence in, and the kids would just hop it anyway."

"What about HFPD patrolling the area more often? At least on the weekends," Cal said.

"They don't have the resources," Em said. "And I've already talked to Gabe about me doing it and was told he'd tack on another two weeks to my"—she made air quotes—"vacation time if he heard that I was hanging out at Seaton House."

"So I'm guessing you didn't tell him you were investigating May and Clara's murders," Josh said.

Cal looked from Josh to her. "What do you mean you're investigating their murders?"

"Thanks a lot," Em said under her breath to Josh before raising her voice and saying to her brother, "What of it? I'm curious."

"You're supposed to be relaxing and enjoying your vacation time, not chasing down leads for a case that was closed a hundred years ago," her brother said.

Cal probably didn't want to hear that, for her, digging into the case would be enjoyable. As much as Brad wanted her to have a life outside of her job, so did her brother.

Josh put an arm around her shoulders. "Don't worry, buddy. I've got it covered. I'm going to make sure Em enjoys her vacation time."

Cal crossed his arms. "Just so you know, I don't find that a comforting thought either."

"Okay, enough talk about what I do or don't do on

my vacation. We're wasting time. The kids will be at the house in forty-five minutes," Em said.

"I know you've been trying to shut down Abby's podcasts from Seaton House, but maybe it's not a bad idea, Em," Quinn said. "It'll satisfy everyone's curiosity about the place."

Raine nodded her agreement. She must've noticed Quinn glance her way because she stopped nodding and lifted an elegant shoulder. "Just because I agree with you about this, doesn't mean I agree with you about anything else. We don't have a single thing in common, and—"

Quinn interrupted her. "Other than Izzy and wanting the trauma center to succeed, you're probably right."

"That's rich," Raine said. "How can you say you want the trauma center to succeed when it's because of your demands that we're two months behind schedule?"

"The reason we're two months behind schedule has nothing to do with me. It's because you didn't provide your budget to the oversight committee, and you didn't file for your permits on time."

She threw up her hands. "It has everything to do with you! You're the town manager! I don't have time for all your red tape. You put up roadblocks at every turn."

"Sounds to me like you could use a holiday, Raine. When's the last time you took time off?" Josh asked.

Quinn snorted. "Time off? She doesn't know the meaning of the words."

"Are you insinuating I'm a bad mother because I don't take time off? Because that's sexist if you ask me. You work as much as I do."

"Don't put words in my mouth. I never said you were a bad mother. All I asked was for you to make some time for us. That's it. That's all I wanted." He looked at her. "You could've just told me you weren't interested."

"I never said I wasn't interested. I just got overwhelmed trying to juggle work, having time for Izzy, and dating you."

"You expect me to buy that?"

"Why wouldn't you? It's the truth."

"Really? So you were taking part in the speed dating for a lark?"

Em looked at Josh. "You knew exactly what you were doing, didn't you?"

He watched the couple fighting with a smile on his face. "Not exactly. Quinn was complaining that they never spent time together before they broke up so I thought it might be a conversation starter. Our group dinners are more fun when Quinn comes, and he's been a no-show ever since they called it quits. But anyone can see they're into each other. All they needed was to talk it out."

"They're yelling."

"I know. Great, isn't it?" He glanced at his phone. "We should probably head to the house without them." He whistled, waving a hand to get their attention. Bri and Cal, who'd been trying to mediate, looked at Josh while Raine and Quinn continued arguing.

"Em and I are going to the house. You guys hang out here and talk it out. Plenty of wine and beer in the fridge and snacks in the second cupboard—just leave Em's Sour Patch Kids alone."

"And my Pop-Tarts."

"Trust me, Freckles. No one in this room is interested in eating your Pop-Tarts." He looked down at Gus, who was lying at his feet. "No humans, at least."

"I'm coming too," Raine said, face flushed, eyes bright.

Em took in her high heels. "Not in those you're not. You can borrow a pair of my sneakers."

"Crap, we don't have a key to get in the house," Josh said as he nudged Gus out of the way and stood up. "It's too late to call Jenny and Steve."

"I texted Jenny to let her know what's up when you took Gus for his walk and asked her to leave a key in her mailbox."

Josh grinned. "We make a great team."

"Except your plan got vetoed," Cal reminded him.

"I'll come up with another one. I'm good at thinking on the fly," Josh assured him. "Em, do you have any lanterns or flashlights?"

"Yep." She nodded at the buffet table in the dining room where she'd placed two battery-operated lanterns and two flashlights. "I've also got a bat and two walking sticks."

"I'd kiss you right now, but you'd probably slug me," Josh said.

"If I didn't, Cal would," she said, noting the way her brother was looking at his best friend.

"Seriously, bro? As if I'd hit on Em. We're friends."

"As long as you don't become friends with bene—"

"Cal!" Em and Josh yelled, cutting her brother off.

"What? It happens all the time."

"I'm more worried about why Em and Josh think we need a bat and walking sticks," Bri said. "I thought we agreed we're not scaring the kids, so there's no reason for us to even be in the house."

"What we agreed is that, one, we're going to keep the kids safe, and two, make sure they have no interest in coming back to Seaton House. Which means they have to get into the house, and we're there to ensure that no one gets hurts."

"They won't come into the house if we're there, Josh," Em said.

"They will if they don't know we are," Josh said, grabbing a flashlight and the bat before heading for the door. "I'll get the key and meet you at the house. You can explain why we need the bat and walking sticks."

Cal followed Josh to the door. "I'll go with you."

"Me too," Quinn said.

Em handed Bri and Raine each a lantern and a walking stick. "Trust me, you'll feel better armed. Pest control isn't coming until Monday." Em told them about the wildlife they'd encountered at Seaton House the other day.

"Oh good, I thought you were going to tell me the place really is haunted," Bri said.

"I'm more worried about rabid raccoons and rats," Raine said, looking like she was having second thoughts about joining them. Then she sighed. "But if Izzy's with them, I should be there."

Em walked to the entryway closet and grabbed a pair of sneakers for Raine, who looked at them and said, "Do you have a pair of boots instead?"

"That's not a bad idea." Em retrieved a pair of hiker boots for herself, handing rubber boots to Raine and to Bri. Once they'd put them on, Em gave Gus a quick head scratch. "We'll be back soon," she promised, locking the door behind them.

Em turned on her flashlight, stuck it under her chin, and said, "Boo."

"No wonder you and Josh get along so well," Raine said. "But do you really think fake-dating him is a good idea?"

"Yeah, it's a good cover for both of us. It'll keep the women of Highland Falls off his back and the matchmakers of Highland Falls off mine." She glanced at Bri and Raine as she lit their way along the gravel road to Seaton House. "Why? Do you think it's a bad idea?"

"I think it's a great idea." Bri smiled, elbowing Raine. "You do too, don't you?"

"Um, yes?"

"Could you sound any less enthusiastic?" Admittedly, Em preferred Raine's skepticism to her best friend's obvious delight at the idea.

"I'm sorry. I guess I'm jaded when it comes to dating, even if it's fake-dating. I'm obviously no good at it." Raine kicked a stone. "Do you know not one of the men I met tonight wanted to date me?"

"Why would...," Em began at the same time Bri said, "I'm sure that's not..." Em gestured for her best friend to continue. "You're the expert, not me."

"I'd rather you finish what you were going to say, Em. Bri is too nice to tell me the truth."

"Hey, I always tell you the truth," Bri protested.

"Yeah, but you sugarcoat it. And sometimes people need you just to lay it out there," Em said. "What I was going to say, Raine, is why would any of those guys put themselves out there when it was obvious you had eyes for only Quinn?"

"That's not true."

"I was sitting beside you, and I know what I saw. And if I did, so did they. If it makes you feel better, I doubt any of the women Quinn met tonight wanted to date him. He spent the entire time watching you."

"Really?"

"Yeah, really. So why don't you just admit you're in love with him and try to make it work?" She frowned at Bri who was grinning at her. "What?"

"Look at you, all romantic."

She shrugged. "None of us know how long we have with the people we love. It's stupid for Raine to keep Quinn at arm's length just because she's afraid of getting hurt." Em caught Bri and Raine sharing a glance and decided a subject change was in order. "So, I should probably tell you Seaton House is haunted."

"Why are you just telling us that now?" Raine asked.

"Because we're here, and I thought you might like a little warn—"

"Boo!" Josh popped out from behind a bush, the flashlight under his chin illuminating his ghoulish grin.

Raine screamed, and Bri jumped, grabbing Em's arm. "Really? I did the same thing, and you didn't react."

"Face it, Em. I'm better at it than you are," Josh said, opening the gate for them and then glancing up the road at the sound of several vehicles headed their way. "It could be the kids. We'd better get out of sight."

"Where are Quinn and Cal?" Bri asked as they hurried after Josh.

"Doing a sweep of the main floor," he said just as the front door swung open and Cal and Quinn ran out.

"I think you forgot to tell us something, bro," Cal said.

"Oh right. The house is haunted."

"You two suck," Raine said, crossing her arms. "Now what are we supposed to do?"

Josh held the door open. "Stick to the plan and keep the kids safe." Approaching headlights illuminated the gravel road, and he ushered everyone inside, closing the door behind them. "Okay, so we're going to split up. Cal and Bri, you take the kitchen. There's a broom closet you can hide in." He glanced at Em. "Don't worry, I checked. Jenny must've cleaned it sometime this week. Leave the door open a crack and leave the lantern on the kitchen table," he instructed them.

Bri and Cal looked down the hall. "I'm not sure this is a good idea," Cal said, reaching for Bri's hand.

"If it makes you feel better, Em and I are taking the upstairs. That's where we saw the ghost."

"So you really did see a ghost?" Bri asked.

"We think we did." A door slammed upstairs, and Em winced. "Sorry," she murmured, thinking she'd offended the ghost. "We saw a woman in the turret window, and we heard a lot of door slamming." A red ball bounced down the stairs.

Josh grinned. "And Em played ball with a ghost kid."

Quinn swore under his breath, putting an arm around Raine's shoulders and drawing her close. "Your plan isn't going to work, Josh. Not if the kids hear or see any of what you're talking about. They'll be back every weekend."

"Let me worry about that. For now, put your lantern on the fireplace mantel, Raine, and then you and Quinn hide in here." Josh walked to the wall beside the fireplace and pressed his palm against it. A segment of wood paneling popped open, revealing a hiding place. "Cool, eh? Neil told me about it. There's a peephole so you'll be able to see what's going on."

He typed on his phone, and theirs all pinged. "It's a link to an alarm like the one Em mentioned. If you press activate, a siren will blare, and lights will flash. So if the kids get out of hand or we think someone's going to get hurt, we'll sound the alarm. I texted Izzy so she knows what to expect. She'll tell the kids the house is monitored and to get out before HFPD arrive."

Raine sent a nervous glance up the stairs. "Why can't we just do that now?"

"Because, if everything goes according to plan, they're going to come in and look around and see nothing but an old house in need of renovating." Car doors slammed, and they could hear kids laughing. "Places, people." He motioned for Em to follow him, lighting the way with the flashlight on his phone.

"Okay, so how do you plan to get the ghosts to cooperate?" Em asked, sprinting up the stairs after him.

As they hurried past the bedrooms to the front of the house, he called out quietly, "May, Clara, Willy, we know you're here, and Em is going to help Jenny clear your names. But right now, we need you to stay quiet. Just until the kids leave," he said as they reached the turret room.

Em stared at him. "You actually think that'll—" She broke off at the sound of a woman softly weeping.

"Did you hear that?" she asked Josh, who'd crouched near the window, looking outside.

He nodded and then turned to her, mouthing *Show-time*. Staying low as he crossed the room, he motioned for her to get behind the half-open door and joined her there.

Downstairs, the front door opened. "It's just a lantern. Don't be a bunch of lame-asses. Mike's dad must've been working here and left them on. Come on, or do you want me to hold your hands?"

Josh rolled his eyes, obviously recognizing the voice. Em imagined he knew the majority of the kids coming into the house. And from the stampede of footsteps, there were a lot of them.

As if he read her mind, he held up his hands, closed his fingers, and held them up again. At least twenty teenagers. He must've seen them coming up the path. They were roaming around downstairs. "Hey, don't touch anything. It's private property, Drew."

Izzy, Em mouthed, and Josh nodded.

"You're such a goody-goody." It was the smart-ass kid who, Em figured, must be Drew. "Let's check out upstairs. You should probably stay down here, Johnson. We wouldn't want you to freak..." A high-pitched cry was followed by, “What the hell was that?” The panic in Drew’s voice came through loud and clear.

Josh muttered, “Damn it.”

A bunch of the kids started laughing. “She got you good, Drew.”

“Maybe I should lead the way,” they heard Izzy say. “We wouldn’t want you to *freak out*, Drew.”

Em and Josh smiled and high-fived each other. Ten minutes later, they did it again when some of the kids started complaining that coming to Seaton House had been a lame idea. At the sound of them heading down the stairs, Em and Josh stepped out from behind the door in the turret room.

“Okay, I have to admit it. Your plan totally work—” Em began.

She was cut off by a muffled scream coming from the living room, a scream that was echoed by several of the kids, followed by the pounding of feet as they raced for the front door.

Josh bowed his head when it slammed behind the kids before raising his gaze to hers. “Looks like we’ll be spending our Saturday date nights hanging out at Seaton House.”

From downstairs they heard Raine say, “I couldn’t help it. A rat ran across my feet!”

Chapter Fourteen

♥

Josh walked down the hall of Highland Falls Elementary. It was a stone's throw from the high school, which made it easy for his mom to have him run errands for her. Today was her volunteer day, and she'd forgotten her lunch.

She'd called him ten minutes ago, asking him to pick her up something to eat. He'd been too busy to leave the campus and brought her his lunch instead. But as he approached the kindergarten classroom, he heard a familiar voice and knew he'd been had.

He leaned against the doorjamb, watching Em, who sat in a kid-size chair at a round table finger painting with a group of kindergarteners. She wore jeans, a green sweater, and a frown on her face.

"Thanks. I like your tree," she said to the boy beside her, who was holding up his artwork.

"It's not a tree. It's my dad," the boy said, and Josh pressed his lips together to keep from laughing.

"Oh, he's, uh, tall," Em said and went back to dabbing

her orange-and-yellow-coated fingers on the paper in front of her.

"Do you like my painting?" the little girl beside Em asked.

"I do." Em nodded. "You did a good job painting your dad."

"It's not my dad. It's a tree. Like yours," the little girl said, her bottom lip pushed out.

Josh could almost hear Em swearing in her head. She leaned over as if getting a better look. "You're right, it is. Only your tree is better than mine."

The little girl beamed, and a dark-haired little girl with pigtails across from Em held up her painting. "What about mine?"

"It's really good," Em said.

"No, you're supposed to say what it is," the dark-haired little girl said in a demanding voice that didn't bode well for Em if she guessed wrong.

Josh pushed off the doorjamb. "Hey, how come no one told me it was finger painting day?" He grinned at Em, who looked like he'd saved her from a fate worse than death.

"Look at mine, Coach. Look at mine!" several of the kids in the class called out, holding up their artwork.

He usually stopped in once a day when his mom was volunteering. Although he'd recently begun staying away when he'd discovered Allison Parker, a woman he'd dated six months ago, was their substitute teacher. She was at the speed-dating event Saturday night, and she'd opted to give him a second chance.

"Wow. They're amazing." He leaned over Em. "Good job, Picasso. Is that Gus?" he teased, knowing full well it was a tree stump.

"No, it's you." She glanced around the table as if it had dawned on her how the kids might misconstrue her words. "I'm just joking," she said, but it was too late.

"Is Officer Em your girlfriend?" the dark-haired little girl asked.

His mom, who'd been helping at another table, looked up with a smile. As if sensing he was about to say no, she sent a pointed glance in Allison's direction.

Josh nodded slowly. "Yes, she is."

His answer resulted in Em bowing her head with a groan and a barrage of questions about when they were getting married shouted by half the class while the other half sang about him and Officer Em sitting in a tree k-i-s-s-i-n-g.

They were cut off by Allison moving to the front of the classroom and clapping. "All right, boys and girls. Let's thank Officer Emma for spending the morning with us."

When Em stood up, the kids at her table begged her to stay. "I'd love to but I really have to go. Thanks for having me, and thanks again for my gratitude rocks." She held up her hands. "I just need to wash up."

Allison directed her to the tiny sink at the back of the classroom. While Em washed her hands, Josh admired the paintings being thrust his way as he walked over to his mom, handing her his lunch bag.

"What's this?" she said, frowning at the bag.

"The lunch you asked me to bring you."

"Oh right." She peeked inside. "Salad and an apple, how nice."

He took back the bag. "I'll eat this, and you can eat the lunch you have hiding in your cubby."

She wrinkled her nose. "You know me too well. But I wanted you to see Em with the kids. Wasn't it just the cutest? They loved her, and she was so good with them."

He glanced over his shoulder. Several of the kids had followed Em to the sink like she was the Pied Piper, and they were foisting their paintings on her as she dried her hands. She gingerly accepted them, promising to put the paintings on her fridge at home.

"Yeah, she is pretty cute," he said, as Em gave him a wide-eyed look when the kids started hugging her. Then he realized what he'd said. "Don't get any ideas, Mom. You know the deal."

She ignored him, walking to Em instead and giving her a hug. "It was so sweet of you to drop in today. You have to do it more often. The kids loved having you, and so did I."

"Yeah, it was...fun," Em said, looking down at her sweater that was now dotted with red, yellow, and orange paint from the artwork she'd pressed to her chest when his mom hugged her.

"It'll wash out," his mom assured Em, patting her arm. "Don't forget our family dinner on Sunday."

"Family dinner?" Em asked, looking from his mom to Josh.

"Josh, did you not tell Em?" His mother waved her hand. "I knew I should've sent the invite directly to you,

Em. Anyway, yes, dinner's at five, but you come early. We can have some girl time."

Em narrowed her eyes at Josh before she smiled at his mom. "Okay. Sure. Sounds good."

She'd never say no to his mom, but Josh had a feeling he was going to hear about this. Placing a hand at the small of Em's back, he nudged her forward, and they waved goodbye to the kids.

"A little warning would've been nice," Em said as they walked into the hallway.

"Sorry. She sent me the invite just before I went out on a call last night, and I forgot about it."

"Not about that, although yeah, I would've appreciated knowing we were expected for dinner at your parents'."

"Oh, you meant about me telling the kids we were dating."

"No, that wasn't what I was talking about either, but yeah, what were you thinking?"

"I was thinking about the reason why this works for me as much as it does for you."

"I'm having second thoughts about that now," she said, turning down the hall toward the office. "Your mom might've been happy I was there, but Allison wasn't. You could've told me she was one of the women you dated and dumped."

"I didn't dump her. I just didn't ask her out again, which, by the way, was the reason I said you were my girlfriend and why our fake-dating works for me as much as it does for you. But how was I supposed to know you were going to show up here today?"

"Sorry, you're right." She smiled her thanks at the secretary who buzzed them out. "You should probably send me a list of the women you've dated so I'll be prepared for the bitchy looks and cold shoulders."

"Okay, I guess I can do that."

She looked at him. "Exactly how long will this list be?"

"Long," he admitted sheepishly.

She shook her head and headed for her car.

"Hey, Em," he called after her. "Don't forget to bring Gus to practice this afternoon."

"Why? Aren't you picking him up?"

He rubbed the back of his head. "I kind of told the guys my girlfriend would be showing up at practice today, and I expected them to be on their best behavior."

* * *

Josh nearly swallowed his tongue when Em walked onto the field later that afternoon. There was nothing remotely sexy about her outfit. She wore a gray *It's Football Y'all* sweatshirt with a pair of denim shorts and white sneakers. The problem was her legs—long, tanned, and toned. He knew Em worked out and was in great shape, but he could've done without visual confirmation. And her hair, shiny and loose, swinging across her shoulders like she was in a shampoo commercial, didn't help either.

She didn't look like Em, his best friend's kid sister, the girl he'd known since grade school. She looked like...someone he'd like to date. He'd had the same reaction Saturday night at Highland Brew, and he wasn't sure what to do about the inappropriate tightening in his gut as she closed the distance between them.

Run, was the first thought that popped into his head, but instead he said, "Why did you get all glammed up? It's just a football practice."

She looked down at herself. "What are you talking about? I'm wearing shorts and a sweatshirt."

She raised her narrowed gaze. Her lashes were darker, thicker, longer, making her eyes stand out more than usual. He was as tongue-tied as he'd been the day he'd first noticed there was nothing ordinary about Emma Scott and her eyes. He'd been nineteen, and she'd been seventeen. He'd shut down the feelings as fast as they'd appeared, unwilling to damage his long-standing friendship with Cal.

Josh crouched to hug Gus and then took his time working the football jersey over the dog's paws in an effort to get his head straight. *It's just Em*, he told himself as he stood up. He tugged on a long strand of her auburn hair, wondering if it had always been this silky.

"You have your hair down, and you're wearing makeup, Freckles." He teased her like he always did. Only this time it felt different. He was using her nickname to remind himself of the girl she used to be. Ironically, calling attention to the cinnamon sprinkles scattered across the bridge of her nose and the top of her high cheekbones had the opposite effect. There was nothing cute about her freckles today. They looked come-to-me sexy.

He curled his fingers into a fist to keep from touching

her soft, flushed skin, from tracing a line from one freckle to the other. There was something seriously wrong with him. The best thing he could do, for both of them, was end their fake relationship. Laughter drew his attention from Em and the running commentary in his head. His team walked across the field, reminding him of the reason he'd suggested fake-dating in the first place.

Em followed his gaze. "You told the guys on your team that I was your girlfriend. So I thought I'd better look like someone you'd date."

"Okay, just to be clear. I'm not shallow. I don't choose who to date based on what they look like."

She raised an eyebrow. "You sent me your list, remember? I checked them out, and you have a type. None of them were plain Janes or sporty girls, and neither was your ex-wife. Oh, and do yourself a favor, don't go on their social media."

Leave it to Em to investigate the women he dated. "How bad is it?"

"Let's just say you probably need to fake-date me more than I need to fake-date you."

So much for putting an end to their charade. But as much as Em said it benefited him more than her, he couldn't shake the memory of her confession by the river. So, as he'd done more than a decade before, he shut down his inappropriate thoughts and feelings. He could do this. He could do this for Em.

His cell rang, and he pulled it from the pocket of his shorts. It was his assistant coach. He didn't know why he was surprised.

"What's up?" Em asked once he'd disconnected.

"Assistant coach can't make it. It's the fourth time he's bailed since the start of the season. Never has a problem making it to our games though."

"I can give you a hand," Em offered, completely serious. As though she read his mind, she said, "Josh, I played competitive soccer and was on the varsity cross-country team; I think I can handle running a few drills."

"Sure. Okay," he said as the team crowded around. Josh introduced them to Em.

She gave Drew the once-over. The kid thought he was God's gift to women of all ages, so he probably assumed Em was checking him out. If he only knew she most likely wanted to drop-kick him for what he'd said to Izzy the other night at Seaton House. The thought gave Josh an idea, and he hoped Em caught on and rolled with it.

"Em lives on Sugar Maple Road, just down from Seaton House. You've probably seen her around, Charlie," he said, adding for Em's benefit, "Charlie lives at the far end of Sugar Maple Road."

Em nodded, crossing her arms. "You didn't happen to see a bunch of kids at Seaton House Saturday night, did you?"

Charlie's Adam's apple bobbed. "No, ma'am."

"That's Officer Ma'am to you," Em said.

Oh yeah, Josh thought, she was rolling with it—like a steamroller. He probably should've given her a heads-up. He felt bad for putting Charlie on the spot. He was a good kid. Shy and quiet, he was still finding his place on the team. Neil's son Mike sidled closer to

Charlie, lending him support. He was a lot like Charlie, only he tried harder to fit in. Gus, who'd no doubt seen Officer Hard-ass in action, moved to sit between Charlie and Mike, offering the teens emotional support.

"Yes, ma'am. I mean, Officer Ma'am," Charlie said, patting Gus's head.

Drew and his crew snickered.

Em pinned Drew with a stare that had him flushing to the roots of his blond surfer dude's hair. "Which one of you drives a red Ford Explorer?" she asked, reeling off the license plate so that Drew had no wiggle room.

"It's my dad's," Drew admitted.

Em raised an eyebrow.

"It's my dad's, Officer Ma'am," he said, glaring at his friends when they snickered.

"So your father was at Seaton House Saturday night." Em pulled out her cell. "I'll just give him a call."

"No, please don't," Drew said.

The pleading note in the kid's voice confirmed Josh's concerns about Drew's father's treatment of his son. Josh had seen him in action at a couple games last season and had taken him aside, threatening to have him removed from the stands if he ever heard him yell at his son like that again. When Drew's father complained to the principal, she backed Josh. So had the school board. To say the man wasn't a fan of his was an understatement.

"Who was at Seaton House Saturday night?" Em asked. Drew and his crew exchanged sidelong glances and then reluctantly raised their hands. "First-degree trespassing is a class two misdemeanor, which means the possibility of sixty days in jail and a thousand-dollar fine. Lucky for all of you, the owners of Seaton House don't want to press charges. But if this happens again, I'll be advising them to do so. Got it?"

They nodded. "Got it, Officer Ma'am."

The boys didn't catch Em's lips twitching but Josh did. Probably because they kept drawing his attention. She must've put on lipstick or lip gloss. Her mouth was plump and shiny and looked ripe for a kiss. He groaned. In his head.

"Drop and give me twenty," Em said.

The boys looked at Josh, and he shrugged. "She's taking over for Coach Delaney at today's practice." Like him, they were smart enough to groan in silence.

When the seven boys dropped to the ground, Em joined them. They stared at her. "You were there?" Drew asked.

"Who do you think you heard scream? A ghost?"

Josh got on the ground beside her, and the boys treated him with the same shocked stares. "You ruined our date," he said.

Em glanced over her shoulder. "What are the rest of you doing standing there? You're a team, aren't you? One for all, and all for one?"

Josh snorted a laugh, and Em lifted a shoulder. Then she grinned. "I bet I can beat you."

"You're on." He completed his twentieth push-up ten seconds before she did.

"You might've beaten me time-wise, but I had better form. I'll beat you next time."

It took a concerted effort not to focus on her *form*,

which might've been why his voice came out a little husky when he lowered it and said, "Anytime, anywhere, Officer Hard-ass." He needed to stop calling her that. His mind went to where it shouldn't. She walked over to the cart, bending over to pick up the bags for drills. He needed to come up with a new nickname for her ASAP.

The boys fell over themselves trying to help her. "We've got it, Officer Ma'am."

"Em. You can call me Em," she said and smiled.

Josh had a feeling half his team had just fallen in love with Emma Scott. He didn't worry about falling in love with her. Falling in lust with her? Yeah, he was a little worried about that.

Chapter Fifteen

♥

"Two feet now," Em said, running the agility drill with Charlie and Mike. The six blue step-over bags were laid out in a straight line one yard apart from each other. "Hut," she called, watching as Charlie and then Mike ran through the drill. "Two taps," she reminded them. "Knees up."

"Good job," she said when they completed the drill for a second time. They were hot and sweaty but she liked how they didn't ask for a break, eager to please and to improve.

They were the youngest players on the team, and it was obvious they were having trouble fitting in with their teammates. She remembered what that was like. She hadn't fit in either. Only she hadn't cared. Mike did while Charlie seemed to take it in stride.

"Okay, three taps now." She sensed their hesitation. "I'll do it too." She demonstrated once, slowly, and then a second time, arms pumping. "Don't look at your feet. Keep your eyes straight ahead," she said as she reached the second-to-last step-over bag.

But as she went to shuffle over it, Josh moved into her line of sight down the field. He lifted the hem of his T-shirt to wipe his face, giving her a tantalizing look at a glistening, golden brown eight-pack. Em tripped over the bag. She managed to keep herself upright through sheer force of will. She didn't want Josh to think she'd fallen because of him and his glistening abs. The man was a total thirst trap.

"And that's why you don't look at your feet," Em said, acting as if she'd tripped on purpose and not because Josh had gotten her all hot and bothered. It wasn't the first time she'd found herself looking at him during practice. As much as she'd told herself it was because she wanted to make sure she was doing the drills right, it had nothing to do with the drills and everything to do with Josh. Her gaze drifted back to him. He lowered his shirt and blew his whistle. Practice was over. She no longer had to worry about embarrassing herself. No, what she had to worry about was that under the relief was a hint of disappointment she wouldn't get to moon over his tantalizing abs, tight butt, and sigh-inducing arms.

She blew out a frustrated breath and smiled at Charlie and Mike. "Nice work," she said as she reached for one of the bags.

"Thanks for doing the drills with us," they said, coming to give her a hand.

"I've got it, thanks. You guys need to hydrate." She wondered if that was her problem. Maybe she was dehydrated.

They nodded and straightened. "Are you coming

to the game Friday night?" Charlie asked before they walked away.

Given her reaction to Josh and his abs, a reaction that was uncomfortably similar to how she'd acted when she'd been crushing on him at seventeen, she thought putting some distance between them might be a good idea. "I don't think so. I'm behind at work."

Work as in investigating a hundred-year-old cold case. But instead of being deterred by how difficult the case would be to solve, she was looking forward to digging into it. Which reminded her that she was having dinner with Jenny and Steve tonight. She was hoping to pick Jenny's brain about the case.

She briefly closed her eyes. She was supposed to invite Josh to the dinner. If she got lucky, he wouldn't feel like coming. After all, he had worked a twelve-hour shift at HFFD the day before.

"Oh, okay." Charlie gave her a weak smile, looking disappointed.

She'd learned his mom was a single parent who rarely made it to his games due to working two jobs, and Em felt herself caving. "On second thought, I should probably come and see you guys put into action the plays we worked on."

Charlie brightened, acknowledging Josh with a smile. "Hey Coach, Em's coming to our game. Can she stand behind the bench?"

Josh seemed to hesitate before nodding. "Yeah, sure. Now go grab something to drink." He glanced at her when they ran off. "He's got your number, Officer Marshmallow."

She snorted, patting Gus, who'd abandoned her for Josh during the practice. The dog licked her knee and then took off to where the rest of the team were guzzling water. "Me? A marshmallow? I don't think so."

"I know so." He glanced at the kids. "You working with Charlie and Mike one-on-one was a good idea. Although I think the other guys are jealous they got all your attention."

"Please. I doubt they even noticed," she said, helping him load the rest of the bags onto the cart.

"Oh, they noticed all right," he murmured as he walked to the practice dummy, glancing at her as he easily picked it up. "Steve texted me and mentioned we're having dinner with them tonight?"

"Yeah, but I figured you'd be too tired to come," she said, trying not to stare at his impressive biceps as he placed the practice dummy onto the cart. "I can make your excuses. I'm sure they'll understand."

"Is there a reason you don't want me to come?"

"No. I just didn't think you'd want to after working a twelve-hour shift yesterday."

"I probably shouldn't but Steve finished the prototype for his latest game."

"Really? You two are going to play video games?"

"Yeah." He waggled his eyebrows. "You can play too."

She rolled her eyes. "Thanks, but I think I'll pass."

He frowned.

"Come on, Josh. As if you thought I'd want to play video games."

"What? No." He lifted his chin. "I'm just wondering

why your boss is walking this way, and he doesn't look happy." Josh glanced at her. "What did you do?"

"Why do you think I did something?" she hedged, having a fairly good idea why Gabe was here.

"You were nosing around, asking questions about the Seaton sisters, weren't you?"

"No," she said slowly. Technically, she didn't question anyone. "I did some research at the library, that's all."

"The way the library ladies talk, you might as well have posted what you're up to on social media." He gave her elbow a squeeze. "I'll let you two talk in private."

As Josh walked away, he shared a few words and a couple laughs with Gabe.

"Hey, Chief," she said when her boss joined her.

"Em." He glanced over his shoulder. "So, you and Josh," he said, before returning his attention to her. "He's a great guy. I'm happy for you."

Gabe was a smart man and an excellent cop so she was surprised he couldn't see through their act. Glad that he couldn't, but surprised. "He is, but I don't think you're here to talk about my love life, are you?" She briefly closed her eyes. Dating. She should've said *dating life*.

"I'm not." Gabe shoved his hands in his uniform pants pockets and rocked on his heels. "We have a problem."

Hmm, maybe he didn't know she'd been at the library earlier this afternoon going through the *Highland Falls Herald*'s archives. "What's going on?"

"You nosing around in the Seaton sisters' deaths has stirred things up in town, just like I warned you it would."

Em scoffed. "Like Jenny's book and the promotional events Abby has planned for *The Haunting of Seaton House* haven't already stirred things up."

"You're a cop, Em. It's different. They're not trying to exonerate May Seaton and solve a murder."

"Possibly two murders, and technically, that's not true. Jenny implies in her book that both May and Clara were murdered."

"But she doesn't name names or speculate who did it. People around here know your reputation, Em. They know you won't give up, and they know you're very good at your job."

"Thanks, I guess, but it's a hundred-year-old cold case. The chances I can solve it are slim to none. Besides that, whoever was involved in their murders is long dead."

"Yeah, but no one wants their family name associated with murder. Even a murder that took place a hundred years ago."

"This isn't just hypothetical, is it? Did someone call the station and threaten me?"

"No. Jenny found a letter in her mailbox two hours ago." He pulled out his phone and showed her the screenshot. The words *Leave town now or you'll be sorry* were scrawled in red ink on lined paper. "We'll see if we can lift any prints, but I doubt we'll be able to."

"It's a fairly generic threat, Gabe. And it might have nothing to do with the murders. It's possible it has to do with Seaton House or Jenny herself."

"How do you figure?"

"Maybe with the uptick in interest in Seaton House, the people who sold it to Jenny's grandfather for a song want to buy it back and recoup their losses. The only way Jenny will sell is if they decide not to stay in town. She's been open about her plans. And she's just as open that she believes she's a witch, even if it's not in the same context that people assume."

"Half the folks in town believe the Sisterhood are witches, so I'm not buying that has anything to do with the threat. Trying to run Jenny and her family out of town to get a deal on Seaton House, that's a little more believable."

"I'll look into it. Quietly," she assured him.

"Okay, I don't know how many times I have to tell you before it sinks into that hard head of yours, but you are on vacation, Em. Besides, I've already put Todd on the case."

She fisted her hands on her hips. "You tell me I'm stirring things up but you're putting Todd on the case?"

"Not the cold case. The threatening letter case."

"Oh good, because I'm too busy…" She trailed off, catching herself before she said *working on the Seaton sisters' murders.* "…Too busy relaxing and hanging out with my boyfriend to get involved in Todd's case."

She smiled at Josh, who was walking over to place a stack of orange cones on the cart. He stopped in his tracks, his expression a cross between shocked and panicked.

"Isn't that right, *honey*?" Em called out in an effort to convince her boss of their dating status. Because the way Gabe was looking at Josh suggested he was now questioning whether Em was using their relationship as a cover.

"Umm, yeah, that's right," Josh said as he placed the cones on the cart. He joined them, glancing at Em as if he too wondered what she was up to.

Which didn't help her cause as evidenced by her boss's narrowed gaze. She laced her fingers through Josh's, giving them a subtle squeeze in hopes he'd get with the program. "If you're all set, we should probably get going, honey." She smiled at Gabe. "Big date tonight."

"Are you celebrating something special?" Gabe asked.

Of course her boss couldn't just let it go. She looked at Josh, willing him to come up with a believable answer, but all he did was stare at her as if he had no idea what had come over her. "Date number three. Josh doesn't usually make it past date number two."

"I guess that is a big deal. Congratulations," Gabe said, and Em could tell he was trying not to laugh. "I'll let you two get to it then."

As soon as Gabe was out of earshot, she said to Josh, "Why are you acting so weird?"

"I'm acting weird? You called me *honey* twice, and you're holding my hand." He held up their linked fingers.

And maybe because he'd drawn attention to it, she became aware of how her hand felt in his. There was something strangely intimate about holding a person's hand, his hand, and she immediately let it go. She hadn't held a man's hand in over seventeen months and felt almost guilty for holding Josh's.

"So? That's what people do when they're dating," she said, knowing exactly where the defensive note in her voice was coming from.

It wasn't like Brad would care that she'd been holding Josh's hand. This was what he wanted for her. Except this wasn't real. And maybe that's why she felt guilty. Because earlier, when she'd been watching Josh coach the boys and they'd shared a smile when Gus ran interference and caught the football, their fake relationship had felt real in that moment, and she'd liked it. She'd liked it a lot.

"Yeah, when they've been dating for a couple of months. Maybe a couple weeks for the hand-holding."

He was right. She hadn't held hands with Brad for the first six weeks of their relationship or called him *babe* or *honey* until they'd been together for months.

"But we've known each other forever," she said, defending the hand-holding and endearments. "It makes sense that we'd skip a few steps."

"If we were actually dating it would, but we're not."

"You say that like you think I need a reminder."

He said something under his breath. She didn't catch it because the team were calling out their goodbyes and heading off the field. Both she and Josh waved goodbye at the same time they yelled for Gus, who was trotting after Charlie and Mike.

"You're right," she said, instead of asking what he'd

been muttering before he'd been interrupted. She was afraid she wouldn't like his answer. "This is good for Gus."

Josh nodded as he grabbed hold of the cart's handle. "It's good for the team too, especially Charlie and Mike. They like having him around." He glanced at her as they walked across the field. "I didn't have a chance to ask you earlier, but how did you know which car Drew drove?"

"I saw him getting something out of the Explorer when I pulled into the parking lot. A couple of his friends were with him, and I heard them call him Drew. What's the deal with his father?" she asked, patting Gus when he joined them.

Josh filled her in about his run-ins with Drew's father, Peter.

"He sounds like a jerk. Wait a sec. Drew's father wouldn't happen to be Peter O'Brien, would he? The guy who's running for mayor?"

"One and the same."

"Huh. He was the only one I spoke to who wanted to shut down Abby's podcast as much as I did."

"I guess it makes sense why Drew wouldn't want him to know he was at Seaton House."

"Yeah, but after what Gabe told me, I'm wondering if there's more to Mr. O'Brien's desire to shut down Abby's podcast." She told him about the letter Jenny had received. "That's why Gabe dropped by. He blames me for stirring the pot."

"And you wanted to convince him you were too busy with me to investigate the Seaton case," he said, seeming relieved.

Good thing one of them was. After how she'd reacted to seeing Josh on the field, Em was feeling awkward around him—a little like she had when she was seventeen. "Yeah, and you weren't very helpful selling our fake relationship."

"You caught me off guard. I'll do better next time." He pulled the cart to the closed gymnasium doors and removed a set of keys from his pocket. "You don't think Drew's father had anything to do with the letter, do you?"

She shrugged. "I've got to start somewhere, and he fits the profile."

"How do you figure?"

"For one, the letter was delivered when the majority of kids were in school, and if it was a kid, it'd be more likely they'd direct message Jenny on social media. Plus, the O'Brien family made their money in real estate. Something Mr. O'Brien felt compelled to share with me several times."

"From personal experience dealing with O'Brien, you might want to keep your investigation into him quiet until you have actual evidence, Em," Josh said as he fit the key into the gymnasium doors.

She nodded, pulling her phone from her pocket. "I'll give Todd a call."

"Are we still on for dinner at Jenny and Steve's tonight?"

"Looks like," she said, scrolling through her recent messages. "Jenny hasn't canceled. But do me a favor and park at my place in case Gabe does a drive-by. I wouldn't put it past him to check up on me."

"Sure." He glanced behind her. "Hey, guys. What's up?"

She turned to see Charlie and Mike, shuffling their feet. "We, ah, were wondering if Em could give us a drive to my house?" Charlie said. "My mom was supposed to pick us up, but she had to work overtime."

"Sure, no problem. I'll see you tonight, Josh." She noticed the way the boys were watching them and wondered if they expected them to kiss goodbye. They probably did, she thought with a sigh. That's what a real couple would do.

She leaned toward Josh, and he leaned back, staring at her with a look of alarm on his face. She didn't know whether to be offended or amused. But when he caught Charlie and Mike sharing a glance, he blew out what she could only assume was a relieved breath. He lost the freaked-out expression and smiled, offering her his cheek.

She resisted the urge to fist her hands in his T-shirt and plant a hard kiss on his mouth. Not a long, passionate kiss that would gross out the boys—even though she was kind of worried that she wouldn't be grossed out—but one that would widen his eyes with panic. He deserved some payback after his years of teasing her. Instead, she pressed her lips to the corner of his mouth.

From the look on Josh's face as the gymnasium door closed behind him, she might as well have given him a long, passionate kiss. Weird. This whole situation was weird. But worth it, she thought when her cell rang and Abby's name appeared on the screen.

"I'm over there." She pointed out the Camaro to the boys and then connected the call. "Yes, I'm still dating Josh. And it's going really well," she said before Abby got a word in. She'd phoned Em the day before with three prospective candidates for when Josh inevitably dumped her after date number two.

"I'm glad to hear that, but Em, everyone knows what Josh is like. The odds are a hundred to one you won't make it to date number four."

"You guys are betting on us?"

"Not your family and friends, although I did see Todd's name on the betting list at Highland Brew. If you're wondering, he's betting you guys go the distance."

"The distance?" Thanks to her mind inconveniently flashing to an image of her and Josh naked and in a bed, Em's voice cracked on a sudden flurry of nerves.

"Yeah, you know, the whole nine yards. Wedding bells and then a baby carriage."

"I've got the picture, thanks," she said, her voice sounding raw. It felt like Abby had pulled the scab off Em's wound. "But if I were you, I wouldn't bet against Josh and me making it to date number four." She cursed her competitive nature for wanting to prove to everyone, everyone but Todd, that they were wrong. She just couldn't seem to help herself.

"Okay, I'll spread the word. And I am happy for you, Em. You and Josh. You're like a rom-com cliché."

"A what?"

"You know, best friends becoming lovers."

Em wanted to cover her ears and hum, but she couldn't unhear what Abby had said. "On that note, I have to go."

"Wait. I'm not calling about you and Josh."

"Could've fooled me," she muttered, suddenly in a bad mood. "So if you're not calling about us, what are you calling about?" She needed to dial down her irritation. It wasn't Abby's fault the conversation had upset her.

"I'm hosting a party Friday night, and I wanted to invite you."

"Thanks, but I'll be at the football game."

"That's fine. The party doesn't start until ten. It's women only though, so you'll have to leave Josh at home. Bri's coming."

"Oh, okay, sounds good." She beeped open the locks on the Camaro's doors as she crossed the parking lot. "I'll see you Friday at ten. Should I bring something?" It would be a good way to get rid of one of the casseroles in her freezer. She'd just have to make sure none of the guests at the party had made it for her.

"We're good, thanks. I've got everything covered. But Em, you can't back out. I have a waiting list. Besides that, I really want you there. Coming, honey. I've gotta go. Can't wait to see you Friday!"

"Abby, what exactly—" The line went dead. "Go ahead and get in the car," she told Charlie and Mike.

"Sweet ride," the boys said as they climbed inside. Charlie patted the seat, encouraging Gus to join them in the back, while Em looked up coming events on Abby's podcast. And there it was. Abby was holding an event at

Seaton House with the Sisterhood on Friday night. The entertainment for the evening? A psychic medium who would communicate with the ghosts of May and Clara.

Rolling her eyes, Em typed out a text to Abby, telling her she couldn't make it. She hesitated before pressing Send. If she wanted to solve the case, and if this psychic medium was the real deal, she could help Em interrogate May and Clara.

Em tapped her phone on her forehead. Gabe was right. She really did need to take some time off.

Chapter Sixteen

♥

Josh grabbed the bouquet of fall flowers from the passenger seat and got out of his truck. He was late. He was never late for a date. It's not a date, he reminded himself. It was just dinner with Em and some friends. The reminder did nothing to calm his nerves. And that was something else he'd never been before a date—nervous. It was why he was late. Em calling him honey, holding his hand, and kissing him at practice today had messed with his head. He'd acted like an idiot. He was surprised Gabe hadn't noticed. Em certainly had, and he supposed that was the problem.

He was afraid she'd eventually figure out why he'd been stunned stupid. But really, how could she? It wasn't as if she could see what was going on in his head or feel how he'd responded to her hand in his and her lips pressed to the corner of his mouth. She'd made his heart race and his gut tighten with desire simply by holding his hand and giving him an innocent kiss. Feelings he'd never felt with any of the women he'd dated this past year. It was why he'd never gotten past date number two.

There'd been no chemistry. He'd felt like he was on a date with a friend. Now here he was having feelings for a woman who was an actual friend. A woman who was still in love with her dead fiancé.

Josh wouldn't let himself get involved with another woman who had unrequited feelings for another man. It had taken him a while to recognize that Amber hadn't gotten over her ex. Looking back, the signs had been there from the beginning, but he'd ignored them. Their chemistry had been off the charts, and he'd fallen hard for her. It wasn't the same with Em. They had too much history. They'd been friends too long for his feelings for her not to be complicated. He hated complicated. He glanced at the keys in his hand and thought about getting in his truck and driving away.

A car pulled in behind him, blocking his escape. Todd got out of his vehicle. He nodded at the flowers. "Nice to see you putting in the effort."

"What are you talking about?"

"I've heard about your dates with Em, bro. They're not up to your usual standards. Just because you guys have been friends since you were kids doesn't mean you can skate by. I have a vested interest in you two going the distance. Since I'm pretty much the only one, I can clean up big time. I've already got my eye on a sherpa-lined leather peacoat. So do a bro a solid and don't mess this up."

"There's a betting pool on us?"

"Yeah. I'm surprised you haven't heard about it. A couple of your HFFD coworkers were at Highland Brew the other night and started it."

It was probably the new guy. Cody. They'd worked together the night before, and he'd been overly interested in Josh and Em's dating life. When Josh shared that their two dates had consisted of hanging out at Seaton House, Cody had fist bumped one of their coworkers. His reaction now made sense.

Josh's phone pinged, and he pulled it from his pocket. It was a text from Em, wondering where he was. He replied that he was on his way. "If you're looking for Em, she isn't here. We're having dinner with Jenny and Steve."

"Do you mind if I tag along? I want to run a few things by Em."

"I'm guessing you were looking for a free meal to go along with the advice."

Todd grinned. "She has a freezer full of casseroles, and I didn't think she'd mind sharing."

"I'm sure she wouldn't, and just as sure Jenny won't mind feeding you."

"So, the flowers aren't for Em, are they?"

"Em isn't exactly a hearts-and-flowers kind of woman. She'd be happier if I bought her a couple doughnuts and some Sour Patch Kids."

"True that," Todd said as they walked along the side of the gravel road. He nodded at Seaton House when it came into view. "This place sure has someone riled up."

Josh shared Em's thoughts about the letter writer.

"Yeah, she called me earlier."

"Do you think Jenny and Steve have reason to be concerned?"

"That's what I wanted to talk to Em about. They weren't the only ones who received letters. I just came from Abby's and the Three Wise Women Bookstore."

"Same type of threat?"

"Pretty much. 'Stop promoting the book or else.'"

"We both know that's not going to happen," Josh said, glancing at the house as they walked by. As far as he knew, pest control had gone in today, and Neil hoped to have the roof and exterior work completed within a couple of weeks.

Todd nodded. "Abby has an event planned at Seaton House Friday night, and she's adamant about not canceling. The owners of the bookstore feel the same way. Some members of their families tried to dissuade them, but they felt better when Abby mentioned Em would be there."

"I'm surprised Em's going," Josh said. "She spent last week trying to shut down Abby's podcasts at the house."

"I was surprised too. Em's not exactly a fan of the woo-woo, and a medium is going to try and contact May and Clara." Todd grinned. "Then again, maybe it makes sense that Em would go. If there's a chance the medium makes contact with the Seaton sisters, she'll want to interrogate them."

"So you know she's investigating their murders?"

"Yeah. I would've been worried about her if she wasn't. The chief won't be happy about it though, especially now."

"What do you mean?"

"Em didn't get a letter but a call came into the station warning her to drop the investigation or she'll be sorry. The voice was distorted so it was hard to tell if it was male or female, but we're running it through speech recognition."

If anyone could handle themselves, it was Em, but that didn't mean Josh wasn't concerned for her safety. Something he knew better than to share with her. "She's been careful to keep the fact she's looking into the case quiet but she told me she spent the afternoon at the library. Do you think the caller could've been there?"

"It wouldn't be hard for someone to guess what she was up to. Every article she looked up on microfilm was related to the Seaton sisters. I'll get a list from Em of who was at the library and take it from there."

"How worried should I be about her?" Josh asked.

"She's one of the best investigators I've ever met, and between you and me, her talent is wasted here. But she's also cocky, and not that I'd ever say this to her, she's overly confident in her ability to handle anything and anyone on her own. And when I tell her she should be careful until we figure this out, I can almost guarantee she'll laugh in my face."

"I bet she won't. She'll brush aside your concerns, for sure. But she won't laugh in your face," Josh predicted as he knocked on Jenny and Steve's door.

Forty minutes later, Todd muttered at Josh, "I should've taken you up on your bet."

They were sitting at the kitchen table with Em, Jenny, and Steve. Charlotte had just gone to play fetch in the backyard with Gus, which was why Todd had no doubt felt comfortable sharing an update on his case and suggesting Em be careful. She'd laughed in his face.

"I understand why you might think this is funny, Em," Steve said. "I'm sure, as a police officer, you've been threatened before, but this is new to us. I'm worried about my daughter and my wife's safety. And our baby's." He rested a protective hand on Jenny's stomach.

Em's face went blank. The laughter in her eyes vanished as if someone had flipped off a switch. Josh wondered if she was remembering how protective Brad had been of her and their unborn child, how he'd insisted she stay in the vehicle, not wanting any harm to come to them. Josh wanted to take her hand. But he didn't think she'd welcome his comfort or sympathy.

"Are you forgetting the threats I received when I first started my program at Georgia U, Steve?" Jenny pushed back from the table. "Anyone want seconds, or are you ready for coffee and dessert?"

She'd served an apple chicken stew with homemade bread for dinner.

"I forgot about that," Steve admitted sheepishly. "But, honey, they weren't the same as this."

"No, they weren't. They were far worse. And I'm not about to let anyone chase us from our home."

"Our home?" Steve looked stunned. "I thought we agreed to sell Seaton House after the renovations were completed."

As if sensing this might devolve into a family argument, Todd pushed back from the table. "I should probably get going. Thanks for the meal, Jenny. It was great."

Jenny pursed her lips at her husband and then said to Todd, "Are you sure you won't stay for coffee and dessert?"

"Honestly, I couldn't eat another bite." He came around the table and patted Steve's shoulder. "We'll catch whoever is making the threats, but until we do, we'll do extra patrols of the area."

"I live down the road, Todd," Em said. "I think I can handle patrolling the area on my own."

"Just what our boss will want to hear," Todd said dryly as he headed for the door.

"He won't hear about it unless you tell him," Em said.

Josh was relieved she sounded like herself. It was difficult not being able to comfort her. He could do something though. He could show her that she could find joy in life despite her heartbreaking losses. So far, he hadn't done a very good job of it. Todd was right. He needed to take her on a real date. A real *fake*-date, he reminded himself. Remembering why he'd come up with the idea in the first place helped alleviate his worry that he was in over his head. He just had to keep his feelings for Em firmly in the friend zone.

Todd stopped with his hand on the doorknob and turned. "Fine, but we work the case together. I mean it, Em. You have to keep me in the loop. No holding back."

She nodded and got up from the table. "I'll walk you to your car."

Josh wondered what new information she'd uncovered that she had to share with Todd. He figured she'd tell him later. At least he hoped she would. He wanted to be kept in the loop too so he knew what she was dealing with.

He said goodbye to Todd and stood, helping clear the table. "I'll go play catch with Charlotte and Gus. Give you guys a chance to talk," he said as he placed the dishes and cutlery beside the sink.

"Thanks, but it's getting late, and Charlotte has to get an early night. She's starting school tomorrow," Jenny said with a pointed glance at her husband.

Steve blew out a breath. "I agreed that Charlotte attending school here was a good idea, honey. But us living here permanently at Seaton House?" He shuddered. "No, I didn't agree to that." He got up from the table and walked to the sliding glass doors. "I'll round up Charlotte and Gus."

Jenny gave Josh an embarrassed smile as the door slid closed behind Steve. "I'm sorry. I didn't mean for you guys to get caught in the middle of our spat."

"Don't apologize. Charlotte has a big day tomorrow, and you and Steve obviously have a few things to work out. We can do coffee and dessert another time. Food was great, and so was the company. Don't give it another thought."

"That's sweet of you to say, and I wish you weren't right, but you are. Steve and I obviously aren't on the same page." She picked up a pie. "Please take this. It's caramel apple, and I have two."

"I'd never say no to caramel apple pie, and Em would probably shoot me if I did. Thanks, Jenny. It smells great," he said, accepting the pie. He didn't want to break his promise to Steve, but it might help for Jenny to know where her husband was coming from. "Steve is pretty open about his feelings for ghosts and the supernatural so it isn't surprising he's uncomfortable at the thought of living in a haunted house." Terrified would probably be more accurate. "I'm sure most people feel the same way he does. But you might find he'll be okay with living there once the house is renovated and the ghosts are gone."

"I really hope so. I've fallen in love with Highland Falls. The people are so warm and welcoming." She smiled. "Well, most of the people."

"Yeah, I'm sure the letter hasn't helped make your case for staying here, but let Em and Todd worry about it. They'll make sure you and your family are safe."

He turned as Steve opened the sliding glass door, ushering Charlotte and Gus inside. "Come on, boy," Josh said, heading for the front door. "Thanks again for dinner. You have a good day at school tomorrow, Charlotte."

"I'll walk you out." Steve joined him. "Sorry for ruining the evening, Josh," he said once he'd closed the door behind them.

"You didn't, and I need an early night anyway."

"Thanks, but I'm sure I'll hear about it from my wife. She's not happy with me at the moment."

"Cut yourself some slack. Between the accident and the threatening letter, you've had a lot to deal with in a little more than a week. You both have."

"Don't forget the rodent- and ghost-infested house." He glanced down the road where a full moon shone down on Seaton House. "There's nothing I wouldn't do to make my wife happy, my daughter too, but honestly, Josh, I don't think I can live in that house."

"I could be wrong, but it sounded to me like Jenny loves the idea of living in Highland Falls as much as she loves the idea of living at Seaton House. If you can't see yourself being happy there once the house is renovated and ghost-free, maybe Jenny would be willing to compromise. You guys could sell Seaton House and find a place in the area that you're both happy with."

Steve nodded slowly. "That might just work. Thanks, Josh."

"No problem. Have a good night," he said with a light tug on Gus's leash. "Get your nose out of the bushes, buddy. It's time to go home." He met Em on the road and held up the pie. "Are you going to invite me for dessert?"

"Really? You eat pie?" she asked, taking it out of his hands as they continued down the road to her place.

"I eat clean ninety percent of the time. But Jenny's a great cook, so I'm betting it'll be worth it. Besides, it has apples in it."

Em glanced over her shoulder and lifted her chin at Jenny and Steve's. "Are they okay?"

Josh shared his conversations with the couple.

"Smart. The way Jenny was talking earlier, I think she'd be willing to compromise."

"How did your conversation go with Todd?"

"We spent most of the time talking about his love life, or I should say lack thereof."

"The guy from speed dating didn't work out?"

"An hour into their date, he told Todd he had a guy who would be perfect for him." She looked at him and grinned. "I'll give you one guess who."

"Matteo."

"Yep, so now Todd's decided he's giving up on dating to focus on work."

"Not a bad idea." Josh stood back as they reached Em's front step, letting her by.

"Well, he'll have more time to dedicate to the case now, which works for me." She opened the door. "I convinced him of a possible connection between the letter writer and May and Clara's murders, so he's agreed to help with my investigation. And as long as Gabe agrees the two cases overlap, Todd won't have to sneak around. We, or I should say Todd, might even be able to bring Gwen in on the case."

"That's great." He unclipped the lead from Gus's collar, feeling better knowing Em wouldn't be working the case on her own. "Did you get a chance to talk to Jenny about the murders?"

"Better than that." She reached into her pocket and held up a thumb drive. "She downloaded all her research for the book onto the drive, including the journals. I'm hoping I can find something she missed or left out of the book." Em pocketed the drive and opened a kitchen drawer. "Do you want me to heat up your piece of pie?"

"Sure. Do you have any ice cream?"

"Is that a trick question?"

"Okay. Any ice cream other than Moose Tracks?"

"There should be some vanilla in the freezer," she said, cutting them each an overly large slice of pie.

Josh set the vanilla ice cream on the counter and then leaned across the sink to close the window. The days were still relatively warm but it was getting cool at night. "Do you want me to put on a fire?"

She licked some caramel apple off her finger and nodded. "Go for it."

Five minutes later, they were settled on the couch with pie and ice cream. He nodded at Gus asleep in his dog bed by the fire. "Charlotte must've worn him out."

"Charlotte and football practice," Em said, scooping up a forkful of dessert. "I had an interesting conversation with Mike and Charlie."

"About?"

"The O'Brien family. Don't worry," she said at the face he made. "I know how to question someone without them guessing why. Besides, I asked about other team members too."

"So you really think Peter O'Brien is behind the letters and calling in the threat to you?"

She nodded. "I didn't put it together until after I talked to Mike and Charlie. Remember the Henderson farm?"

"Sure. We used to go there every Halloween. Fright Fest was the best." He glanced at her. She seemed to be waiting for him to make another connection. He thought about it for a minute. "Right. O'Brien is a distant relative and recently inherited the Henderson farm. But other than one of his relatives supposedly being murdered by May a hundred years ago, what does this have to do with him?"

"I'm not exactly sure, but O'Brien is a real estate developer and the Henderson farm and Seaton House share a property line. So maybe he wants to buy out Jenny and doesn't want to pay fair market value. He's also running for mayor. So he might not want a scandal coming out in the middle of his election campaign."

"Wait a sec. Are you saying that you think Edward Henderson's younger brother avenged his death by killing May and Clara Seaton?"

"First, I don't know if I agree with Jenny's theory that May was murdered. I have a feeling she might have died from natural causes. But I do agree with Jenny's suspicions that Clara's death wasn't accidental. And second, while I was initially looking at Edward's younger brother—he was the one who accused May of murder, after all—I think I might've found someone I like better for Clara's murder."

"You're the expert but Jenny made a pretty good case for both May and Clara being murdered. And who'd have better motivation to kill them than the dead man's younger brother?"

"I might be wrong, but I don't think I am. At least about May dying of natural causes." Em licked the last of the caramel apple off her fork and placed it and her plate on the coffee table. "When I went back to the library after dropping off Charlie and Mike, I checked back issues of the *Herald* for the days immediately following Clara's death, and I came across something interesting. A man was reported missing the day after

Clara died. He was the Hendersons' farmhand. I have to do a deeper dive and widen my search parameters, but as far as I can tell, he was never seen alive again." She smiled, looking pleased about finding a new suspect.

At least she had until Josh said, "But what reason would the Hendersons' farmhand have for killing Clara?"

Chapter Seventeen

♥

If someone had asked about her favorite way to spend a Friday night, Em would've automatically said sitting on the couch eating takeout and watching *Stranger Things* or *The Haunting of Hill House.*

But now standing under the lights cheering for the hometown football team with their handsome coach by her side ranked as her favorite way to spend a Friday night. She couldn't remember the last time she'd been this nervous or had this much fun.

The team was five minutes away from beating their top rivals for this year's football championship. She looked from the clock to the field, sucking in a shocked breath when Charlie intercepted the ball.

"Go, Charlie!" she yelled as the other team's players converged on the small but speedy teen.

She hadn't realized she'd grabbed Josh's hand until he gave hers a reassuring squeeze. "They've got him," he said, lifting his chin at Mike, who ran interference for his best friend while two of their teammates cleared the path to the goal line.

Charlie was inches away from a touchdown when both he and Mike were tackled from behind. Highland Falls fans—including Em and Josh and the offensive line on the bench—groaned while the opposing team's fans cheered. Their roles reversed when the game buzzer went off three minutes later. Highland Falls High had won the game twenty-three to twenty.

Em cheered and threw her arms around Josh, who hugged her and spun her around.

"Aww look at the lovebirds! Aren't they the cutest?" cried a voice from the stands, a loud and familiar voice that could be heard above the cheering crowd.

Josh froze mid-spin and set Em back on her feet while shooting a *zip it* look at Patsy, who was standing and clapping—for them as much as for the team, Em suspected. Apparently Em's brother thought so too because his gaze narrowed on her and Josh. But unlike Patsy, he obviously didn't think they were *the cutest*.

Em didn't have time to worry about her brother or what her and Josh's PDA might look like to anyone else. The offensive line had run off the field and Charlie and Mike were soaking up another round of praise and shoulder slaps from their teammates. Josh and Em joined them, congratulating the boys and then lining up to shake hands with the other team.

As they walked back to the bench, Josh nudged her. "You deserve a lot of the credit for that, you know."

In response to his smile and compliment, the muscles in her stomach fluttered. She'd like to ignore her reaction to him or pretend she had no idea why her stomach was acting this way, but every time he'd glanced at her or smiled at her throughout the game, those very same butterflies took flight.

"You're giving me too much credit. I've worked with them for like three practices. If anyone deserves the credit, it's you, Josh. You're a great coach."

It wasn't as if she was using the compliment to distract him. She really did admire his coaching abilities and how he interacted with the kids on the team. He knew the plays inside out, and he knew how to get the best out of each of his players. He was tough but fair, and always quick with a word of encouragement. It was obvious the boys respected and admired him. She did too. A lot.

"Thanks, but I didn't just mean for Charlie and Mike's newfound confidence on the field. I meant for how the guys are pulling together as a team. For me, that's just as important as them winning the game."

And that was just one more reason she admired him. Although an hour later, she wasn't feeling the warm and fuzzies for the man walking her to her car. "Josh, you and Cal don't have to hang out at my place. It's not like we'll need backup." It was the night of the séance at Seaton House.

He shrugged. "Cal and Steve think it's a good idea, and so do I. You never know, Em, things could go sideways. The person who made the threats might make an appearance."

"You do remember I'm a cop, don't you? If things go sideways, which they won't, I'm trained to handle them."

He nodded while texting on his cell phone.

"You didn't hear a word I said, did you?"

"You're a cop who is exceptionally good at her job and who doesn't need anyone's help."

"That's not what I said."

He looked up from his phone and smiled. "We're hanging out at Steve's place instead of yours."

* * *

They'd woken up Charlotte when they'd arrived, and Jenny was putting her back to bed with some help from Gus, who was having a sleepover. Josh and Cal were sitting on the couch focused on the TV screen while Steve explained the object of his new video game—*The Haunting of Seaton House*. From what Em could tell, players earned points by retrieving certain objects in the haunted house. In their quest, they had to evade ghosts and wild animals and the other players.

If a player succeeded in retrieving said objects, which according to her brother and Josh would never happen, the ghosts and wildlife disappeared. Apparently, Steve was working out his issues with Seaton House in his video game.

Lights shone through the pebbled glass insert in the front door, and Em opened it, sticking her head out to look down the street. There was a line of cars parked on the side of the road. "We should probably head out now," she said to Bri, who was waiting with her in the entryway.

Steve glanced at her. "I'd feel better if Jenny went with you, Em. She shouldn't be long."

Em held back a sigh. She'd thought she'd alleviated Steve's fears about the letter writer but clearly she hadn't done a very good job. Despite the hype for Abby's party tonight, no one had received another threatening letter, and no one had called in another threat against Em at the station. HFPD hadn't been able to lift any prints off the letters or the envelopes or identify the caller who'd phoned in the threat, but Todd had paid Peter O'Brien a visit anyway.

Todd had used the mayoral candidate's well-documented attempts to shut down Abby's podcast at Seaton House as a reason to question him. Peter hadn't appreciated being treated as a suspect and had filed a complaint with Gabe, suggesting Em was probably behind the threats given *her* previous attempts to shut down the podcasts.

"Sure," Em said, figuring it was a waste of energy trying to reassure Steve. Just as she was about to text Abby that they'd be late, Jenny appeared in the living room. She kissed Steve on the cheek, gave him last-minute instructions about Charlotte, and then headed to the entryway. "I'll just grab my jacket," she said, nodding at the closet.

Cal and Josh got up from the couch, and Em had a moment of panic that her fake boyfriend might kiss her to keep up appearances for Steve and Jenny. Instead, he pulled her aside.

"Promise me you'll be careful," he said in a voice only she could hear.

"Josh, it's a house party."

"Yeah, with a bunch of women trying to raise the dead."

Em snorted. "Not a bunch of women, just one woman, and she's trying to communicate with the dead, not bring them back to life."

"It's not funny, Em."

"It is when an image of a bunch of zombies walking around Seaton House pops into your head."

His lips quirked at the corner, and then he tried covering his amusement with a serious expression. "Em, you're digging into a family for murder."

"A murder that happened a hundred years ago, and no one, other than you, me, Jenny, Steve, and Todd have any idea I'm actually looking into it so there's nothing to worry about."

"Really?" He moved closer, reaching around her to pat the waistband of her black jeans. "So if you're not worried something will go wrong, why do you have your gun?"

Leave it to him to notice. She wore a leather jacket over a baggy black sweater in hopes no one would. "It's just a precaution."

Someone cleared their throat, and they turned to see Cal staring at them with his arms crossed. "Would you mind telling me why you keep *hugging* my sister?"

Em turned away from her brother, saying under her breath, "Don't you dare tell him I have my gun."

With his back to her brother, Josh put his other arm around her and drew her close. "Okay, but he obviously thinks I was copping a feel of your butt, so I have to hug you," he murmured before telling Cal, "I'm wishing her luck."

"Is that right? So why were you hugging her at the game tonight?"

Josh slowly lowered his arms and moved away from Em, staring at her brother as if surprised by his overprotective attitude. And maybe a little hurt by it. "Because Em's been working with Charlie and Mike at practices, they nearly scored a touchdown, and we won the game."

Em was ticked, and not just because her brother had obviously forgotten that Steve and Jenny weren't in on the fake-dating arrangement but because he'd made Josh feel bad. He was his best friend!

"Josh, you don't have to explain anything. My brother seems to forget I'm a grown woman who can speak for herself." She jabbed her finger at Cal. "Stay out of my love life. I can hug, kiss, or do whatever I want with whomever I want."

To make her point, she fisted her hands in Josh's sweater and pulled him toward her, kissing him full on the lips. She'd meant to give him a quick kiss but her lips had a mind of their own and lingered on his. Maybe because she'd spent her teenage years fantasizing about kissing him, she was curious as to whether it would live up to those imaginary kisses. She was a curious person, after all.

Her lips softened, parting on a gasp when Josh drew her flush against him. He murmured a soft curse against her mouth before gently breaking the kiss. She stepped back, shaken by the buzz of attraction quickening her pulse.

The moment her heartbeat returned to normal, she was swamped by guilt and briefly closed her eyes. She shouldn't have enjoyed the feel of his mouth on hers as much as she did or the feel of his hard, muscular body pressed against hers. She opened her eyes to see everyone staring at her.

"Get over it," she muttered, avoiding Josh's gaze. She opened the door and stomped outside.

"Em," Bri called, hurrying after her.

"I don't want to talk about it." She glanced at her best friend. "But you need to talk to your husband. That was uncalled for."

"I know. In his defense, he's worried about you."

"I can take care of myself. I don't need a keeper."

"He knows that. It's just hard for him sometimes. You've been through a lot. The accident shook him."

"What he said in there had nothing to do with the accident. He made Josh feel like an ass, and that's unfair. And not only is it unfair, it's ridiculous. He knows there's nothing going on between us. We're fake-dating!"

"You and Josh aren't really dating?" Jenny asked.

Em bowed her head. She hadn't realized Jenny was behind her. She waited for her to join them on the side of the road and explained about her arrangement with Josh, quietly in case any of Abby's guests were hanging around near the cars lining the road or walking the path to the house.

"Oh, okay. I never would've guessed. You guys are so great together," Jenny said.

Em had to change the subject before Jenny asked

about the kiss she'd just witnessed. "It looks like there'll be standing room only. We'd better get in there or they'll start without us."

"They'll wait for us," Jenny said, holding up the silver locket she wore and pointing to the ring on her pinkie finger. "The medium says she needs something that belonged to May and Clara to connect with them."

"She's holding the séance in May and Clara's house, and from the evidence, it appears they're still there. Shouldn't that be enough?" Em asked as she pushed open the gate, unable to keep the skepticism from her voice. It sounded like a bunch of hooey to her.

"She said it's difficult to get a clear reading when there are so many energies."

"She thinks there are more ghosts than May, Clara, and Willy?" Em asked, glancing at the house. The windows were illuminated by flickering lights that appeared to be candles. A dumb idea if you asked her. The house was old, and the interior mostly wood.

"I think she was talking about the energies from all the people who've lived there," Jenny explained.

The front door opened, and Bri's sister, Ellie, stepped outside. She hugged Bri. "I was just coming to get you. What took you so long?"

Afraid Bri might mention Em and Josh's kiss, Em said, "Nice dress. All you need is a pointy hat and a wand."

Ellie laughed. "What's a nonbeliever like you doing at an event like this?"

"I was invited," she said, and then she introduced Jenny to Ellie. "I'm her bodyguard." Em held open the door, ushering the women inside. "Hang on for a minute," she said to Bri's sister, closing the door halfway. "So this woman Abby hired, do you think she's the real deal or is this some kind of scam?"

"According to Abby, she's legit. She checked her out when the woman contacted her about appearing on her podcast."

"The woman contacted Abby, not the other way around?"

Ellie nodded. "She told Abby she was intrigued by the stories about Seaton House and volunteered her services."

"Volunteered as in she's not getting paid?"

"You sound like Granny. She says there's something fishy about the woman. But honestly, I think she's just put out that Abby didn't ask us to conduct the séance."

"Do me a favor, and see if you can get a read on the woman." As much as Em didn't believe in the woo-woo, she couldn't completely discount Ellie's abilities. Ellie had consulted on a couple of cases for the North Carolina State Bureau of Investigation. So there had to be something to it.

"Em, I don't read people without their permission."

"I'm guessing you heard about the threatening letters Abby, Jenny, and the bookstore received?"

"I did, but what does that have to do with Madame Zola?"

Em snorted-laughed at the woman's name then cleared her throat. "Maybe nothing, but at this point, I'm not ruling anything or anyone out, and I agree with Granny McLeod, something doesn't feel right about this." She held open the door. "Now that I think about it, see if you can pick up anything from the other women in attendance."

Ellie's lips twitched. "Does that include you?"

"No, it doesn't include me." Em mentally slammed down the walls in her mind. The last thing she wanted was Bri's sister poking around in her head, especially after the kiss Em had shared with Josh.

"You're just like my husband. I can't read him either." Ellie stepped into the house and lowered her voice. "So what exactly am I supposed to be picking up on?"

"Someone who isn't here for the thrill. Someone who's angry." Bri's sister swayed, and Em reached out to steady her. "Are you okay?"

Ellie nodded. "It happens sometimes when I open my mind. There's a lot of emotion in this room, in this house."

Before Em could question her further, an older woman sitting behind a card table in the center of the living room pinned Em with a penetrating stare. She wore a black dress, a thick silver amulet at her throat, and heavy rings on her fingers. Madame Zola, Em presumed.

"Okay, there's one person who's angry," Ellie whispered.

"I knew it," Em said out of the side of her mouth. "Is she angry because I'm looking into May and Clara's murders?"

"You are? Who do you think—"

Madame Zola cut off Ellie with an impervious wave of her bone-white hand. "You are late. You have disturbed the energy in the house." The woman waved Jenny over, pointing at the chair across the card table from her. "Sit."

Em nodded at several people she knew as she moved to the front of the semicircle the women had formed around the table. She'd promised Steve she'd stay close to Jenny.

There were about thirty women crowded into the living room. She spotted Abby, who appeared to be live streaming the event.

"You have the items I requested?" Madame Zola asked Jenny.

Okay, that was something Em needed to ask about. It sounded like the medium had specifically requested the ring and locket. Madame Zola accepted the items from Jenny, placing them in her palm. She folded her fingers around the jewelry, rubbing the open palm of her other hand over her closed fist. She tipped her head back, closing her eyes and murmuring words Em couldn't make out. She'd ask Jenny what the woman had said later.

Em watched Madame Zola closely. She wasn't about to let her pull a sleight of hand and pocket Jenny's family heirlooms. There was a loud bang, and several women jumped, followed by a nervous titter of laughter. Em glanced around. Bri was standing in the far corner of the room with several members of the Sisterhood, including Granny MacLeod, who caught Em's eye and waved her gloved hands. Em smiled and nodded before continuing her search for Bri's sister, but she couldn't spot her in the crowd.

"Yes, yes, I hear you," Madame Zola said, her voice several octaves higher than her speaking voice.

At the sound of a low moan, several women near Em took nervous steps backward.

"Yes, I feel your pain. I want to help you. Will you let me help you?" the medium crooned, her gaze moving around the room.

The woman's red-slicked lips tightened, and Em glanced over her shoulder to see what had gotten her attention. It was Ellie. She was tiptoeing up the stairs. The table appeared to rise off the floor and then fall with a loud bang. Several women cried out in alarm, and Em took a protective step toward Jenny.

Jenny gave her head an almost imperceptible shake, and then Em noticed her finger resting on her knee, pointing at Madame Zola's lap under the table.

Em nodded, glancing at Abby, wondering if she'd caught it. But the angle of the camera was off. Em had a feeling Madame Zola had told Abby where to stand. Another question that would have to wait until later.

The medium fell back against the chair, her body shaking as if she were having a seizure. Then she stiffened and jerked upright, saying in a guttural voice, "Leave. Our. Home. Now."

After uttering the words, Madame Zola collapsed face-first onto the table. The women in the room glanced nervously at each other as if wondering if they should go to the medium's aid but within seconds she lifted her head, looking around as if she'd come out of a trance.

Clutching her amulet, she sat up. "You must leave this house. Leave the Seaton sisters alone or you'll be sorry." The medium turned her head, her gaze flicking from Jenny to Abby. "You'll all be sorry."

Em was about to tell Madame Zola it was her who would be sorry if she didn't return Jenny's jewelry but was distracted by the swirl of emergency lights through the living room window. She walked over to look outside. The front yard was filled with cops making their way across the lawn with flashlights.

This wasn't something she'd expected. Turning to the women in the living room, she said, "We're about to have company. Everyone back against the far wall and let me handle this."

The door burst open, and cops filed into the house with Gwen and Todd leading the charge, guns drawn. "You're a little late for the party, guys. Now put your guns away."

"Em?" Todd looked around the room while holstering his gun. Gwen did the same. They glanced at each other, muttering, "We've been swatted."

"Of course it was a hoax call. What did you expect to find?" Em asked.

"A human sacrifice," Gwen admitted sheepishly.

Something about that bothered Em but she didn't have time to question them further. She'd just noticed Madame Zola wasn't in the room. Em was mentally kicking herself for being an idiot when a familiar voice called out, "Help! I need help."

Em ran toward the voice with Todd following her.

She found Granny MacLeod in the kitchen, lying on the floor, her hands wrapped around Madame Zola's legs. "I've got her," she said.

"Way to go, Granny," Em said, clamping a hand on Madame Zola's shoulder while extending her other hand to help Bri's grandmother off the floor. Em looked up to see Bri and Jenny and half the Sisterhood crowding into the kitchen.

She pulled out a chair, firmly pressing Madame Zola into it. "Search her for a ring and silver chain and locket, and I want to know who hired her," Em said to Todd.

Then Em guided Bri's grandmother into a chair. "Someone get Granny MacLeod a glass of water."

"I'd prefer a cup of tea, if you don't mind. And some cookies," Granny MacLeod said. Her friends hurried off to do her bidding.

Em heard Cal and Josh arguing with Gwen in the entryway, and she leaned back. "You can let them through, Gwen."

Josh's gaze roamed her face as he strode down the hall into the kitchen. "Are you okay? What's going on?"

"We're all fine, and I'll explain everything in a minute, but first I need to know if a reporter for the *Highland Falls Herald* is out there with a photographer?"

Josh nodded. "Yeah. It looked like he was interviewing a cop and Peter O'Brien."

"That's what I thought." Em glanced at Todd, who was questioning Madame Zola. "Todd, would you mind interviewing her in the living room?"

"No problem." He helped the woman off the chair,

rolling his eyes when the medium said, "You'll get nothing out of me. Nothing. I want my lawyer."

Once they were out of hearing range, Em said, "Okay, everyone, listen up. A reporter's outside interviewing Peter O'Brien. HFPD got a call that there was a human sacrifice taking place here, you're all dressed in black, the Sisterhood have been labeled witches before, and the mayor is a founding member, so it's not hard to figure out what O'Brien is up to. It's entirely up to you if you want to deal with it head-on or you can take the path through the woods and avoid O'Brien and the press altogether."

"I vote for taking the path through the woods," Granny MacLeod said to her friends. "O'Brien will end up looking like the fool if none of us are here."

The women argued back and forth but eventually ceded to Granny and some of the older members' wishes. "Okay," Em said. "Bri, Cal, Jenny, and Josh, you guys can distract the reporter, cameraman, and O'Brien so that the ladies can get into their cars unseen."

Everyone agreed. The Sisterhood left through the back door while Cal, Bri, and Jenny headed for the entryway.

Josh hung back. "What are you going to do?"

"There's someone I need to talk to."

"Fine, let's go talk to them." He crossed his arms when she opened her mouth to object. "I'm not leaving until you do."

She sighed. "Okay. Come on." She looked around the entryway and the living room for Bri's sister but couldn't see her. "Ellie must be upstairs."

They found her sitting on the floor in the turret room, her face streaked with tears.

Em and Josh rushed to her side. "What's wrong? Are you hurt?"

She shook her head before lifting her eyes to Em. "You need to help them. They can't move on unless you do. There's a box. I'm not sure but I think it's a wooden box, a little bigger than this." She indicated the size with her hands.

"Did they say anything else?" Em asked. "Did they tell you if they were murdered, and if they were, by whom?"

"No. But I feel like the answer is in the box."

Chapter Eighteen

♥

I hope I'm not interrupting anything," Todd said, waggling his eyebrows with a grin on his face when Josh opened Em's door the next morning.

Em's spoonful of Froot Loops froze midway to her mouth, and Josh rolled his eyes. She was acting as if Todd had caught them in bed together.

Then again, maybe she had a point given how gossip with little or no basis in truth spread in Highland Falls. Josh was about to clear things up for Todd. The last thing he needed was for Cal to think he and Em were sleeping together. The kiss had nearly sent his best friend over the edge, something he didn't want to think about now—not to mention his own reaction to it.

But it wasn't as if he could tell Todd they'd left Seaton House at two in the morning and he'd crashed on Em's couch. He didn't want to blow their fake-dating cover. Although last night, he'd come close to pulling the plug. It wasn't the most romantic or passionate kiss he'd ever shared with a woman, but it was the first time he'd kissed, and been kissed by, Emma Scott, and he'd wanted to keep kissing her. He'd wanted to take his time exploring her sweet, soft mouth and drawing another breathy sigh from her lips. He wanted to… He swore under his breath when an image of him in bed with a naked Em popped into his head.

Both Em and Todd looked at him. "Stubbed my toe," he said, turning to close the door.

He considered *thunk*ing his head against it to rid himself of the X-rated image and the tightening in his gut that accompanied it. He looked at Em instead, thinking that would help. She was sitting at the table wearing an oversize sweatshirt and baggy sweatpants with her face makeup free and her hair a tangled mess, chowing down on a breakfast better suited to a twelve-year-old. It didn't help. He was still turned on.

"Stop waggling your eyebrows at us," Em said to Todd. "Nothing happened. We just wrapped up at Seaton House six hours ago, and Josh slept on my couch."

Okay then, they were going with the truth. Maybe it was better that they end the charade anyway. He was getting worried about his ability to keep Em in the friend zone. On his part, at least. She didn't seem to have the same problem keeping him there, which, he had to admit, was a slight blow to his ego. She'd acted as if kissing him was about as big a deal as kissing Gus.

Todd looked from him to Em. "Why?"

"Because he was tired," she said, shoving another spoonful of Froot Loops into her mouth.

"I meant why was he not sleeping with *you*? Did you guys have a fight?"

"No, we didn't have a fight. Not everyone jumps into

bed with someone after a couple of dates. Not like some people I know," she said around a mouthful of cereal.

"Hey, I'll have you know that Matteo and I dated for weeks before we *jumped* into bed together."

"There you go. We've only been dating for a little more than a week," Em said.

Okay, so she wasn't going to tell Todd the truth. Josh considered doing it himself but he'd started this to help Em. It had to be on her time line. He just hoped the conversation about their non–sex life stopped. "You want a cup of coffee, Todd?"

"Thanks." Todd nodded as he pulled out a chair at the table and went back to talking about the sex Josh and Em weren't having but Josh was afraid he wouldn't stop thinking about having whenever he was around her now.

"Yeah, but by my calculation, you guys are with each other every day, so you're on at least date number seven. Even if they were kind of lame dates." He looked at Josh. "I thought you were going to up your game, bro. Football practices and a football game don't exactly cut it."

Josh silently urged Em to tell Todd the truth. She didn't. "What are you talking about? I love helping Josh at the practices and working with the kids. And being behind the bench at the game was fun."

Admittedly, Josh enjoyed her helping at practices, and he'd really enjoyed having her behind the bench with him. A little too much, now that he thought about it.

"I guess that makes sense. You two have a lot in common. Which is why I figured you two would be getting down and dirty." Em shot him a glare. "Doing the nasty? Shagging?" He shrugged. "Whatever. You've been friends since grade school, so that means your seven dates are equivalent to a brand-new couple going on their twenty-first date, and I guarantee they'd be having sex."

Josh couldn't take it anymore. "Enough with the sex talk," he said, wincing at the sharpness in his voice. "Sorry. I didn't get much sleep. But I doubt you came to talk to us about our sex life, Todd." He hoped he hadn't.

Josh handed Todd his coffee and then pulled out a chair at the table and sat down across from Em. Avoiding her gaze, he took a sip of his own coffee and nearly burned off his tongue.

"I feel your pain, man."

Josh had a feeling he wasn't talking about him burning his tongue.

"Todd," Em muttered, then nodded at the newspaper in his hand. "Let me guess, Peter O'Brien's on the front page of the *Herald* demanding Seaton House be torn down."

"Pretty much. He's painting the Sisterhood as a coven of witches who are using Seaton House as a meeting place to call on evil spirits." He lay the newspaper out on the table.

Em scoffed. "Next he'll be telling people in town to lock up their virgin daughters on Halloween so the Sisterhood can't make them light the black candle and achieve immortality."

Josh laughed. "*Hocus Pocus.* My sister loved that movie."

"I loved it too," Todd said. "But I hate to tell you, kids, that's the rumor spreading around town."

"Oh come on." Em shoved the cereal bowl away from her. "People can't seriously be buying that crap."

"Have you been on social media in the last five years?" Todd asked.

"Yeah, and anyone who spreads malicious lies should be shut down."

"Agreed. But that's way above our pay grade. And there's a little thing called free speech."

"Yeah, well, if you publish crap that's a blatant lie that puts people's lives and their livelihood at risk and encourages hate, that crosses the line in my books."

"Preaching to the choir, sister. But as I said, our hands are tied."

"Not if we can prove that Peter O'Brien was behind the letters, the phone call threatening me, or the 911 call you guys responded to."

Todd groaned. "Don't remind me. Last night had to have been the most embarrassing night of my life." He cocked his head. "Scratch that. Second most embarrassing. The most embarrassing was when I proposed to Matteo and he rejected me."

Em sighed. "Give the guy a break. You dated for six months. And it looks to me like he was right. If you really loved him, you wouldn't have broken up with him because he needed more time."

Todd's jaw dropped. "You're supposed to be on my side."

"I am, which is why I'm being honest with you." She

put her hand on his arm and shook it. "You've been miserable. Give the guy another chance."

"What if he rejects me?"

"Then you'll know he's not your one."

Todd looked from Em to Josh. "Listen to her. You really are good, man." He grinned. "Sherpa coat, here I come."

"What are you—" Em held up her hand. "Never mind. I heard all about the betting poll. Did you know they're taking bets on how long we'll last at Highland Brew?" she asked Josh.

He nodded. "Todd is the only one who thinks we'll go the distance."

"Not anymore I'm not. If the odds keep dropping, I may have to go for the bomber jacket and not the full-length coat."

Em picked up the newspaper. "Did you get anything out of Madame Zola that connects her to O'Brien?"

"I didn't get a word out of her, but Ellie's husband did. He's one scary dude, hot too, and he wasn't happy his wife was upset or that Madame Zola got in a scuffle with Granny MacLeod. Even if Granny got her bruises from throwing herself at Madame Zola, who by the way, has a list of aliases a mile long."

"I thought Abby checked into her," Em said.

"She did. Her website looks legit, and Abby even called some of the people who left glowing recommendations. She did her due diligence. It's just that Madame Zola has been doing this a long time. As for a connection between her and O'Brien, that would be a no. She swears she targeted Abby because of her podcasts and the talk about Seaton House. It fits her MO."

"What about her repeating the threatening letters verbatim?" Josh asked. "I mean, I know they're pretty generic threats, but still…"

"Same. Abby posted the letter on social media and talked about it on her podcast."

"So we're back to square one." Em rubbed her face. "Only now we also have to deal with the fallout from O'Brien's smear campaign."

"It sounded to me like the Sisterhood have a handle on it. I got the impression they've dealt with this kind of thing before. And, according to Granny MacLeod, Abby's cooking up a plan to counter O'Brien's narrative."

"Was that supposed to be comforting?"

Todd got up from the table. "Be grateful you've got another week of vacation. If you're lucky, this will blow over by the time you come back to work."

"He's right, you know," Josh said after Todd left five minutes later.

Em carried her bowl and mug to the sink. "You can't seriously believe this will blow over in a week?"

"No, but you and I both know that the Sisterhood can deal with O'Brien's idiotic claims and the *Hocus Pocus* rumors. I meant Todd is right about you having one week left of vacation. You should enjoy it, have some fun."

"The Sisterhood shouldn't have to deal with this, but yeah, I know you're right. As to me taking time to enjoy my last week off, you heard Ellie. I need to figure out what happened to May and Clara, and to do that, it looks like I need to find the box."

"We searched Seaton House from top to bottom, and we didn't have any luck." That's what they'd been doing until two this morning.

"It was dark. If we go back today, we might have better luck."

"We had flashlights. Besides that, Neil and his crew are working there today." An idea came to him. "They'll probably rip up floorboards and walls and parts of the ceiling. Good places to hide the box if you didn't want anyone to find it. We'll tell Neil to keep an eye out for it. Charlie and Mike are working with him on the weekends, so we can get them looking for the box too."

"That's not a bad idea but we'd have to make sure no one knows why we're looking for the box and that it might hold the key to solving the case."

"Right. What if we tell them Jenny thinks her ancestors buried a box of family heirlooms?"

"That might work. But we'd have to make sure they didn't open the box or tell anyone if they find it."

"We could tell them there's a finder's fee. That way they'd keep quiet about it to ensure no one else comes looking for the box. And we could say the box is rigged and can only be opened by a member of the family or it explodes."

Em laughed. "You lost me at the exploding box. But the finder's fee is a good idea."

"I can't take credit. Remember Steve's new video game? A box is one of the objects the players need to find. They get points if they do. Similar to a finder's fee."

"That's pretty coincidental, don't you think? I wonder if there's a mention of a box in the journals."

"Let's leave that for later. We've taken care of the search for the box, so why don't we just enjoy the rest of the day?"

"What do you have in mind?"

"I was thinking we'd go biking on Blue Mountain, check out the fall foliage."

"Sure. I just have one thing I want to do before we go."

* * *

"You might've mentioned the thing you had to do was connected to the case," Josh said an hour later as he drove along the dirt road to the mayor's greenhouse. Raine's mother, Winter Johnson, owned Flower Power on Main Street, and she grew most of her flowers on her farm on Honeysuckle Ridge Road.

He'd gone to Seaton House to talk to Neil and the boys and then headed home to shower and change before returning to pick up Em and Gus. But Jenny had asked if the dog could spend the day with them. More for Steve's benefit than Charlotte's, according to Jenny. She figured Steve could use the emotional support after the fallout from the séance the night before.

"I promise, we won't be long," Em said. "We'll have lots of time to hit the trails."

"As long as the rain holds off." He pointed out the dark cloud looming over the mountain.

"I don't mind biking in a little rain," she said, looking out the windshield. "Is it always this crowded at the greenhouse?"

"I'm not sure. I've never been before, but it's busier than I expected." He pulled the truck between a car and an SUV.

"Me too. I thought I'd get Winter alone. I need a cover story for why I'm here. I don't want anyone thinking I'm questioning her about O'Brien's accusations."

"Or anyone guessing that you're asking if May could've unintentionally killed her neighbor with an herbal remedy."

Edward Henderson had been known to suffer from migraines, and in his statement to police, his younger brother had said he'd gone to May hoping for a cure.

"You're right, I don't, so you'll have to distract her customers when I'm talking to her." She undid her seat belt. "And since ninety percent of them are female, you shouldn't have a problem."

"Thanks for your vote of confidence," he said as he got out of the truck, waiting for her to join him on the side of the road. "I think I've figured out your cover."

"Yeah, what is it?"

"You've got a front garden full of gratitude rocks and nothing else. We can pick up some plants while we're here." He pointed to a woman loading the back of her pickup with hay bales, pumpkins, and cornstalks. "Maybe pick up a few pumpkins and hay bales for your front steps."

"Or we can pick them up for your front steps."

"Come on. You used to love decorating for Halloween." He nudged her. "Get in the spirit, Freckles."

"I've got the spirit thing covered, thanks. We've spent half our time in a haunted house communing with ghosts."

He smiled, nodding at several women who called out to him. "Hi, how's it going?" he said, and slung an arm around Em's shoulders. She looked at him with her eyebrows raised. "What? I can't help it if I know a lot of people. I've been coaching and teaching gym at the high school for seven years."

"Really? It's been that long?"

"It has."

"You love it, don't you?"

"I do. Kids are great, and so are the people I work with." He removed his arm from her shoulders and took her hand as they walked along a narrow path to the greenhouse. He glanced at their joined hands, wondering when holding Em's hand had begun feeling natural, normal. She must've felt the same because she didn't pull her hand away.

"What about you?" he asked. "Are you glad you moved back home?"

She thought about it for a minute. "I didn't think I would but I guess it's growing on me. For the most part, I like my job, even if it's boring at times."

"It hasn't been boring this past week."

"You're right, it hasn't." She laughed. "Which would explain why I'm happier this week than I have been for a while." Her laughter faded, and she looked away, letting go of his hand. "There's Winter."

"She's busy with customers. Why don't we check out the pots of chrysanthemums?"

"Look at you knowing the names and everything."

"Em, everyone knows what a chrysanthemum is."

"Not me." She bent down and picked up a pot of purple chrysanthemums. "Okay. I'm done."

"Are you kidding me? You need at least five pots of flowers for your garden." He looked around. "I'll get us a cart. I saw a stack of them outside beside the hut." When he came back with the cart, Em was talking to Raine, Quinn, and Izzy.

"Hey, kiddo," Josh said, tugging on Izzy's curly dark hair. He nodded at Raine and Quinn.

Izzy crossed her arms instead of giving him her usual hug. "You're not checking up on me too, are you, Uncle Josh?"

"Ah, no. Em and I are buying flowers. Why would I be checking up on you?"

"Ask them," she said and stomped to the small hut, opening the door and walking inside.

She joined another teenager who was cashing out a customer.

"What's that about?" he asked Raine and Quinn.

"We were concerned there might be fallout from the article in the *Herald*," Quinn said. "But it doesn't look like it's affecting Winter's business."

"I was more worried there'd be protesters here," Raine said, shaking her head. "I can't believe people are taking the accusations seriously. You should see some of the comments online."

"Todd mentioned Abby's coming up with a plan to counter O'Brien's narrative. Do you know anything about it?" Em asked.

Raine nodded. "They're holding a town hall meeting Friday night with the Sisterhood, and Jenny is the speaker. She's going to talk about the history of witches."

"Not a bad idea," Em said, and Josh agreed.

Quinn raised an eyebrow. "They're selling T-shirts and mugs that say 'Embrace Your Inner Witch.' "

"Okay, so they're leaning into the controversy big-time," Em said. "It'll be all hands on deck at HFPD. I should probably give Gabe a call."

"You're on vacation," Josh reminded her.

"Doesn't mean I can't attend. What?" she said when Josh raised an eyebrow. "You want me to have fun, and this definitely sounds like a fun event."

"Yeah, if you like murder and mayhem," he said.

Her face lit up with a smile. "You know I do."

"Tickets go on sale tomorrow," Raine said.

Em frowned. "They're selling tickets?"

Raine nodded. "The proceeds go to the affordable housing project Abby's spearheading. It's what my mother is campaigning on." Raine sighed at Em's blank look. "You have no idea what I'm talking about, do you?"

"I don't follow politics."

"You'd better start. Because if Peter O'Brien's elected mayor, the first thing he'll do is squash the project."

"What can he possibly have against affordable housing?"

Quinn explained. "In their will, the Hendersons gifted their property to the town, but as their sole surviving relative, O'Brien contested it on the basis they weren't of sound mind and that they'd been coerced by Winter and the town council. He wants to build big-box stores."

"That's it. That has to be it," Em said.

"What are you talking about?" Raine asked.

"I've been racking my brain trying to figure out O'Brien's motivation, and I think you just gave it to me."

Chapter Nineteen

♥

Thunder rumbled and raindrops splattered against the truck's windshield. "It looks like we're not biking Blue Mountain today," Em said, a little surprised at how disappointed she was.

"Don't worry. There's always tomorrow," Josh said. "But I have an idea how we can still enjoy our day without the rain interfering."

Her gaze strayed to the way the black Henley clung to Josh's chest, showing off his impressive pecs and abs. Which might explain why a highly inappropriate idea came to mind as to how they could enjoy their day despite the rain. It involved snuggling in bed with Josh.

Except she'd been thinking about Josh in her bed before they'd gotten caught in the rain filling the back of the pickup with pots of chrysanthemums, hay bales, cornstalks, and pumpkins. She'd been thinking about it ever since Todd had put the idea in her head this morning, and she couldn't seem to get it out of her head no matter how hard she tried, and she'd been trying really hard.

Even talking to Raine, Quinn, and Winter and

feeling like she'd finally gotten a break on the Seaton case hadn't been able to push the thoughts completely from her mind. But it wasn't just the thoughts about Josh in her bed that she'd been preoccupied with. Honestly, the way the man looked, she didn't blame her mind for going to sexy times with him. What had been more concerning was how she'd reacted to holding his hand. Or more to the point, how she hadn't reacted. Her hand in his had felt perfectly normal, perfectly right.

However, the revelation that she'd been happier this past week than she'd been in a long time was troubling…because it was true. She hadn't even realized it until she'd made the offhand remark. But there was nothing offhand about her feelings. She'd been happy, happy hanging out with Josh. She rubbed her chest as if it would take away the guilty ache. Other than the moments after she'd kissed Josh last night, she'd gone days without thinking about Brad, and she hadn't even noticed until now.

"What's up? Are you okay?"

Afraid he'd notice the tears welling in her eyes, she glanced out the passenger side window. "Just thinking about the case."

"I get it, okay. But Em, you can't let it consume you. You've figured out O'Brien's motivation. And after talking to Raine and Winter, it's looking as if May died from natural causes like you suspected, and Winter's going to go over the herbal remedies you found in the journal and see if there's a chance the sisters could've unintentionally poisoned Edward Henderson. So for now, put it aside and enjoy the rest of the day."

Em had to see if she could get records from the jail to confirm Raine's theory, but it made sense. May had had her baby while she'd been in custody, and Raine suspected she hadn't received the proper care after a complicated birth, resulting in a series of medical issues that had been left untreated. The next mystery Em had to solve—who was the baby's father? Her gut said it was Edward Henderson. Proving it would be another story.

"Em?"

"You're right. What's your plan for the day?" She looked out the window and frowned. "Why are we at the grocery store?"

"Trust me, it'll be fun." He smiled, pulling into a parking space.

Fun, she thought. This was what Brad wanted for her. He wanted her to be happy. No, he needed her to be happy and to move on with her life, for both his and the baby's sake. She hadn't thought that was possible, and now she was afraid that it was. As hard as it had been to let him go, facing the reality that she might be ready to move on was harder.

Josh grabbed her hand, and they ran across the parking lot. "Bet you want to jump in a puddle, don't you?"

"No, I don't want to jump in a puddle. We're already soaked."

"That's the point. We can't get much wetter than we are," he said and jumped in a small pool of rainwater.

She looked down at her water-splattered sweatshirt. "Seriously?"

"We're done with serious for the day," he said, his eyes shining.

"We'll see about that." She jumped in the middle of the puddle, ensuring Josh got even wetter than her.

"Look, Mommy, look!" a little boy cried, running over to jump in with them.

"Okay, that mom was not happy with us," Em said as they walked into the grocery store five minutes later.

"Yeah, but her little guy loved us." Josh pushed his hair back from his face with both hands, his biceps flexing.

Em looked away. The man was ridiculously hot. She sniffed at a familiar smell wafting past her nose.

Josh laughed. "You look like a bloodhound."

She sniffed again. "I smell pumpkin spice coffee." She looked around.

He took her by the shoulders, steering toward the coffee bar. "How do you not know your way around the grocery store?"

She shrugged. "I order it and have it delivered to the station."

"Ah, a grocery store virgin. This is going to be fun." He paid for her pumpkin spice latte and handed it to her before buying himself a green smoothie.

"Thanks," she said, making a face when he tipped his head back and took a long swallow of his smoothie. "How can you drink that? It smells like a cup of grass, and it looks gross."

"Don't knock it until you try it," he said, wiping the back of his hand over his mouth and offering her the bottle.

"I'll pass, thanks."

He grabbed a cart, steering it toward colorful bins of

veggies and fruit. "Let me introduce you to the produce aisle, Freckles."

He stopped at every bin, holding up a fruit or a vegetable while he explained its nutritional value. Then he'd ask if she wanted said fruit or vegetable, and she'd say no, and still he'd put it in the cart.

"If you keep this up, the store will be closing before you're finished shopping."

"No it won't because we're not shopping in any of your favorite aisles. Wave goodbye to the junk food aisle and the cereal aisle," he said as he walked past them.

"That's just mean."

He grabbed her hand when she began walking down the cereal aisle. "Oh no, you don't. You have two boxes of Pop-Tarts in your cupboard."

"Not the one with sprinkles, I don't. What are you making anyway? I mean besides fruit salads and cooked vegetables."

"I'm not making fruit salad or cooked vegetables for you. Those are for me. Although I plan on leaving some of the bananas, apples, and oranges at your place. I'm making white bean chicken chili for dinner. Or I should say, we are." He leaned over, plucking a loaf of bread off a rack. "Before you get too excited, we're having it with sourdough bread instead of nacho chips."

She leaned over one of the coolers in the bakery section. "Okay, if you get to pick what we're having for dinner, I get to pick what we're having for dessert."

"I already did," he said, nodding at the fruit.

"Good try." She grabbed a box and held it up.

"Pumpkin pecan cheesecake. It's got vegetables and cheese in it so don't complain."

It took them over an hour to get out of the store. It was as if half the town was in the meat department or going through the checkout, and Josh knew every one of them.

"What was up with that guy?" Em said when they finally left the store, their arms loaded down with brown paper bags. The rain hadn't let up, and they made a run for the truck, this time dodging puddles instead of jumping in them.

"His son's on my team. He was upset I've cut back on practices and tackle and live drills," Josh said, opening the door to unload his bags into the backseat. "He calmed down once I shared the recent studies that show kids are more likely to suffer head injuries during practices and tackle and live drills than during the game."

"That makes sense," she said as she unloaded the bags. She got into the front seat and put on her seat belt. "You're a good coach, Josh. The kids are lucky to have you."

"Thanks." He smiled, turning the heat on high. "You're not so shabby yourself. The boys enjoy you coming out to practice."

"I don't think your assistant coach feels the same way."

"He doesn't but he's no longer my assistant coach. He called to resign after the game Friday."

"Because of me?"

"No, because I told him I'd fire him if he didn't make the next practice. It doesn't set a good example for the team." He turned onto Main Street. "I'm going to drop off my groceries and pick up some dry clothes. Do you mind if I shower at your place?"

"Nope," Em said, praying he didn't hear the nervous squeak in her voice. Her mind had provided a visual of Josh in her shower, which she could've done without.

* * *

Josh looked up from filling the dog's bowl and grinned at her as she walked into the kitchen. He'd gone to Jenny and Steve's after his shower to pick up Gus. "You were hoping I'd go ahead and cook without you if you stayed in there long enough, weren't you?"

That, and trying to clear her head of images of Josh in her shower, Josh in the grocery store, Josh jumping in puddles, and Josh at the greenhouse. Her mind was filled with images of Josh, and it was ticking her off. The more she tried to stop thinking about him, the faster the images would come.

"No," she lied. "*Someone* used all the hot water, so I took a nap while the tank refilled."

"I had a five-minute shower. You were the one who was in there for twenty minutes." He rubbed the back of his head and looked away.

Maybe she wasn't the only one having inappropriate shower thoughts. She crouched and gave Gus a hug and then stood, leaning against the island. "So, how's Steve doing?"

"Unhappy about the 'Embrace Your Inner Witch' event from the sounds of it."

"I can't say I'm surprised. Did you tell him that Abby's

husband is former special forces, Granny MacLeod's fiancé is former CIA, Ellie's husband is an agent with NCSBI, Bri's cousin is married to an FBI agent, and my boss's wife is a member of the Sisterhood too?"

He laughed. "I did. But all he seemed to care about was that you'd be there. I told him you would, and I also shared where you were at with the investigation. I didn't think you'd mind."

"No, that's fine. I'd planned on telling them anyway. Did you ask Steve and Jenny about the box?"

He nodded while setting out ingredients for the chili on the cutting board. "Steve said he hadn't read anything about a box in the journals or Jenny's manuscript. He said it was just something that worked for the game. As far as Jenny knows, there was no mention of it in the journals either. They did agree that it was a good idea to have Neil, Mike, and Charlie looking for the box while they work at the house." He tapped a knife on the board. "No more talk about the case, we have work to do."

It was surprisingly fun cooking with Josh. Although she supposed she shouldn't have been surprised. He had a knack for making the most mundane thing seem fun; he always had. He cupped his hand under the spoon. "Give it a try."

It smelled delicious. She leaned in and took a tiny taste. "It's good."

He ate the rest of the chili off the spoon. "It's not good. It's amazing. I might just make a cook out of you yet." He reached for the bowls on the top shelf of the cupboard, the bottom of his sweatshirt riding up to reveal a dark happy trail that disappeared under the waistband of his gray joggers.

"In your dreams," she murmured, thinking he'd probably play a starring role in hers tonight.

"Couch or the table?" he asked, turning to fill the two bowls with chili.

"What?" Her voice went up an octave, and she mentally slapped her forehead. He wasn't asking whether she wanted to make out on the couch or the table. He was asking where she wanted to eat. "Couch. Couch, would be good."

The couch wasn't good. The couch was bad, very bad. The chili had been great, the pumpkin pie cheesecake even better, but sitting under the blanket with Josh binge-watching *The Haunting of Hill House*? It was as if her teenage fantasies had come true.

His phone pinged, and he leaned over to grab it off the coffee table. He glanced at the screen. "So you know how I said we'd go biking tomorrow?"

"Yeah, but don't worry if something else came up." She thought she could use a day away from him. Maybe five.

He showed her the screen. "My mom. She's decided we should go on a family outing before dinner."

She'd forgotten they were supposed to have dinner with his parents the next day. "Where does she want to go?"

"The apple orchard. But if you'd rather go biking, I'm good with that. Don't feel obligated to say yes."

She hesitated and then realized Patsy and Phil would provide the distraction she needed. She wouldn't fantasize about Josh with his parents there. "The apple orchard sounds good."

* * *

Em awakened to the sound of the TV and blinked her eyes open, praying she was experiencing a particularly vivid dream. She slowly lifted her head and immediately closed her eyes. This was no dream; this was embarrassingly real. She was sprawled on top of Josh's hard body, and if she wasn't mistaken, a part of his anatomy was happy to have her there. She rested a hand on the back of the couch to ease herself off him without waking him up.

His eyes slowly opened, and then he squinted at her as if trying to figure out if she was real. She knew the moment he realized he wasn't dreaming. His jaw went slack, and two red splotches colored his stubbled cheeks, and then he practically threw her off the couch. She put out her hand to save herself from landing on the coffee table.

Pushing himself into an upright position, he scrubbed his hands over his face. He looked at her over his fingers and winced. "Sorry about...you know. It has nothing to do with you. It's just an early morning thing."

For some reason, his explanation ticked her off. "I might be a grocery store virgin, but I'm not a *virgin* virgin, Josh."

He groaned. "Really, Em?" He swung his legs off the couch. "I can't believe we fell asleep."

"We had a late night the night before." She didn't

think that was it, at least not for her. The fire had been crackling in the woodstove, the rain tapping on the roof, and she'd been warm and cozy snuggled up with Josh, and she hadn't wanted to move. She'd wanted to stay like that for as long as Josh would let her. She swallowed at the thought. She knew what she had to do.

"Josh," she said at the same time as he said, "Em."

"You go ahead," he said.

"I don't think we should keep fake-dating. It's been great and everything. But you know, with how Cal reacted..." She trailed off, not sure what else to say.

He blew out a breath, looking relieved. "Yeah, I was thinking the same thing. It was good though. For both of us. You seem comfortable hanging out and dating now, making small talk, that kind of thing, and I've proven I'm not just a two-date guy."

For some reason, the fact that Josh was relieved bugged her. No, it didn't just bug her, she realized, it ticked her off. She'd thought he was beginning to feel something for her but obviously not. Ugh. What was wrong with her? She didn't want him to feel anything for her. Just like she didn't want to feel anything for him. That was why she was breaking up with him...fake breaking up with him. This was the stupidest idea she'd ever had. Except it hadn't been her idea, it had been Josh's. She wanted to punch him.

Instead, she changed the subject. "So what are we going to do about dinner with your mom and dad?"

"Would you mind if we still go? They knew we were fake-dating anyway so it's not like they'll be upset.

They'd be more upset if you didn't show up. You know how much they love you."

She felt the same way about Patsy and Phil. At that moment, she liked them a heck of a lot more than she liked their son. She nodded. "It'll be nice to spend time with them. So we're still on for the apple orchard too?"

"Unless you have other plans."

It sounded like he was trying to get out of it, and because she was ticked at him and feeling contrary, she said, "No, I'm looking forward to it."

"Oh, okay, good." He stood up, holding the blanket in front of him. "What about practices? You still good to come? I know the guys would be disappointed if you didn't. No pressure though."

She nodded. "I'll still come to practices. Although once I'm back at work, I might not be able to make it to all of them."

"That's okay. Even if you can make a couple practices, and a game or two, it would be good for the guys to see that we're still friends."

With that one word, the spark of anger inside her fizzled and died. It wasn't Josh's fault that her feelings for him had crossed the line from friendship to something more. She remembered the night down by the river. He'd been a good friend. She couldn't have asked for better. He'd kept her confidences. He'd been there for her. She needed to be there for him.

"I agree. And don't worry, I'll make sure everyone knows that I broke up with you."

Chapter Twenty

♥

Josh frowned up at Em and rubbed his head. She stood on a stepladder reaching through the leafy branches for another shiny red apple. She'd just dropped the first one she'd picked onto his head, and he was pretty sure it had been intentional. "You did that on purpose, didn't you?"

She glanced at his parents, who'd moved to an apple tree farther up the row, and whispered, "Yeah, and if you act the way you did when your mother mentions someone else I should date, I'll drop this one on your head too." She held up an apple that looked as if it was on steroids.

He stepped out of range. "All I said was Cody wasn't a good choice. He's a nice guy but he's a player."

Em gave him a look he was familiar with, her full cherry-red lips flattening, irritation sparking in her bottle-green eyes. But instead of the look ticking him off as it had in the past, it turned him on. They should've stopped fake-dating the night of the football game. Before Em kissed him at Jenny and Steve's, and before he'd woken up with her on top of him, wanting nothing more than to roll her beneath him.

She stepped off the ladder. "You said the same thing about every guy she suggested, and worse, you acted like you were jealous."

"No, I didn't. I acted like a guy who cares about you and who doesn't want you dating a player." Player*s*, because his mother had come up with a list of five men within minutes of them telling his parents they were no longer fake-dating.

In all honesty, he'd been shocked when his mother had immediately tried setting Em up with someone else. He'd been prepared for another reaction entirely. He'd been positive she'd try and convince them to keep fake-dating in hopes that it would turn into something more. If she only knew, that for him, it had. It was why he'd been going to put a stop to their fake-dating but Em had beaten him to it.

"What you did was play right into her hands. She was trying to make you jealous." Em raised her eyebrows at him and bit into the apple.

He had a sinking feeling she was right, and not just about his mother's true intentions. "I'm not jealous, Em." He picked up the basket of apples. "And what was with your reaction? You acted like you were considering dating again. Wasn't that the reason we started fake-dating in the first place? You didn't want people setting you up?"

She shrugged. "Fake-dating you opened my mind to the fact I'm probably not as bad at it as I thought. I mean, it's not as if I want to marry anyone." She grinned around the apple. "Maybe I'll take a page out of your playbook and become a serial dater. Two dates and I'm done."

"That's not funny," he muttered.

"I wasn't trying to be. You were the one who made me promise I wouldn't slip back into my old ways."

He had. And as much as he knew that they had to stop fake-dating, he'd been worried about what that would mean for Em. "I meant you working twenty-four seven. Be honest, if it wasn't for me, you would've been working the Seaton sister case every chance you got. You need to have a life that doesn't revolve around work, Em."

"I've already decided not to take any extra shifts when I go back after my vacation, and I told you, I'm still going to help with the team." She caught sight of someone and waved. "It's Cal and Bri. Come on. Let's go tell them our news."

He sighed. Em had spent half the time at the apple orchard sharing their news with whomever they met, even when she barely knew them. He'd tried telling her not everyone in Highland Falls knew they'd been dating or that they cared, but it hadn't stopped her. He'd suggested she take out a billboard, and for a second there, he'd thought she might be considering it.

He glanced at Cal, who didn't look overjoyed at seeing him with Em. At least that was one positive that came from breaking up with Em. He didn't have to worry he'd lose his best friend because their friendship had begun feeling the strain. Which Josh still couldn't wrap his head around. Cal knew they were fake-dating.

Unless his best friend, who'd known him since he was a kid, had realized even before Josh had, that there was nothing fake about his feelings for Em.

"You guys checking out the corn maze?" Em said as they reached Cal and Bri. The couple had been caught making out in the corn maze last fall, and it had nearly cost them their relationship. Leave it to Em to tease them about it.

Cal's eyes narrowed at him. "No. Have you?"

"No, the hay loft," Em said, all serious-like. She reached up as if pulling something from her hair and then angled her head toward him. "Can you check if I still have hay in my hair, Joshie?"

"You're a brat," he said, tugging on her hair. "She's teasing you, Cal. We're not fake-dating anymore." He glanced at Em, praying she didn't tell Cal where and when exactly they'd decided to end the charade.

"It's about time," Cal said. "I don't know what possessed you to fake-date in the first place. It was a stupid idea."

"Cal!" Bri said.

"What? It was," he said to his wife, who was frowning at him.

"You know what? Your attitude is ticking me off, big brother. And not that I care what you think, fake-dating Josh wasn't just a good idea. It was a great idea. Thanks to him, I'm ready to start dating again."

Josh appreciated Em defending him to Cal. He wished she didn't have to, but given Cal's reaction, apparently she did. But he could've done without her mentioning her plan to start dating again because now he had to keep from giving himself away. He'd been told he didn't have a poker face, and he'd been told that by the man currently studying him with his arms crossed.

"Look at this, Phil, exactly the two people I was hoping to see," his mother said, brushing past Josh to get to Bri and Cal. She hugged them both. "Josh and Em are having dinner with us, and I was going to call and ask you two to join us."

Cal raised an eyebrow at Josh, and he was tempted to flip him off. Em wasn't the only one ticked at her brother. Cal looked as if he was going to make an excuse not to come, which suited Josh just fine. He didn't know how much longer he could put up with his best friend acting like a jerk without calling him on it. Josh was easygoing, and it took a lot to make him mad, but Cal had been pushing his buttons since the night of the séance at Seaton House.

"I'm not sure if—"

Bri cut off her husband. "We'd love to."

"Wonderful!" Josh's mom rubbed her hands together. "It'll be just like old times." She looked at the basket of apples in Josh's hand and smiled. "Between us"—she nodded at the basket in his dad's hand—"we'll have enough to make apple crisp and apple dumplings for dessert. We should probably head out now, Phil. I have lots to do."

"I'm happy to help, Patsy," Bri offered. "I love making apple dumplings."

"Perfect. Then you might as well all come over now. We'll make a day and a night of it."

Josh groaned, wincing when everyone looked at him. He thought he'd groaned in his head. He rubbed his back. "I must've pulled something."

"That's what you get for sleeping on Em's couch, sweetheart. You should've slept in her bed."

Josh briefly closed his eyes. Leave it to his mom. He glanced at Em, figuring she'd be holding back a laugh. She had a dry sense of humor, and the way she was feeling about her brother at that moment, Josh imagined she'd like nothing better than to make Cal squirm.

Except she wasn't laughing. She was chewing on her bottom lip and nodding as if she'd come to a decision. And he had a feeling he knew what she planned to do.

His mom, who'd never been able to read a room—something he'd been accused of in the past—smiled as if she hadn't just lobbed a grenade in the middle of their little group. "We'll see you soon."

His dad, who'd been about to follow his mother, frowned. He glanced from Cal to Josh. "Everything okay here, son?"

"All good, Dad," Josh said, staring down Cal. If he said anything derogatory to Josh in front of his father, all bets were off. Josh wasn't about to let his parents be drawn into this. They loved Cal, the same as they loved Em. They thought of them as family, and they'd be upset if they thought there was a rift between them.

As his parents walked away, Em said, "Josh, I'll get a ride with Bri and my brother. There are a few things I need to tell them. Don't worry about picking up Gus. We'll talk at my place."

"Come on, Cal," Bri said, casting Josh an apologetic smile as she steered her muttering husband away. "We'll wait for you at the Jeep, Em."

Josh reached for Em's hand, tugging her off the path to a quiet place under an apple tree. The orchard was busy, and he wanted to give her some privacy. "You're going to tell them, aren't you?"

She nodded. "Cal's being a jerk. He needs to know the truth. He needs to know why you suggested that we fake-date each other."

It was something he'd hoped she'd do. He believed it was one more step in her journey to healing. But he didn't want her to do it for him. He wanted her to do it for herself. "Don't do this for me, Em. Cal and I will work it out."

"It's not fair to you, Josh. I put you in the middle. I made you keep my secret."

"Hey." He gave her hand a gentle squeeze. "Em, look at me. You didn't make me do anything. I'll take your secret to my grave if you want me to."

"But you think I should tell them."

"You know I do, but only when you're ready. I'll be by your side if you need me. Whatever you need from me, you've got it. You always will. I hope you know that."

She gave him a weak smile and hugged him. "I know." She stepped back, squaring her shoulders and taking a deep breath. "We'll probably be awhile."

* * *

Two hours later, Josh looked up from raking leaves in his parents' backyard. Cal slid the patio door closed and walked to the picnic table. He sat down on the bench, buried his face in his hands, and cried.

Josh bowed his head. He knew exactly how his best friend was feeling. Leaning the rake against the tree, Josh walked to the table. He sat on the bench beside Cal and put his arms around him, holding him until his sobs subsided.

Cal straightened, dragging his forearm across his eyes. "I should've stayed. I should've been there when she lost the baby. I should've known something more was going on."

"You're not a mind reader. You couldn't have known. She doesn't blame you, Cal. Don't blame yourself. It won't help either of you."

Cal glanced at him, his bloodshot eyes shadowed by grief and guilt. "I'm sorry. I've been a jerk. I should've known you'd never take advantage of Em."

"Yeah, you have, but you're her brother. You wouldn't be you if you didn't protect her. You went above and beyond for Em when she lost Brad, Cal. Don't ever doubt that you did everything in your power to help her."

"I don't understand why she didn't tell me or Bri. She didn't have to carry that burden on her own. It was bad enough that Brad was gunned down on their wedding day, and she was there. But then to lose the baby a week after burying him?" He shook his head. "Who thinks they can deal with something like that on their own?"

He stiffened, feeling defensive on Em's behalf. "She dealt with it the only way she knew how. No one knows how they'd handle something unless they go through it themselves. But she's told you now. You and Bri."

"And you. She told you before she told us."

He shrugged. "I caught her at a weak moment."

"You should've told me, Josh. You should've told me and Bri."

"I promised Em I wouldn't. She needed someone to confide in, and I was there. I wasn't about to abuse her trust."

"Sorry, you're right. I'm glad you were there for her." He glanced over his shoulder. "Do you think she really saw and spoke to Brad? Or do you think it's a sign something more is going on, like mental health–wise?"

He hoped Cal hadn't said that to Em. "Your sister is the biggest skeptic I've ever met. If she said she saw and spoke to Brad, I believe her. And with what's happening at Seaton House, I'm surprised you'd have to ask. I think Gus and Jenny and Steve's little girl felt Brad's presence too."

"I haven't had a chance to talk to Bri about it, but I have a feeling she's on the same page as you."

"For the sake of your relationship with Em, you'd better get on it too. It helped her, Cal. Talking to Brad and being able to say goodbye to him, it helped her let him and her guilt go."

"I'm not sure she has. I worry she's just going through the motions."

Josh had worried about that too. Except his worries had been for selfish reasons. He didn't think she'd be able to get over Brad and move on with someone else, someone as in him. "How is she?"

"Better than me. I mean, it was obviously difficult for her to tell us. It was as if she was reliving it all over again. But after she'd told us, she seemed...I don't know, more like the old Em, if that makes sense."

"It does. I'm glad she told you. I think it's been weighing on her. How's Bri?"

"She held it together for Em. She cried with her, of course, but Bri shines in these types of situations. She knows exactly what to say."

"It's what she does for a living, buddy. Any chance she talked to Em about therapy?"

He nodded. "Em agreed. But she won't see anyone other than Bri."

The patio door opened, and Josh glanced over his shoulder. It was his dad. He had three bottles of beer in his hands. He walked over, nudged his head at Josh to move over, and sat between him and Cal. He handed each of them a beer. "You boys doing okay?"

His dad's eyes were shiny, and his voice was gruff. "Em told you and Mom, didn't she?"

He nodded. "Your mom could tell something had happened. She's not easily put off." He took a long pull on his beer. "Poor Emmy. My heart just about broke for her."

Josh moved to get up from the bench.

"Your mom's got this, son. Doesn't matter how old a woman is, sometimes they need a mom. Even if that mom's not their own." Em and Cal's mother had died suddenly of a brain aneurysm when they were away at college.

When his father decided they'd given the women their privacy for long enough, they walked into the house. Bri and his mom stood at the kitchen counter finishing up the apple dumplings and apple crisp while Em sat at the table with her feet up on a chair having a beer.

Her bloodshot gaze was wary as it moved over the three of them. "Could've called it," Josh said, shaking his head. "Slacker."

She smiled, and the tension left her face. "You know the saying, too many cooks in the kitchen."

"Emmy's right. Game's on in the living room if anyone wants to join me," his dad said, and then, because he wouldn't be able to help himself, he leaned over and dropped a kiss on the top of Em's head.

She glanced away, lifting the beer bottle to her lips, her fingers tightening around the bottle in a white-knuckle grip.

Josh took the seat across from her and gently pushed her feet off the chair, replacing them with his own in hopes of distracting her. "Hey, Mom, do you know anything about the Hendersons?"

"Of course I do, honey. Your grandma dated one of the Henderson boys but your great-grandma put a stop to it. She had a lot to say about LeRoy Henderson, and none of it was good. Your great-grandma liked his older brother Edward though. Said how it was a shame the Seaton girl hadn't murdered LeRoy instead of Edward. He was a bad seed, that one. According to your great-grandma, the parents knew it too. Rumor at the time was that they planned to cut him out of the will. I guess it was lucky for LeRoy that Edward died."

Em smiled at him, a luminous smile he'd seen once before. Only then she'd been smiling at her fiancé's ghost. This time that smile was meant for him.

Chapter Twenty-One

♥

Em placed a hand on her stomach in order to calm the nervous flutters while walking across the field to where Josh was setting up the step-over bags. The flutters refused to cooperate. The closer she got to him, the faster they danced. Aside from a couple of texts, she hadn't seen him or spoken to him in three days. As evidenced by the butterflies doing the "SexyBack" dance in her stomach, she was excited to see him. She wondered if he'd be able to tell. Her face felt flushed.

She'd worked on mindfulness techniques with Bri the day before and wondered if they'd help in this situation. Except Em was supposed to focus on what she was feeling in the moment, and she didn't think focusing on how excited she was to see Josh would get rid of the butterflies or the flush heating her cheeks.

She also wasn't supposed to judge what she was feeling, and she was feeling pretty judgy. It's what she did, who she was. She followed the evidence and came to a logical conclusion. In this case, the evidence confirmed what she'd already begun to suspect. She was falling for Josh Callahan.

"Hey, Em," Charlie and Mike called, running toward her. "I've got the picture you wanted," Charlie whispered when he reached her side, glancing at Josh.

"Great," she said, accepting his baby photos and sliding them into her jacket pocket.

She was using Josh's birthday on the twenty-eighth as an excuse to confirm her theory that Willy was Edward Henderson's son. There was a photo of Willy at about a year old in *The Haunting of Seaton House*, and Em wanted to compare it to Drew O'Brien's baby picture. It wasn't as if she could ask him for one—she'd come up empty on her internet search—so she'd used a sweatshirt bearing the team's baby photos for Josh's birthday as an excuse. It wasn't the best idea she'd ever come up with to gather evidence, but the players were excited about it. Everyone wanted to see if Josh could guess who they were.

"I forgot mine," Mike said and pulled out his phone. "I'll get my dad to drop it off." He gave her a shy smile. "He's looking forward to your date tonight."

"Yeah, me too," she said, returning his smile, hoping it passed for an excited smile and not a *what had she been thinking?* smile.

Her excitement at seeing Josh today might've confirmed her feelings for him just now, but her reaction to the promise he'd made to her under the apple tree had thrown up the first red flag that she'd gone from crushing on him to something more.

The second red flag had started waving after she'd spilled her guts to Cal and Bri and then to Phil and Patsy. She'd caught a glimpse of Josh comforting her brother on the picnic bench, and then Josh had known just what to do to distract her after Phil's fatherly kiss, saving her from having an embarrassing meltdown at the Callahan's kitchen table.

Josh was always there for her, for her brother, for his family and friends, his team, and his community. He was caring, constant, and kind. He was one of the best men she knew…and that was the thought that had sent her into a panic. Up until that moment, she'd thought of Brad as the best man she'd ever known, and it felt as if she was replacing him by falling for Josh.

And that was why, when she'd been checking out Seaton House with Jenny the day before and Neil had asked her out, she'd agreed.

Josh looked up from hugging Gus. "Hey, long time no see. How's everything going?"

"Good. Keeping busy." She had been, but she'd also been avoiding him. It had been a bonus that, in trying to avoid him, she'd had extra time on her hands and had gotten into the Halloween spirit. And she'd had a lot of fun doing it. Maybe too much fun given the balance in her bank account.

"So I've heard. The kids have been talking about your place. Sounds like you'll take first prize in this year's Best Decorated Halloween House competition."

One of the boys must've overheard him because he said, "You should see it, Coach. Em has these really cool animatronic witches. They look just like the Sanderson sisters from *Hocus Pocus*. She's even got a cauldron and a graveyard. It's the best."

"I'll have to get over there and check it out," he said, his eyes dancing with amusement.

"If you don't want to get stuck in a lineup, go right after dinner or late at night," the teen advised before running off to join his teammates and Gus on the field.

"Now I know why the *Herald* hasn't included your place in their Halloween house coverage. You're really leaning into the controversy, aren't you?"

She unzipped her jacket, flashing him her *Embrace Your Inner Witch* T-shirt. "I'm happily stirring the pot and supporting the Sisterhood and the mayor while doing it. I have her campaign sign front and center."

He rubbed the side of his face. "By any chance has Peter O'Brien done a drive-by?"

"I'm not sure. Why?"

"Because he's walking this way, and he doesn't look happy." He glanced at her and cleared his throat. "You might want to zip up your jacket."

She did as he suggested but they soon learned it was Josh the man was unhappy with, not Em. O'Brien was there to complain about the new practice schedule. Josh's explanation didn't appease him the way it had the father at the grocery store.

"I don't care what the statistics say. What I do care about is that my son is being scouted, and by limiting his practice time and contact drills, you're putting his football career at risk."

"Better to put his football career at risk than his life,

don't you think?" Em said. "Or are you not as worried because, as a quarterback, he's at less risk than his teammates?"

"And that's another thing. Why is this woman acting as your assistant coach and not Delaney?"

Em crossed her arms. "This woman has a name, which I'm pretty sure you know since we had a conversation about Abby Mackenzie's podcast."

"Em, why don't you do the warm-up with the team?"

"Sure. But if it's okay with you, I want to talk to them about swatting first," she said to Josh while holding O'Brien's gaze. "You may not be aware of this, but HFPD was a victim of swatting Friday night at Seaton House. You were there, weren't you? Using it as an opportunity to defame your opponent, which I'm sure your lawyer has already advised put you in legal jeopardy. If they haven't, I'm happy to provide you with the exact laws you've broken."

"You obviously have an agenda, Officer Scott, and I won't allow you to use your volunteer position on this team to push it. I advise you to fire her today, Callahan, or you might find yourself without a job."

"Actually, I'm here speaking in my role as community outreach officer with HFPD. We believe a member of this team made the call Friday night." She held his gaze, and then she turned and walked away.

She called Gabe as soon as she was out of hearing distance. Although she didn't think O'Brien would hear her if she was standing right beside him. He was too busy yelling at Josh. Em had no idea how Josh remained calm in the face of the man's threats. He was far too chill and easygoing. And because he was, Em decided she'd pay O'Brien a visit when she was back on the job next week and give him a warning based on what she heard coming out of his mouth.

Gabe answered, and Em filled him in. He wasn't exactly thrilled with her, especially because there was no evidence linking a member of the team to the call. But he did agree that the high school student body should be made aware of the dangers of swatting, which resulted in Em being awarded the position she claimed to hold. She was now acting community liaison with HFPD. Or she would be once she was back on the job.

After a brief talk about swatting, Em put the team through the warm-up routine. She hadn't seen any indication of guilt on the boys' faces. But she did see humiliation and anger on Drew's face every time his gaze strayed to his father. He caught her watching him and ducked his head.

"Okay, guys, take a five-minute break and grab a drink before we start drills," she said, wondering where Josh was. He'd finished up his *conversation* with O'Brien ten minutes ago.

"Em, can I talk to you for a minute?" Drew asked.

"Sure. What's up?"

He raised a shoulder, looking uncomfortable. "I just wanted to apologize for my dad. You're a great assistant coach, and I don't want you to leave because of what he said. None of us do. Me and the guys will talk to the principal or the board if you need us to."

"Thanks, Drew, I appreciate it. I enjoy helping with the team. You're a great bunch of kids, and I don't plan on going anywhere." Unless she put Josh's job at risk. She looked down at herself. "I'm sorry about the T-shirt. I didn't consider how it would make you feel."

He grinned. "It's okay. My mom has one too."

"Cool. But it can't be easy for you right now with the election campaigns heating up, so if anyone gives you a hard time, let me or Coach know. We're here for you if you ever need to talk, Drew."

"Thanks." He glanced at Josh, who joined them. "Sorry about that, Coach. You know what he's like."

"We've talked about this before, buddy. It has nothing to do with you, but if you ever need to talk, you know where to find me."

"Thanks, Coach."

"Go get something to drink." He gave Drew's shoulder a squeeze and then called, "On the field in five, guys."

"Where did you go?"

"To give the principal a heads-up." He held her gaze as he pulled a photo from his pocket. "I ran into Neil on the way back. He asked me to give you this."

"He shouldn't have given you the photo. It was supposed to be a surprise. Don't let the team know." She filled him in on her plan.

"Em, Drew isn't O'Brien's biological son. He's O'Brien's wife's son from her first marriage. But they do have a daughter, and you've already met her."

"I have?"

"Yeah. Finger painting day with my mom's class. Remember the dark-haired little girl I rescued you from having to guess what she'd painted? That was O'Brien's daughter. But Em, two kids looking alike doesn't prove anything. Unless you had a DNA match..." His eyes roamed her face and he groaned. "You have got to be kidding me."

"What? They wouldn't even know. All I'd need is a water bottle or, in the case of a kindergartener, a juice box."

"Don't tell me. I don't want to hear about it. But I'd suggest you talk to your boss before you do anything, and while you're at it, you might want to tell him about your conversation with O'Brien. Because I guarantee, he'll be giving him a call."

"I already did." She told him about her new assignment at HFPD, and Josh started laughing. "It's not funny," she muttered.

"You're right. It's not funny. It's hysterical." His laughter faded almost as fast as it began, and he put his hands in his pockets. "So when were you going to tell me you have a date with Neil tonight?"

"I don't know. It's not a big deal. It's just a date."

"A date isn't a big deal for some people, but it is for you. This is your first date since Brad died."

"No, it's not. You were my first, second, third, and fourth date. Unless you're counting football practices and the game."

"Em, those weren't real dates."

They felt real to her, and it bothered her that he so easily dismissed them. "Whatever. We're just going out for dinner. I think I can handle it."

"Where are you going?"

"Zia Maria's," she said, referring to the Italian restaurant on Main Street.

"Really? I guess I'll see you there."

"No. No way. I don't need a chaperone or you mouthing conversation starters at me."

"What are you talking about? I'm not going to chaperone you. I have a date too."

Her stomach felt like it was weighed down by a lead balloon. "Oh yeah, with whom?"

"You wouldn't know her."

* * *

Em sat across from Neil at a table for two. A candle wedged into a wicker-wrapped Chianti bottle cast a warm glow over the red-and-white-checked tablecloth. The fact the table was tucked away in a far corner worked for her. She had a feeling the date wouldn't go well and didn't want any witnesses to her failure. And the reason she didn't think the date would go well had nothing to do with her being a pessimist. It was based on the evidence. Neil had blanched when Zia Maria assured them that it was the most romantic table in the restaurant, and he seemed unable to stop talking about his wife. It was as if he'd been storing everything up for the past three years, waiting for Em and for this moment.

The restaurant door opened, ushering in a gust of cool air, a few colorful leaves, and a short woman with spiky magenta hair on the arm of a tall, redheaded man, who looked a lot like Neil, probably because he was his brother. Em stared down her coworker, but Gwen refused to look her way.

"Sorry, Em. All I've done is talk about my wife."

Neil must've noticed the face Em was making at Gwen, and assumed it was directed at him for monopolizing the conversation.

"No. I think it's great that you talk about your wife. Really," Em added when he cast her a doubtful look.

Gwen caught her eye and gave her an excited thumbs-up. Em pursed her lips at her, letting her know she wasn't pleased she was here spying on them.

Apparently, Neil didn't notice. "I don't talk about her. To anyone. You're the first person I've felt comfortable talking about her to." He unfolded and refolded the napkin. "You've lost someone you love too. No one else understands what it's like for me. They all think I should be able to turn off my feelings for her and move on."

"I think they just want you to be happy, Neil."

"How can I be? I lost the love of my life."

"You have Mike, and your business. Family who loves you," she said, sending a *knock it off* look at Gwen, who mouthed for the third time, *How's it going?*

The restaurant door opened again, and this time, along with cool air and colorful leaves, Em's brother and her best friend breezed through the door. Unlike Gwen, they discreetly snuck a peek in Em's direction while avoiding making eye contact.

"I know, and I know for Mike's sake I have to move on, but to be honest, Em. I'm not sure that I can."

"Or that you want to?" she asked, knowing only too well what that was like.

He nodded. "I knew you'd understand. I can't tell you how good it feels to talk to someone who does."

"But Mike understands how you feel, Neil. He's suffered the same loss."

He shook his head. "It's not the same. He loved his mom, sure, but he's young. He's got friends, family, and one day, he'll meet someone and fall in love. But I won't."

Neil sounded a little selfish to her, as if he was the only one who was suffering. She wondered if she'd sounded the same to her family and friends, and then she felt bad for judging him. But she also felt bad for Mike. She'd gotten to know him better the past few days. He'd come over after school with Charlie, and they'd helped set up her Halloween display. They were nice boys and good friends, but Em had sensed a sadness in Mike, a loneliness, and wondered what his home life was like. She knew Mike and Neil had a good relationship and loved each other very much, but she was worried about Mike. She knew Josh shared her concern.

"How is the reno going at Seaton House?" she asked, deciding to change the subject instead of mentioning her worries about Mike. She had a feeling Neil wouldn't appreciate her interference.

"Good," he said, leaning back from the table when the server arrived with their meals. He placed a bubbling cheese pizza in front of her and a seafood platter in front of Neil.

"You haven't seen any sign of the box?" she asked as the server walked away.

"No sign of the box or the ghosts." He smiled, raising his wine glass. *"Buon appetito."*

She touched her beer bottle to his wineglass. "So no slamming doors, unexplained shadows, crying women, or rolling red balls?"

"Not that I've seen or heard, but I've worked in old homes before, and most of what you're talking about can be explained," he said, and then he shared his theories about the ghostly sights and sounds at Seaton House.

"Mike and Charlie will be disappointed. They swear Seaton House is haunted," she said. It wasn't an offhand remark. She wanted to work Mike back into the conversation in hopes she could convince Neil to talk to him about his mom.

His mouth tightened. "Mike wants to believe there's an afterlife."

"And you don't?"

"No. I don't." He pointed his fork at her pizza. "You should eat before it gets cold."

They didn't talk much during the meal. Neil savored his while Em wolfed hers down. He talked more during dessert. He'd ordered a specialty coffee, and Em had ordered tiramisu.

He went back to talking about his wife, everything he missed about her, about the dreams they'd had for their future. Em pointed out that Neil could take Mike on the wonderful holidays he and his wife had planned, but he shook his head.

"You know, I've started therapy recently, and it's

made a difference." She'd had one therapy session but Neil didn't need to know that. He also didn't need to know how much a role Josh had played in getting her to the place she was now, which was miles from where she'd been a matter of weeks ago. "I think you and Mike would benefit from talking to someone, Neil."

"I don't know. I'm not big on that kind of thing."

"I get it. Neither was I." She scooped up the last of the tiramisu with her spoon, savoring the final bite before continuing. "You know, just because you smile and laugh and maybe meet someone and fall in love, it doesn't mean you're dishonoring your wife's memory and the love you shared. It doesn't mean you love her any less. You can still love your wife and make room in your life and in your heart for someone else." She put down the spoon, wiping her mouth with the napkin. "If you'd died instead of your wife, you wouldn't want her to be lonely and sad and stuck, would you? I know I'd want my fiancé to move on and have a wonderful life."

He bowed his head, nodding before raising his tear-filled gaze. "I don't know how to go on without her."

She covered his hand with hers and then pushed back from the table. "I'll be back in a minute," she said and headed for her brother and best friend's table.

"Em! What are you doing here?" Bri asked, acting like she was shocked to see her there.

"Stop with the act. I can see right through you."

"I don't know what you're talking about. We come every Wednesday night for pasta fazool, don't we, honey?" she asked Cal, who was hiding his face behind the menu, his shoulders shaking.

Bri pursed her lips at him. "Fine. We just wanted to be here for you if you needed us."

"It's not as if I'm having open-heart surgery," she said, and held out her hand. "I need one of your business cards. I've got a new client for you. Or I should say, two clients, Neil and his son."

"So the date isn't going well?" her brother asked.

"It was more of a therapy session than a date. But it's okay. The pizza was great, and my tiramisu was amazing. And Neil's a nice guy."

In a way, Em supposed it had been as much a therapy session for her as it had been for Neil. She'd realized something important. She didn't need to move on for only Brad and their daughter's sake, she needed to move on for herself.

And as the restaurant door opened again, Em's stomach fluttered and twirled like the colorful leaves on the sidewalk. She didn't feel guilty or sad when her pulse leaped at the sight of Josh walking into the restaurant. She was grateful that she was no longer stuck like Neil.

Someone nudged Josh from behind, and he stepped aside. She took a moment to brace herself for the sight of him with another woman and then burst out laughing when she saw his date. It was Todd. The two of them spotted her and walked over.

Josh frowned, glancing at Neil sitting at the table in the corner, talking to Gwen and his brother. "What's going on? I thought you were on a date with Neil."

"And I thought you had a date with a woman. Anything you want to share?"

Todd snorted. "No one in his little black book was available on short notice."

"I knew it," Em said. "You made that up so you could check on me."

"Yeah, and apparently I wasn't the only one," Josh said, looking around the restaurant.

And that's when Em noticed the other couples in the darkened corners. Half the Sisterhood had shown up with their significant others. But instead of being ticked, she was grateful she had so many people who cared about her, especially the man watching her with a smile in his eyes.

Chapter Twenty-Two

♥

"We didn't lose because Em's not here, guys. What do I always say?" *Always* was a stretch. They rarely lost.

"Sometimes you win. Sometimes you learn," Charlie and Mike said from where they sat at the end of the bench, dangling their helmets between their knees.

Quinn and Cal glanced at him with their eyebrows raised. He'd asked them to fill in for Em. The Embrace Your Inner Witch town hall meeting was tonight, and it had started at the same time as the game. He figured the guys would be stoked. Cal played football in high school with Josh, and the boys always enjoyed when he came to help at practice, and Quinn had played in the NFL for three years before he blew out his knee. But clearly, no one could replace Em. Admittedly, he missed having her behind the bench too.

Bri appeared with two large plastic containers. "Good game, guys."

"Thanks," several of the team murmured while a few of the players looked at her as if wondering what game she'd been watching.

"Em was disappointed she couldn't be here to cheer you on. She made you cupcakes to make up for it," Bri said, opening the lid.

Josh leaned in to get a look at the cupcakes. They were dark chocolate and decorated to look like witches' hats. Half of an Oreo cookie sat in the middle of green icing the color of Em's eyes with a chocolate kiss on top.

"My sister doesn't bake," Cal said, frowning at the cupcakes.

Josh reached into the container, picked up a cupcake, and took a bite. It took a minute to swallow it. "Clearly, she baked these."

"Oh, yeah?" Cal grinned and took one for himself before Bri started passing them around to the team. Cal made a face and swallowed. "I think she forgot the sugar."

Bri glanced at her husband, fighting a grin. "She made sugar-free and gluten-free cupcakes for Josh. She added the icing and decorations for the boys." She pulled a cookie from her pocket. "She didn't forget about you, Gus."

Josh focused on the players' faces as they bit into the cupcakes. Every one of them acted as if they were the best cupcakes they'd ever tasted. He reached in his pocket for his phone and took a photo for Em and then sent it. He scanned the latest texts from her, hoping for an update from the town hall meeting. He was concerned it would get out of hand. But her last text was from Wednesday night when she'd let him know she'd gotten home okay from the restaurant.

He was going to ask Quinn if he'd heard anything but then Josh got busy. The team was as down in the dumps after they'd showered and changed as they were right after the game. Josh gave them another pep talk before they left the locker room. Cal and Quinn were waiting for him in the parking lot. "You guys didn't have to stick around."

"A few of the parents wanted to chat about your revised practice schedule," Cal said.

Josh imagined they did. He'd heard some grumblings in the stands at the end of the game. They blamed tonight's loss on the reduced practice time.

"Don't worry. We backed you a hundred percent."

"Yeah, I don't think you'll be getting any more complaints. Cal had the stats to back you up," Quinn said.

"Thanks. Hopefully they'll let Peter O'Brien know," Josh said, taking his car keys from his pocket. "So how did the town hall go?" he asked Quinn.

"According to my mother, Em was the hero of the night."

"Why? Did it get violent? Is she okay?" Josh asked, ignoring Cal, who was looking at him as if his reaction was over the top.

"It got a little rowdy but Em and a few of her colleagues from HFPD shut the protesters down before it got out of hand," Quinn said.

"I don't get it. How's she a hero?"

Cal grinned. "She used her voice and not her fists or her gun."

Quinn held up his phone and pressed Play.

Em stood at the front of the town hall with a microphone in her hand. She had on the same dress she wore to Saturday Singles Night at Highland Brew. She looked just as beautiful too, which might've been why Josh didn't notice Peter O'Brien right away.

The Sisterhood and Jenny sat on the stage, their expressions tense as O'Brien stood at a podium a few feet in front of Em, spouting his lies about the mayor and the Sisterhood. Lies that apparently a good number of the locals had bought into. According to O'Brien and Winter's campaigns, they were in a statistical tie.

"Em looks like she wants to hit him with the microphone," Josh said.

Cal laughed. "She hit him with her words instead."

"This I've gotta see," he murmured.

"Mr. O'Brien, you've read the rules just like everyone else and agreed to abide by them. Slander is not allowed."

"I'm not lying. Everything I've said—"

Em cut him off. "Is a lie. You have no proof. But I have a question for you. Other than dividing the community with your fearmongering—"

"I resent that. I'm not the one people are afraid of, it's them." He pointed at the women onstage.

Em glanced over her shoulder and then raised an eyebrow at O'Brien. "You're afraid of Granny MacLeod?" She listed several of the women in the Sisterhood who ranged in age from their late seventies to their mid-nineties, who sat on the stage looking like everyone's favorite grandmothers. Half of the audience laughed, earning them a scowl from O'Brien.

"Way to go, Em," Josh murmured. She never could stand a bully. It was like watching her back in the day, and he loved every second of it.

"It's okay. I didn't expect you to answer. They don't exactly fit your narrative, do they? But maybe you can answer this for me. What have you done for the people of Highland Falls, Mr. O'Brien? What are you planning to do to make our lives better?"

"My development will improve the lives of everyone who lives in Highland Falls. They'll reap the benefits of the low pricing that only big-box stores can provide and a wide range of goods and services, and the stores will draw people from the surrounding counties."

"And decimate the merchants on Main Street?" She nodded. "But that's not what I was asking about. I'll give you an example of what I'm looking for," she said and began reciting the charitable organizations spearheaded by the group of women on the stage.

"The youth program at the community center, the community garden, Help for Farmers Foundation, Project Brodie that's funded the summer camp for at-risk youth, the Snowsuit Foundation, Knit for Kids, the animal shelter, the food bank and holiday food drives, the I Believe in Unicorns Festival, the Fall Festival... There are honestly too many festivals to name, just like there are too many charitable organizations to list that the Sisterhood not only created but also volunteer for." She turned to the women on stage. "Thank you, ladies. For everything you've done and continue to do for us."

Tucking the microphone under her arm, Em clapped, smiling when the audience jumped to their feet and gave the women on stage a thunderous round of applause. Josh hadn't realized he was clapping until Cal and Quinn started to laugh.

He shrugged. "Em's right. I don't think I even realized just how much the Sisterhood has done for Highland Falls."

"She's not finished yet, buddy," Cal said, nodding at the screen.

When the applause died down and everyone took their seats, Em continued. "The Sisterhood are the best of Highland Falls. They *are* Highland Falls, and they've done more for this community than you could hope to do in three lifetimes, Mr. O'Brien, which you wouldn't because you don't care about Highland Falls. You care about your bank account. If it were up to me, I'd vote that we give the Sisterhood the key to the town, and they can run it for the next hundred years."

Josh tucked his hands in the pockets of his black pants and pressed his lips together, afraid he might blurt out his feelings for Em. Although from the expression on Cal's face, he was just as proud of Em as Josh was. But Josh wasn't just proud of her, he was in love with her. And the realization nearly knocked him on his ass. He glanced at Cal. The last thing he wanted to lose was the friendship of his childhood best friend, but if he had to choose, he'd choose Em.

"Everyone's celebrating at Highland Brew. You two heading over?" Quinn asked.

"Is Em there?" Josh would be surprised if she was. He hoped she wasn't. He wanted to talk to her in private. He didn't want to wait to tell her he was in love with her. He was in love with Emma Scott, he thought, unable to get his head around it.

"Oh yeah, she's there." Cal held up his phone. It was

a photo of Em laughing, surrounded by members of the Sisterhood, with Gus sitting on her lap.

"What's Gus doing there?" Josh asked.

"Bri brought him with her," Cal said. "He's getting special treatment because Em is the town's hero tonight. I'll catch a ride with you."

"Sure." Of course Cal assumed he'd go. Josh had never been one to miss a party.

He pulled his truck out of the high school parking lot and glanced at Cal. He was staring at the photo of Em with a soft smile on his face. "I can't tell you how good it feels seeing her like this." He turned the screen to him. "She looks happy, doesn't she?"

Happy and so damn beautiful that his chest hurt. Josh nodded, chewing on his bottom lip. He wanted to tell Cal how he felt about Em but he wasn't sure she felt the same way about him. The way she'd looked at him at the apple orchard, at the dinner with his parents, and at Zia Maria's the other night gave him hope that she did. But he didn't want to pressure her either.

There was something else holding him back that he didn't want to acknowledge but he knew it was there, the niggle of doubt that she was ready to let Brad go. That she was ready to give her heart to someone else. As much as he didn't want to admit it because, to his mind, it didn't speak well of him, but he needed to know he wasn't a stand-in for the man she'd loved and lost.

"What's up? You're quiet," Cal said.

"Just tired. It's been a busy week."

"You sure it's not something more? You're not worried about your job, are you?"

"I wasn't until you asked. Do you know something I don't?"

"No. It's just that O'Brien might try to get you fired if he's elected mayor."

"He's tried several times but the principal and the board have always had my back. Then again, if we don't win the championship game, they might not be as willing to go to bat for me. But I'm not the only one whose job would be at risk if he got in—so would Em's."

Cal nodded, looking concerned, as Josh pulled into the parking lot at Highland Brew. "Don't mention it to Em. She's doing well right now, and if she lost her job, I worry it would set her back."

Josh's cell rang as they got out of the truck. "Go ahead. I've got to take this." He brought the phone to his ear. "Hey, Mom, what's up?"

"I'm making the menu for your birthday party, and I was wondering if you want ghost pizzas, monster wraps, or franks in a blanket? You know the ones I mean? They look like severed toes in bandages."

It was like his mom forgot he was turning thirty-three and not thirteen. "Mom, I'm just having a few people over. You don't have to go to any trouble."

"It's no trouble. You know how much I love throwing a party. And your birthdays are especially fun."

Since his birthday was October twenty-eighth, his mom had always gone with a Halloween theme. At least she had when he was a kid. He thought about reminding her that he was throwing the party instead of her but he didn't want to hurt her feelings. Besides that, he was using his birthday as an excuse to throw the party. It had been a while since he'd had one. And he always enjoyed Halloween.

"You know what, I'm going to make all three. You always get a good crowd at your parties. Do you think Emmy will come?"

"I hope so." He smiled at the thought of her being there. Then he realized he was getting ahead of himself.

"Oh, me too. I can't stop thinking about what that poor thing went through. And all by herself." His mom paused and then said, "You might not have noticed, but I was upset when you and Em stopped dating."

"Mom—"

"I know it wasn't real, but you know how much I've always hoped that you two would get together. But you were right, Joshie. And as much as I love Em, I know how hard it was for you when Amber left you for her ex. You deserve someone who loves you with their whole heart. And Em, she gave her heart to that poor boy. She'll never recover from that loss. But you know what, she can still be happy and have a wonderful life, and we're going to make sure that she does, aren't we?"

"Yeah," he said past the wedge of emotion stuck in his throat. "I've gotta go, Mom. I'm at Highland Brew."

"Okay, sweetheart. Have fun."

He said goodbye and disconnected, thinking he should get back in his truck and head home. His mom was right, there was no hope for a future with Em. She'd never be able to move on from Brad. Cal had said the same thing. But Josh wanted to tell Em how proud he was of her, and that wouldn't change even if she couldn't love him.

Highland Brew was packed, and everyone was in high spirits. Josh spotted Em with her friends, sharing a laugh. He walked over to the bar to get a beer. He'd wait to talk to her. He needed a few minutes to get his head straight anyway.

"Thanks," he said when the bartender handed him a beer.

"Hey, pal." Cody, his coworker at HFFD, took the barstool beside him and ordered a beer. "So listen, I was wondering, now that you and Em are no longer dating, how you'd feel about me asking her out?"

Josh forced a smile when all he wanted to do was rip Cody's head from his shoulders. "Sure. Go for it." This wasn't about Josh and his feelings. This was about Em. She deserved to get out and have fun, even if it wasn't with him.

"Thanks, pal." Cody grinned, then slapped him on the back before walking away.

"I hope that doesn't come back to bite you in the ass, buddy," said a deep voice beside him. Josh glanced at the man leaning against the bar. It was Ellie's husband.

"What do you mean?"

He pointed his beer bottle at Em and Cody, who were now talking in a corner. "I've been where you are. Actually, I was sitting on that very stool when I told a man he was welcome to date Ellie. And I have a feeling the reason I did is the same as yours." He clapped a heavy hand on Josh's shoulder. "Take my advice. If you love the lady, let her know."

Josh didn't correct Ellie's husband. He just nodded. But their situations were far from the same. Ellie had dumped her fiancé long before she'd gotten involved with her now-husband. She wasn't still in love with her ex-fiancé like Em was in love with Brad. Ellie's husband hadn't been competing with a ghost.

A wet nose nudged Josh's hand, and he looked down to see Gus staring at him with his sad eyes. "Hey, boy," Josh said, sliding off the barstool. He crouched in front of Gus and accepted a hug. "Thanks, buddy. I needed that."

Chapter Twenty-Three

♥

"Okay, what is going on with you? You're all smiley, and it's freaking me out," Todd said to Em as he parked his butt on the edge of her desk.

"Of course I was smiling. Gwen just told me her dog loves my biscuits, and she ordered three dozen more."

Gwen swiveled in her chair, facing them. "She doesn't love your biscuits. She adores them."

Todd crossed his arms and cocked his head. "Really? You're not just trying to stroke Em's ego so she'll take a shift for you?"

Em hadn't been back from vacation for more than a day before Gwen asked her to take one of her shifts—which Em was proud to report she hadn't—so there might be some truth in Todd's remark. Still...

"Hey," Em said, "I'll have you know Gwen's dog isn't the only one that loves my biscuits. The chief's dog loves them too, and so does Gus. I already have orders for ten dozen more."

She'd gotten bored on the weekend. It wasn't the same without Josh hanging around. But they weren't fake-dating anymore so she hadn't been sure how he'd feel about an invitation to hang out. Actually, after he'd talked to her at Highland Brew Friday night, she'd had a feeling he wouldn't be receptive to the idea of spending time with her. He'd thanked her for the cupcakes, mentioned he'd sent her a pic of the team eating them, and talked about the game and about how proud he was of her for standing up for the Sisterhood at the town hall meeting—a normal conversation that hadn't felt normal at all.

So instead of risking rejection, she'd filled her time making doggy biscuits for Gus. She'd made so many of them that she'd brought them to work with her Monday morning, and they'd been gone before noon.

"Okay, don't get defensive. It's just that I've sampled your cupcakes." Todd shrugged. "I guess dogs aren't as fussy as humans."

Since Em had sampled one of her cupcakes, she understood what Todd meant. She had no idea why dogs seemed to like her cookies either.

Gwen held up her phone. It was a photo of her shih tzu with two of Em's cookies on Instagram. "I told you to come up with a name for your business, Em. Everyone's asking who made the doggy biscuits."

Todd leaned in to check out the photo. "Okay. Those pumpkin and witch cookies are adorbs. I even want to try one. Gwen's right. You need a name for your business if you want to capitalize on the publicity." He tapped his forefinger on his lips. "How about Pawsitively Delicious?"

"Umm. I—" Em began before Gwen cut her off.

"Barks and Biscuits!"

"The Dogmother!"

Em held up her hands. "Stop. As much as I appreciate your ideas, I'm not starting a doggy biscuit business. I'm just doing it for fun. It's relaxing. I bake when I'm watching TV."

"Oh, like knitting," Gwen said. "I do the same thing."

"I do paint-by-numbers," Todd said.

Em pressed her lips together, trying not to laugh.

"Hey." He swatted her. "They're high-end–looking paintings, even if they are paint-by-numbers." He opened his phone, showing her what looked like a professional oil painting on the wall.

"Oh wow, that's really beautiful," Em said, and she wasn't kidding.

"Em's right. It's a gorgeous painting, Todd. If I didn't know—" The sound of someone clearing their throat interrupted Gwen.

They looked over their shoulders to see their boss standing there. "If the three of you are finished talking about your hobbies, I'd suggest you get back to work. Todd and Gwen, I expect an update on the threatening letters and swatting incident at Seaton House by two. Em, the Chamber of Commerce has a meeting tonight at seven. I'd like you to attend as community liaison to discuss their plans for Halloween."

"Sure." So much for fulfilling her dog biscuit orders tonight.

As soon as the chief disappeared from view, Gwen moved her chair in front of Em's desk. "The *Herald* has been asking the chief for a statement about the swatting at Seaton House. They're inferring that someone in the department messed up and that O'Brien has been falsely accused."

Todd hopped off her desk, grabbed his chair, and rolled it beside Em. "Any ideas? Gwen and I don't have anything. We contacted the telephone company to trace the spoofed phone number and came up empty."

"First of all, no one accused O'Brien," Em said. "So my guess is, if he is behind it, he's using the *Herald* to find out where we're at on the case." Em woke up her computer. "It's not like someone needs technical expertise to spoof a caller ID, right?"

"No. But I did a little research into swatting and the first instances seemed to have been in the online communities, especially the video-gaming streams. So what do you think? O'Brien's son is probably into video games and more technically savvy than his old man. Any chance he put the kid up to it?"

"A couple weeks ago, I might've said yes, but I've gotten to know Drew. He's a good kid, and his relationship with O'Brien isn't great. I can't see him doing something like that for his stepfather. Plus, when I lectured the team about swatting, I didn't see any signs of guilt on his face. His or anyone else on the team for that matter."

But another suspect came to mind. Someone who was very involved in video games, and someone who had as strong a motive as O'Brien to get Jenny to leave town. Maybe stronger, because as far as Em knew, O'Brien had no idea that Jenny might also have a legal claim to Henderson Farm.

Except Em had no idea if her suspicions were anything more than that. She had no hard evidence to back up her theory that Edward Henderson was Willy's father. At this point, it was just a gut feeling. She also hadn't come across anything to validate her suspicions in Jenny's research material. Willy's birth certificate listed his father as unknown.

Em shut down her computer and pushed back from her desk. "There's something I have to check into," she said, grabbing her jacket from the back of her chair. "I won't be long."

Josh glanced at his phone. "It's almost lunch. I'm going to grab a bite. You want anything, Gwen?"

She rolled back to her desk and held up a bagged lunch. "I'm good, thanks."

As soon as they'd pushed through the exit doors of the station, Todd said, "Out with it, and don't tell me you have no idea what I'm talking about. I saw the expression on your face."

"It's just a hunch. And to be honest, I hope I'm wrong. You'll know as soon as I do."

"Okay. Where are you on the Henderson case?"

"About the same place as I was when we talked about it yesterday. No real evidence. Just a lot of supposition."

"Share away." When she hesitated, he said, "You promised to keep me in the loop, Em."

"Okay. I pretty much verified everything Josh's mom said about Edward's younger brother, LeRoy. His name showed up several times in back issues of the *Herald*, mostly for drunk and disorderly. He was wild with a bad temper and prone to fights, and he didn't settle down when he got older," she said as they walked across the parking lot together.

When she reached the Camaro, Em leaned against the car and continued. "According to everything I've read about Edward, he was the exact opposite. Strong and steady, a quiet, well-respected man. And, as Patsy indicated, it was apparently common knowledge that their parents planned to leave the farm and property to Edward. And I found proof. There was a will on file in the records of the Hendersons' attorney that predated Edward's death, and the bulk of the estate was to go to him."

"So you believe that LeRoy murdered his brother to ensure his inheritance?"

She nodded. "I do. And if I'm right that May's son is Edward's, it makes sense that LeRoy framed May for his brother's murder, not only to protect himself but to get her and her son out of the picture. It's not a bad plan when you think about it. Poison is the weapon of choice for the majority of women, especially at that time, and the Seaton sisters had ready access to a wide array of toxic substances."

"True. But while you believe May died of natural causes, which the records from the doctor who worked at the jailhouse seemed to support, that leaves us with Clara, who you believe was murdered."

Jenny hadn't been able to find anything in the jailhouse records to corroborate her theory that May was murdered—she'd based her supposition on the suspicious timing of the sisters' deaths. But with help from Todd and Gwen, Em had found the doctor, whose practice had been passed down through the family, and his great-granddaughter had been happy to share his notes.

"It does, and I do. Jenny was able to get a copy of the file because Clara's case had never been officially closed. There was nothing about Clara having evidence that exonerated May, but there was a note in a Jackson County attorney's calendar about a meeting with Clara Seaton, scheduled for three days after she died."

"So what are you thinking? That she'd found proof of her sister's innocence and someone killed her before she could give it to the attorney?"

"Yeah." She nodded. "Have you had any luck finding out where the farmhand disappeared to?"

"None. But I think I might've found a relative on his mother's side. He's ninety-five and lives in a seniors' residence in Jackson County so I thought I'd take a drive over after my meeting with Gabe. Any chance you want to join me?"

"Do you even have to ask?"

He laughed and walked to his car. "I'm counting on you to figure out who our swatter is before our meeting with Gabe."

"No pressure," she said, unsure what to do if she was right.

By the time she'd pulled into her driveway, she still had no idea what she'd do or how she'd broach her suspicions with Steve. But she did have an excuse for popping over. She needed to get the sweatshirt done in time for Josh's birthday, which was two days away.

She unlocked her front door and sprinted into her

bedroom, grabbing the sweatshirt and the team's baby photos off her desk where they had sat this past week. Hopefully, she'd not only figure out if Steve was behind the swatting, he'd also create an online photo template for Josh's sweatshirt while she questioned him.

Sometimes she hated her job, she thought as she locked her front door and headed down her driveway. The low whine of saws and the pounding of hammers at Seaton House followed her all the way to Steve and Jenny's.

When Steve answered the door with a sweetly befuddled smile, Em was tempted to pretend she'd just gotten a call and had to leave.

As she trudged back to her house without the sweatshirt and the baby photos fifteen minutes later, she wished she had gotten a call. She knew what she should do but she was torn given the consequences of what that would mean to Steve, Jenny, and Charlotte. Which was probably why, when she slid behind the wheel of the Camaro, she called the one person she could confide in. Or maybe she was just using it as an excuse to talk to Josh. She missed him; she missed them.

The phone rang several times, and Em tapped a finger on the steering wheel, wondering if Josh was avoiding her calls. She was about to disconnect when he answered. He sounded busy and a little abrupt.

"Bad time to call?" she asked.

"Yeah. Sorry. I just spilled coffee all over my desk."

"I should let you go," she said, hoping he didn't hear the disappointment in her voice. She never would've fake-dated him if she thought it would ruin their friendship, and that's what this felt like.

"Yeah. I...No wait. What's up? Is everything okay?"

"Are you sure you have time? I don't want to—"

"Em, talk to me."

She told him about her suspicion that Steve was behind the swatting and how the evasive way he responded to her questions made her think she was right. "I should've come out and asked him directly, but part of me didn't want to because then I'd have to do something about it. What do you think? Do you think Steve did it?"

"I wish I didn't, but yeah, I think you're right. And we know exactly what Steve's motivation is. He doesn't want to live in Seaton House, and it's obvious that Jenny does. Whereas O'Brien's motivation isn't exactly clear."

"Well, we know he wants to win the mayor's race at any cost so he can build his big-box stores. Steve's swatting HFPD created the perfect opportunity for O'Brien, and he took advantage of it."

"But O'Brien has no way of knowing about your theory that Willy was Edward Henderson's son and that Jenny could have as much right as him to claim the Hendersons' estate."

"Jenny might even have a stronger claim," Em said.

"So what are you going to do about Steve?"

"That's what I wanted to talk to you about. There's a part of me that wants to let it go and keep an eye on him. I really like him and Jenny, and it's not like Steve would follow through with the threats."

"I don't think he would either. But the swatting thing could've been dangerous, Em."

"I talked to him about what could've happened. I didn't accuse him of swatting HFPD—which I doubt we could prove anyway—but I made sure he knew that I suspected he was behind it without coming out and saying it."

"I guess... Hang on a sec, Em."

She heard someone talking to him in the background and felt bad for calling him at work. "Don't worry about it, Josh. You sound busy. I'll let you go."

"Yeah, thanks. It's been one of those days."

"I'll see you at your..." She trailed off at the sound of dead air. He'd just hung up on her! She didn't understand what was going on with him. Had she completely misread his feelings for her? She rested her head against the seat, replaying their conversation in her head. Maybe he was just having a bad day. Maybe he...

Her cell phone ringing cut her off mid-thought. Her heart leaped thinking it was Josh calling to apologize for hanging up on her without saying goodbye. But it was Todd. His meeting with the chief had been postponed so he'd moved up his meeting with the farmhand's cousin.

"Sure. I'll meet you at the seniors' residence in fifteen minutes."

She arrived at the residence at the same time as Todd. It took almost twenty minutes for them to find the farmhand's cousin. He was taking part in a pumpkin-carving contest in the arts and crafts room. They waited for him to finish up.

"Great looking pumpkin," Em said, offering to carry

it to his room. The older man looked like a strong wind would blow him over, but he was spry and could easily pass for someone twenty years his junior.

"I could've done better but I didn't want to put Addie to shame." He winked. "I'm hoping she'll go to the Halloween costume party with me." He opened the door to his room and offered them something to drink.

"We're fine, thank you," Em said, following him inside. She set the pumpkin on the table. "We wanted to ask you a couple questions about your cousin. He was a farmhand for the Henderson family and disappeared right around the time of Clara Seaton's death."

The older man nodded, gesturing for them to have a seat as he put on the kettle. "I was born five years after my cousin disappeared but my family talked about the events of that spring all the time. I suppose it's not surprising given the upset it caused in the family. My mother was the youngest of six girls. They were a close family, and my cousin leaving like that devastated everyone."

"So he'd never told anyone he planned on moving away?" Todd asked.

"No. Never said a word. By all accounts, it was completely out of character for him. As out of character as him stealing money from the Hendersons."

"LeRoy accused him of stealing money?" Em asked.

"Yep, said it right to my uncle's face when he went looking for his son."

"You don't believe your cousin would've stolen the money?" Todd asked.

"No. He was raised better than that, but even if he

hadn't been, he never would've stolen from the Hendersons. Edward was his best friend." He unplugged the whistling kettle and walked into a small sitting room. He rummaged around in a drawer and returned with a photo album. He set it on the table, flipping to a page in the middle of the album. He tapped a gnarled finger on a black-and-white photo that had yellowed with age. "There he is with Edward." He tapped another photo. "Here too. My aunt used to say he was closer to Edward than his own brother. Edward's death hit my cousin hard. They said he wasn't the same after. If anything, the family thought he was getting worse, and then he disappeared."

"And no one ever heard from him?" Em asked.

"Not a word."

"So what do you think?" Todd asked Em ten minutes later as they walked across the parking lot. "Did his cousin avenge Edward's death by killing Clara and then disappear because he couldn't live with his guilt or face his family?"

"It's possible he could've blamed Clara for Edward's death. The town believed that Clara and May were both witches, after all. But why would he wait for more than a year to seek his revenge?" She shook her head. "No, I don't think he had anything to do with Clara's murder, but I also don't think it's a coincidence he disappeared around the same time as Clara died."

"Agreed," Todd said, opening his car door. "Are you heading back to the station or are you off to football practice?"

She glanced at the time on her phone. Her shift was

technically over and there was a practice today. She opened her mouth, thinking she'd get Todd's opinion on her conversation with Josh before she decided whether or not to go to the practice. And that's when she knew how bad she had it for Josh.

"I'm heading home. I have ten dozen dog biscuits to make."

Chapter Twenty-Four

♥

Em parked in Bri and Cal's driveway on Marigold Lane on Saturday night. They lived across the street from Josh. His front yard looked like the gates of hell had opened, spilling its demons onto his lawn. Em shuddered at the sight of a seven-foot-tall, two-headed animatronic clown monster near the front door. She hated clowns, which Josh knew from when they watched the *It* miniseries as kids and she'd run screaming from the living room.

But she was one hundred percent positive Josh's two-headed clown monster had nothing to do with her. She couldn't say the same about his display though. She should've known he'd compete with her for Best Decorated Halloween House. He was one of the most competitive men she knew, she thought with a smile. But her smile faded when she remembered their last conversation. All she'd been able to think about for the past two days was how to repair their relationship.

She glanced at the bags on the passenger seat. If she didn't chicken out, she was hoping he'd know when she gave him his birthday gift that she was ready to move on, start fresh with him, and date for real this time.

The door opened, and Bri stepped onto the front porch.

Em grabbed the gift bags off the passenger seat. "Let me guess, you and Cal are going as Barbie and Ken."

"Blame Izzy. It was her idea. And you're going as...you?"

"I just got off work, and I didn't have time to change. Hey, buddy," she said when Gus scampered down the porch steps to greet her.

"Izzy, Auntie Em and I are heading to Josh's," Bri called into the house. "Text if you need us."

"We'll be fine," Izzy said, coming to stand in the doorway. She frowned at Em. "You can't go in your uniform."

"I can, and I am. Besides, it's not Halloween yet."

"So you'll dress up for Halloween?"

"Ah, no. Here. Catch." She tossed a bag of doggie treats to Bri. They were her most popular cookie, peanut butter and pumpkin.

Bri caught the bag and peeked inside. "Em, these are adorable."

She shrugged. "Dogs seem to like them. I've got orders coming in from half the station now." She'd had to refuse a few of them. She wasn't about to let her new hobby take over her life.

After she'd finished decorating another batch of cookies last night, she'd gotten to work on her therapy homework. Bri had suggested she make a list, a life list, not a bucket list, and Em had an epiphany. There wasn't anything on her list she couldn't do alone or enjoy doing by herself, but when she pictured herself leaf peeping, biking, hiking, or paddling, Josh was with her. Now she had to work up the nerve to ask him out. After their conversation Thursday afternoon, it would take a lot of nerve.

"Look at you, Auntie Em. You've got a side hustle," Izzy said, reaching into the bag for a treat. Em thought she was going to give the cookie to Gus but she bit into it and then nodded. "They're good." She waved them off. "Have fun. And tell Uncle Josh to save me some food. I'll bring him his present tomorrow."

Em glanced at Bri's empty hands. She didn't want to be the only one giving him a gift. He'd clearly stated *no gifts* on the e-invite. "Did you get Josh a present?"

She nodded. "Cal took it over earlier."

Em lifted her chin at the front yard. "It looks like Josh has been busy trying to one-up me for the Best Decorated Halloween House."

"It wasn't Josh. Patsy and Phil were out there the entire day setting up the displays. Patsy has basically taken over his party."

"You know Patsy. She loves a celebration."

"Yeah, but she's never taken over Josh's birthday before. The menu is one thing, but the decorations and guest list? Cal thinks she's concerned about Josh. He hasn't been himself. Cal's worried about him too."

"He doesn't think there's something physically wrong with him, does he?" she asked, unable to keep the worry from her voice.

"No. It's just...he's acting very un-Josh-like. You

know how he's always up for a good time? He left early from Highland Brew last Friday, and Cal says he doesn't seem into the party. It's weird. He's acting more like you, and you're acting more like him these days."

"Please. I haven't turned into Suzy Sunshine, and I'm not easygoing. I still don't like small talk, no matter what it looked like last Friday, and just ask Todd and Gwen. I'm as grumpy as always at work."

It was mostly true. But the other day, Gwen had called her Suzy Sunshine. Em had found it annoying and slightly worrisome. But she didn't want Bri to connect Em 2.0—that's what Todd called her, mostly because he knew it bugged her—to Josh in case he didn't want to date her after all.

A car pulled out of a driveway up from Josh's, and Em took Bri by the arm. They'd been standing in the middle of the road.

"So you really think Josh is acting like me?" she asked as they stepped onto the sidewalk. To Em that implied he was missing her as much as she missed him.

The only reason she wasn't moping around too was because that's what she'd been doing for the past six months. She didn't count the first year after losing Brad. She was entitled to grieve. But looking back, it was easy to see how she'd allowed her grief to suck nearly every ounce of pleasure from her life.

"I do, and so must Patsy because she invited Robyn to Josh's party."

Em knew who Robyn was, and she also remembered that Josh had seemed interested in the attractive paramedic at Saturday Singles Night. And just like that,

Em's hopes for tonight fell at her feet and died. She bent down and picked up the gift bags she'd just dropped on Josh's front lawn, checking to see if the bottle had broken. It hadn't but now she didn't think she could work up the courage to give it to him.

And then something else occurred to her. "But why would Patsy set him up with Robyn? She's always wanted Josh and me to get together, and she wasn't shy about letting us know."

Em loved Patsy and Phil, and she loved that they loved her for their son. Even when she hadn't known she'd one day fall in love with him. It was just nice to know that she was loved by the two people who at one time she'd hoped would fill parental roles in her life. She didn't know what hurt more, Josh dating someone other than her or his parents picking someone other than her for him.

Bri put a hand on Em's arm, stopping her just before they reached the front door. Then Bri looked at the two-headed clown monster towering over them and pulled Em a couple feet away.

"I know there's something going on with you and Josh." She shook her head when Em opened her mouth. "Don't bother denying it. Your reaction to Patsy inviting Robyn just confirmed it. As much as I wish you'd shared with me about Brad and the baby last year, I understood why it was hard for you. But this, Em, this is something you're supposed to share with your best friend. We always talked about who we had a crush on."

Bri sounded hurt, and Em felt awful. "I couldn't talk to you about my feelings for Josh because I hadn't told you about Brad visiting me or about the baby. And now I don't feel like I can because you're married to my brother, and you saw how he acted when Josh and I were fake-dating."

"I have a feeling he acted that way because it felt more like you guys were real-dating than fake-dating."

"Either way, he acted like a jerk, and I'm not putting you in the middle."

"I've talked to Cal about how he acted. He's a guy so it's not always easy to get to the heart of the matter, but reading between the lines, I think he sensed you were holding something back. He took on the role of your parents—both mom and dad—when you guys were young, and old habits die hard. It doesn't matter that he loves Josh like a brother and that you're thirty. In Cal's eyes, you'll always be his little sister."

"Yeah, well, he doesn't need to protect me anymore. He can protect you and Izzy."

"You, out of anyone, should be able to empathize with Cal, Em. You acted just like him when you tried to keep us apart."

"I don't know what you're talking about."

"Really? You don't remember letting your brother believe I'd left for Europe when I was right across the road? Or how about—"

Em winced. It hadn't been her finest moment. "Okay. I get your point. But Josh won't date me if it upsets Cal. He made it clear he'd choose his friendship with Cal over a relationship with me." She caught the worry in Bri's eyes before she blinked it away. "You don't think that bodes well for us, do you? Don't bother answering.

I know it doesn't." She sighed and looked down at the gift bag. "I don't know why I thought it would work out between us anyway."

"Em, you don't know if he still feels that way. Give him and your relationship a—" The two-headed clown came to life, red eyes glowing in the dark, its heads moving from side to side, and Em and Bri let loose earsplitting shrieks. Strobe lights swirled in the yard, and from somewhere close by, speakers pumped out Michael Jackson's "Thriller."

Em heard a chuckle and turned to see Phil coming around the side of the house. "Got them good, Cal," he called over his shoulder.

After saying hi to Phil and assuring him the front yard display was terrifying, Em went in search of Josh. She wanted to get it over with before the guests started arriving.

"Emmy." Patsy enfolded her in a warm, motherly hug. Then, with her hands on Em's shoulders, she stepped back to look at her. "You need a costume, sweetheart. I have a few at home. Which would you prefer, sexy nurse, sexy schoolgirl, sexy French maid, or sexy witch?"

Em had a feeling the costumes had been worn by Patsy and wondered how Josh would react when she told him about the offer. "I think I'm good, Patsy. But thanks anyway." She looked at the buffet tables set up in Josh's living room. "You've put out quite the spread. It looks great." Every dish on the table went with the Halloween theme including the purple-marbled deviled eggs with one eye in each. "Is Josh around?"

"He's in his bedroom. Putting on his costume." Patsy

reached out and fluffed Em's hair. "Undo a couple buttons on your shirt," Patsy said, popping Em's collar as she reluctantly did what she suggested.

Patsy's narrowed gaze moved over Em's face. "Hang on a sec." She reached for a purse under the table and pulled out a tube of siren-red lipstick, slicking it over Em's lips. "There you go." She patted Em's cheek. "You're a sexy cop, or as sexy as we can manage without the short leather skirt. Phil and I better get our costumes on. Guests will be arriving anytime." She hustled off, calling for Phil.

Em had stayed for a week at Josh's with her brother so she knew he was the third room on the right at the end of the hall. She knocked. "Josh, it's Em." She heard the nervous quiver in her voice and cleared her throat.

"Come on in. I'm decent."

She kind of wished he wasn't. "I'm not," she said as she walked into his bedroom. "Your mom turned me into a sexy cop. I should say she *tried* to turn me into a sexy cop."

"You had it right the first time," Josh murmured, and then he looked like he wanted to clunk his head against the bureau where he stood painting a line of blood at the corner of his mouth. The black pants he wore with a white dress shirt and the black cape lying on the tub chair in the corner of the room were a dead giveaway he was going as Dracula.

"What's up?" he asked.

His bed had a beautiful rustic wood headboard and an incredibly comfy mattress that she sank into when she sat on the edge of the bed. His leaf-green comforter was as cozy and welcoming as the mattress, and she found herself stretching out on the bed with her head propped on the pillows.

"You tired?" he asked, a trace of amusement in his voice, but there was a touch of something else that she hadn't heard before when Josh spoke to her. A distance, a coolness she didn't like. She needed to get them back on track, the same track they'd been on a little more than a week before.

"Did your mom tell you I paid a visit to the kindergarten class yesterday? We did a read-aloud of Halloween stories." She'd planned to call him as soon as she'd left the class later in the afternoon but Patsy had told her he'd taken another shift at HFFD. It seemed like he was the one working all the time now.

Josh turned and leaned against the bureau. He crossed his arms, the white dress shirt pulling tight and showing off his broad shoulders. "Please tell me you didn't try and get O'Brien's daughter's DNA."

She dragged her gaze to his face. "No, I didn't need to. Charlotte and O'Brien's daughter could be identical twins." She lifted her hip to pull out her phone, turning the screen with the picture of the two girls to him.

He leaned in without coming closer, as if he didn't want to get near the bed with her in it. "Em, you can't take their picture without permission."

"I'm just showing it to you, and then I'll delete it. But it's incredible how much they look alike, isn't it?"

"Yeah. Mom said a few people have commented on it." He turned back to the mirror, adding more blood to the side of his mouth. "So where does the case stand now?"

She sat up, swinging her legs off the bed. "I'm taking a wait-and-see approach with Steve. I haven't completely ruled out O'Brien after learning that Assistant Coach Delaney has been hanging around with him, and supposedly he's a huge gamer."

"He is. And Delaney wants my job so he'd do whatever O'Brien asked him to, even if it was illegal. I actually hope it's him and not Steve."

Josh was right. It had been obvious that Delaney thought he should've been awarded the job instead of Josh. Delaney had been the team's assistant coach under the previous coach.

"I hope so too," she said, glancing at the gift bags on the bed. She should do it now and get it over with. Instead, she said, "Todd and I interviewed the farmhand's cousin the other day."

"That's great. Did they have any idea where he ended up?"

She told him what the farmhand's cousin had said.

"It keeps circling back to LeRoy," Josh murmured.

"It does. But the thing I found most interesting was how close Edward and the farmhand had been, and how his grief had seemingly increased a year after Edward's death."

"So the farmhand would have been motivated to find out the truth if he believed LeRoy had killed Edward."

She nodded and got up from the bed. "I really need to find that box."

"I hear Neil and his crew are ripping apart the second floor so maybe they'll find something." Josh glanced at the door as the sound of laughter and conversation drifted into the room. "We should probably get out there." He walked over to get his cape and was putting it on when Em thrust the gift bags at him. "The sweatshirt is from the kids. The other thing is from me. Happy birthday."

He set both bags on the bed and then pulled out the navy sweatshirt. He laughed. "This is great, even though you did it to get evidence for the case."

"Yeah, but the boys don't know that. And let me tell you, it wasn't easy superimposing their baby faces over their teenage faces."

"You did it yourself?"

"I might've had some help from Steve."

"Was that before or after you accused him of swatting HFPD?"

"Around the same time. Anyway, the guys will be quizzing you on Monday, so you better work out who's who tomorrow."

"I will, and thanks, Em. It's a thoughtful gift even if you hadn't intended it to be." He lifted the other bag. "What's this?"

"It's something from me." As much as she didn't want to tell him why she'd gifted him a bottle of cologne, without an explanation it might seem an odd choice, an intimate choice. But the explanation was also her way of showing him that she was ready to move on with him. At the same time protecting her from humiliation if he didn't feel the same.

"It's cologne?" he said, opening the box.

She nodded. "Montblanc Legend. It smells good but there's a gift receipt in the bag if you want something else."

He sat on the bed, uncapped the bottle, and sniffed. "It smells great." He smiled. "It's about time I changed cologne. Amber bought the Armani for me every birthday and every Christmas. I have three bottles left."

She took a deep breath. It was now or never. "Brad used to wear Armani. I brought the last bottle with me when I moved back home, and I'd spritz it on my sweatshirts."

He got a pained look on his face. "And every time we were together, I'd sniff your shoulder and ask if you'd used my cologne. I'm so sorry, Em."

"You didn't know. I should've told you." She focused on the bottle in Josh's hand instead of on his handsome face. "I threw out the last of Brad's cologne."

He got up off the bed and came to stand in front of her, tipping her chin with his knuckle, his eyes searching hers. "What are you trying to tell me, Em?"

"That I'm ready—"

"Knock, knock." Patsy poked her head around the door. "Joshie, Robyn's here."

"Mom, just give Em and me a minute. I'll—"

"I don't think that's a good idea, sweetheart." She looked over her shoulder. "He's here, Cal."

Chapter Twenty-Five

♥

It was Halloween, and Em had a roomful of witches in her house on Sugar Maple Road. Bri as Glinda the Good Witch, Izzy as Hermione Granger, and Raine as Maleficent had decided to get ready at her place for the All Hallows' Eve party at the community center. The party would get underway right after the kid's Halloween Parade on Main Street. The street was closed to cars from five thirty to seven, and all the local businesses handed out candy to trick-or-treaters under the age of thirteen.

Em didn't believe the three witches were at her place because they thought it would be fun to get ready together. She knew darn well they were here to make sure she wore a costume and didn't chicken out like she had at Josh's birthday. As she'd tried to explain to Bri, she hadn't chickened out. She'd gotten cut off by his mother, who appeared to want him to go back to his serial dating ways, which Em found strange. And then, when half the women attending his party in their sexy costumes kept *accidentally* falling into Josh's lap as he played his guitar, Em had had second thoughts about the whole thing.

"I still don't understand why you didn't ask him to the All Hallows' Eve party when you were at his place Saturday night," Bri said as she fitted the blond wig on Em's head.

Em was going as Sarah Sanderson from *Hocus Pocus*. According to Bri and Izzy, Sarah was a sexy witch, and they thought it was time Josh saw Em's sexy side. They said her sexy cop from his party didn't count or cut it.

"I wasn't going to ask him in front of everyone, and he was never alone."

"Okay, but his party was Saturday, and it's Tuesday. You had plenty of time to ask him to go to the All Hallows' Eve party with you, and then you wouldn't be stressing about what to do on your date," Bri said.

"I don't know why you think I'm stressing about it. I just showed you my list of potential date ideas."

"You showed us your list too," Izzy added unhelpfully.

Em had also shown the list to Todd, which was a big mistake because she hadn't noticed Gwen had returned to her desk. Gwen hadn't been pleased to learn that the date ideas had nothing to do with Neil and everything to do with Josh. And in an effort to soothe her coworker's hurt feelings and her worry about Neil, Em had promised to help Gwen find him someone to date.

"If you weren't stressing about it, you would have asked him out already, which is why I'm worried you're going to chicken out again," Bri said as she added more shadow to Em's eyes. Apparently Bri was going for a smoky eye, whatever that meant.

"Hello. It was the lead-up to Halloween," Em said. "I've been a little busy. You may not be aware of this but every house in the Silver Creek neighborhood was TP-ed late Saturday night, and then we had a gang of pumpkin smashers running amok in the chief's subdivision Sunday night, and last night, someone soaped half the shop windows on Main Street." She held up her hands as proof that she'd spent part of her morning cleaning windows. "But why are you just harping on me about chickening out? Raine did too."

Em was beginning to wonder if something was going on with the mothers of thirtysomething-year-old sons because Quinn's mom had set him up with his date for the party, the same as Patsy had set up Josh with Robyn. Except unlike Quinn's mom, who did not like Raine, Patsy loved Em. And yes, she was still trying to figure out why Patsy had set up Josh with anyone other than her.

"I didn't chicken out. This is all Bri and Izzy's idea," Raine said, admiring her long black nails. "I don't know why I should be the one to ask Quinn out anyway. He should ask me out."

"He has, Mom. Three times."

"Izzy's right, Raine," Bri said. "You can't expect Quinn to put himself out there again when you keep rejecting him."

"I didn't reject him. I...I've just been busy. Between my mother's campaign and getting the trauma center up and running, as well as having a seventeen-year-old daughter, I don't have a moment to myself."

"Bock, bock, bock," Em said, which earned her a pursed-lip look from Maleficent.

"The time for chickening out is over," said Glinda the Good Witch. "You're both going to embrace your inner witch. And you'll have Izzy and me there for support. Izzy, you'll be your mom's emotional support person and coach, and I'll be Em's."

"I thought I'd just bring Gus," Em said.

"Dogs are allowed in the parade but they're not allowed at the party," Izzy reminded her. "Someone's doing a doggy daycare in the park, I think."

"You and your friends aren't working it?" Em asked her.

"No, we have other plans tonight," she said without meeting Em's gaze. "You need more mascara, Mom."

"How can she need more mascara? She's wearing fake eyelashes." Em crossed her arms. "Izzy, what are you guys up to tonight? And it better not be hanging out at Seaton House."

"I told you before, Aunt Em, I'm not a narc. But I promise, we're not going to Seaton House."

"All you guys could talk about was Seaton House so excuse me if I don't believe that you're not planning to go to the local haunted house on Halloween night," Em said.

"Fine. We were, but Mike told us it isn't safe. They've ripped apart the second floor, and they have propane blowers drying out the place. Drew didn't want to go anyway." She bowed her head. Obviously that was a tidbit she hadn't meant to share.

"Are you dating Drew O'Brien?" Em asked.

"Honestly, Em, I don't know where you get your ideas." Raine waved her hand as if swatting away Em's question like it was an annoying fly. "Of course Izzy isn't dating Drew O'Brien. She's focused on school and her friends, not boys. But if she did date someone, it certainly wouldn't be the son of the man who's been slandering her grandmother."

"Drew isn't like his father, Mom," Izzy said hotly, totally giving herself away.

"You are dating him!" Raine bent over her phone, frantically typing a message.

Em leaned over and glanced at the screen. "So the first person you turn to when you're upset is Quinn."

"I don't have to tell Cal. Bri's here." She looked at Bri. "Feel free to step in at any time."

"Izzy is seventeen, Raine. And you know as well as I do, she's smart and responsible and an excellent judge of character."

Izzy gave Bri a grateful smile. "Bri's right. I am seventeen, and I can date whomever I like." She shrugged. "I like Drew, and trust me, I thought he was a jerk too. Hot, but a jerk."

Raine groaned, and Bri and Em laughed. "Don't worry, Raine," Em said. "Drew is a good kid. A really good kid. I'm glad he has Izzy to talk to. The campaign hasn't been easy for him either."

"Thanks, Aunt Em. Drew hates his stepfather. He's horrible to him, and he doesn't want him to win the election. He spent all day Sunday putting out Gran's flyers with me."

"I hope his stepfather doesn't find out," Em murmured.

"He wore a hoodie and shades." Izzy said with a smile that indicated he'd looked hot in his disguise, which Raine obviously noticed because she said, "I think we need to have another of our mother-daughter chats."

"Thanks, Mom. But we had the birds-and-the-bees conversation when I was twelve, and you and Dad had the sex chat with me when I was fifteen, so I've got this."

"I'm sure you do, but if ever you have any questions about anything, you know you can talk to the three of us, individually or as a group," Bri said.

"Group chat works for me," Em said, holding up her phone. "We're all on WhatsApp together."

Izzy's grin faded. "Aunt Em, don't tell Uncle Josh, but Drew doesn't want to play football. He loves being on the team because of his friends, and he thinks Uncle Josh is the bomb. He really likes you too. But the only reason he plays is because his stepfather makes him. Mr. O'Brien hired Assistant Coach Delaney to practice with Drew every day after school. He's nasty to Drew. I think he's jealous because Drew is such a good quarterback but doesn't want to play. Coach Delaney wanted to play but he wasn't good enough. He doesn't like Uncle Josh or you, and when Drew stands up for you guys, he works him twice as hard. He makes Drew do full-contact drills with some of his friends, and they're big guys. I'm afraid he's going to get hurt, Auntie Em." She chewed on her thumbnail. "Is there anything you can do?"

There were plenty of things she'd like to do, but they were illegal. "I'm glad you told me, Izzy. And trust me, one way or another, I'll make sure Delaney doesn't get near Drew again," she said and stood up.

"Em, where are you going?" Bri asked.

"To have a chat with Delaney and O'Brien."

"Aunt Em, you can't go now. You're dressed like a witch."

"And you're supposed to be going to the All Hallows' Eve Party," Bri said.

Em checked her phone. "It's only six. The party doesn't start until seven."

* * *

Em drove to the O'Briens' house in the Bragg Creek subdivision. The homes were large and nestled among the trees on one-acre lots. Several of the homes on O'Brien's street would give Em and Josh a run for the money for Best Decorated Halloween House. Not O'Brien's though. He'd doubled down on his attack on the Sisterhood and earlier in the week had started a war against Halloween so it wasn't like he could decorate his house for the holiday.

Em felt bad for his little girl. She'd been as excited for Halloween as the rest of the kids in her class. Although no one in the kindergarten class was as excited for the holiday as Charlotte. The family were going as Darrin, Samantha, and Tabitha, characters from the sixties' sitcom *Bewitched*.

Em had been keeping a close eye on Steve, and there'd

been no more threatening letters, calls, or swatting incidents. Steve was probably resigned to the fact that he couldn't change his wife's mind. As Jenny had proven, she wasn't easily scared away.

Em sympathized with Steve. If he was behind the letters and swatting, she understood why he'd resort to extreme measures he never would've considered in the past. After all, the family had nearly drowned, and the man was clearly terrified of wildlife and ghosts. But lately, he seemed to be doing better. They'd been at Josh's birthday party, hanging out with a few couples from the neighborhood, and Steve had begun teaching classes at the community center.

But while it looked like Em no longer had to worry about Steve, Peter O'Brien was another story. She couldn't rule out that he'd been behind the letters, call, and swatting, and the election was still a few days away. And if he won, Em might be looking for another job. Josh might also lose his head coach position.

Em glanced at herself in the rearview mirror and considered going home to change but by the time she got re-dressed and redid her makeup, she'd be late for the party, and Josh might go home early. She wanted to do this tonight. She didn't think he'd say no, but if he did, she had the perfect cover. Between the music and the lights from the disco balls, she could easily get away with pretending he'd misheard her.

The front door opened, and Drew came out, yelling something over his shoulder. Em got out of the car, and he stared at her.

"It's Em," she said, closing the car door.

"Cool costume." He jerked his thumb at the house. "But we're not giving out candy this year."

She rolled her eyes. "I'm not trick-or-treating, Drew. I've come to talk to your mom and dad about your after-hours football practices with Coach Delaney."

"I told Izzy not to say anything." He looked away, hitching his backpack higher up his shoulder. "It's no big deal, Em. I can handle it. It's not for much longer anyway."

"Does your mom know how you feel about football, Drew? Has she seen the note Josh sent home with you guys?" Em knew Josh had laid out the reasons why he was decreasing practices and contact drills in the message to the parents.

"Peter took it from me before my mom saw it, and he told me that I'd be sorry if I mentioned it to her."

There were those three words again. Maybe her initial suspicions had been correct and O'Brien, not Steve, had been behind the letter writing, calls, and swatting.

Drew continued. "I can't tell my mom I don't want to play ball. She'd stand up for me, and it'd get ugly. I can't put her in the middle of it."

The front door opened. "Drew, who are you talking to?" O'Brien called out.

Drew got a panicked look on his face. "Don't say anything about the practices with Delaney, please, Em."

She nodded and stepped away from him. "Officer Scott, Mr. O'Brien. I'm responding to a call that someone's being murdered on your property. Maybe a couple of witches?" She winked. "Don't worry, I figured it was a prank. Lucky for you I did or you would've had twenty cops and the media showing up at your door. Not a great look with the election a few days away.

"Anyway, I have to do a walk-through and speak to any other members of your family...Thanks for your cooperation, Drew," she said, then walked toward a glowering O'Brien. "He cleared you if that's what you're concerned about."

But somehow Em had to ensure that the after-school practices stopped. An idea came to her. "Drew, promise me, no horsing around tonight, no rough stuff with your friends, and that goes for the next few days too. The last thing any of us want is for you to be injured. Josh says he's heard from several scouts who'll be attending the championship game."

By the time Em got home, it was almost seven. She wanted to take Gus for a quick walk before she headed to the All Hallows' Eve party, and while she trusted Izzy, she wanted to take a look around Seaton House. She attached Gus's leash to his collar and grabbed a flashlight.

It was a beautiful autumn night. The stars and quarter moon shone bright in the black velvet sky. The air was cool and smelled like woodsmoke, fall flowers, and decaying leaves.

Gus nosed around a bush, and Em gave the leash a light tug. "We're not taking a nature walk tonight, buddy. Do your business, and then we'll check out Seaton House."

His ears perked up at the mention of the house, and he quickly got his business out of the way. Em pushed open the gate and shined her light along the path and around the front yard. There was no sign of anything out of the ordinary. She hadn't really expected there to be—not this early. If Josh agreed to go out with her, maybe they could have their first real date here tonight at midnight. If she were a teenager, that's when she'd come.

Gus barked, straining at the leash as he pulled her after him. "What's up, boy?" She looked around as he dragged her up the stairs to the front door. And that's when she heard it, someone calling "Help."

She tried the door. It was unlocked. As she walked inside, she heard Mike and Charlie's voices coming from the kitchen. They were pounding on a door, yelling for help.

"We're coming!" she called out, shutting the door behind her. There was a loud blowing noise, and she looked up the stairs. A large commercial propane blower sat on the landing. Izzy was right. It would be dangerous for anyone to come here tonight. Em and Charlie and Mike were going to have a serious chat.

When she reached the kitchen, Gus was sitting at the basement door, barking. She reached for the knob but she couldn't get it to turn. "Guys, back up in case the door swings into you. I might have to give it a shove."

Eventually she got the door to open, and the boys raced to her, throwing their arms around her. "We didn't think anyone would ever come," Charlie said.

She patted their backs. "What were you two doing here? Or more to the point, what were you doing in the basement?"

"Trust me, we didn't want to go in the basement," Mike said. "But we think Willy was trying to tell us something. Maybe about the box?"

Em's pulse kicked up at the thought she might finally solve the case. "Why do you think Willy was trying to communicate with you?"

Charlie took the red ball out of his pocket. "It rolled down the stairs, and then it kept rolling right to the basement door. So we opened the door, and it rolled down the stairs and stopped near a shelf kind of thing, maybe a workbench? We couldn't see anything. We didn't have a flashlight, and we'd left our phones upstairs. But you have one, Em. We should check it out."

She was going to tell them to stay in the kitchen but she needed to know the exact location the red ball had rolled to. "Okay, but as soon as you show me where the ball stopped rolling, you come back and wait for me here."

They shared a look and nodded. "To be honest, we don't like it down there. It's creepy."

"Gus will stay with you," she said and then started down the stairs with the boys and Gus following close behind. When she reached the bottom of the stairs, she raised her flashlight. There were signs that the basement had been home to rats and raccoons, and spiders, a lot of spiders going by the number of cobwebs on the shelves that held dust-coated cans and jars.

"Where abouts did the ball stop?" she asked the boys.

"Here," they said, pointing to the right of Em's foot. She was standing beside a workbench that looked like it hadn't been used in decades. The tools were buried under a thick layer of dust and cobwebs. "We'll help you look, Em."

She glanced around the workstation. It would take her less time to search the area if the boys helped, and she'd have a chance of making it to the party on time. Ten minutes later, they'd searched every nook and cranny, underneath the workbench and in every drawer, and still they came up empty.

Em heard a *whoosh* and turned. The basement door slammed shut, and the doorknob fell off and rolled down the stairs. The boys sent her panicked looks.

"Don't worry. We won't be locked down here all night." She didn't scare easily but this place was even creeping her out. She checked her phone. No cell service. "Okay. You guys have been working with Neil for a while now so you probably know a thing or two about tools." She picked up the doorknob and walked over to the workbench. "There must be something here we can use to reattach the knob."

Above them, something crashed and banged several times. Em couldn't be sure but it sounded as if something was rolling down the stairs. Something heavy, something metal, something like the propane blower, she thought with a touch of alarm.

She hurried up the stairs and pressed her ear to the door. Whatever had rolled down the stairs crashed at what she suspected was the base of the staircase. She heard running feet and then the front door slammed, the wood shuddering beneath her ear. She wondered if O'Brien had followed her to Seaton House. The thought had barely crossed her mind when she smelled something. Something familiar… Burning wood.

Chapter Twenty-Six

♥

Here you go, buddy. Nice costume," Josh said to the little girl dressed up as a firefighter. A couple of guys had called in sick at the last minute, and he'd volunteered to give out the Halloween treats for HFFD. He didn't mind. All he had to do was stand at the end of the parade route, handing out treats to the kids.

He looked up Main Street. There were a couple stragglers making their way to him as one by one the store's lights blinked out. He glanced at his phone. It was five after seven.

He waved the stragglers on, directing a couple of people to the community center for the party. He planned to head there himself. He was hoping to see Em so they could finish the conversation they'd started on his birthday. He'd gone to her house a couple times to talk to her but she hadn't been home.

With the uptick in Halloween pranks, it was a busy time for HFPD. He'd just missed her when he'd gone to help clean up at Silver Creek. Then he'd gotten busy himself and it wasn't something he wanted to talk about over the phone.

"Okay, it's your lucky day, guys," he said, emptying the boxes of mini chocolate bars into their pillowcases. They were dressed like the kids from *Stranger Things*. A couple of them looked older than thirteen, but he didn't call them on it. He figured if a kid put the effort into dressing up, they deserved a treat.

As he walked over to help move the barriers blocking Main Street, he heard what sounded like *Em needs you.*

Josh rubbed his ear and looked around. There was no one there. He started walking again and another whisper sent a chill down his spine. It was a male voice, and this time it was stronger and insistent. *Em needs you. Fire. Seaton House.*

If Em hadn't told him she'd seen and spoken to Brad, Josh might've hesitated, he might've second-guessed himself, but he couldn't take the chance this was real and Em was in danger.

He raced across the road to his truck and pulled out his phone. "Report of a fire at Seaton House. I'm on my way." He disconnected from HFFD and jumped in his truck. His tires squealed as he backed onto Main Street and turned the wheel sharply, pressing the pedal to the floor as he headed for Sugar Maple Road.

He tried calling Steve, and then Charlie's mother, thinking they might have gone home after the parade. They were close to Seaton House and could rescue Em, if she needed rescuing. Neither of them answered. Josh tried Em but it went straight to voice mail, and then he started to pray.

Swaths of light from the street lamps illuminated the interior of his truck, and he looked around. There was no one in the cab with him. He didn't know what he'd been expecting. Maybe that he'd see Em's fiancé's ghost like she did or at least sense a presence? But there was no discounting the voice he'd heard. Besides that, he believed Em.

"I'm driving as fast as I can, Brad, but I might need some help keeping her safe. I know you loved her first, and I know how much she loved you, loves you still, but I'm hoping she has enough love left for me. Because I've gotta tell you, man. I'm in love with her."

And right now, he couldn't care less if he was Em's second choice or if she didn't love him as much as she loved the ghost of her fiancé. If she told Josh she loved him and wanted to be with him, no one would be happier than him.

He slowed down as he reached the hairpin curves along the river. He wouldn't do Em any good if he died. Even though Brad didn't know what he was thinking, he felt bad for the thought. "Unless someone has figured out a way to throw their voice and they're pranking me, which to be honest, I'm kind of hoping is the case because that means Em isn't in danger. But after what she's told me, I have a feeling it's you, Brad. Any chance you can give me a sign that I have your blessing? I know I don't need it but I'd like to know you're okay with Em moving on with me," he said, looking around the truck.

He didn't know what he was expecting. Maybe lights to flash or his radio to turn on and off. But none of that happened; the only he thing he smelled was his old cologne. The scent filled the cab of his truck.

Josh smiled. He wasn't wearing Armani; he was wearing the new cologne Em had given him. He'd thrown out the last of the Armani the night of his party. "Thanks, man. I appreciate that more than you know. Em told me what you said to her, that you wanted her to move on, find love again, and be happy. I'll do my best to make her happy, and if she comes out of this okay, and I've gotta believe she will, you and the baby can move on. You don't have to worry about her anymore, Brad. I've got this."

He turned onto Sugar Maple Road. The Camaro was parked in Em's driveway. He considered checking her place first, but then he saw the smoke billowing up into the night sky. It was coming from Seaton House. He sped down the gravel road and jerked the steering wheel to the right, driving his truck through the gate. He braked hard in front of the steps. As he jumped out of the truck, racing for the front door, he heard the sirens. They were close.

He touched the doorknob. It was hot. He jumped off the steps and ran around the side of the house, heading for the kitchen door, praying that the fire hadn't gotten that far. But it wasn't the flames he had to worry about; it was the smoke. He took off his jacket and tied it around his mouth and nose and then he went in through the kitchen door. It was smoky and the fire was spreading fast but he had a feeling, thanks to Brad, he'd gotten there in time. Now he just had to find Em. He called her name.

"Here! We're trapped in the basement," she yelled, pounding on the other side of the basement door. Gus was there too and it sounded like Charlie and Mike were also locked down there with them. Josh tried the door but he couldn't get it to open. The fire was licking up the walls in the entryway.

"Stand back from the door."

"Okay. We're good," Em called a few seconds later.

He took a run at the door, putting his shoulder into it. The door shuddered but didn't open. It took him three tries. On the last try, the door flew open, hitting the basement wall. "Come on!" Josh beckoned them with his left arm, so relieved to see Em—even if she didn't look like his Em—that he barely felt the pain in his shoulder.

"Out the kitchen door," he told the boys as they ran past him. Em disappeared from view. He started down the stairs. "Em, what are you doing?"

She came back in sight holding a flashlight and ran up the stairs with Gus following her. "How did you know we were here?"

He lifted his chin. "Later. We've gotta get out of here."

Several firefighters ran into the kitchen. "Anyone else in the house?"

Josh looked at Em. She shook her head. "No. It was just us."

"I'm going to get them away from the scene," Josh told one of the firefighters as he ushered Em, the boys, and Gus away from the house. "We'll be across the road if anyone needs to speak with us. I'll have someone check them over."

The firefighter gave him a thumbs-up while relaying Josh's message over his radio.

"I'm fine," Em said as they hurried along the path to the road.

"Humor me, please." He leaned forward, looking past the emergency vehicles to get the four of them safely to the other side.

The front yard at Seaton House was lit up like it was two in the afternoon. It was crawling with members of the fire and police departments. An HFPD patrol car pulled alongside the road and Todd jumped out, heading their way.

Em and the boys were on their phones. Josh murmured to Em, "Just go along with what I say." He planned to tell her the truth when they were alone but no one else. They'd think he was crazy.

She frowned, searched his face, and then nodded. "I texted Bri and Cal and your parents so they know we're all right."

"Thanks, and now, if you don't mind, I need to kiss you."

"Good." Her face relaxed, and she smiled. "Because I need to kiss you too." She glanced at Charlie and Mike, who were grinning. "Close your eyes, boys. You too, Gus," she said as she put her arms around Josh's neck.

At the weight of Em's forearm on his shoulder, his knees buckled, and his eyes watered. But when her soft, warm lips touched his mouth, the excruciating pain lessened on a flood of emotion.

Someone cleared their throat, and they raised their heads to see Todd grinning at them.

"I knew you two were meant for each other," he said. "But it would've been nice if you figured that out sooner. Like before they paid out on the betting pool." His expression became serious as his gaze moved from Em to the kids to Gus. "You're all good? No one's hurt?"

The boys and Em nodded. "We are, but we wouldn't have been if it weren't for Josh." She looked at him. "You never told me. How did you know we were trapped in the house?"

Okay, so she just blew his cover. He was going to say she'd called him. He had to think of something else.

Josh got a reprieve when Charlie's mother and Neil ran down the road, calling their sons' names. The boys ran into their parents' open arms. After they'd ensured their children were okay, the questions came.

"What were you thinking, Mike? You too, Charlie. I told you guys I didn't want you hanging out at the house," Neil said, raking his hands through his hair.

"We didn't have anything to do with the fire, Dad. It wasn't our fault," Mike said.

"I can't believe you'd disobey Mr. Sutherland after all he's done for you," Charlie's mother said to her son.

"It was my fault," Em said. "They were looking for something for me."

Mike and Charlie sent her grateful glances, and Josh was almost positive there was more going on.

Neil stared at Em. "Really? They're kids. They're not cops. And I don't appreciate you using my son and his friend—"

"Dad, stop. It's not Em's fault, and it's not Charlie's fault. It's mine. I asked Charlie to come with me."

"Why? What were you doing?" his father asked, glancing at Em, who stepped closer to Mike, placing a hand on his shoulder.

"I read that the veil thins between heaven and earth on All Hallows' Eve. I got a Ouija board and asked Charlie to come with me. I know you don't believe it, Dad, but Seaton House is haunted. And I thought maybe that would help me connect to Mom's spirit." He shrugged. "I just wanted to talk to her."

"I never should've taken the job," Neil said, looking in the direction of Seaton House before turning to Mike. "Your mother's gone. She's not coming back, and you can't communicate with her—"

Charlie's mother and Em gasped, no doubt in reaction to the harshness of Neil's voice.

"What? You think I should lie to him. Pretend that there's—"

Cal and Bri ran down the road. "Em! Josh!"

"Relax. We're fine," Em said, but it was obvious she was upset with how Neil was handling his son.

Josh knew how she felt, and he opened his mouth. He didn't care if people ended up thinking he was crazy. Mike needed to know that whether he could see or feel his mother's presence, our loved ones' spirits live on, and Em needed to know Brad was her hero, not Josh. They all did.

But before Josh got a chance to say anything, Todd said, "If we don't want to be here all night, I need to get everyone's statements."

Josh figured he'd get his chance to say what he had to say soon enough and waited with Em and the boys on the side of the road while they gave their statements. Em said something that didn't jibe with what Josh had seen, and he opened his mouth. Then he shut it. If Em was holding something back, she had a reason.

Todd turned to Josh. "How did you know Em and the boys were trapped in the basement?"

His gaze drifted over Mike and Neil before coming to rest on Em. "I didn't. Brad, Em's fiancé who died eighteen months ago, told me."

"Say that again," Todd said, looking at Josh as if he suspected he'd been drinking.

"I know it sounds crazy, but not everything in life can be explained. Brad told me Em needed me. He told me there was a fire at Seaton House. He's the hero, not me. If he hadn't found a way to reach me, we might've had a tragic outcome instead of a happy one."

"You believed him, and that makes you my hero, Josh Callahan," Em said, stepping closer and taking his hand in hers. Because of the love shining in her tear-filled eyes, he was able to hold back a groan of pain.

"Josh isn't imagining things, Todd. And Mike, even if you can't hear your mom or sense her presence, trust me, she loves you, and she's always with you. You too, Neil. Brad came to me after the accident at the river. I saw him. I spoke to him. Did you see him and talk to him?" she asked Josh.

"I didn't see him, and other than him telling me you were in danger, he didn't say anything else. But I did ask him a question, and he gave me a sign."

"What was your question?" she asked with that very un-Em-like smile on her face.

He gently wiped the tears from her face. "I told him I loved you, and that if you felt the same way, I would spend the rest of my life making you happy. I asked for his blessing."

"Did he give it to you?"

He nodded. "I asked for a sign, and my truck was suddenly filled with the smell of Armani cologne."

She sniffed his neck and smiled and then pressed a kiss to the underside of his jaw. "I'm glad he gave you his blessing. But you didn't need it, you know. You already had mine."

He was about to try and wrap both his arms around her when Cal said, "Okay, this has gone past the point of being ridiculous," and clamped a firm hand on Josh's uninjured shoulder, drawing him away from Em.

"I swear to God, Cal, if you so much as touch a hair on his head, I'll never speak to you again," Em said.

"I'm going to do more than touch a hair on his head, Freckles. I'm going to put his shoulder back in place. And trust me, I'm going to enjoy every second of his pain as I do."

Em studied Josh, no doubt taking in the way his arm hung limply at his side. "You dislocated your shoulder when you broke down the door, and you didn't think you should tell me?"

"It was worth it. Your kiss took away my pain. And once your brother fixes my shoulder, you can—" He wasn't sure if he screamed when Cal popped his shoulder joint into the socket, but he did come close to passing out. "—kiss it better," he finished weakly.

She didn't look impressed or like she planned on kissing him. "Josh Callahan, if you ever do that again—"

"Do what? Tell you I love you?" He gently pulled her against him with his uninjured arm, and she wrapped her arms around his waist. "You must've put a spell on me, Emma Scott. Because I'm thinking we should skip the whole dating thing and just get married."

Chapter Twenty-Seven

♥

I hope I'm not interrupting anything," Todd said, waggling his eyebrows with a grin on his face when Em opened her door the next morning.

"Nope, you're not." She ushered him inside.

"Seriously? What is wrong with you two?" he asked, shaking his head. Then his face lit up when Josh sauntered out of her bedroom with sexy bedhead and his arm in a sling. "Thank God. I was starting to worry about the lack of sexy times with you two."

"Don't talk to me about a lack of sexy times," Josh grumbled, leaning in to kiss Em before heading into the kitchen. "You want a coffee, Em? Todd?"

"I'll get the coffee. You go sit." She gently steered Josh to the kitchen table, pulling out a chair for him.

"Oh, okay, I get it now. I forgot about your shoulder," Todd said, reaching for a chair. "Sucks for you guys though."

Josh gave Todd a look before saying to Em, "I'm fine. You don't have to baby me."

"Not that fine or you wouldn't be so testy." Todd put

an elbow on the table and cupped his chin in his hand. "I don't think I've ever seen you grumpy. It's kind of a hot look on you."

Em held back a snort of amusement. Todd was right. Josh was grumpy...and hot. "I'm not babying you. I'm taking care of you just like you took care of me. Enjoy it while it lasts." She kissed his stubbled cheek and walked into the kitchen. "So what brings you here this early?" she asked Todd, reaching for the mugs in the cupboard.

"Fire chief cleared us to go into Seaton House, and I figured you'd want to join me."

"I do." She poured their coffee, added cream and sugar, and brought them over to the table. "Did you talk to Gwen?" she asked, handing Josh and then Todd their drinks. Gwen had been providing security for the house last night at Em's request.

"I did, and you were right. Steve showed up an hour ago. He brought coffee and muffins as an excuse for coming."

Jenny had arrived five minutes after they'd finished giving their statements last night. She had Charlotte with her but not Steve. They'd learned he had a cold and had stayed home. Steve had shown up a few minutes later. Supposedly his cold medicine had knocked him out, and he hadn't noticed the sirens or emergency lights until just then.

"Gwen didn't let him in, did she?"

"No. She said he didn't seem interested in going inside. He was more interested in showing them the damage the rocks had left on the window frames and where he'd cleaned up the egg."

Steve had said he wasn't surprised by what had happened. Jenny had acknowledged that he'd shared his concerns with her, and she felt bad for going ahead with the Embrace Your Inner Witch town hall meeting, fearing that she'd made things worse. But Steve had placed the blame on Peter O'Brien for stirring the pot, which, according to Steve, had resulted in rocks being thrown at the windows and the house being egged.

"None of which actually happened because you'd been keeping an eye on the house," Josh said.

"Not to mention that was the first time I'd heard about it from Steve," Em said.

"Which he realized when you gave him your cop's stare, and why he tried to draw Neil into it," Todd said.

"Neil didn't exactly corroborate his story," Em said.

"Probably because he was still trying to process his son's confession about trying to connect with his mom and then you and Josh sharing that you see dead people."

"Dead person would be more accurate," Em said.

"No. I'm pretty sure it's dead people," Josh said, taking one last swallow of his coffee before pushing back from the table. "We saw the woman in the turret window."

"Right." She frowned when he got up from the table. "Where are you going?"

"To grab a shower and then I'll go with you to Seaton House. I don't have a class until ten."

Short of calling in sick for Josh, Em couldn't figure a way to get him to stay home for the day and rest. He wasn't impressed when she kept checking in with him as they did a walk-through of Seaton House. The main floor had suffered significant damage from not only the fire but from the water.

"I'm a volunteer firefighter, Em. I've done this before so go do your thing and don't worry about me."

"You haven't done it in a sling so just be careful."

Todd grinned. "You two are so cute."

"Shut it," Em and Josh said at the same time and then smiled at each other.

"You don't have to be so cranky. No one's going to want to be around you two until you get some somethin'-somethin.' "

Josh rolled his eyes. "I'll be right back," he said and walked outside. The doors and windows had been left open to deal with the smoke.

"Has anyone ever told you have a one-track mind?" Em asked Todd as she crouched beside the propane blower and looked up at the landing.

"Yeah. You. What are you looking at?"

She nodded at a brick on the third stair from the top. "We're supposed to believe that the brick was thrown through that window, hit the propane blower, which sent it rolling down the stairs, and then set the area rug on fire. Except there's barely any glass on the landing or on the stairs."

Josh came back inside. "There's barely any glass inside because it's on the ground below the window. The brick wasn't thrown from the outside. It was used to smash the glass from the inside."

Em smiled. "Which is why there are no dents or scratches on the propane blower that would indicate it had been hit by a brick." She rolled the blower onto its side. "But there is an imprint of a shoe. It looks like a man's size eleven, and by the tread, my guess is it's a tennis shoe."

"I didn't have to go outside and investigate, did I? You already had it figured out," Josh said.

She shrugged. "Let's just say you confirmed my working theory."

"Look at him. He's so into you, it isn't funny. You two really are annoying to be around. I'm going to interview our number-one suspect." Todd glanced at Em. "Unless you want to."

"No. I'd rather it was you." She was a hundred percent certain Steve was responsible, and she was angry at herself for not holding him accountable for the swatting.

"Hey, don't beat yourself up," Josh said, reaching for her with his uninjured arm. "Neither of us suspected Steve would go this far."

"But he did, and Charlie and Mike could've died."

"And you and Gus." He drew her closer. "But you're all okay."

"Thanks to you." She played with the knot on his sling.

"Me and Brad."

She moved her hand, cupping the side of his face. "I love you, you know. I love that you believed me and that you didn't question that Brad was there, but most of all, I just love you for being you."

He turned his face and kissed her palm. "Todd's right. I'm completely into you. You're very hot when you're in cop mode."

"I'm glad you think so, but between Steve and my

inability to solve Clara's murder, I feel like I've lost my mojo."

"Let's go check out the basement again. It was dark when you were looking, and you had two scared kids with you."

"You're right. And it makes sense that the box would be hidden down there. They've basically torn the second floor apart and haven't found it."

"Plus, Willy sent the boys to the basement," Josh pointed out.

"And Clara died there," Em said, pulling on the string that dangled from a bald light bulb at the top of the basement stairs. "Weird," she said when the light bulb turned on. "It didn't work last night."

"Maybe someone changed the bulb. HFFD would've come down here to check it out."

Because his arm was in a sling, Josh couldn't crawl around on the floor with Em, but while she shined her flashlight in every nook and cranny, he hammered on the wall, looking for a hollow space, a secret compartment like there was in the living room.

He swore and dropped the hammer on the workbench.

"Are you okay?"

"Yeah. I... Ah, Em, you're going to want to see this."

She moved to his side. The hammer had landed at an angle on the workbench, revealing a crack. "I think it's a secret compartment," he said, wedging a flat-head screwdriver into the space. He popped it opened, and they both gasped. There was a wooden box inside.

Em shook her head as she reached inside, pulling

it out. "If you hadn't dropped the hammer, we never would've found it."

He held up the hammer. "I thought the head was rusted, but when I started hammering in this area, it caught the light. I don't think it's rust, Em. I think it's blood. It's why I dropped it."

"Okay. I'll bag it as evidence." She looked around the basement. "I have a feeling this is a crime scene. I don't think Clara is the only person who was murdered here."

"The farmhand?" Josh asked.

She nodded. "That would be my guess. Let's get out of here. We can look through the contents of the box upstairs. I want to put gloves on anyway."

A grim-faced Todd met them at the top of the stairs. "Steve confessed. He's here and would like a word before I bring him to the station."

Steve sat on the couch with his face buried in his hands. He raised his head when they walked into the living room. "I'm so sorry. I don't know what possessed me to do what I did. But, Em, you have to believe me. I had no idea you and Gus or Charlie and Mike were here." He bowed his head, and his shoulders started to shake. "I couldn't have lived with myself if something happened to any of you," he sobbed. "I never meant to hurt anyone. I just...I wanted to get rid of the house and the ghosts."

At a muffled cry, Em looked over her shoulder. It was Jenny, her face streaked with tears. "I'm so sorry, Em," she whispered. "I had no idea."

A stricken expression crossed Steve's face. "Jenny had nothing to do with this, Em. It's all on me. You have to believe me."

"I do. I believe you, Steve. Jenny won't be held accountable for any of this." Jenny's eyes met hers, and Em nodded. "You'll have to face the legal consequences, Steve, but I'll do what I can to help you."

"And we'll be there for Jenny, Charlotte, and the baby," Josh promised, sitting on the couch beside Steve.

He nodded and wiped his eyes. "Thank you," he said, his voice broken.

Jenny sat on the other side of Steve and wrapped her arms around him. "We'll get through this."

Todd walked over.

"Give us a minute," Em said, holding up the box. "I think we should all be here for this."

Jenny gasped. "You found the box."

"Actually, Josh did." Em smiled at the man she loved and asked Todd for a pair of gloves. "Thanks," she said when he handed them to her. "I'll get you to record it too."

Inside the box, they found the farmhand's confession. He'd witnessed LeRoy adding something from a brown bottle to Edward's morning coffee on three separate occasions. He hadn't known it at the time but put it together after Edward's death was ruled murder by poison. The farmhand had confronted LeRoy but he had told him that May had given him the medicine for Edward's headaches, and he didn't know it was poison.

The farmhand had believed in LeRoy's innocence and kept his secret, until the day LeRoy got drunk and started ranting about Clara's attempts to exonerate her sister and how he wanted to get rid of her. Her and his brother's son. He wasn't about to share his inheritance.

Afraid that he would go to jail because he'd kept LeRoy's secret, the farmhand wrote out his confession and must have hidden it in the workbench until he could give it to Clara.

"Will this be enough to have May exonerated and LeRoy Henderson charged with Clara's and the farmhand's murders posthumously?" Jenny asked.

"I'll do whatever I can to make that happen. We'll have a stronger case if we find the farmhand's body. My gut says we'll find it either buried in the basement or somewhere on the Henderson or Seaton property, and I'm hoping we will be able to use genetic genealogy to compare DNA from the hammer and the farmhand's remains that will help prove our theory. But Jenny, you can let everyone know the truth. May is innocent, and LeRoy Henderson murdered Clara and the farmhand."

From behind Em, a woman whispered *Thank you*, and a child laughed. "Ah, Em, you might want to turn around," Josh said.

She turned as a stream of sparkling light illuminated two women and a little boy on the stairs. The women smiled, and then the three of them disappeared.

There was a loud *thunk*, and Em turned to see Todd on the floor. He'd fainted.

Chapter Twenty-Eight

♥

"You put a spell on me," Cal said in what Josh assumed his best friend meant to be a lovestruck voice. It sounded more idiotic than lovestruck. Which Josh supposed made sense since he'd felt like an idiot after he'd said it to Em Halloween night.

Cal and Quinn smirked and fist bumped each other. It was the championship game today, and his friends had volunteered to give the team a pep talk. Josh was just glad they were hanging out in his office while the boys dressed.

He didn't want the members of his team hearing that he'd basically proposed to Em, and she'd looked at him and laughed. It was bad enough Charlie and Mike and their parents had heard him. But Josh had covered up with a joke, and he figured everyone bought it, including Em. Not Cal though.

Josh's *You put a spell on me* line might've been total cheese but the line that followed was the absolute truth. He wanted to marry Em. He still did.

"Okay. It's getting old," he said to Cal and Quinn.

They'd been teasing him for the past three days, sending him clips of the Sanderson sisters' singing "I Put a Spell on You" in *Hocus Pocus*.

"Where is your little witch?" Cal asked.

His best friend was in much better spirits and still his best friend even though Josh had basically proposed to his baby sister. It was the proposal that had won Cal over. As he'd told Josh the next day—after he'd finished singing an off-tune rendition of "I Put a Spell on You"—Cal had been afraid Josh wouldn't be able to make a commitment after his disastrous marriage and subsequent divorce.

"You might not want to let Em hear you call her a little witch," Josh said, getting up from behind his desk. "As to where she is, she's talking to the judge about the most expedient way to have May Seaton fully exonerated and to have Clara and the farmhand's death ruled as murders." The judge lived at the inn on Mirror Lake and was a well-respected and well-connected former superior court judge.

"I'm surprised you finding the box wasn't enough to woo your girlfriend into saying yes. You basically solved her case for her," Cal said.

"Em had solved the case long before I found the box. And the only reason I did was because I freaked out thinking there was blood on the hammer's head and dropped it." As it turned out, he'd been right. It was blood and the farmhand's body had been found buried in the basement.

Josh picked up his iPad and walked out of his office. Cal and Quinn joined him.

"The energy in this room does not bode well for the game," Quinn murmured.

Josh looked over his team. Quinn was right. The boys sat with their heads bowed, shoulders slumped, dangling their helmets between their legs.

"What's going on with you, guys? And don't tell me it's because Em's not here. I told you she—" A loud banging on the door interrupted him.

"You guys decent?" Em called from the other side.

The guys brightened but not by much. Josh brightened by a lot. He'd been worried she wouldn't make it in time for the game. He should've known better. She'd promised she would, and Em didn't break her promises.

"Are you kicking the..." he began as he opened the door. Em wore a baseball hat in the team's colors, her ponytail pulled through the hole, his football jersey, black leggings, and tennis shoes, and a smile that lit up her beautiful face. Not that long ago, he'd considered it an un-Em-like smile, but lately it was the only smile he'd seen on her face. He loved that smile, and he loved that face.

As he'd suspected, she had been kicking the door. Her arms were full with plastic containers. Wearing his team jersey, Gus trotted over to Mike and Charlie.

"Em, the guys can't have cupcakes before the game," Josh said, taking them from her.

"I know. They're for after the game." She looked up when a couple guys groaned. "Hey, my cupcakes weren't that bad. But I didn't have time to bake anyway. I went to Bites of Bliss." She lifted the lid of one of the containers, showing the boys. "Look great, right?" She frowned at their lackluster response and closed the lid. "What's up with you, guys? You're acting like you lost the game, and you haven't even played yet."

"That's what I want to know," Josh said. "Come on, guys. Tell us what's wrong."

"They don't want to say anything because of me," Drew said, then looked at his teammates. "I told you guys; you can talk trash about him all you want. It doesn't bother me. I feel the same as all of you."

Em nodded. "Okay. I think I get it."

"Good, then maybe you can enlighten us," Josh said.

"They're worried you'll lose your job. Am I right?" she asked.

They nodded, and one of the boys spoke up. "My mom's on the school board, and I heard her talking about it with my dad last night. She's worried that if O'Brien gets elected, the first thing he'll do is push for Assistant Coach Delaney to take your place, Coach."

That resulted in some trash-talking of Delaney, which Josh put a stop to, even though he'd felt basically the same after learning about Delaney's after-school practices with Drew. But Em's visit to O'Brien on Halloween had ended the practices.

"If we win the game tonight, we might be able to save your job, Coach. But we're worried we can't beat them." They were playing the team that they'd lost to last week.

"I love coaching football, and I love coaching you guys, and you have to know that I'll fight to stay on as head coach. Just as hard as I'll fight to ensure Assistant Coach Delaney doesn't replace me. But guys, on the off-chance that happens, and trust me, I don't think it will, it's not like I can't hang out with you and play ball and help with your game. I'm not going anywhere no matter what happens. And my fate doesn't hinge on this game. Whether you win or lose, if O'Brien becomes mayor, he'll go after my job. So your job today is to do your best and above all else, have a good time doing it."

"You are so hot when you're in coach mode," Em whispered when Quinn started his pep talk. "That speech just earned you a gallon of Moose Tracks."

He whispered in her ear what he'd prefer over a gallon of ice cream. She shivered and kissed his cheek. "I think that can be arranged."

Josh supposed it spoke to his priorities these days that he couldn't wait for the game to be over so that he could take Em home with him.

* * *

Em's throat ached from screaming. Once again, Charlie intercepted the ball, but this time he passed it to Mike. The crowd roared as Mike raced for the goal line with Charlie doing the same, mere inches behind him. The opposition took Mike down, and the crowd groaned. But wait, Mike didn't have the ball. Charlie had faked the pass. Em looked at the clock. There was less than a second left in the game. It felt as if time stood still, as if Charlie was running in slow motion. He crossed the line. Touchdown! They'd won the championship. The team went wild, the fans in the stands went wild, and so did Em and Josh.

They continued the celebration back at Josh's house. Patsy and Phil had gone ahead to get everything ready. They had a fire lit in the pit and pizzas and salads scheduled to arrive from Zia Maria's by the time members of the team and their families got to Josh's.

Patsy smiled at Em as they plated the pizza slices and Phil and Josh poured the drinks. "I always knew you two would end up together," Patsy said smugly.

Em arched an eyebrow. "I seem to remember you setting Josh up with Robyn less than a week ago."

"Yes, and you should've seen your face. Josh's too." Patsy sighed happily. "I can't wait to start planning your wedding. What do you think about a New Year's Eve wedding?"

Phil rolled his eyes. "Patsy, they just started dating for real three days ago. I think you could give them at least a month to think about it."

Em was glad Patsy was happy that she and Josh were together for real this time, but she couldn't think about getting married now. It was way too soon in their relationship. Em laughed, thinking making light of it was the best way to go. "We're planning on dating for a while first, Patsy." Em glanced at Josh, wondering about the look on his face. "Aren't we, honey?"

"Yeah, of course. And stop with the pressure, Mom." Josh smiled at Em, and her tension disappeared.

Soon after, Cal, Bri, Raine, and Quinn arrived. Raine hadn't chickened out at the All Hallows' Eve party, and the couple were officially dating. Except... "You're what?" Em asked, positive she'd heard Raine wrong.

"Getting married, or I should say remarried," Raine

beamed, holding out her left hand to show off the pink diamond engagement ring.

"Wow, that was fast," Em said, glancing at Josh. He was sitting at the firepit talking to several of the team's parents, the flames illuminating his handsome face. Em had a feeling this is what he wanted.

She hugged Raine and Quinn, congratulating them both. "Izzy must be thrilled."

Raine nodded. "She is, but—" She looked at Quinn, whose phone had just beeped. "Are the results in?"

Quinn nodded and then held up his phone. "Quiet, everyone! They're going to announce the election results." He increased the volume on his phone while everyone pulled out their own, tuning into the live announcement at the town hall. The results were coming in earlier than anyone had expected. They'd planned to head to the town hall in an hour.

Em walked over to Josh. She wanted to be with him when the announcement came in. He pulled her onto his knee. There was a reason they could announce the winner early. Winter had won by a landslide. Everyone cheered, and there were a lot of relieved faces, including Josh's, and she imagined her own.

Or maybe not, she thought when he gently clasped her chin. "Winter won, babe. You're supposed to be happy. Our jobs are safe."

"I am. It's just that Raine and Quinn are getting married and . . . Is that what you really want, Josh?"

"I love you, Em, and I want to marry you. But only when you're ready, and I don't care if it takes you a year or two or the next decade to decide."

"I do want to wait but it has nothing to do with how I feel about you. I love you, and I want to spend the rest of my life with you. There's nothing I want more than for us to be together forever. I just need a little time."

"Take all the time you need," he said, reaching for his guitar.

"Are you going to sing for me?" Em and her brother always joked that a sure sign Josh was going to make a move on a woman was when he picked up his guitar.

"I am." He waggled his eyebrows.

"You never sang for me before, Josh Callahan. You'd better make it good," she said, moving to the arm of his chair so he had room for his guitar.

"Every song I ever sang was for you, Em. I just didn't know it," he said, and then he took off his sling and played his guitar, singing Lonestar's "Amazed" for her.

Epilogue

♥

Halloween, one year later

There'd been a change of venue this Halloween. The party after the parade was being held at Seaton House instead of the community center. It had taken nearly the entire year but the house had been returned to its former beauty and, as far as Em knew, was ghost-free. She kind of missed Clara, May, and Willy but was happy that they'd been able to go to the light. Not that everyone in town believed that they had, thanks to Abby.

Jenny had decided to open the house as a museum and a tribute to the Seaton sisters. Abby was doing her podcast from there tonight, hence why she'd resurrected the Seaton sisters, at least in the citizens of Highland Falls' imaginations.

The change of venue worked out well for Em. All she had to do was walk up the road to take part in the festivities. And unlike last year, she was looking forward to it. The past year had brought quite a few changes to Sugar Maple Road.

"Hi, Em!" Neil called out as he jogged across the

road. "Nice costume!" These days, Neil and Mike basically lived on Sugar Maple Road with Charlie and his mom. Mike and Charlie were inseparable as always, and Neil and Charlie's mom seemed happy and in love.

"Thanks. I like yours too," Em called out. She was Sarah Sanderson again. It wasn't like she'd gotten much use out of her costume last year. But she had a new addition to her costume this year.

"Hi, Em!" Jenny, Steve, and Charlotte called out as they hurried across the road. They were dressed respectively as Dorothy, the Tin Man, the Wicked Witch of the West, and their baby boy—named Emerson after Em—was a lion.

Steve had served only a short jail term because it was their property and no one actually lived in the house at the time, and it had been obvious to the judge that Steve felt deep remorse and hadn't meant to hurt anyone. Em imagined Steve's lack of priors and the fact he was in all other ways an upstanding citizen were also reasons for his relatively light sentence. Steve had taken it upon himself to do community service, and he and Jenny were in couples' therapy. They'd bought the house they'd been renting, and they seemed to be doing well.

"Hey, Aunt Em!" Izzy called as she got out of a Ford Explorer. She was dressed as Hermione Granger again. "Hi, Em!" Drew waved. He was dressed as Harry Potter.

Em waved at the couple. They'd been dating for a year now. Drew was no longer the quarterback on the varsity football team but he never missed a game, cheering for his former teammates. His mother had filed for divorce from Peter after Drew, with some encouragement from

Josh and Em, had finally told her how his stepfather had treated him. After losing the farm to Jenny, Peter had left town for greener pastures two months before.

Izzy was waiting for Em at the gate. "Aww," Izzy squealed. "You dressed her as a witch." She peeked into the stroller. "Hi, Baby Willa."

Yes, Em had a baby girl. She was two months old, and just like Granny MacLeod had predicted, she had beautiful sky-blue eyes like her daddy, whose hair was the color of ravens' wings.

As though he sensed they were there, Josh turned, and a smile lit up his face. He was working at the bonfire, which was fine with her. She always loved how he looked in his uniform. He didn't volunteer with HFFD as much as he used to though, just like she'd didn't take extra shifts. They didn't need a lot to make them happy. They had Willa, each other, Gus, and their family and friends. They'd bought the bungalow on Sugar Maple Road, and Josh sold his house on Marigold Lane, moving in with her and Gus a few months before their wedding in May.

"Here they come," Izzy said, at the stampede of excited women headed their way.

Ten seconds later, they were surrounded by cooing members of the Sisterhood. "My turn first," Patsy said, leaning in to unbuckle Willa from the stroller. "You don't mind, do you, sweetheart?"

"Of course not." Em smiled. She couldn't ask for better in-laws. "While you cuddle her, I'll go cuddle my husband." She leaned in and kissed her daughter's soft, sweet-smelling cheek.

Josh, who was talking to their family and friends, lifted his arm as she approached, wrapping it around her as soon as she got close. He ducked his head, giving her a quick kiss. "How are my little witches?"

Em laughed. "We're fine, thanks." She looked around. "Where's Gus?"

"Chasing Todd and Matteo's cat."

Yes, Todd and Matteo were back together. They were getting married in December. Em was Todd's best woman, although he'd threatened to replace her with Josh if she didn't stop siding with Matteo over the wedding plans. She frowned. "When did Todd and Matteo get a cat?"

Josh grinned. "Five minutes ago. They adopted the black cat from Seaton House."

"Nice. We don't have to worry about Gus hurting him, do we?"

"Nah. The cat looks like he can handle himself. He lived in the house with raccoons after all."

"And ghosts, rats, and spiders," she said, leaning against him, enjoying the heat from the fire and the low murmur of familiar voices.

"Are you planning on falling asleep on me?" he asked, sounding amused.

"I might," she said, relaxed and happier than she'd thought possible a little more than a year before. And as she stood with the man she loved, surrounded by their family and friends, she looked up at the starlit sky and whispered *Thank you. I hope you're as happy as I am.*

Acknowledgments

This is the last book set in Highland Falls, and I want to give a shout-out to all the wonderful readers who have shared their love for this series and my other series with me. Thank you for your reviews, emails, and social media posts, your enthusiasm and support. I'm honored so many of you have stayed on this journey with me, and I hope we can continue it together for many more years to come.

Thank you to my dedicated editor Alex Logan, for always being so generous with her time and her talent. This is our twenty-eighth book together, and she never fails to make each story better. Thank you to the sales, marketing, publicity, production, and art departments at Grand Central/Forever for all you do on behalf of my books. None of this would be possible without you.

I'm grateful to my wonderful agent Pamela Harty for her friendship and support, and all her efforts on my behalf.

Thanks so much to my family and friends for always being there for me. Please know how grateful I am to have you in my life. And to my wonderful husband, amazing children and their equally amazing spouses, and our adorable granddaughters, thank you for your love and encouragement and for supporting me in doing what I love to do. You are my world.

About the Author

USA Today bestselling author **Debbie Mason** writes small-town romance with humor and heart. The first book in her Christmas, Colorado series, *The Trouble with Christmas*, was the inspiration for the Hallmark movie *Welcome to Christmas*. When Debbie isn't writing or reading, she enjoys cooking for her family, cuddling with her granddaughters and granddog, and long walks in the woods with her husband.

You can learn more at:
AuthorDebbieMason.com
Twitter @AuthorDebMason
Facebook.com/DebbieMasonBooks
Instagram @AuthorDebMason

Looking for more second chances and small towns? Check out Forever's heartwarming contemporary romances!

REUNITED ON SUGAR MAPLE ROAD
by Debbie Mason

Ever since her fiancé's death over a year ago, Emma Scott's been sleep-walking through life, and her family is growing increasingly worried about her. Enter Josh Callahan, high school football coach and her brother's best friend. Though he may drive her crazy, his suggestion to fake-date is brilliant because there are no feelings involved. And his plan works… until Josh realizes that the feelings he has for Emma are all too real. But is Emma ready to share her heart again?

THE CORNER OF HOLLY AND IVY
by Debbie Mason

Arianna Bell isn't expecting a holly jolly Christmas. That is, until her high school sweetheart, Connor Gallagher, returns to town. But just as she starts dreaming of kisses under the mistletoe, Connor announces that he will be her opponent in the upcoming mayoral race…even if it means running against the only woman he's ever loved. But with a little help from Harmony Harbor's matchmakers and a lot of holiday cheer, both may just get the happily-ever-after they deserve.

Connect with us at Facebook.com/ReadForeverPub

Discover bonus content and more on read-forever.com

THE HOUSE ON FIREFLY BEACH
by Jenny Hale

Sydney Flynn can't wait to start fresh with her son at her sanctuary: Starlight Cottage at Firefly Beach. That is, until she spies her childhood sweetheart. Nate Henderson ended their relationship with no explanation and left town to become a successful songwriter—only now he wants to make amends. But when a new development threatens her beloved cottage, can Sydney forgive him and accept his help? Or will the town they adore, and the love they had for each other, be lost forever?

THE INN AT TANSY FALLS
by Cate Woods

When her best friend dies and sends her on a scavenger hunt from beyond the grave, Nell Swift finds herself setting off for a charming little Vermont town, where she's welcomed by friendly locals, including an adorable Labrador and a grumpy but attractive forester and his six-year-old son. Is Nell willing to start her life all over again and make this new town her forever home? Includes a reading group guide!

Meet your next favorite book with @ReadForeverPub on TikTok

Find more great reads on Instagram with @ReadForeverPub

PRIDE & PUPPIES
by Lizzie Shane

After years of failing to find her own Mr. Darcy, Dr. Charlotte Rodriguez swears off dating in favor of her new puppy, Bingley. And there's no one better to give her pet advice than her neighbor and fellow dog owner George. When their friendly banter turns flirtatious, Charlotte finds herself catching *feelings*. But will Charlotte take one last chance with her heart before they miss out on happily-ever-after?

A CAT CAFE CHRISTMAS
by Codi Gary

In this laugh-out-loud, opposites-attract romance, veterinarian and animal lover Kara Ingalls needs a Christmas miracle. If Kara can't figure out some way to get her café out of the red, it won't last past the holidays. Marketing guru Ben Reese hatches a plan to put the café in the "green" by Christmas, but they will need to set aside their differences—and find homes for all the cats—to have their own *purr*-fect holiday… together.

Follow @ReadForeverPub on Twitter and join the conversation using #ReadForeverPub

THE FOREVER FAMILY
by Shirley Jump

The youngest of three close-knit sisters, Emma Monroe is the family wild child. Maybe that's why a yoga retreat leads to a spur-of-the-moment decision to marry Luke Carter, a man she's met exactly three times. The next morning, Emma sneaks back home, where she should have nama-*stayed* in the first place. When her brand new husband arrives to convince her to give their marriage a chance, can she envision a future where her biggest adventures come not from running away but from staying?

SWEET PEA SUMMER
by Alys Murray

May Anderson made the biggest mistake of her life when she broke up with her high school sweetheart, Tom Riley. Now he's back in Hillsboro, California, to take over his family's winery—and wants nothing to do with her. But when they're forced to partner for the prestigious Northwest Food and Wine Festival, their plans to avoid each other fall apart. When working side by side causes old feelings to surface, can they find the courage to face the fears that once kept them apart?